Sour Grapes

ELIZA LENTZSKI

ISBN: 9798833166796
Imprint: Independently published

WORKS BY ELIZA LENTZSKI

Don't Call Me Hero Series
Don't Call Me Hero
Damaged Goods
Cold Blooded Lover
One Little Secret
Grave Mistake

+ + +

Winter Jacket Series
Winter Jacket
Winter Jacket 2: New Beginnings
Winter Jacket 3: Finding Home
Winter Jacket 4: All In
Hunter

http://www.elizalentzski.com

OTHER WORKS BY ELIZA LENTZSKI

Standalones

Sour Grapes
The Woman in 3B
Sunscreen & Coconuts
The Final Rose
Bittersweet Homecoming
Fragmented
Apophis: Love Story for the End of the World
Second Chances
Date Night
Love, Lust, & Other Mistakes
Diary of a Human

+ + +

Works as E.L. Blaisdell
Drained: The Lucid (with Nica Curt)

CONTENTS

DEDICATION

To C

CHAPTER ONE

My in-car navigation system and the directions on my phone's map application didn't match. My phone told me to continue driving straight while my car's navigation system said I needed to turn around. I'd never possessed a talent for navigating from Point A to Point B, and reliance on technology had only made my sense of direction worse. Alex used to say that I couldn't find my way out of a paper bag. It was one of the things we'd routinely fight over after I'd managed to get us famously lost even with the use of a smart phone.

I slowed down and peered beyond the lazy back and forth of my car's wipers at the stretch of indistinguishable county highway before me. I touched my forehead against my steering wheel and sighed in defeat; I was lost. This, combined with the fact that it was a rare rainy day in Napa County, seemed to signal that maybe I was making the wrong decision.

I pulled over at the next gas station along the empty rural roadway. At first glance, the business looked abandoned—the name on the sign was a person's instead of a corporation, and the gas pumps had no option for credit card transactions—but the gas prices affixed to the analog sign reflected current rates. I heard the distinct sound of a bell as my car wheels rolled over a black hose stretched across the rain-soaked concrete.

I intended on going inside the small shop, but before I could even unfasten my seatbelt, a figure in a yellow rain jacket, its bright hood covering the person's head, hustled outside and approached the driver's side door. I rolled down the automatic window and kept my car running.

The gas station attendant, an older man with a tan as deep as his well-earned wrinkles, leaned his head toward my open window. "Fill it up?" he questioned.

"Sorry, no," I apologized. "It's electric. I'm just looking for directions."

The man leaned back and sucked on his teeth. "A winery," he guessed.

I felt simultaneously ashamed of my electric vehicle and of my destination.

"Your high-tech car doesn't have navigation?" he posed.

"It does. And I've got a phone," I said. "But they can't agree on where I'm supposed to go."

The man grinned, slow and wide. "The robots are fighting. Or maybe they're working together to drive you off a cliff."

His teasing caused me to bristle. It pained me to ask for help in the first place without being the target of ridicule. "I'm sorry to have bothered you," I said tightly. "I'll figure it out myself."

The man held up a finger. "Hold on, sweetie. Just a second."

He turned on his heels and trotted back towards his store. He threw open the glass-pane door and disappeared inside. My car continued to idle while I stared out my still-open window. Errant raindrops splashed on the window sill and ricocheted in my direction. I wanted to close the window while I waited for the man's return, but it seemed like an obnoxious move; he was the one in the rain, not me.

The door of the gas station shop opened again and the man in the yellow rain jacket reappeared. He shuffled back to my car, still smiling despite the persistent rain.

"What you need is a time machine," he announced. He sounded proud of himself.

"Time machine?"

He tapped a thick stack of multi-colored paper against the open window sill. "This, my dear, is called a map. Back in the Dark Ages, this is how people traveled."

I stifled the urge to roll my eyes. Despite my desire to drive away, maybe splashing the gas station attendant in the process, I needed this man's help.

He unfolded the accordion-style paper map to a close-up of Napa County and spread it across the window sill. "Where are you trying to go?" he asked.

I had to consult my navigation app. I hadn't yet memorized the address. "Lark Estates. It's supposed to be just off the Silverado Trail."

The man peered at the details on his paper map. "Bachelorette party?"

"Pardon?"

"The vineyard," he noted, "are you going to a bachelorette party or something? Seems to be all the rage these days."

"Oh," I said, catching on. "No. No bachelorette party. I, uh, I just bought the place."

I internally winced. *God.* I sounded so pretentious with my electric car and my San Francisco parking decals, driving to the vineyard I had just bought.

The man looked up from the map. I watched his eyes travel from my face to the back of my vehicle, which was packed high with luggage and whatever household items I didn't think I could survive without. "Fancy."

I wanted to launch into the complicated history of how I—June St. Clare, a forty-year-old graphic designer from the Bay Area—had come into possession of a twenty acre micro-winery in Napa Valley. But it was a long story, and the man in the yellow jacket was still standing in the rain, which was progressively getting worse.

I smiled mildly instead. "How about those directions?"

The gas station hadn't been very far from the property. A few more turns off of the county highway, and a handful of miles down narrow paved roads, led to the property that had only recently come into my possession. The purchase was so recent, the For Sale sign was still visible on CA-128. I put on my blinker even though there were no other vehicles on the road and turned onto the long driveway that served as the entrance to Lark Estates.

I'd only been to the vineyard once. We'd been staying at a Napa bed and breakfast that had included a complimentary tour and tasting at the micro-winery. I'd never heard the term before that day, but it was exactly what you might expect; the property only produced about

10,000 cases of wine each year. The big producers in the area spilled more wine in a year than what this vineyard created. But that was exactly why Alex had wanted it.

I leaned forward in the driver's seat to get a better view of my surroundings. A thick fog had settled across the road; without the morning sun, the cloud cover had gotten trapped in the valley. Gravel churned beneath my tires. I drove slowly, yet the treads still spit up small rocks that pinged off the bottom of my car.

My eyes swept back and forth across the lean landscape as I continued down the long, vacant driveway. The grounds looked much different in April than in the idyllic late summer when Alex and I had made our first and only visit. I remembered tall, blooming, wild flowers and ample sunshine. But the sky was currently grey, and the native flowers hadn't yet bloomed. The valley was immersed in a thick fog, and instead of lush, green vines crowded with tight bundles of grapes, the vineyard was barren of all life.

A few hundred yards into the property was a large barn that doubled as a tasting room as well as the production site for the wine itself: crusher destemming machines, a juice press, and giant steel fermentation tanks. Like many of the smaller wine producers in the area, access to the tasting room was by appointment only. The parking lot adjacent to the barn was empty. On a drizzly, overcast Tuesday in April, no one had apparently scheduled a visit to the winery.

I didn't stop at the barn. I continued to slowly drive down the bumpy gravel road and beyond more acreage of hibernating grape vines. The dormant vines were neatly spaced from each other like rows of solemn soldiers awaiting their orders. I'd never been this deep on the property before. The public tour had brought us into the corrugated metal barn that served as the public-facing space and production room, and we'd also been taken into the subterranean cellar where hundreds, if not thousands, of French oak barrels sat, each at their own stage in the wine-aging process.

At the edge of the property sat a white farmhouse. The previous owners hadn't lived on the vineyard, and the dilapidated structure was evidence of that fact. Alex had been excited about the prospect of us fixing up the farmhouse together. I didn't know the first thing about home improvement apart from the HGTV shows I watched. I'd always lived in apartment complexes and condos. When something broke, I called the property manager. I didn't even know how to operate a lawnmower.

Alex hadn't let my lack of homeowning experience dampen her excitement about the property though: "Don't worry about it, babe," she'd told me. "I'll take care of everything."

I pulled to a stop and parked in front of the farmhouse, mildly aware that I'd have to arrange for an EV charger to be installed on the property, otherwise my electric car would be useless. I exited my vehicle and shut the driver's side door behind me. I scanned the horizon for something—I didn't know what—for some sign of life, maybe, for some indication that this was the right choice. But the landscape offered me nothing. No joy. No life. No sense that I'd inherited more than a strange forest of bald, miniature trees or perhaps rows and rows of old men, bent over their walking sticks.

I opened the back hatch of my vehicle and began to unpack the back of my car. I expected a small moving truck to arrive later in the week with the rest of my belongings. If I'd been more organized, my things would have been waiting for me at the farmhouse. But Alex was the organized one, not me. If she had a spreadsheet for everything, I had post-it notes clinging precariously to various unstable surfaces.

I grabbed a small table lamp and a piece of luggage and carried them to the front door. My best friend Lily had offered to help with the move, but I'd stubbornly refused the kindness. I didn't know what I'd been trying to prove, or to whom, by insisting this was something I needed to do on my own, but now I was regretting not having the extra set of hands or at least a friendly, familiar face amongst these unfamiliar surroundings.

I cried out in surprise, but not pain, when my foot landed on the first step of three that led to the farmhouse's front porch. Instead of a solid foundation, my foot went straight through what turned out to be a rotten board. I stared down incredulously at my right leg, half of which had disappeared into the step. I didn't linger for long, however, as I immediately considered all of the creepy crawly things that might be living under the front stoop. I wretched my foot free, miraculously unhurt.

I was more careful ascending the final two steps; the boards were more generous than the first and thankfully didn't fail me. I looked down to the first step and the new foot-shaped crater. A mental To

Do list began to take shape in my mind: Fix the front stairs. Install an EV charger.

I sighed, struggling beneath the weight of my luggage and my new reality. "What the hell have you done, Alex?"

After unloading the boxes and luggage in the back my car, I went to bed early. It was only a two-hour drive with traffic from San Francisco to Calistoga, but I was fatigued from more than the rainy drive. I didn't bother to unpack any of the moving boxes or my luggage; there would be plenty of time for that later. I'd had the foresight to pack a small bag with toiletries, along with pajamas and clean sheets so I hadn't needed to rummage through every box to find what I needed for bed.

I claimed the downstairs bedroom for myself. The upstairs had two additional bedroom-shaped rooms and a larger bathroom than the smaller three-piece bathroom on the ground floor, but I wasn't ready to spread out and claim the entire house as mine. I'd never really lived someplace on my own. Alex and I had lived together nearly as soon as we'd started dating, close to twenty years ago. Before that I'd had roommates in college and before that I'd lived with my parents.

Being alone in the San Francisco condo I'd once shared with Alex hadn't felt too out of the ordinary. Alex often traveled for work, especially over the past few years as she tried to make as much money as possible for our 'early retirement.' Plus, I'd been surrounded by my belongings, which fostered familiarity. But now I was in a strange, empty home, on a property that I didn't know, in a part of California that I'd rarely visited. It made me feel like an uprooted plant, ripped from the soil, with my raw and vulnerable roots left to dangle in the wind. The metaphor was appropriate, perhaps, considering my new location. I needed to find a soft place to land, somewhere to re-establish my life, a place where I could recover and eventually thrive.

+ + +

I woke up the next morning feeling disoriented. I'd slept without dreaming with a little help from my new best friend melatonin. I hadn't been able to fall asleep lately without the assist. I was looking forward to going into town for a strong cup of coffee and a preliminary grocery run, just to get the lay of the land, but a shower beckoned me before I could make that happen.

The pipes in the walls of the downstairs bathroom made a disgruntled noise when I first turned on the shower. The old metal groaned and loudly clanged. After a worrisome lag, hot water shot out of the showerhead. The vacant farmhouse reminded me of a grumpy old man who'd been sitting in one position for too long and was now being asked to move. Everything in the house creaked and groaned and complained when I pushed a button or twisted a knob. The hot water stayed hot for the duration of my shower, however, so I considered that a victory.

After showering, I inspected my naked figure in the foggy mirror above the bathroom sink. I'd lost weight in recent months; without Alex to cook for, I hadn't found the energy or inspiration to prepare a real meal. Cereal, salad in a bag, and the occasional sandwich had served as dinner as of late. But I hadn't resorted to frozen TV dinners—yet.

I twisted in the bathroom mirror and continued my appraisal of the woman who stared back at me. Despite having recently celebrated my fortieth birthday, my skin was still youthful with minimal lines or wrinkles. My breasts were full and firm, although not quite as perky as they'd been in my twenties. My stomach was flat with some definition, although my hips had definitely become more full since my college years.

God, I reflected with a wistful sign, *college felt like a lifetime ago.* I'd secured a graphic designer position at a marketing agency in San Francisco straight out of college. I'd gradually worked my way up to Creative Director of the agency after a dozen dedicated years filled with late nights and truncated vacations. At the time I'd told myself the sacrifices would all be worth it. But then I'd given all of that up for Alex's master plan.

I frowned and made a face at the blue eyes staring back at me. The woman in my mirror's reflection wasn't quite a stranger, but she was different. Everything these days was different.

The farmhouse wasn't in total disrepair, but it was definitely rough around the edges. The kitchen appliances and basement laundry might have been older than me. The aged windows throughout the house were definitely not energy efficient. I could already anticipate how they might shake and rattle during a thunderstorm or how much the winter chill or summer heat would sneak beyond their single pane of glass.

I opened the cabinets in the kitchen, equal parts curious and horrified by what I might find. No one had lived in the rundown farmhouse in some time—human at least. I prayed I wouldn't stumble across the decomposing remains of any former wild animal tenants.

I found an impressive collection of cleaning supplies stored beneath the kitchen sink. The sight of so many disinfectants and surface cleaners momentarily derailed my plans to drive into Calistoga for groceries. Everything would be better once I had a cup of coffee, but I knew myself too well; until the farmhouse had been scoured from top to bottom, I wouldn't be able to unpack and get settled. The cobwebs, dust, and grimy buildup would have to be vanquished first. I resolved to unpack all of my boxes and to clean the whole house from top to bottom that day. I hadn't been able to control much since leaving San Francisco; having a clean and organized living space would be the first step to regaining control of my life.

I was up to my elbows in Comet scouring powder in the kitchen's enamel-coated cast iron sink when I heard a knock at the front door. It was cold that day—sunny but brisk—and I'd opened all of the windows that hadn't been painted shut. I'd left the front door open with only the screen door between myself and the elements to air out the house and make sure I didn't pass out from cleaning supply fumes.

I heard an upbeat, female voice call to me from the front porch: "Yoo hoo!" The screen door rattled against the doorframe with a second knock.

I stopped my obsessive cleaning to greet whomever was at the front door. As I walked closer, I spotted a woman peering through the door's worn screen.

"Hi!" she called to me, her voice chipper and bright. "Is your husband around?"

I pulled off my yellow rubber dish gloves and held them loosely in one hand. "Husband? I'm sorry—I think you have the wrong place."

The woman consulted the screen of her phone and made a humming sound. "I'm looking for Alex Marchand. I was told he'd just bought the property."

"Oh. You mean *Alexandre* Marchand," I spoke through the closed screen door. "Alex is a girl."

"Oh my gosh! I'm *so* sorry! I saw the name on the paperwork and I just assumed."

I wiped my hands on the back of my jeans. "Don't worry. It happens."

The woman continued to look flustered by her *faux pas* despite my assurances.

"What can I do for you?" I asked. That she knew of Alex's existence but not her pronouns was curious.

"It's more like what *I* can do for *you*."

"Come again?"

"I'm Belinda Reynolds," she introduced herself. "—the seller's real estate agent. The Mitchells had a conflict, so they asked me to give you a little tour of the place and make some introductions with the staff."

Belinda Reynolds was a short, and aggressively perky woman. Everything about her appearance seemed to ooze money and luxury, from the designer sunglasses perched on her nose to her tailored blazer and skirt. The sticker price on the oversized SUV idling in front of the farmhouse had probably cost more than twice my own car.

I touched a self-conscious hand to the loose bun fixed on top of my head. "I'm sorry. Who are the Mitchells?"

"The previous owners." The woman gave me a curious look as if she was starting to doubt I actually belonged on the property.

"Oh. I-I didn't know their names," I struggled. "Alex took care of all of those details."

The realtor—Belinda—peered through the closed screen door that separated us and looked beyond me. "Is Alex around? I'm sure she'd appreciate the tour, too."

"She … she won't be able to join us today. But I can fill her in on all the details afterwards."

I opened the screen door, but only long enough for me to exit and shut the main door behind me. The woman digested my appearance as I stepped outside. I hadn't consulted my reflection recently, but I imagined my disheveled appearance. I'd pulled my hair back in a haphazard top bun. A rolled blue bandana served as a headband to keep the flyaways out of my face. My clothes had become grimy like a dust rag. I wore an old, tattered sweatshirt pulled up to my elbows. Stains of various shapes and sizes covered the material. My jeans were similarly old and a boot-cut fit that was no longer fashionable.

Standing on the front porch, the Belinda Reynolds looked torn. Who was this messy woman squatting at Lark Estates? She was taking my word that I was supposed to be there. In a different scenario, she might have pressed me harder for why Alex couldn't come along on the tour, but she'd already tripped over Alex's gender and pronouns. I doubted she wanted another opportunity to offend me.

Belinda affixed a tight, but cheerful smile to her painted lips. "Okay," she chirped. "Let me introduce you to your head winemaker first and then we'll do some exploring."

"Watch your step," I announced in warning. "That last step is a little tricky."

Belinda looked down at the steps that descended to the gravel driveway and at the obvious foot-shaped hole in one of the wooden planks. "I suppose you're second-guessing waving that home inspection," she chuckled.

"Yeah," I returned with a nervous laugh. "But Alex really wanted this property, warts and all."

It wasn't a long or arduous walk between the farmhouse and the tasting barn, but Belinda insisted on driving us in her car. She claimed to be a full-service realtor, but she probably didn't want to muddy her designer boots in the soft, uneven terrain. I flipped down the passenger seat visor to inspect my face and hair. I licked the pad of my thumb and wiped at a dark smudge just below my right eye. I didn't know if it was old, traveling mascara or if the farmhouse was really that dirty.

As we approached the large, metal barn, I began to second-guess my outfit. First impressions were terribly important, so why was I about to meet the vineyard's head winemaker in clothes I wouldn't even go to the grocery store in? I considered asking Belinda to turn us around so I could freshen up, but before I could vocalize my misgivings, she'd parked her SUV and had shut off the engine.

"You're going to love Rolando," Belinda gushed, exiting the vehicle. "He's one of the Valley's most respected winemakers. You and Alex really lucked out. This place practically runs itself."

I climbed out of the SUV and stared up at the tasting barn. Hidden away in the farmhouse, I'd fallen into a false sense of comfort. Owning and managing an actual vineyard had existed in the abstract for such a long time, but now it was going to become a reality.

Belinda opened an unmarked door on the side of the barn and gestured for me to go inside. I sucked in a deep breath as I walked through the barn door. The bottoms of my tennis shoes scuffed against poured concrete.

"We're not open to the public, miss," a clear male voice called out. "You'll have to make a reservation on our website for the tour."

"Oh ... I-I'm not a tourist," I fumbled. The interior of the barn was dark, and my eyes struggled to adjust to the dim lighting. A single figure sat alone at a wooden picnic table only a few yards from the door.

The man was older, maybe in his late sixties. His face was deeply tanned with fine wrinkles at the corners of his mouth and eyes. His denim shirt hung loosely on narrow shoulders that curved forward. He had a full head of hair, dark grey in color, with lighter streaks of silver near his temples. His hair was combed and parted to one side.

Belinda entered the barn just behind me. "Good afternoon, Rolando!" she greeted.

"Belinda?" The man sounded confused by her presence. "*Que pasa?*"

"I'm here to introduce you to ..." She turned in my direction and blinked a few times. "I'm sorry. Who are you?"

I realized I'd never told the woman my name. "June," I said quickly. "June St. Clare."

"June and her ..." Belinda stopped again. She didn't know who Alex was to me and obviously didn't want to make another mistake.

I swallowed. "My partner, Alex. But not like business partner. Like, life partner." *God, I sounded so stupid.*

Rolando stood from the picnic table, abandoning the remnants of a sandwich and an apple. He wiped at the corner of his mouth with a paper napkin. "Forgive me. The Mitchells told me they'd found a buyer, but I didn't realize the sale had already gone through."

I held out my hands. "Please, don't let me interrupt your lunch," I insisted. "There will be plenty of time for introductions later."

Rolando nodded his head. "If you want to drop by tomorrow morning, I can give you a tour." He gestured to the barren, sleeping landscape beyond the barn's windows. "There won't be a lot to do outside for a few more weeks, but I can orient you to the production side of things."

"That would be great," I enthused. "Thank you."

I would have been satisfied to return to the farmhouse and come back later the next day, but Belinda was still committed to giving her version of the property tour. She corralled me back into her SUV and continued to drive away from the barn and the farmhouse.

I stared out the passenger side window as we bumped along a gravel roadway deeper onto the property. The horizon seemed to stretch on forever with only a few gnarled oak trees to break up the monotony.

"It's not much to look at, huh?" I thought aloud.

"Nothing above ground, no," Belinda agreed. "But beneath the soil, the vines are expanding their root systems. They're storing carbohydrates in their trunk. Kind of like me after a big bowl of pasta," she joked. Her laugh was sharp and loud.

"So as you know," she continued, "the property is twenty acres with seven of that planted with cabernet sauvignon. The property includes the barn, which we just saw, and the farmhouse. Unique to the area, you'll also find natural hot springs scattered around the property. The Mitchells had planned on building a day spa until they ran into some health issues and had to sell, but you and your wife might consider following through with those plans."

I licked my lips, taking it all in. "Maybe down the road. Right now I'd like to make the farmhouse a little more livable before considering new construction."

"Of course." Belinda bobbed her head as she drove. "If you change your mind, the Mitchells included the city-approved blueprints for the spa construction with the property's other paperwork. No sense re-inventing the wheel."

The land became more wild and the road less groomed the deeper we ventured onto the property. My throat constricted as the drive continued. Twenty acres hadn't sounded like much land when Alex had first proposed the purchase, but as Belinda continued to drive toward the edge of the property, I couldn't help but feel overwhelmed. At least there was no grass to mow.

"How big is an acre?" I wondered aloud.

Belinda hummed in thought. "Mmm … about the size of a football field."

I was no sports fan, but I tried to picture twenty football fields attached together. Before my anxiety could completely take over, Belinda slowed her SUV, and the vehicle came to a rolling stop. She put the car in park, but kept the engine running. "Come look," she encouraged. "You need to see your multi-million dollar view."

I exited the vehicle and followed Belinda to the property's edge. A metal stake in the ground signaled the property line. We stood at the top of a gently rolling hill, not quite large enough to call itself a mountain, but high enough that it offered an expansive view of the valley. A wide river wound back and forth in the distance. A thick bank of clouds had collected on the valley floor.

"Not too shabby, right?" Belinda observed.

I hugged my arms around my torso and inhaled. The view was a far cry from the congested city vista we'd enjoyed at our condo. I considered myself a city girl, but I'd enjoyed vacations Alex and I had taken to more rural locations. This was no vacation though.

"Not bad at all," I murmured.

Not too far in the distance I spotted a formidable log home on a flat piece of land in a small clearing.

"Who lives over there?" I pointed.

"That's Rolando's house," Belinda revealed. "The Mitchells sold his family an acre about thirty years ago. It's probably the only reason he hasn't gone to another, bigger vineyard. I'm sure he gets other job offers all the time."

I peered down the rolling hill at the wooden construction below. The home looked rustic, but more updated than the farmhouse. Half a dozen of the same hunched-over dormant vines I'd seen elsewhere on the property had been planted close to the house.

"He has his own vines?" I questioned aloud.

"I guess so," Belinda shrugged. "You'll have to ask him about it though. That's as far as my intel goes."

I turned to the real estate agent. "Thank you, Belinda," I said in earnest. "I appreciate you stopping by. You've been very thorough."

"Oh, I'm happy to help!" she gushed. "The commission on the property is more than enough to pay for my son's college, so I feel pretty indebted to you gals."

The reminder of just how much we'd sunk into the property and how much we'd mortgaged our future on this gamble shattered my temporary moment of euphoria. I cleared my throat: "Glad to have helped."

"Do you want me to come back tomorrow and show Alex around?" she offered.

I wrapped my arms tighter around my torso and continued to stare across the picturesque vista.

"No, that won't be necessary."

I could feel Belinda's eyes on me as if she expected more of an explanation.

I couldn't explain why I wasn't more forthcoming with the realtor about why Alex hadn't been around for the tour. I'd had plenty of time to wrap my brain around our situation; I'd had months to adjust to what had happened. But it almost felt like Coming Out all over again—when people would ask me about Alex, I found myself getting tongue-tied and making excuses instead of just telling them the truth.

Alex wouldn't need a tour of the property. Alex was dead.

CHAPTER TWO

I tugged on the brim of my baseball cap as I crossed the short distance between the farmhouse and the tasting barn. I was admittedly nervous and not a little bit terrified for my first official day of working with Rolando, the vineyard's head winemaker. He'd done nothing during our brief, initial meeting to give me cause for such emotions, but I was still an anxious mess.

I hadn't had a first day of work at a new job in over a decade. I was technically the vineyard's owner, not a new employee, but I still wanted to make a good impression. Added to the first day jitters was the very real fact that I had no idea what I was doing. Buying a winery had been Alex's idea. As part of her sales pitch, she'd convinced me that I really wouldn't have to do much—maybe help out with marketing or social media or design wine labels since that was in my wheelhouse. She'd promised that she would take care of the rest.

I kicked angrily at a small rock and watched it bounce across the gravel driveway. "So much for that plan," I huffed to myself.

I hadn't even known what to wear that morning, but I'd eventually settled on jeans, a long-sleeved t-shirt, and duck boots, with my hair in a ponytail, woven through the back of a baseball cap. I'd gone through more outfit combinations than if I'd been getting ready for a first date—something else I really had little experience with.

Dating long term the first woman with whom I'd ever gone on a date had saved me from those kinds of awkward experiences later in life, but in other ways it had sheltered me from having to pivot or adjust or muddle through that uncomfortable knot in the pit of one's stomach. Without Alex to help me navigate, it was like experiencing the world for the first time. I was stripped down, sloughed of old skin and calluses that had built up over the years. I was a newly scrubbed infant, pink and raw and vulnerable, stumbling through unfamiliar territory.

It was a brisk morning with little wind and no frost on the winter-hardened ground. Looking around at the grey landscape, it was hard to picture that in a few months the vineyard, in theory, would be alive with new growth. For the time, however, I would just have to trust that Alex hadn't invested our entire life savings on acres and acres of brittle-looking, slumped over trees.

The air temperature outside was chilled, but a blast of warm air met me when I entered the tasting barn. I found Rolando, the head winemaker, sitting alone at the picnic table inside, just as I'd found him the previous day. It made me wonder if he'd moved at all. As I approached, he didn't look away from the carefully folded newspaper that he held in one hand.

Rolando wasn't an overly tall or overly short man. His shoulders were slightly slumped forward as he drank from a ceramic coffee cup. His fingers curled around the mug as though it was a natural extension from his hand. I felt better about my outfit selection when I observed his blue jeans, boots, and faded flannel shirt.

"Good morning," I greeted.

Rolando's dark eyes slowly lifted from the newspaper, and he offered me a kind smile. "Good morning, June."

He held out his free hand across the table as a sign that I should take a seat. I became nothing but gangly legs and awkward arms as I climbed over the bench seat to join him at the picnic table. I couldn't help the small, frustrated grunts and noises of complaints that tumbled from my lips. It was like I'd never seen a picnic table before or had never tried to sit at one.

Rolando silently observed my inelegant arrival as I eventually took up the empty space across from him. He gestured to a folding table behind me where I saw a silver coffeemaker and a stack of similar nondescript mugs as the one from which he drank. "Coffee?" he offered.

"I'm good, thanks."

I probably would have helped myself to a cup if I wasn't so worried about having to get up and then sit down again. I didn't trust myself to ever stand up again.

Rolando took another careful sip from his coffee cup. He watched me with curiosity, which had me tugging my baseball cap even lower on my forehead. I wondered what he thought about me, or what he might have learned since my arrival the previous day. Without actually knowing, I was certain I didn't resemble someone who owned a vineyard. But what did a vineyard owner even look like? Male, probably. Older, definitely. Maybe a button-up shirt and a Patagonia vest.

Before I could entirely wither beneath Ronaldo's silent gaze, the barn door slid open again and the sound of two male voices filled up the space.

"You're crazy if you think Canelo could beat Chavez in his prime. They didn't call him *El Gran Campeon Mexicano* for nothing," one of the men boasted.

"You can't judge Canelo yet," the other man countered in a more reserved, reasonable tone. "He's the best pound-for-pound fighter, and he's just getting started."

"Pound-for-pound because the others have all retired," the first man all but scoffed. He was a small, but muscular man, like a featherweight boxer or an elite long-distance runner.

Neither of the newcomers looked in Ronaldo's or my direction. They walked directly for the informal coffee bar and helped themselves to free caffeine.

"Legacy. Longevity," the second man ticked off. He taller than the first, but was more narrowly built. His face featured straight lines; along with a thin nose, a broadly drawn mouth topped a thin mustache. He spoke in a softer and more understated tone than the other man. "That's what's important. After Chavez lost to De La Hoya, he was never the same."

"I'd be embarrassed to have lost to that pretty boy, too," the first man grinned.

"Carlos, Oscar," Rolando named the men. "Stop your gossip and meet our new owner, June St. Clare."

Rolando's phrasing made me uneasy. I didn't own *them*, after all. And technically the vineyard belonged to the bank until I successfully chipped away at the outrageous mortgage Alex had negotiated.

I stood with the intention of shaking hands with the two men, but the toe of my right boot snagged on the bench. I caught myself just in time and narrowly avoided face-planting across the picnic table. I was sure everyone had noticed me tripping all over myself, but they had the kindness or tact not to point out my awkwardness.

"It's nice to meet you both," I said, addressing each man individually. I would have to determine which one was Carlos and which one was Oscar when I wasn't so frazzled. "I look forward to working with you in the coming months."

I wanted to come across as competent and sincere, but my words felt robotic and forced. I was used to managing people, but my natural habitat was a sea of cubicles in a big city high rise, not a corrugated metal barn on a rural vineyard.

Rolando took another drink of his coffee before standing from the picnic table. Even though he must have been at least twenty years older than me, he stood without a telling groan. He also removed himself from the picnic table without getting tangled with the bench seating as I had.

"I suppose we should go for a walk," he said in a slow, careful drawl, "and you can see what you've gotten yourself into."

He offered me another gentle smile, so I didn't take offense to his choice of words.

Rolando opened the main barn door and we stepped outside. It wasn't cold enough to justify a winter coat, but I regretted not dressing warmer. I self-consciously rubbed at my arms, which had only the thin cotton material of my long-sleeved t-shirt. The action didn't go unnoticed.

"Do you need to get a coat?" Rolando asked me.

I stubbornly shook my head. "No, I'll be fine."

It only occurred to me in that moment that we would probably be spending a lot of time outdoors. I grew frustrated with myself for not having the foresight to be more prepared. I'd fretted for so long about my stupid hat and which shoes to wear that I apparently forgot that grapes grow outdoors. I choked down the urge to sprint back to the farmhouse, get in my car, and leave this whole experience in my rearview mirror.

Ronaldo took another sip from the coffee cup he'd brought along. He seemed to be admiring the landscape even though it was a view, I was sure, he experienced every morning.

"This is the sleepiest time on the vineyard," he identified, "so there's not much to see. We've already put the vines to bed with cover crops to keep the roots warm, and we've pruned back the vines to the rootstock. Around now is when we perfect our blends and top off the barrels in the cellar."

"Blends?" I was acutely aware of how ignorant I was when it came to wine.

"Most wines aren't one hundred percent varietal specific," he explained. "In California, cabernet sauvignon can contain up to twenty-five percent of non-cabernet sauvignon. An under-ripe cabernet might be improved with a small addition of a spicy merlot or a bold, fruity zin."

I blinked a few times as my brain struggled to make sense of his words. *Varietal. Under-ripe. Fruity Zin.* "Oh." I tried to keep from fidgeting. "Ronaldo?"

The head winemaker turned away from the terrain to face me. "Yes?"

I bit down on my lower lip. "I don't know anything about making wine."

Rolando rewarded my transparency with another warm, patient smile. "Your secret's safe with me, June. I appreciate your honesty." The longer he smiled, the better I felt. "And I'll tell you a secret of mine: I didn't know anything about making wine at first either. And look at me now."

"But I'm a quick learner," I said in earnest. "And I want to learn. I want to do a good job."

"It's easy to get caught up in the romance of wine making," Ronaldo noted. "You're taking a pretty common plant and transforming it into something totally different. But growing grapes and making wine is just a farm."

His words were intended to ease my anxiety, but they brought a grimace to my lips instead. "I've never even had a garden."

"Well, there's no time like the present to get started." He took a final sip of his morning coffee before tipping the mug over and emptying the dregs of his drink onto the ground.

Rolando started to walk towards one of the tilled plots and beckoned for me to follow. He moved as if he was never in a rush. It wasn't the slow, jerky shuffle that comes with age, but rather a smooth, fluid gait like a cat crossing a room. It forced my own stride to slow down beside him, which I discovered took some conscious effort. I'd internalized San Francisco's frenzied pace after close to a decade and a half of living and working in the city.

"Our entire operation is dependent on a robust grape harvest every year," he started. "We're a vertically integrated winery, not a *négociant* who gets their grapes from someone else."

"People buy grapes to make their wine?" I asked. The thought had never occurred to me, not that I often thought about wine making.

Rolando nodded. "You can have a wine label without owning a vineyard. And you can also run a vineyard without ever making wine. We, however, do it all."

Rolando stopped at the edge of a barren plot, empty except for the short, gnarled, sleeping grapevine. "Winter pruning takes place in January and February. The previous year's growth is cut back. We choose the best canes—these horizontal branches," he gestured, "to grow new shoots for the coming year's harvest. It's a critical moment that determines the future of the vine."

"Poorly chosen canes grow weak harvests," I guessed. I committed the information and vocabulary to memory. *Cane equals horizontal branch thingie.*

Rolando bent and scooped up some of the loose dirt, which better resembled the ash bin from a fireplace. It coated the ends of his fingers like wood ash or dust. "We call this moon dust," he said. "The soil is classified as gold ridge sandy loam. It drains very well."

"It's very fine," I said, not knowing how else to respond.

"This is three to five million years old ocean floor. Just about three feet down from the surface is a layer of fossilized sea shells. Grapevines love this kind of soil because it drains well; it doesn't retain much moisture, and the roots of the grapevine loves that. Cabernets especially."

"And we make cabernets," I recalled from Belinda's brief tour of the property. "So what's next? What work needs to be done?" I was eager to do more than a walking tour.

"We'll keep perfecting what's in the barrels until bud break," he said. "Sap rises from the roots, and we see first signs of new growth on the vineyard. New canes will grow on the old wood," he said, tapping at a grey-colored stalk. "We'll get one to two inches of growth a day."

"A day?" I gaped. "That's remarkable."

"It's exciting," he confirmed with a nod, "but also perilous. The new buds are very delicate; spring hail storms can destroy them and shorten the growing season, reducing the ripeness of the resulting wine."

"What about water usage?" I questioned.

As a lifelong Californian, I was deeply aware that half of the state was on fire at any time because of recent historic droughts.

"Water isn't as big of an issue in the Valley as in other areas," he told me. "We get enough rainfall on average to sustain the vines. We have irrigation tubing throughout the property, but Calistoga has the highest amount of rainfall in the valley, so we can typically dry farm. Plus, grapes don't really require too much water; grapevines thrive where little else will grow."

I nodded, silently grateful for the admission—one, because the state could hardly afford diverting more water for a nonessential item like wine, and two, it signaled less overhead that might eat into my already miniscule savings.

I looked away from Rolando and the empty vines when I heard the sound of car tires crunching along a gravel road. A white SUV with gold trim accents drove down the long driveway that led to the tasting barn.

"Are we expecting someone?" I asked.

"That would be Natalie. We must have tours today."

I swallowed hard. I'd already embarrassed myself in front of the vineyard's other employees that morning. Might as well go for a full sweep.

Rolando strode back in the direction of the barn, and I followed a step behind. He walked with that same, no-rush gait. This time I didn't need to consciously slow my pace. Maybe I was already becoming more in tune with rural life.

We reached the tasting barn just as the sliding door opened and a woman stepped out. She struggled with the awkward shape and weight of a freestanding blackboard.

Rolando quickened his actions when he saw her try to drag the signage outdoors. "Hold on, Nat. Let me get that for you."

The woman stood back and allowed Rolando to take over. I stood a few awkward steps away and watched him set up the sign just beyond the barn's main entrance. Someone had written across the blackboard with vibrantly colored chalk: *Tastings and Tours Enter Here.*

Natalie eventually noticed me. "Oh, hi. Are you here early? We don't officially start things until 1:00 p.m. today."

I opened my mouth, but Rolando spoke before I could: "Natalie, this is June St. Clare. She's the new owner."

The woman's features lit up with new appreciation. "Oh! It's so nice to meet you! I'm sorry I mistook you for a guest. This one," she said, thumbing in Rolando's direction, "should have warned me."

"It's okay," I appeased. "I don't suppose I look like the typical vineyard owner." My misgivings tumbled from my mouth.

"Oh, honey, you say that like it's a bad thing." She shook her head, and with it, her shockingly bright red hair. "The vineyard owners I've met are mostly stuffy, old, white men. It's about time we shake things up," she said with a conspiratorial wink.

"I've got to run into town," Rolando announced. "Nat, would you mind running through the tour script with June while I'm gone? I'm sure it's all material she's heard before, but it's always nice to have a refresher once in a while."

I gave Rolando a grateful smile: *Your secret's safe with me.*

+ + +

"You ready to drink some wine?"

I sat down on a barstool in the tasting room while Natalie uncorked a nearby wine bottle before I could respond. I wasn't wearing a watch, but it seemed a little early in the workday to indulge.

"Not too much," I cautioned as she filled up the glass in front of me higher than expected. "I don't want a hangover my first day on the job."

"No worries," she appeased. "The primary cause of a wine headache isn't sulfites; it's dehydration. Drink eight ounces of water with each serving of wine and you won't feel a thing—well, except the alcohol," she chuckled good naturedly.

Natalie Cook was in her late fifties or early sixties. As tasting room manager, her role on the vineyard was to coordinate on-site tastings and lead the tours. She worked part-time in winter and came on full-time during the growing season. The fine lines around her mouth and eyes revealed a woman who laughed more than she frowned. Her vibrant orange-red hair came from a beautician, not genetics, although I suspected the single thick streak of white in her bangs was a point of pride, otherwise it would have been colored over. Her voice was a little rough and raspy, as if she'd been a smoker earlier in life.

"This is our 2018 cabernet sauvignon," she told me. "It's the world's most popular wine—a cross between cabernet franc and sauvignon blanc."

She set the bottle she'd recently opened in front of me for inspection. "All of our wines are estate wines," she continued, "which means that all of our grapes are grown right here on the property."

"We don't buy grapes from anyone else," I chimed in, recalling what Rolando had taught me earlier.

"Exactly." She tapped manicured fingernails on the square label on the bottle before me. "Everything you need to know about a wine is right on the label. Three-fourths of the grapes have to be grown in the Valley for it to have 'Napa Valley' on the label. The year, or vintage, is when the grapes were harvested. This particular wine is a single-varietal, meaning it was made with one or mostly one grape variety, although we do have several blends, especially field blends, which are made with different varieties harvested and vinified together."

My brain was spinning from Natalie's soliloquy. She probably could recite the tour in her sleep whereas I had never heard of half of those words.

I reached for the wine glass, but Natalie stopped me. "This one gets better with a little air. I wasn't expecting you, so I don't have anything already decanted. Let that sit in your glass for a while," she instructed, "and I'll tell you a bedtime story."

I had no idea what she was talking about, but she had such an easy confidence that I had no choice but to sit back on my stool and smile.

Natalie cleared her throat before beginning. "We think of wine today as a fancy indulgence—something you might pair with a fancy dinner out or as a celebration drink. Or maybe Mom has had a hard day," she laughed to herself. "But wine has much more humble roots. Before our modern-day water purification systems, alcohol was the most hygienic beverage out there. People needed wine. Columbus had wine on his ships. The Puritans and Pilgrims had beer. It wouldn't go bad or stale like a cask of water would."

"Huh," I mused aloud. "That makes a lot of sense. The fermentation, right?"

"Bingo," Natalie confirmed. "California wines started 240 years ago out of the Mission de Alcalá in San Diego. After the Gold Rush in 1849, wineries become popular in Sonoma and Napa Valley, and the industry took off. Unfortunately," she noted, tilting her head to one side, "the industry would soon be hit by a double-whammy that spelled the end for many wineries. A San Francisco earthquake and fire in 1906 resulted in the loss of three-fourths of the state's wine supply. And then in 1910, the dreaded *phylloxera* virus spread through the valley, killing off more than ninety percent of the vines."

"*Phylloxera?*" I struggled with the word.

"It's a fancy-sounding name for a louse that attacks grape wine roots," she told me. "Because of *phylloxera*, most vines in the region aren't that old. Varietals from the oldest wines are some of the rarest and therefore most sought after. But that infestation was only the first challenge to California's wine industry."

"Prohibition?" I guessed.

"That's number three on the list," she clucked. "Don't worry; we'll get there."

"Are you like the resident wine historian?" I marveled.

"Nothing so pompous as that," she laughed. "A lot of folks these days are getting degrees in viticulture and enology. But when you've been around winemaking as long as me, you start to pick up on a few things."

"How long have you worked at Lark Estates?" I asked.

Natalie batted her mascara-coated eyelashes. "A lady never reveals her age."

I smirked at the response. "Fair enough. So what was the wine industry's second challenge?" I pressed. "And when do I get to drink this wine?"

Natalie laughed, loud and without a filter. "Go ahead, honey."

I took my first experimental sip while Natalie continued her history lesson: "In 1915, the region experienced its next big set-back. The Panama-Pacific International Exposition was supposed to be California's moment to shine. But because of World War I, the industry's traditional big hitters like France, Germany, and Italy didn't attend. And then," she said, her voice lilting up, "the Prohibition era kicked in, nearly bringing an end to Napa Valley all together."

I set my wine glass back on the bar top. "That's good," I approved, pointing to the beverage. I didn't have the lexicon to describe why I liked the wine, but it wasn't too dry to make my throat burn.

"Thanks, darling," Natalie approved. "The Santiagos definitely know their way around a wine cellar."

"How long has Rolando worked here?" I asked, "or do ladies not reveal that either?"

"Oh, you're a quick one," Natalie chuckled. "I think we'll keep you."

I smiled, privately pleased, and brought the wine glass back to my lips. Even if I tripped and bumbled through interactions with everyone else, I had a feeling that Natalie would be a soft landing place.

"I believe Rolando is going into his fortieth harvest this season," she told me.

"Fortieth?" I gaped. "That's practically longer than I've been alive."

"He's been married to this vineyard longer than most people have been married to their spouses," she confirmed. "Speaking of wives, where's yours?"

My throat constricted at the question. "Oh. Uh."

"Sorry to put you on the spot," Natalie chuckled. "Belinda is a good friend of mine. She called me up to warn me she'd epically failed yesterday when she misgendered your partner. She didn't want me to make the same mistake."

I licked at my lips. They tasted like wine. "Alex is ... Alex ... she, uh ..."

God, why couldn't I just say the words?

Behind me, I heard the barn door slide open. I took the interruption as an opportunity to avoid Natalie's question. I turned on my barstool and saw one of the two men—Oscar or Carlos—I still didn't know who was who.

"Carlos," Natalie greeted, "what can I do for you?"

Carlos. I committed the name and the man's face to memory. He'd been the smaller, but more muscled of the two men. I wondered if they were related to each other.

"I came to get her," he said, nodding in my direction.

"Me?" I all but squeaked.

The man gave me a broad smile. "Can't drink the profits all day, *Jefa*. It's bad business. Ready to get your hands dirty?"

I looked from Carlos, back to Natalie, and then down to my barely touched wine glass. It seemed like such a waste of a very good wine, but I didn't want them thinking I was lazy or was in this business for the wrong reasons.

I hopped down from the barstool. "Thanks for the history lesson, Natalie. I'll be back another time for the rest."

"Don't let those boys work you too hard, June," she advised me. "Remember who's the boss."

I tried to smile at the affable woman, but I was sure it looked more like a grimace. I certainly didn't feel very boss-like.

I didn't make it back to the farmhouse that night until after sunset. We were deeper into the spring season, with little fear of frost, so Carlos had tasked me with helping plant new vines in areas of the vineyard where older vines that no longer produced fruit had been removed from the earth. It had been hard work, and I'd certainly gotten my hands dirty. But despite how my knees and lower back protested being hunched over for the better part of the afternoon, my body felt satisfied from the day's work.

I anticipated an early morning the next day. I needed to go into town for supplies—groceries and other essentials—but Rolando had promised to give me an overview of the wine-making process when I returned. I'd been a timid mess on my first day, but I was determined to be less awkward on day two.

An antique clawfoot tub awaited me in the upstairs bathroom, but until a general contractor could inspect the farmhouse, I didn't want to risk filling an already heavy bathtub with gallons of water. If the front stoop hadn't been able to handle the weight of my body, I didn't want to test the limits of the second floor. My muscles and joints would have benefited from a long soak, but I opted for a hot shower instead.

Dinner consisted of macaroni and cheese out of a blue and yellow box. I discovered that only three of the electric stovetop burners actually worked, so I added that to my growing list of maintenance needs. I didn't anticipate crafting gourmet meals that would require more than a serviceable microwave or hot plate, however. I forced myself to eat the uninspired meal at the table in the eat-in kitchen. I had no cable or internet service in the farmhouse yet, so it wasn't like I could have watched brainless television to distract me from the one-pot meal.

As I sat at the kitchen table, shoveling elbow noodles into my mouth, I was struck by the silence of the farmhouse. It was so quiet, almost unbearably so. I'd become accustomed to condo and apartment living where the low murmur of a television show in the next apartment or the heavy steps of an upstairs neighbor could be heard. But the farmhouse had no discernable sounds beyond a few wooden creaks as the result of wind or the house's foundation settling.

I still had cheesy noodles in the bottom of my bowl, but I called my best friend Lily in hopes of filling the silent emptiness of the night. The phone rang and rang and rang with no answer. I began to lose hope of connecting with my friend that evening, but Lily picked up just before the call could go to voicemail.

"Junie!" she exclaimed. She nearly sounded breathless. "How are you doing? Are you all settled in?"

I wanted to pour my heart out to my friend and describe each of my worries to her, but the sound of thumping base reverberated through the phone call.

"Where are you?" I asked instead. I pulled the phone away from my ear and winced. "It's so loud!"

"I'm sorry," Lily apologized, nearly shouting to be heard over the music. "I'm at a burlesque show in the Castro. Everybody!" I heard her call out, "say hi to Junie!"

I had no idea who 'everyone' included, but I heard a chorus of greetings in the background and not a few sentiments of people missing me and wishing I was there. I gripped my phone a little tighter as a wave of longing and regret crested over me.

What was I doing here? Why was I suffering, alone and disoriented? Why had I left the city and my friends?

"I miss you guys, too!" I managed to choke out.

Lily's voice returned to the call. "I'm sorry, sweetie, but I've got to go. The show's about to start, and I don't want to be rude."

I swallowed down my feelings of disappointment. "No, no. It's okay," I reassured her. "I was just calling to say hi."

"Let's catch up soon, okay?" Lily declared. "I want to hear all about how much ass you're kicking up there."

"Right," I said weakly. "Totally slaying."

CHAPTER THREE

Rolando held a small, dark berry between his middle finger and his thumb. He held it up to the morning sun like a jeweler inspecting a precious gem. "This," he announced proudly, "is a wine grape."

I stood with Ronaldo at the edge of one of the tilled plots the next morning, not far from the tasting barn. After a brief run into town for groceries and other necessities, I'd returned to the vineyard for more of my wine education. Rolando plucked another leftover grape from the closest grapevine and handed it to me. I cupped the slightly shriveled berry in the palm of my hand.

"It looks more like a blueberry than a grape," I noted.

"Wine grapes are different than table grapes," he said. "They're smaller and sweeter with seeds and thicker skin. The valley," he continued, "is perfect for growing wine grapes. Hot summer days provide color and big berry flavor. Cool nights maintain acid balance and retention. And Calistoga has the highest percentage of volcanic soils which yield more minerals in the wine itself."

I thought about the tiny shoots I'd planted with Oscar the day before. "How long does it take for a new plant to start growing fruit?"

"Fruit that you'd actually want to use?" he qualified. "Three years. Before that we either compost or find a buyer who doesn't mind young grapes."

"I knew wines got better with age, but so do grapes?"

Rolando nodded. "The quality of the berry increases, but older vines also produce less fruit. You really want to have a mix of young and old vines on the farm."

"How old is the oldest vine on our property?" I asked.

"Close to fifty years old," he replied. "But that's about as old as you want. At fifty years, the vine is hardly producing any berries."

"Huh," I considered. "I don't know why I had this picture in my head of ancient grapevines that were centuries old."

Ronaldo rested his hand on one of the cut back vines. It looked like a low, twisting crutch. "These old rootstocks and canes might look like they've got no more life in them, but I promise you that in a few weeks, they're going to amaze you."

I let Rolando's optimism influence me. If the head winemaker was confident, I had no reason not to be.

"Let's head back inside," he suggested, "and I'll show you how the wine gets made."

The tasting barn was empty when we returned; Carlos and Oscar were elsewhere on the property, and Natalie wasn't scheduled to come in until later that day. I found the silence of the farmhouse in the evening to be off-putting, but the quiet of the barn was almost restorative. Offices were typically filled with the constant jangle of telephones, the erratic clicking of fingers against keyboards, and competing voices that filtered above the half walls of cubicles. The scent of microwaved lunches had always annoyed me; the vineyard's barn smelled of cool concrete, dirt, and yeast. I surprisingly enjoyed the latter. It was like proofing bread in the moments before it went into a hot oven.

The barn was a wide open space under a corrugated metal roof and frame, divided into different sections. An employee's only section consisted of the picnic table where Rolando drank his morning coffee and Carlos and Oscar gathered for lunch. A small office with a proper door and four walls was the economic center of the business and the only space with internet access. Natalie commanded another corner of the building as the start and finish point for guest tours. A few backless stools had been pulled up to a makeshift bar that was really only a few empty wine barrels tipped onto their sides. The rest of the barn was dedicated to the production of wine once the grapes had been harvested in September and October.

Ronaldo walked me through the barn's impressive and expensive-looking machinery. Everything was turned off, but in late fall, a wide conveyor belt allowed workers to pick through newly harvested grapes. Leaves, stems, and berries that had become rotten or sun dried would be removed by hand. Anything that shouldn't make it into the wine would be disposed.

The remaining grape clusters were then transported, very gently, on a second conveyor belt that reminded me of an escalator to be dropped into the crusher destemmer. The destemmer mechanically separated the berries from their stems. The stems were later composted and would go back into the vineyard.

After that, the berries went through a second sorting. A shaking table removed tiny bits of stems that the destemmer might have missed. Rolando told me it was a trick adapted from blueberry sorting; little horizontal slats allowed for tiny wooden stems to fall through. The whole apparatus reminded me of mining gold in the Klondike. But we were making liquid gold instead.

The final mechanized ride was another escalator trip that transported the berries to massive, stainless steel fermentation tanks, not unlike tanks one might find in a brewery. The separated grapes sat in the tanks for a specific amount of time, producing CO_2 and alcohol, all carefully monitored by Rolando. The resulting fermented juices would eventually be divided into smaller oak barrels to be stored and aged in the subterranean cellar.

I took in everything—the silent, giant machines and currently empty fermentation vats. I tried to imagine the constant hum of machinery towards the year's end and the organized chaos of harvest time.

"So it's just you, Carlos, Oscar, and Natalie doing all of this work?" I asked. It seemed like a massive undertaking for such a lean team.

"For a little while longer," Rolando confirmed. "We'll take on more workers once the growing season begins and especially during harvest," he told me. "But you don't have to worry about that. I have a very good relationship with some seasonal workers who come back year after year, and they all bring at least one friend whom they can vouch for."

I recalled the realtor, Belinda, and her earlier words about the vineyard. "It sounds like a well-oiled ship," I remarked.

I should have been reassured, even relieved, by this fact, but I discovered only disappointment. Rolando and his tight-knit staff seemed to have everything covered.

Did I really need to be here? I silently lamented. *What was I supposed to do? How could I make myself useful?*

"Ahhh. Just in time," Rolando approved. His eyes focused on something behind me. "Here's our most valuable employee."

I turned around, fully expecting to see another person—a fifth employee, perhaps—but a notched-ear barn cat slunk into view instead. The lean animal approached us with caution, one quick step in front of the other. It stopped and stared up at me with green eyes. Its fur was mostly dark grey, but its white chin gave the impression of having a beard.

"We have a cat?" I questioned.

"We do," Rolando confirmed. "But you don't have to worry about Gato," he assured me. "There's enough critters on the property that he stays better fed than the rest of us."

My Spanish wasn't very extensive, but I knew a few common words and phrases. "Wait. The cat's name is *cat?*"

Rolando grinned, showing off two charming dimples. "We save the creativity for the wine making."

I bent over and leaned closer to the cat who was currently rubbing his body against Rolando's work boots. I wasn't exactly a cat person—Alex had had allergies, so we'd never had a pet. "Hey, Gato," I softly greeted. I reached out a tentative hand. "I'm June."

I tried to pet between the cat's ears, but Gato had other plans. He maneuvered away from my outstretched fingers and swiped at me with his right paw. I jerked my own hand away to avoid getting scratched, and the cat scampered away.

"Don't worry," Rolando assured me. "He'll get used to you."

I righted myself when the door to the tasting barn unexpectedly swung open. A figure, backlit by the day's sunshine, stood in the doorway. "They sold us?!" The voice was shrill, but decidedly feminine. "I leave for a few months," the newcomer seethed, "and they sell the place right from under our feet?!"

A woman strode aggressively into the barn, leaving the door wide open.

"Who is that?" I murmured for only Rolando's ears.

"*That* is your assistant winemaker," he returned.

"She doesn't sound very happy," I continued in my hushed tone.

"She takes a while to warm up to change," he whispered back. "She's like her mother in that way."

I arched an eyebrow at his words.

Ronaldo shrugged. "She's my daughter."

Daughter?

"I wasn't expecting you back so early," Rolando called out to the fiery woman. "You're usually not here until after bud break."

"Carlos called me about the sale," the woman all but growled. "I booked the first flight back."

"*Ven acá, hijita,*" Ronaldo coaxed. "There's someone I'd like you to meet."

"Can it wait?" The woman looked apologetic, but annoyed. "I've been traveling all day. My body doesn't know if it's night or day."

"It'll only take a minute," he promised.

I heard her displeased grumble and the muttering of unintelligible complaints, but the woman crossed the barn to join us near the fermentation tanks. As she approached, her features came into finer detail.

She looked younger than me, but not by much. We were close to the same height with her a little taller. I noticed her high, sweeping cheekbones first and then her wide, serious mouth. Her complexion was lighter than her father's, but they shared the same dark, expressive eyes and thick eyelashes. She had a high forehead, a long, narrow nose, and thick, but not unruly eyebrows. Her hair was long, straight, and dark; she wore it parted down the middle. Her figure was lean and angular. The scoop-neck t-shirt she wore hung low across her chest, revealing a mesmerizing clavicle. I tore my eyes away from the exposed skin when I realized I'd been staring.

"Lucia, this is June St. Clare," Rolando introduced with his gentle, appeasing smile. "She just bought the vineyard."

Lucia snapped her head in my direction. She pinned me in place with a pointed stare. "You?"

"T-technically," I stuttered, "my partner Alex bought it; it's her name on the mortgage." I felt myself shrinking under the woman's heated, incredulous scowl. "But I'm eager to learn the business and help out."

"Learn?" Lucia sneered. "You bought a vineyard without knowing anything about viticulture?"

"I-I ..." The venom and disdain in her voice took me by surprise. Rolando had only shown me kindness; why was his daughter so angry at me?

Rolando clapped his hands together. I flinched at the sharp sound. "I have a wonderful idea," he announced. "Starting tomorrow, June, you'll shadow Lucia. Lucia, you'll teach June everything you know about making wine."

"I'm not a babysitter!" Lucia hotly exclaimed. "I'm assistant winemaker!"

"Exactly," Rolando confirmed. "And as *assistant* to the head winemaker, I've decided that you'll show June the ropes."

The glare Lucia gave her father suggested that the only ropes she wanted to introduce me to were the hangman's noose.

I started to protest. "Rolando, I—."

"I've made up my mind," he said with finality. "Lucia will be in charge of your orientation."

"I don't have time to do my work *and* teach her," Lucia bitterly complained.

"Do this thing," Rolando bargained, "and I'll consider giving you ten percent of this year's harvest to make your own blends."

Some of the animosity faded from her features. Lucia seemed to consider the offer. "Twenty five."

Rolando chuckled, sounding amused. "Be satisfied I'm giving you any fruit at all, *mija*."

"Ten is perfect," Lucia rushed before Rolando could change his mind.

I looked between father and daughter. "So what do I do now?"

Lucia's lip curled. "I'm going to bed; I'm jetlagged as fuck. We'll start tomorrow at 6:00 a.m."

"So early, *mi hija?*" Rolando looked concerned. "Is that really necessary?"

"If I'm the one babysitting, I say when the day starts," Lucia countered.

"6:00 a.m. is great," I jumped in. It was a much earlier start than what I was accustomed to, but I didn't want to be a source of conflict between Rolando and his daughter.

Lucia looked me up and down a final time. She said nothing more, but I heard her indignant huff before she turned and walked away.

I licked my lips and watched the dour woman's exit. "Think she'll get used to me, too?" I wondered aloud.

Rolando stood beside me and rested his hand on my shoulder. "You'll probably have better luck with the cat."

+ + +

I bent at the waist and itched the small bandage that covered my right ankle bone. I'd been shaving my legs since puberty, but I still managed to routinely nick myself in the shower. When I righted myself, I leaned against the makeshift bar and sighed. It was only my second day on the job and Rolando had already run out of tasks for me. To be fair, none of the staff had been prepared for a novice owner who wanted to learn on the job. Apparently the previous owners, the Mitchells, had never been interested in the day-to-day operations of the vineyard, but rather bragging to friends that they owned a Napa Valley winery.

Rolando had passed me off to Natalie once she'd arrived on the property later that day. There was another private tasting scheduled for me to assist with. I was frustrated to not be able to help elsewhere, but it was clear—despite Rolando's unyielding kindness— that I was a nuisance. There would be simpler, more routine tasks for me later in the season—when things were actually growing on the vineyard—but until then, I worried my days might consist of watching other people drink wine.

Across the tasting barn, on the production side of the building, Carlos was at the top of a ladder, changing out a burned out lightbulb. Oscar stood at the bottom of the ladder and held it steady.

"What are they like?" I wondered aloud.

Natalie paused in setting up a long table with a white tablecloth. She followed my gaze across the barn. "Who? Oscar and Carlos?"

I nodded. Natalie and I had only just met the day before, but she didn't intimidate me like the others.

"You'd be hard pressed to find harder working boys." Natalie continued to set up the table with several sets of evenly spaced wine glasses. "Rolando is very discerning when it comes to the vineyard. Oscar has a talent for plants; his green thumb can nurse back even the most struggling vine," she explained. "And Carlos is Mr. Fix it. If you need something fixed in the farmhouse, more than likely Carlos can figure it out."

"And Lucia?" I found myself asking. After only a brief interaction earlier that day, she'd already made quite a first impression.

"Lucia?" Natalie looked interested. "She's back already?"

I nodded. "Yeah. She, uh, she found out about the property sale."

"And let me guess," Natalie mused, "she stormed in here with her hair on fire."

I pressed my lips together. "Yep."

Natalie gave me a sympathetic look. "Don't take it to heart. That girl can be pricklier than a porcupine."

"She seems … " I paused as I decided on my words. "Intense."

"That's one way to put it," Natalie confirmed with a wry smile. "Lucia grew up on the vineyard, much like a grape herself. There's wine and soil in her blood," she philosophized. "You can be taught the science of winemaking. But not everyone can appreciate its art."

"Any tips?" I pressed. "She's supposed to be taking over my training tomorrow."

"Are you sure you want to do that?" Natalie countered. "You could hang out with me instead."

The corner of my mouth twitched. "She can't be that bad."

The sympathetic look on Natalie's face intensified. "I guess you'll find out soon enough."

CHAPTER FOUR

The flashlight on my cellphone struggled to cut through the early morning fog. A dense fog habitually settled in the valley every morning, blanketing the sleeping vineyard until the sun rose higher in the sky and burned off the ghostly veil. I walked along the gravel road that connected the farmhouse to the tasting barn with another nervous knot in my stomach. Every day seemed to bring new challenges and new anxieties. I hoped that it wouldn't be much longer before I settled into a comfortable routine on the vineyard. But first, I had to prove myself to Lucia Santiago, the assistant winemaker.

I typically got along with people with whom I worked. In my many years as a designer, and then art director, and finally creative director, I could count the serious confrontations I'd had with a coworker on one hand. Conflicting personalities eventually faded with time and collaborations. But my intuition told me it might take more than a shared donut in the company break room to whittle away at Lucia's animus.

As I approached the tasting barn, I didn't see any cars parked in the adjacent parking lot. Maybe I'd beaten everyone to work that morning. The small, triumphant smile on my face faltered, however, when another thought surfaced. I was either the first person to show up or Lucia had tricked me about the pre-dawn start time.

I pulled open the barn's main door, expecting only darkness. An isolated set of lights, however, shone down on the picnic table where

I typically found Rolando with his newspaper and coffee. Instead of the head winemaker, however, his daughter occupied the space.

Lucia sat by herself at the picnic table. Her hair was tied back from her face in a tight braid, which fell down the center of her back. She wore a denim shirt, unbuttoned at the collar, with the sleeves rolled halfway up her forearms. Her shoulders were slightly hunched as she sat, and her features were serious as she inspected the screen of her cellphone. She didn't look up from her phone despite the sound of the barn door opening or my tennis shoes squeaking against the concrete floor.

I approached and offered a tentative greeting: "Good morning."

My words got caught in my throat. She was the first person I'd spoken to that morning.

Lucia barely looked in my direction. "You're late." She sounded bored but annoyed.

I cleared my throat to dislodge the morning fog. "Am I?"

If anything, I might have been a few minutes early. I'd set multiple alarms to make sure I didn't oversleep.

Lucia stood from the picnic table. I watched her stand to her full height. In thick-soled work boots, she was slightly taller than me. I might have weighed more, though. Her frame was slight, almost delicate, if not for her stony exterior.

"Let's get this over with," she said dully.

I frowned at her words, but kept my disappointment to myself. Apparently there would be no opportunity for chitchat or getting-to-know-you.

Lucia strode away from the picnic table in the direction of the production side of the barn. I hastened my step to keep up with her long, impatient gait. Rolando walked as if he was on his own schedule; Lucia's steps were quick and frenetic as if she was going to miss a flight.

I followed her past the crusher destemmer machine and past the juicer. She kept on walking past the giant, silver fermentation tanks to another door at the back of the barn. The door was oversized and out of place. It looked more like the vault door to a bank.

Lucia stopped in front of the closed door and abruptly spun around on her heel. I nearly gasped at her proximity. She raised a single finger. She was so close, her finger almost touched my nose.

She regarded me with a stern expression. "Don't. Touch. Anything."

I nodded my head in silent agreement.

She turned back around and pulled open the heavy metal door.

A dimly-lit staircase, constructed of rust-colored bricks, led down to the underground wine cellar. I remembered the subterranean area as part of the vineyard tour I'd been on with Alex the previous summer. I'd been struck at the time at the temperature change. The day had been hot, but it had been several degrees cooler—almost like air conditioning—within the solidly constructed cellar. I had an urge to touch my fingers to the carved out walls as we walked along a narrow corridor, but mindful of Lucia's warning to not touch anything, I kept my arms and hands pinned to my sides.

The shallow hallway opened up to a larger room with a vaulted ceiling. The height of the room was particularly impressive, especially considering we were underground. Large wooden barrels, stacked high on top of sturdy-looking shelving units lined either side of the cavernous space. In the middle, more stacked barrels formed neat, symmetrical rows.

"This," Lucia announced, "is where the magic happens."

Some of the annoyance had left her tone. She might have been upset that her father had tasked—in her words—to babysit me, but maybe her animosity was only at the surface. I hoped it was only a matter of time before that stubborn veneer wore away.

Lucia turned on her heel to face me, almost as if she was leading a private tour. "This is where the wines develop their flavors," she said. "The oak barrels are slightly porous, allowing oxygen to interact with the wine, but not too much oxygen," she noted, "otherwise it would go bad. The smaller the barrel, the more contact the wood has with the wine, intensifying its flavor."

I looked among the rows and rows of oak barrels. "How long do they age before bottling?"

Lucia stood beside one of the barrels and touched the horizontal cask. "Red wines take a little longer than whites, but anywhere between six months to three years." She touched the container reverently, her fingertips moving across the cooperage almost like a loving caress. "This room holds our oldest vintage, which will be ready to bottle in fall."

"How many bottles of wine are in each barrel?" I wondered.

"These smaller ones are thirty-gallon barrels," she said, tapping the cask closest to her, "which is about 150 standard bottles per barrel. We have sixty-gallon barrels in the other room, which is 25 cases or 300 bottles each."

I whistled lowly as I continued to scan the room. The space where we stood held too many barrels to count, not that I'd ever had a talent for math. "That's a lot of wine."

She curled her lip. "Well, we *are* a winery."

I followed Lucia to the next cellar space, which mirrored the previous room with the exception of containing larger barrels. They looked large enough for an adult to squeeze inside, not that I had any interest in trying.

"These sixty-gallon barrels are pretty standard, but they're as big as we'll go, without sacrificing the integrity of our wine," she explained, gesturing to one of the larger wine barrels. "Larger wineries less concerned with quality might use huge steel vats infused with oak chips to make the consumer think they were aged in real oak barrels. Their wine gets packaged on huge assembly lines, churning out thousands of bottles an hour." Lucia's tone was one of judgment and disapproval. "They can sell in the grocery store for the same price as a two-liter bottle of soda."

"But doesn't that democratize wine?" I proposed. "Making it accessible to everyone, not just people with money?"

Lucia wrinkled her nose. "Nothing more than Two Buck Chuck."

A third room, slightly smaller than the first two cellar spaces seemed to be the last underground space. I had thought Lucia and I were alone in the cellar, but both Oscar and Carlos were waiting in the final room. It almost felt like an ambush, but I shoved those undeserved emotions to the side.

The two men cut short whatever they'd been doing or talking about before our entrance. The man I recognized as Carlos got behind the wheel of a forklift. The other man, Oscar, grabbed a ladder and positioned it next to a stack of oak barrels.

"Are we moving barrels to another room?" I guessed.

"No." Lucia didn't bother to elaborate. She left me and walked in the direction of Carlos and the forklift.

I rocked back and forth in my tennis shoes, uncertain if I was intended to follow. I was supposed to be shadowing Lucia, but instead of a discrete observer, I felt like a persistent puppy or an obnoxious gnat, glued to the woman's side. She made no indication if I should stay put or if I was missing out on an important lesson. Instead, she spoke with Carlos while I strained to eavesdrop or at least read their lips.

Before I could completely melt from awkwardness, Oscar came to stand beside me. "Good morning," he softly murmured.

"Morning," I responded tightly.

"We're racking the wine."

I turned to appraise the man more closely. Where Carlos was compact like a runner or a featherweight boxer, Oscar was long and lean. His hair was closely cropped and he wore thin, circular, wire-rimmed glasses that made him look like a poet or philosopher.

"Racking?" I asked.

"Moving the wine from one barrel to another," he explained. "Separating the clear wine from sediment that's fallen to the bottom of the barrel."

"Oh." I appreciated Oscar's attempt to fill me in, but I still didn't really understand. "Sediment from what?"

"Dead yeast cells," he said. "After primary fermentation, the wine sits in these barrels for a year, year and a half, while it goes through something called malolactic conversion. Fermentation is still happening in the barrels, with millions of little yeast cells floating around and gobbling up any trace amounts of sugar. As that yeast dies," he said, "it sinks to the bottom of the barrel, forming a layer of sediment call lees."

"And we don't want that sediment in the wine," I guessed.

"Sometimes, yes. Sometimes no," he told me. "Sometimes the lees is useful; we can regularly perform *bâtonnage*, which is basically scraping the bottom of the barrel," he explained, "to mix the lees back into the wine. Aging wine on the lees tends to give the wine a softer mouthfeel, more complexity, and a more robust body."

I frowned as Oscar listed off a new set of unfamiliar wine industry words. I made a mental note to bring a notepad with me the following day.

"June!" Lucia called out. "Get over here."

I flashed Oscar a quick, but grateful smile. "Thank you."

He nodded in return, slow and thoughtful.

I hustled across the room to Lucia, Carlos, and the forklift, feeling moderately more at ease armed with Oscar's information.

I came to a stop beside Lucia. "So we're racking wine today?" I said, a smile in my tone.

Lucia frowned. Her dark gaze flicked from my face to the direction where Oscar still stood. I wondered if she would be cross with him for telling me anything. "Not if you're including yourself in that Royal We," she rejected. "It takes an experienced touch to access the clean wine and to leave the sediment behind."

I resisted rolling my eyes. Less than twenty-four hours of being around Lucia and I could already anticipate her responses. I took a cleansing breath. "Okay. No racking. What am I allowed to do?"

"Pressure clean the barrels."

I nodded grimly. It was far from a glamorous task, but I was eager to get to work and prove myself.

Carlos got behind the wheel of the forklift. He expertly maneuvered the machinery in the small confines of the room. The lift slid beneath one of the larger barrels and hoisted it a few inches off of the ground. I would have appreciated Oscar's play-by-play to let me know the purpose of these details, but I figured I was on my own from now on.

Lucia grabbed a long metal rod that seemed to have a spear on one end. It looked almost like an underwater spear gun that might make an appearance in a spy-thriller film. She loosened and then removed the oversized cork at the bellybutton of the wine barrel.

"Here," she called to me. "Catch."

I didn't have much time to react before she tossed the large cork in my direction. I never had a chance; I'd never been very athletic. My arms and hands crossed in front of my body as I tried to catch the projectile. The cork bounced off of my forearm and fell to the floor.

I quickly scooped the object off the concrete and held it up. "Got it!"

Lucia rolled her eyes and mumbled something under her breath before returning to her task. She stood on her tiptoes and dipped the silver spear into the newly opened barrel. A clear, bendable tube was connected to the end of the spear that wasn't submerged in wine.

Without needing to be told, Carlos left the forklift and grabbed the flexible end of the metal spear. He sharply sucked on the open end of the clear tube until it produced a purple-colored liquid. He dropped the gushing end into a nearby silver tank and the wine inside of the oak barrel began to empty into the separate holding tank.

Carlos grinned broadly. "Better than siphoning off gasoline, eh?"

I realized then that they'd elevated the wooden barrel to create a siphon, which would then allow gravity to do the rest of the work. It was actually pretty ingenious, but I kept my compliments to myself.

Lucia concentrated on a metal and glass joint that connected the metal spear to the plastic tubing. The viewing glass revealed a deep purple color rushing from the oak barrel to the waiting steel holding tank.

"That's a tri-clover sight glass." Oscar spoke to me in a hushed tone as if sharing proprietary information. "It helps us make sure we're only moving the clear wine and not the lees."

"Oscar!" Lucia barked.

Oscar's head snapped up, and he seemed to jump away from me like a teacher had called us out for talking during class.

Lucia glared in our direction. "Would you like to be in charge of her training?"

Oscar held up his hands and took a few steps backwards. He seemed to retreat. I wondered if either Carlos or Oscar would risk speaking to me ever again.

Lucia leveled her heated gaze on me next. "You," she grunted. "Stop playing with your bunghole and get over here. I don't want the wine in this holding tank forever."

I glanced in Oscar's direction, hopeful for a little more clarity.

"The cork is called a bung," he quietly supplied.

I hustled over to Lucia with the oversized plug in hand. I tried to give it back to her, but she gruffly shook her head. "It's not time for that yet. Grab one of those trays," she said, nodding in the direction of a stack of plastic containers. They looked similar to the flat containers one might put belongings into when going through airport security.

I did as I was told and waited for more instructions.

"Slide that under the barrel," she told me next. "Reach under the barrel and find the second bung."

I positioned the tray under the large barrel, anticipating its purpose. I blindly reached for the second cork, not wanting to go completely beneath the precariously balancing barrel. Even without wine inside, it must have weighed at least one hundred pounds.

I grimaced as my fingers slipped over the lip of the stubborn cork again and again. I couldn't quite wiggle it free.

"Oscar, help her," Lucia declared. She sighed and sounded impatient.

"No, I've got it," I insisted. I closed my eyes as if I could transfer my sight to my fingertips. It seemed to work, however, as I successfully loosened and then removed the bung with a satisfying pop.

A wet, thick liquid noise followed. The wine sediment flowed out of the barrel's second hole into the waiting plastic container below. It looked like loose blueberry yogurt that had been left in the sun. When the flood of liquid slowed to a trickle, indicating that the majority of the lees had been emptied, Oscar reached beneath the barrel and removed the plastic tray.

I thought that might have been my job since it seemed the most unpleasant until Lucia pressed a thick rubber hose into my hands. "Get cleaning."

I still had no idea what I was doing, but the oak barrel only had two holes. If I pressure cleaned from the bottom whole, I imagined a purple yogurt Old Faithful in the wine cellar.

I experimentally twisted the metal attachment at the head of the hose. Clean water rushed out more quickly and with more power than I anticipated. An unflattering squeal escaped my lips as I hastily turned off the water.

"Be careful, *Jefa*," Carlos warned from the his position at the forklift. "Those barrels are $800 a pop."

The cellar was several degrees cooler than above ground, yet I still felt the heated flush of embarrassment reach my cheeks. I collected myself before returning to my assignment. I had to carefully coordinate the timing, but I managed to turn on the pressure cleaner and successfully drop the nozzle into the top of the oak barrel. More purple liquid rushed out of the second hole. It swirled around the cellar floor before disappearing down an in-ground metal drain.

The top hole wasn't large enough for me to stick my hand and arm into it, but I managed to maneuver the pressure cleaner enough so it reached every curve and corner of the barrel's interior. When the escaping water ran clear instead of purple, I turned off the hose, satisfied with my work.

Lucia stood nearby to inspect my progress. "Not bad," she begrudgingly admitted. "One down. Only twenty more to go."

We worked without much conversation for the next few hours. Every time Lucia emptied an oak barrel of its clean wine, I had a plastic tray ready to catch the lees. Oscar continued to remove the tray and dump out the sediment when each barrel was nearly empty while I proceeded to pressure clean the barrel's interior. Once a barrel was sufficiently clean, the process reversed itself with Carlos and Lucia transporting the clean wine in the holding tanks back to their original oak barrel.

"Shit," I heard Carlos curse from the forklift.

He scrambled out of the driver's seat when the latest barrel to be lifted tilted in midair. Oscar rushed to help the other man stabilize the heavy barrel. I didn't intend to get distracted by the circ du soleil act of Carlos and Oscar rebalancing the massive barrel on the machinery's fork, when my attention should have been on my own chore. I couldn't imagine what might happen if the barrel fell and enough liquid to fill 300 bottles of wine spilled across the concrete floor.

With Oscar helping Carlos, I grabbed the plastic tray full of lees with the intention of dumping it out for him. I grabbed the tray from the floor, careful not to let lees spill over the container's shallow edges. I righted myself and turned on my heel. Lucia must have had the same idea; I didn't notice her directly behind me. When I spun around, her proximity startled me.

I could feel the tray start to slip from my grip. Not wanting to let the lees spill on the floor, I overcompensated and pulled the tray closer to my chest. The tray stabilized, but not the thick liquid inside. A tidal wave of greyish-purple liquid sloshed over the edge and drenched the front of my shirt.

I heard Lucia's snort. "Whoops."

I grimaced from the cold, sticky sensation dribbling down my chest and torso. My t-shirt and jeans were probably ruined. I'd once spilled red wine on the grey couch Alex and I had in an early apartment. No amount of internet searching for life hacks had been able to fully remove the stain. A shadow of a red puddle had permanently remained.

"Go home and clean up," Lucia instructed. "We'll try again tomorrow."

"Tomorrow?" I frowned. Despite my ruined clothes and the unfavorable way my soaked socks squished inside of my equally ruined tennis shoes, her dismissal was disappointing. What was I supposed to do for the rest of the day?

"Enjoy this lull," she told me. "After bud break, the work will get harder. And during harvest, we'll be working sixteen-hour days." Her disapproving gaze raked over me, and she seemed to curl her lip. "If you last that long."

CHAPTER FIVE

I stripped out of my wine sediment-soaked clothing the moment the farmhouse door shut behind me. The material had started to dry against my skin; peeling off my t-shirt and jeans had been akin to shedding an adhesive bandage. My bra, underwear, and socks came off next, and I crumpled the entire outfit into a tight ball. I stood naked and slightly sticky in the living room. The curtained windows that faced the gravel roadway in front of the house offered little privacy, but no one would have been this deep on the property to see me.

I needed a second shower of the short day, but I slipped back into my squishy tennis shoes and descended the first floor stairs to the dusty basement in the hopes of salvaging my clothing. When I'd first moved into the farmhouse, I'd spotted a matching washing machine and dryer in the basement. I hadn't been brave enough to test out if they actually worked or not, but that now seemed like an important detail to ascertain.

I stood, still naked except for my ruined tennis shoes, in front of the yellow-green metal laundry machines. I didn't have any detergent, but I found an aging box of soap flakes that was probably older than me. I dumped my wine-soaked ball of clothing into the top loading washer and poured a generous amount of the laundry flakes into the machine's open top.

The controls weren't overly complicated—no advanced options like on a modern washing machine. I pressed and turned a few buttons and the vintage device seemed to power on. I allowed myself a moment to indulge in the small victory; I hadn't experienced a win in what felt like several months. I turned a few more dials and waited for the familiar sound of water being fed into the machine. A frown formed on my face the longer I waited with no satisfying result.

I pressed and turned a few more buttons and dials, hoping to identify the magic combination, but no matter what I did, no water pumped into the washing machine. I slapped my palm against the top of the metal machine as if it only needed to be jolted awake after several decades of neglect. I slapped it a second time, this time to express my own frustration. Rejected, I trudged up the stairs to the first floor like a petulant teenager. I didn't bother retrieving my clothes from the useless washing machine. They were probably too far gone to salvage, and I didn't have the energy or desire to hand wash them in the kitchen sink.

I needed a shower—my hair felt crispy from the now dried wine sediment—but I stood at the kitchen sink and stared out the back window. Like the front of the house, the land was flat and sprawling. Scattered ancient oak trees dotted the horizon. Rather than reach and stretch into the sky, however, they appeared bent and gnarled, like the grapevines themselves. All of the surrounding vegetation looked chained or tethered to the ground.

"Prison," I thought out loud.

My cellphone rang, interrupting my darker thoughts. It was lucky that I'd left my phone behind that day, otherwise it would have probably gotten ruined along with my clothes. My friend Lily's name and face appeared on my cellphone's screen. I didn't feel like talking, but I answered the phone anyway.

"Hello?"

"Junie!" she cheered. "How have you been? How's the wine business?" Her voice was so warm and friendly, it made me want to cry.

"Everyone hates me," I lamented.

"I seriously doubt that," she rejected my melodrama. "Napa Valley is awfully big."

I sighed into the phone. "Okay. So maybe not *everyone*," I conceded. "The head winemaker and the woman who runs the tasting room have been really nice. But that's it. I'm not connecting with anyone else."

"You're not there to make friends," Lily pragmatically pointed out. "You're running a business."

My best friend spoke the truth, but that didn't make me feel any better about my situation. I tugged my hair band off and tried to fluff out my hair. Sticky wine sediment impeded my efforts. "I'm in over my head," I complained. "I can't believe Alex ever convinced me this was a good idea."

"You've always been a bit of a pushover," Lily noted, "especially when it came to her."

I frowned into the phone. "You're not doing a very good job of cheering me up, Lil."

"Oh, is that what I'm supposed to be doing right now? I hadn't realized," she chuckled. "I know what will cheer you up."

I was afraid to even ask.

"Let's go out tonight. We'll have a couple of drinks. Maybe do a little dancing. Make some bad decisions," she proposed.

"On a Tuesday?"

"Aren't you the boss?" Lily pointed out. "Don't you get to make your own rules?"

Lily's rhetorical question left a bad taste in my mouth—or maybe that was the wine lees.

"Yeah. Okay."

"Really?" Lily's voice revealed her surprise. I could hardly believe I'd so readily agreed myself. "Dang, it must be really bad."

I continued to stare out at the lifeless, barren landscape that stretched beyond my kitchen window.

"You have no idea."

+ + +

Calistoga to Guerneville, California was a forty-five minute drive. It was just long enough to be an annoyance, but not far enough away for me to reject Lily's idea altogether. Coming from San Francisco, the drive was more than twice that for her. I sat at the bar, nursing a session IPA. I intended on driving home that night so I alternated between a tall glass of water and the low ABV beer. I'd been to Guerneville before with Alex, but not to this particular bar. The town had earned a reputation as a queer-friendly vacation town, but it was neither vacation weather nor a weekend, and the gay club was relatively empty that evening.

Lily had a longer drive, so I tried to be patient while I sat alone at the bar. I slumped my shoulders forward, curving my body around my pint glass, and hoped my body language was enough to keep the bar's other patrons away. My friend had successfully convinced me that I couldn't hide out in the farmhouse forever, rattling my chains, but that didn't mean I was in the mood to engage with strangers.

I wasn't a frequent visitor to gay bars or clubs. I had been a few times during college, but once Alex and I had partnered up, neither of us had seen much use for strictly queer establishments. After college, when we'd relocated to San Francisco, most restaurants and bars we patronized were gay-friendly, so we hadn't sought out explicitly gay businesses. Lily, however, filled her social calendar with Pride Events—drag brunches, queer karaoke, body-positive burlesque, gay and lesbian film fests. It was like her thirst for gay content couldn't be quenched.

It was one of the reasons why I wasn't surprised when she'd recommended we meet up at one of the more established gay bars in the gay-friendly resort town. I half expected to see her picture hanging over the bar. Alex used to joke with me that Lily was too gay for her. They'd dated in college—briefly—before I'd entered the picture. Strangely enough, Lily and I had become closer friends over the years than Alex and Lily. But maybe I'd been able to stay strictly in the friend zone because I'd never seen Lily naked. It could have been strange to be best friends with your partner's ex-girlfriend, but they'd dated a lifetime ago.

I swiped my finger against the condensation that had collected on the outside of my pint glass. I turned the horizontal line into a smiley face, but the extra moisture bled into my portrait, transforming the smile line into a droopy mess.

"Well, this is disappointing." Lily's judgmental voice sounded in my ear. "I wouldn't have suggested this place if I knew it was going to be so dead." Her critical features turned apologetic. "Sorry," she grimaced.

"You're can say the d-word," I allowed.

Over the past few months, words like 'dead' or 'death' had become forbidden, expunged from my friends' vocabulary. I understood they were only trying to be sensitive to my situation, but regardless of the words they used, Alex was still dead.

I stood from my bar stool to greet my friend. She grabbed my arm and pulled me in for a hug. I let her squeeze me a little tighter than was necessary.

"How are you doing, sweetie?" she asked, arms still wrapped around me.

I breathed in her familiar scent. Coconut and a little earthy. "Ask me something easier."

"What are we drinking?" she posed instead.

Lily released me from her hug and claimed the empty barstool beside me. She motioned to the bartender and ordered herself a well drink.

"Not drinking wine tonight?" she said, noticing my pint glass and beer. "I figured you'd be a total convert by now."

My mind flashed back to earlier in the day and the embarrassment of my wine sediment shower. "I don't know. I may give up on drinking altogether," I said wistfully.

Lily made a noise. "Let's not be hasty." My friend turned on her barstool to better appraise me. "So tell me all about these terrible wine people and why you think they don't like you."

"Later," I promised. "But for tonight can we just pretend we're two friends who live boring, uncomplicated lives?"

I heard Lily's laugh. "Okay. I can do that."

"How's work?"

Lily sucked in a breath. "Wow. You were serious about wanting to be boring tonight."

I flashed my friend a pleading look. She held up her hands and accommodated my request.

"Work is busy," she described. "I don't know why all of these unorganized fools wait until the last minute to do their taxes, but whatever," she said, taking a sip from her drink, "once April is over, I'm going to take a well-deserved vacation."

Lily ran her own accounting firm. I'd always marveled how someone with such an outgoing, almost wild, personality had such a buttoned-up professional life.

"Do you want to come with?" she asked. "I'm thinking Mexico. My three favorite b's: beach, boats, and booze. Maybe some boobs, too," she said with a wiggle of her eyebrows.

"I wish." I heaved out a sigh. "But I'm basically tethered to the vineyard until after this year's harvest. I want to give this my all, you know? I really want them to like me."

"Since you're the one who brought it up," Lily tested, "am I allowed to ask questions about your work now?"

"It's so different, Lil. Everything," I emphasized. "There's not a single thing that feels familiar or comfortable."

"That was kind of the point though, yeah?" Lily said gently. "You wanted different after Alex. A brand new start."

I gave her a smile, but it felt sad and wistful. "I guess so."

Lily leaned in my direction, close enough to connect her shoulder with mine. "I'm doing a shit job at cheering you up."

"It's not your fault," I insisted. I slid my half-finished beer on the bar, from one hand to the other and back. "I'm in a funk. I'm in a rut."

"We could all use a good rut now and again."

I rolled my eyes, but allowed myself a laugh. "I'm no good for anyone yet."

"You don't have to commit long term to the next person you date," she told me. "Hell, you don't even have to date. You're allowed to have uncomplicated fun."

"But I'm so old," I lamented. "Even if I was ready to get back out there—which I'm not," I was quick to add, "I wouldn't even know what to do or where to start."

"There's always online dating," she suggested.

"Pass," I quickly rejected.

"Why not?" Lily pressed. "There's not the same stigma about meeting someone on an app like there might have been when you were first dating, back in the Dark Ages."

"What's wrong with meeting someone the old fashioned way?"

"Getting blitzed on Pride Weekend and waking up in a stranger's bed?" Lily mused.

"No." I smiled mildly. "Like, a coffee shop or the grocery store?"

Lily arched an amused eyebrow. "Honey, what made-for-TV movies have you been watching lately?"

"I don't even have cable anymore!" I protested. "It turns out, owning a vineyard is pretty expensive."

"How about here?" my friend proposed. She swung around on her seat to face the bar's other patrons. "There's got to be at least one pretty girl in this bar tonight." She leaned toward me again. "Present company excluded."

"Charmer," I snorted.

Lily toyed with the stir stick in her drink. "Let's see," she mused. "Who would Junie find attractive?"

My sour mood wasn't entirely forgotten, but I was curious to see if Lily could discern my type. It had been so long though, I wasn't sure I even had a type anymore.

I allowed my gaze to scan the sparsely populated bar. The overhead lights were low, making it more challenging to really make out individual faces. I stopped at a small group of women who stood around a high top table. They casually conversed, periodically erupting into laughter. My attention didn't linger on any particular figure, but I observed their interactions with something that felt like melancholy nostalgia.

Alex and I had built solid friendships with so many people in our nearly two decades of dating. But it had been to Alex that everyone initially gravitated. She was the one with the outgoing, gregarious personality. She had been the one with all of the best stories. I had often felt like a bystander at house parties where Alex was typically the center of attention. I knew people liked me, but with the exception of Lily, few of the people whom I'd considered friends had tried to stay in contact after the funeral.

The women in the small group continued to interact while Lily and I observed them from afar.

"See anything you like?" my friend posed. "I could be your wing lady tonight."

I wrinkled my nose at the description. I started to reject her offer, but my mouth remained wordlessly open when I spied a familiar face across the bar. In a room full of strangers, one of them wasn't so strange. Lucia Santiago—or someone who looked exactly like her— stood among the small group of women. She wore different clothing than what I'd seen her in earlier that day, but her hair was still tied back in a braid.

"Shit," I whispered under my breath. I quickly turned around on the barstool and prayed that I hadn't been spotted.

"What's wrong?" Lily asked.

I slumped my shoulders forward and shielded my face with both hands. "I know one of those women over there. She works at the vineyard."

"Which one?" Lily's voice lilted with interest.

"Blue button-up shirt, hair in a braid." *Had the bar gotten warmer?* I started to fan my face. *Was I sweating?*

"She definitely saw you," Lily murmured.

My throat tightened. "How can you tell?"

"Because she's coming this way."

I didn't have enough time to recover before Lucia's voice was cutting through any extraneous bar noise. "Can I get another gin and tonic?"

I sat, immobile, as Lucia set her empty glass on the bar and occupied the empty space beside me. I observed her out of the corner of my eye and waited for her to notice me.

"Hi," came my strangled greeting.

Lucia briefly nodded in my direction. "Hey."

Her lack of any real acknowledgement made me momentarily wonder if she even recognized me. We'd only met briefly the previous day, and I'd spent the better portion of our remaining time following her around the winery's dimly lit cellar. I supposed I might have looked different when my hair was down and I wasn't drenched in wine sediment.

Lucia turned around and rested her back against the bar top while the bartender mixed her another drink. "Small world," she grunted.

I grimaced. Yep. She recognized me.

Lucia looked beyond me to where Lily sat. "Hey," she said with a brief wave. "You must be Alex. It's nice to finally meet you."

Lily's eyes grew wide, and she looked to me for explanation.

"Oh! This is my friend Lily," I said in a rush. "She drove from San Francisco to meet up with me."

Lucia's stoical gaze traveled back and forth between our faces. "Nice friend," she murmured. "That's got to be a drive."

"Hour and a half if I time it right with traffic," Lily cheerfully supplied.

Lucia looked like she wanted to say more, but then thought better of it. She shook her head as if to knock the words from her mind. "Well, have a good night," she said curtly. She trained her gaze on me. "Don't drink too much, *Jefa*; I won't go easy on you in the morning."

She grabbed her new drink from the bar, nodded her thanks to the bartender, and wandered back to her group of friends.

"She doesn't know?" Lily asked when Lucia was no longer within earshot.

My attention remained on Lucia rather than my friend on the adjacent stool. "Know what?"

I watched Lucia rejoin the small group and clink her glass against another woman's. I studied their faces as best as I could between the distance and the darkness. *Were they friends?* I wondered. *Or something more?* And did this mean that Lucia was gay, too, or did she simply like this particular bar that happened to be gay, in a community close to an hour away from the vineyard, that also had the reputation of being gay? I pressed my fingers against my forehead; my accumulating questions threatened to bring on a migraine.

Lily's voice brought me back to our conversation: "About Alex."

I turned around on my barstool, but I couldn't quite meet Lily's eyes. "No."

"Why not?"

"Everything and everyone is so new," I tried to reason. "I didn't want to complicate things even more by telling them about Alex. And now …" I sighed, "now it's like too much time has passed. How do I bring her up without making it awkward?"

"It's going to be awkward, Junie," Lily observed. "But you have to do it."

I sighed deeper. "I know. And I will."

"What did she call you, by the way? Jah-fuh?"

"*Jefa*," I corrected her pronunciation. "I had to Google it," I admitted. "It's Spanish for girl boss or something. I'm sure it's meant to be ironic."

"She's kind of hot," Lily observed. "In a dark and broody kind of way."

"I hadn't noticed." It wasn't a lie. I had been too intimidated and too afraid to really look at her since we'd met the previous day.

"Yes, she's definitely hot," Lily decided after a moment. "I would let her not take it easy on me any day."

I snorted into my pint glass. "You're terrible."

CHAPTER SIX

I stood on a lofted catwalk in the barn and peered down into one of the massive fermentation tanks. The copper-colored cap that usually covered the silver silo had been removed.

"You want me to do *what?*" My voice echoed in the empty steel vessel below.

I'd heard her the first time, but she couldn't have been serious.

Lucia folded her arms across her chest. She seemed to have a love affair with double denim. I'd only ever seen her in jeans and chambray shirts. "Until I tell you otherwise, your job is cellar rat. We all had to work our way up," she said sternly. "You don't get to start at the top, just because your name is on a piece of paper."

I wanted to correct her that it was Alex's name on all of the paperwork, not my own, but she'd made her point.

I leaned over the edge of the empty fermentation tank and stared. "What exactly am I removing?" From my vantage point, the tank looked clean and empty.

"Wine is made of three kinds of acid," Lucia told me. "One of those acids leaves behind a residue: tartrate crystals. Some people call them wine diamonds," she observed, "but that's just to make the consumer feel better about inferior wine." Even though I continued to gaze into the stainless steel silo, I could feel her intense stare on me. "You don't want to make inferior wine, do you?"

I breathed out deeply like a child resigning to eat their vegetables. "No. I don't."

"Making wine isn't glamorous," she frowned. "It's sanitizing and re-sanitizing equipment. It's hauling heavy loads from one side of the property to the other."

"I know, I know," I huffed. A petulant whine worked its way into my tone; I'd heard her speeches all before. "I get it."

I glanced again into the giant steel vat. It had to have been more than ten feet down. "And you're sure there's not another way?"

Lucia opened her mouth and took a breath, but I cut her off before she could lecture me again about work ethic or integrity or whatever her judgment of the day about me was going to be. I held up my hands in defeat. "I'm going, I'm going."

Lucia's held out a small scrub brush for me to take. It wasn't much larger than a toothbrush. She looked amused at my expense. "Down you go."

There was no easy way to drop into the empty tank. We had to drag a ladder from another part of the barn and carry it up to the catwalk, only to lower it into the fermentation tank. The ladder was still dwarfed by the height and size of the steel silo.

I sat at the catwalk's edge and dangled my feet into the tank. I stretched out my right leg and reached for the ladder. The toes of my tennis shoe barely brushed against the ladder's top step.

I looked over my shoulder to where Lucia stood. "I don't think I can reach."

She folded her arms across her chest. "I'm hearing a lot of excuses, *Jefa*."

I frowned at the name—*Jefa*—and returned my attention to the ladder with renewed focus. I was determined to reach the ladder or break my neck trying. I scooted my backside to the far edge of the catwalk, and stretched out my right leg again. I sucked in a sharp breath and let myself go.

I felt a sensation like free falling before my right foot landed solidly on the top of the precariously positioned ladder. I'd once gone skydiving with Alex on her thirtieth birthday and the gravity-free sensation reminded me of jumping out of that plane. I'd never been a fan of heights; I'd only gone because Alex had wanted to go so badly. She'd been the risk-taker. I preferred having both feet on solid ground.

My right ankle felt sore from the force of my leg jamming down into my foot, but at least I'd reached the ladder. My satisfaction was short lived, however; a moment later, I was flailing my arms to keep from tumbling backwards. Another uncomfortable feeling washed over me—*this is how I die*—until I discovered myself being jerked back to stability. Lucia had managed to grab both of my wrists to keep me from falling off of the ladder.

I stared up at Lucia's determined face and then looked to her strong fingers wrapped tightly around my wrists. She gripped me with such strength, I thought my wrists might be bruised.

"Jesus," she grit out. "Are you trying to kill yourself?"

"But you said—."

"Are you okay now?" she cut me off. "Can I let you go?"

I nodded. Both of my feet were now solidly on the ladder's top step. She didn't let go, however, until I'd descended a few more rungs and had better stability.

When she eventually released her hold on me, I reflexively rubbed at my wrists. My heart was still beating fast from the almost fall. "Think I could file for worker's comp?" I tried to joke.

If possible, Lucia looked even grumpier than before as she stared down at me from the catwalk. "You tell me," she snorted. "You're the boss."

I finished descending the ladder and stood on the bottom of the fermentation tank. Large lights were suspended from the barn's ceiling, but not all of that light reached the bottom of the tank. I leaned closer to the interior metal wall and squinted my eyes to see better in the dim lighting. "Are you sure this hasn't already been cleaned?" I questioned. "I don't see anything that looks like crystals."

"They're small," Lucia assured me from above. "They're there."

I continued to stare at the smooth interior wall. A voice in the back of my brain told me this was some kind of trick, but Lucia didn't seem the type to pull pranks. She seemed downright humorless.

"Lucia?" I called up when I realized I couldn't hear her anymore. "Are you still there?"

I waited a few seconds for a response that never came. I heaved out a giant sigh, ruffling the wisps of hair that had worked their way free from my ponytail.

I set myself to the task of scrubbing out the interior of the fermentation tank. I resolved myself to the reality that I was going to be in the bottom of this tank for a while. Lucia had only armed me with a small abrasive scrubbing brush. I couldn't gauge my progress either since I couldn't tell the difference between the metal I had scrubbed and that which still needed to be cleaned. I also had no cleaning solvent, no water, and no rubber gloves. I knew this was probably some kind of hazing ritual—give the impossible task to the new girl—but I was determined to do my best.

I didn't know how much time had passed. I was on my knees, nearly lost to the monotonous, mind-numbing work when I heard heavy boots ringing against the metal stairs of the catwalk.

I paused my scrubbing to listen to the footsteps above me. "Lucia?"

A face appeared over the edge of the fermentation tanks, but it didn't belong to Lucia. Carlos waved down at me. "Oh. It's you," I heard him chuckle. "I heard a sound and thought a rat had fallen in."

I stood up and grimaced at the ache located behind my kneecaps. My lower body had been motionless for too long and it felt like rigor mortis had set in. I wiped at the front of my jeans. "Nope. Just me."

"What are you doing down there?" Carlos asked.

I showed him my scrubbing brush. "Getting rid of tantric crystals."

"You mean tartrate?"

"Right. That." I hoped I wasn't blushing. Tantric was something *totally* different. Obviously.

Carlos wet his lips. "Tartrate crystals only occur in white wine."

"But Lucia said …" I didn't bother finishing my sentence. "I don't need to be doing this, do I?"

Carlos had the grace to look apologetic. "Sorry. No."

"Hah. Good one. Hazing the new girl." If my features had been flushed before, my cheeks had probably turned the same color as the wine we made. The wine that didn't produce wine crystals. "Did they do this to you, too?"

I heard Carlos' quiet cough. "No."

A veil of red clouded my vision as I scrambled up the ladder to my freedom. Carlos waited on the catwalk and offered me his hand, but I rejected his help and climbed out of the fermentation tank myself.

"Where is she?" My question was quiet, but dangerous.

Carlos gave me another one-worded response. "Lunch."

Lucia ate her lunch with little consideration of the woman to whom she'd given not an impossible task, but rather a wasteful and unnecessary task. I had been ready to accept some kind of needle-in-the-haystack endeavor, especially if it had been something everyone at the vineyard had done as they worked to prove themselves as worthy. I was not okay, however, with being singled out and made to look like a fool.

My anger and embarrassment had only increased as I stomped from the production side of the barn to the employee picnic table. Lucia paid no attention to me even though my heavy, heaving breath must have sounded like a rodeo bull getting ready to buck off its rider. She popped the final bite of her sandwich into her mouth and brushed the crumbs from her fingers.

"Wine crystals?!" I blustered. "How long were you going to let me keep scrubbing?"

Lucia picked up a small green pear and inspected its outer skin. "You would have figured it out eventually."

I swallowed hard and took a few calming breaths. "I know you resent that I own this vineyard," I said in an even tone to match her own, "you've made that abundantly clear. But you need to get over it. I didn't do anything wrong."

Lucia set down her pear and finally turned to regard me. She stared at me with a solemn intensity. "I don't like cheaters."

Her words were slow, almost as if they covered a fire burning just beneath the surface.

"*Cheater?*" My voice pitched. "What did I cheat at?"

"The bar last night," Lucia clarified. "It's none of my business, but I think it's pretty shitty to be out at a gay bar with someone who isn't your wife."

"My wife?" I echoed. Slowly, Lucia's accusation began to make sense. "Oh. You think … Lily and me." I exhaled deeply as my anger began to fade. "Well first, Lily and I are only friends. I've known her forever, and believe me, there's like zero interest on either side. And second …" I licked my lips. "Alex is dead."

Lucia's eyes flicked up to meet mine. "Dead?"

"Sh-she died in January," I revealed. "She was hit by a car."

Although Lucia was finally looking at me—finally giving me the attention I thought I deserved—I could no longer handle her penetrating gaze. I dropped my eyes to the concrete floor.

"That's ... terrible."

I could hear the earnest regret in Lucia's tone. I should have felt satisfied that I'd made her feel guilty for her earlier mistreatment of me, but I only felt remorse as well.

I swallowed hard. "Yeah," I managed to choke out.

With my head lowered, gravity had a better chance of coaxing out the liquid forming in my tear ducts. I lifted my head and rapidly blinked my eyes to avoid crying in front of my assistant winemaker. I'd embarrassed myself enough for one day.

Lucia pointed at my feet. "That's an interesting look."

I looked down to my shoes. The originally white sneakers had become dyed different shades of purple and pink from spilling wine lees on them. My laundry still wasn't working; I'd tried to hand scrub them clean, but the leather material was permanently colored.

Lucia stood from the picnic table in a single, fluid motion. She cleared away the remnants of her lunch. "Get yourself a pair of work boots and a wide-brimmed hat," she instructed. "Your feet and complexion will thank you later."

She left the picnic table and marched in the direction of the production side of the barn. I grimaced, already anticipating what new kind of torture she might put me through that day. I'd already lost the majority of the morning to her unwarranted revenge.

"More cleaning?" I guessed.

"No," she tossed over her shoulder. "I'm going to teach you how we make wine."

"Oh!" My mood instantly brightened, and I hustled to catch up with her brisk stride.

We stopped first at the destemming machine where a narrow conveyor belt ascended and stopped at a metal container that resembled a meat grinder. A giant corkscrew within the metal-framed box separated most of the grapes from their woody vines.

"In early fall, when the grapes are ripe, we'll hand pick the bunches and bring them to the barn." Lucia gestured to the currently silent machine. "This is the crusher or destemmer. Grapes are dumped into the hopper that augers them into a rotating destemmer that knocks the berries off the stems."

I nodded to indicate I was listening. Rolando had briefly described all of these things to me, but I wasn't going to interrupt or cut her off.

"The berries fall through the gap between two rollers set to pop them without crushing the seeds," she continued. "If it crushed the seeds, you'd get too much bitterness."

"I'm assuming no one actually crushes grapes by foot anymore?"

Lucia curled her lip. "Would you want to drink wine that someone's feet had been in?"

"I guess not."

Lucia sighed. "We could do something to entertain the tourists if that's what you're suggesting. We usually compost our young grapes that aren't ready to be wine yet, but I guess we could let visitors stomp around in them first."

A small smile made its way to my mouth. "That's very charitable of you."

Lucia snorted. "Whatever."

We walked next to the trio of fermentation tanks where I'd recently spent my morning. I looked up at the giant steel silos. "I'll probably never look at these things the same." I tried to keep my tone light and teasing.

Lucia's frown deepened. "I'm sorry." She tugged at her long, single braid. "I shouldn't have assumed."

"And I should have told you all about Alex earlier," I admitted. "But anyway," I said, not wanting to linger on the past, "this is where the alcohol gets made, right?"

Lucia nodded. "Naturally occurring yeast grows on the exterior of the grape. Only the skin protects it from that yeast. When the skin is broken, fermentation occurs. It's not rocket science," she admitted. "If you took a bucket full of wine grapes and stomped on them a little, about a week later you'd be making something that resembled wine.

"The yeast eats the sugar, and it makes alcohol," I recalled.

I remembered that part from a brewery tour I'd been on once. The yeast molecules were basically college frat boys—eating, farting, and having sex with themselves to produce the alcohol.

"And CO_2," Lucia added. She wrapped her knuckles against one of the steel tanks. "While the wine is fermenting, CO_2 is released, which causes the skins and seeds to raise to the surface and the juice settles to the bottom of these tanks."

"Do you skim off the skin and seeds then?" I asked. I pictured a wide-mouthed net, like a pool skimmer.

Lucia shook her head. "We want the skins to sit with the juice. The skins are what give red wine its color. The juice itself is clear; it's colorless. It doesn't have the true flavor of the varietal. The true character is really in the skin. The CO_2 pushes the skins to the top, creating a thick cap." She motioned with her hands as if pantomiming the process. "The cap needs to be punched down three times a day to keep the skins moist. It's my favorite part of this whole process."

"Because you like punching things?" I hazarded to guess.

Lucia's mouth twisted. "Who do you think I am?"

"Wine diamonds?" I couldn't help myself.

"I said I was sorry!" Her voice made an uncharacteristic squeak.

I grabbed her forearm to let her know I was only teasing. The motion was involuntary, almost reflexive, but I realized the presumptive familiarity of the touch only after I'd clasped her arm. We both looked down to where my fingers circled around her denim shirt and her thinly muscled arm.

The main barn door unexpectedly opened. My head jerked in the direction of the open door, and I hastily dropped Lucia's arm.

Oscar poked his head into the barn. His body was backlit by afternoon sunshine, but I could make out his slim silhouette. "It's official," he announced.

Lucia rubbed at her forearm—the same arm I'd been holding on to. "What?"

Oscar stepped fully into the barn. "Bud break."

"So soon?" Lucia questioned.

Oscar shrugged delicately. "Mild winter? I don't know: either way, we've got new growth."

"Bud break?" I repeated. I'd heard them say the phrase before, but I hadn't known what it meant.

Lucia looked back in my direction. "The first signs of spring," she explained. "Visible growth on the grape wines."

"Oh! That's good, right?"

Lucia slowly nodded. "We'll be on more stable ground in a few weeks once there's no more threat of frost or hail, but it looks like we made it through another season."

Oscar beckoned to me. "Come see, *Jefa*."

I followed the quiet, slender man outside to the afternoon sunshine. We walked across ground that still felt solidly frozen beneath my shoes. Oscar approached one of the vines closest to the barn. I couldn't see any noticeable changes, but I also didn't know what I was looking for.

Oscar's narrow shoulders curved forward and he bent toward one of the vertical canes. "Look," he said. His low voice sounded almost reverent.

I stooped closer to the vine. It was barely perceptible, but tiny yellow-green buds dotted the old wood. It reminded me of the new buds on a pussy willow.

Oscar delicately touched a tiny green leaf. It looked more like a bud burst than a bud break. "If the buds survive," he said, "they create shoots and flowers. In about two months, those tiny flowers will bloom."

"How do they become a grape?" I wondered.

"Flowers on grapevines are considered perfect flowers; they self-pollinate without need of bees," Oscar noted. "Each little flower will become its own berry."

I stared at the vulnerable looking buds. It was a marvel that something so small would eventually be transformed into something entirely different. "That's kind of magical."

A second voice surprised me: "Green and delicate, yet somehow resilient."

I turned in the direction of the new voice. Lucia stood a few feet behind us. I hadn't realized she'd followed us out to the vines.

She shoved her hands into the back pockets of her jeans. With the exception of the Guerneville bar, I'd never seen her outside of the barn before. I'd never seen her in the daylight. The afternoon sunshine made her glossy black hair nearly iridescent.

"Spring is kind of amazing, don't you think?" I remarked. "A time for rebirth and renewal. Maybe even new beginnings?" I stared purposefully at her, hoping she would get the meaning behind my words: *Let's bury the hatchet. But not in my back.*

Lucia shifted her weight from one foot to another. "Yeah. Maybe."

+ + +

Rain pelted against the windows and periodic gusts of wind rattled the glass in their ancient panes. The sun had set hours earlier, but the inky sky appeared darker than what was typical as storm clouds choked out any light the moon and stars might have provided. I turned away from the rainstorm when I heard the shrill shriek of the hot water kettle I'd warmed on the kitchen stovetop. When I removed the kettle from its burner, the teapot's urgent sound was replaced with something else.

I stood silent and unmoving in the kitchen and focused on the new noise. *Was that a baby crying?*

The low cry sounded human, but not quite. I remained motionless, the tea kettle still in one hand, while I waited for the sound to repeat. The low, mournful wail might have been coming from inside the house, but I couldn't tell. The heavy rain continued to strike the windows like a snare drum solo while the wind produced its own howl.

Great. Not only could I not afford this place, but now it was also haunted. Maybe we could book haunted wine tours, I mused to myself.

I poured the steaming hot water over the waiting teabag at the bottom of my ceramic mug. I paused again when the crying—a siren of some kind?—continued. Was it a tornado warning? If not for the storm raging outside and the failed attempt to get me to scrub away phantom wine crystals, I half considered that maybe Lucia or Carlos was playing a prank on me. Sure, scare the single woman living by herself in the middle of nowhere.

I had no real weapons in the house, but I grabbed a particularly sharp pair of kitchen shears from the butcher block. I stalked slowly toward the front door, which seemed to be the origin of the unnerving cry.

"Very funny, you guys," I called through the closed door. I didn't expect a response, but I hoped I would at least scare them off.

I jerked backwards and nearly dropped the scissors when the front door began to rattle. The aged wooden door was drafty with inefficient gaps on all sides. I thought the brutal wind might have been responsible for the way the door shook on its hinges, but the rhythmic rattling wouldn't stop.

I reached for the door handle with my free hand and gripped the scissors more tightly in the other. I tentatively touched my fingers to the doorknob as if I expected it to bite me. I quickly turned the handle and yanked the door open.

"Ah hah!" I called out, hoping to startle whomever might have been banging on the door.

I stared blankly at the impenetrable darkness beyond my front porch. No one stood on the other side of the door.

"I'm losing my mind," I muttered to myself.

I started to shut the door, defeated by my overly-active imagination. The door was nearly closed when it was unexpectedly forced back open. I spied movement in my peripheral vision as something dark, medium-sized, and close to the ground, forced its way inside.

"Oh shit, oh shit, oh shit," I gasped, worried I'd inadvertently allowed a wild animal—a skunk or racoon—into my home.

I turned on my heel and raised the kitchen shears above my head, although I had no real plan for them. It wasn't like I could actually *stab* whatever had scurried out of the rain. I would probably forfeit my house to its new tenant rather than do that.

I lowered the scissors when I realized what—or rather who—had scurried inside to escape the storm.

"Gato?"

The barn cat looked skinnier than usual with its fur matted flat from the heavy rain. His tail looked pencil thin without its usual fluff and his head drooped low, as if embarrassed to be seen by me.

"Hold on," I told the cat.

I returned the shears to the butcher block and grabbed a tea towel from a kitchen drawer. Gato remained in the same spot, just within the front doorway. I eyeballed the disgruntled-looking animal. He'd never let me pet him before. Would he behave long enough for me to fluff him dry?

I dropped down to my knees beside the cranky feline. "I'm just going to …" I said carefully, more for myself than the cat.

I dropped the kitchen towel on Gato's huddled shoulders and gave him a brisk rub. He made an annoyed noise, but he didn't lash out or run away. I rubbed the open towel over his damp fur, tempting fate again.

"Better?" I asked, as if I expected him to reply.

I couldn't towel him off completely, but he looked moderately drier than when he'd originally scampered inside.

I returned to my feet and opened the front door. I didn't expect him to leave, but I didn't want the outdoor cat to feel like I'd trapped him. Gato sniffed at the open door as if considering his choices.

"Are you in or out?" I asked.

After a moment of weighing his options, Gato turned away from the open door. He found a spot on the woven runner in the entryway near my shoes and began to give himself a bath. I watched for a reaction as I shut the door again. Gato looked unconcerned, however, and continued to groom his fur.

I turned on the porch light and peered into the stormy night. The wind gusts had made the rain practically sidewise. I worried my lower lip. Rolando had once told me that the valley didn't typically get much rain, which was ideal for growing cabernet vines since they required good soil drainage. But what if the vines got too much rain?

Rolando had given me the number to his landline when I'd first arrived on the property. I hadn't had occasion to use it yet despite the numerous questions I'd had over the past few days. I glanced at the clock over the fireplace mantle. It was late. Should I call him? Would he even pick up? He had windows; he would know it was raining. And it wasn't like anything could be done about the storm. We weren't going to stand over the individual vines with umbrellas.

But I knew myself. I knew I would worry all night if I didn't ask my question.

I retrieved my cellphone from the kitchen. I chewed on my lower lip as the telephone rang.

"Hello?" Rolando picked up after the fourth ring. His voice was rough and deep, indicating I'd definitely woken him up.

I briefly considered hanging up, but the damage had already been done. "Hi, Rolando. It's June."

"June? Is everything okay?" I could hear muffled noises as if he was sitting up in bed. I imagined him consulting a clock near his bed to discern the time.

"Yeah, uh, I'm just calling because of the rain."

"Is the farmhouse leaking?"

"No, no. The house is fine. But it's raining." I paused. "A lot. I'm worried about the vines."

"As long as it doesn't hail or freeze tonight, they'll be fine," he assured me. "Or if you see a giant boat outside with two of every kind of animal, then we'll get worried."

I exhaled. "Okay. That's good to know." My former anxiety had my cheeks heating with embarrassment. "I'm sorry I called so late."

"It's okay. I'm glad you're taking this so seriously." Rolando politely rushed me off the phone. "I'll see you in the morning."

"See you in the morning," I repeated before ending the call.

bud break

CHAPTER SEVEN

Lucia stared at the installation, her eyebrows furrowed. She chewed on her bottom lip and looked to be working out a problem in her head. "So are you like an environmentalist or something?"

"I care about the planet, yeah," I said. "It's the only one we've got."

Her features remained pinched while she seemed to supervise the EV charger installation. The crew had installed an EV charging station at the farmhouse earlier in the day. It had taken some time to arrange the appointment, so it only made sense for the company to install a second charging station by the tasting barn while they had their tools and gear already on the property.

"The charging station is a good investment," I reasoned. "Batteries don't stay charged forever. And if someone's driving their electric vehicle during their tour of wine country, they'll come here to charge up."

"So we let them mooch off of us?"

"No," I said calmly. "It takes time to charge. They'll be on a tour or trying our wines in the tasting room while they wait."

Lucia still wasn't convinced. "Nothing guarantees they'll buy anything. We should charge them to be able to use it."

"Do you charge people for using our bathroom?" I countered.

"No," she scowled. "But toilet paper can't be as expensive as this," she said, gesturing to the electricians, tools, and exposed wires.

I considered myself a generally positive, optimistic person, but Lucia's negativity was starting to wear on me. Rolando had said his daughter was slow to accept change, but I hadn't expected resistance to every improvement or change I made to the property. It wasn't like I was butting in on wine making—not that she'd let me do anything but pressure clean the barrels.

"Well, I needed one for my car; an extra charging station isn't hurting anything."

Lucia kicked at a small rock, causing it to launch across the parking lot. "Whatever," she grumbled. "It's your money."

"Yeah. It is," I shot back.

"I'm going back to work," Lucia huffed before storming off.

I watched after Lucia's retreating form as she stomped back to the barn. I didn't really need to supervise the installation technicians, but the alternative meant following Lucia and being subjected to whatever new form of torture she'd thought up for me. I cursed under my breath, but went inside the barn as well.

I paused just within the doorway and scanned the open space, but I didn't immediately see Lucia. I assumed she'd probably gone into the cellar or was hiding behind a fermentation tank to avoid me.

"Oh, June!" Natalie called to me from her post at the makeshift bar. It was still too early in the day for any tours, so she stood by herself. "I've got a present for you."

Thankful for any excuse not to track down the surly assistant winemaker, I crossed the barn to join her. "Present?" I questioned. "But it's not even my birthday."

Natalie gestured to a medium-sized woven basket that sat on top of the bar. "Your neighbors dropped off a welcome to the neighborhood gift."

The basket held two wine bottles—one red and one white—and an assortment of chocolates and salty snacks.

I picked up one of the bottles and inspected its unfamiliar label. "That was thoughtful," I observed. "Who are my neighbors?"

"Bruce and Darcy Jefferson. They make a nice chardonnay," Natalie described. "Fruity and not too oaky, if you're into that."

I returned the bottle to the woven basket. I had no idea if I was into that.

A quick phone search uncovered that the Jeffersons owned the vineyard to the west of Lark Estates. Their winery seemed similar in land size and wine production numbers. I still had more unpacking and organizing and market strategizing to do, but it would be nice to get away from the property to meet my neighbors. The welcome basket seemed to suggest that the Jeffersons didn't view Lark Estates as a rival, but rather a peer.

Similar to Lark Estates, Bruce and Darcy Jefferson's winery—Silver Stag—was only open to the public by appointment. I drove past the signage at their front gates that warned me of that very fact, but no real knowledge if the proprietors would be at home. While Lark Estate's public-facing building was a modest, but serviceable corrugated metal-roofed barn, Silver Stag was far more high end. The wrought-iron fence that surrounded the property should have been my first clue.

I whistled lowly as I came upon the property. I hadn't necessarily been expecting another barn, but I certainly wasn't prepared for a grey lannon stone structure that better resembled a castle. I looked over at the two humble bottles of wine from our vineyard that I'd strapped into the front passenger seat of my energy-efficient car. Maybe I should have brought more.

I parked my car and shut off the engine. I continued to look for signs of human activity as I exited the vehicle and walked up to Silver Stag's imposing front door—two doors, antique or reclaimed wood, studded with metal rivets. The door swung open before I had the chance to figure out if I was supposed to knock or ring a doorbell.

A middle-aged woman in a dark purple blouse and black capris pants looked startled by my presence. "Oh, goodness," she breathed. She pressed a hand to the single strand of pearls strung around her neck. "I didn't know anyone was out here."

I took a step backwards so she wouldn't feel so crowded. "Sorry. I would have rung the bell, but my hands were full."

I lifted my arms, a bottle of wine in each hand.

The woman's features softened. "You're the new owner of Lark Estates."

I cleared my throat. "That would be me."

"Come in, come in!" The woman stepped backwards to make room for me.

I hesitated. "I don't want to be a bother if you were just about to leave."

"No, no," the woman insisted. "It was nothing important. My errands can wait."

I trusted the woman's words and stepped inside.

I stared first at the vaulted ceiling. A mural, not unlike what one might see on the ceiling of a Renaissance Era church covered the interior of the entryway. Rosy cheeked, naked cherubs gazed down on visitors and hid behind grapevines and large clay vessels.

"It's a little much, right?" the woman said, noticing my stare.

"It's nice," I appeased.

The woman made a noise. "I keep telling Bruce that it's hokey, but he likes it. Thinks it classes up the joint or something. I'm Darcy, by the way," she finally introduced herself. "Darcy Jefferson."

"June St. Clare," I returned.

We shook hands, causing the silver bracelets on her right wrist to jangle together.

Darcy Jefferson was a short, blonde woman with a penchant for wedged heels that increased her height by a few inches. Her age was indistinguishable. I suspected her smooth, unlined forehead was the result of facial fillers instead of youth or a regimented skincare routine.

"Thank you for the welcome basket," I said. "I'm sorry I missed your visit, but I wanted to return the gesture." I held up the wine bottles I continued to awkwardly carry with me.

Darcy clapped her hands together. "Oh, you're sweet. I don't usually imbibe this early in the day, but why don't we crack into one of those?"

I followed Darcy deeper into the structure. I still didn't have a word for it. Castle? Manor? The upscale motif continued as we walked: marble tiled floors, dark wood accents, wall sconces, and geometric patterned windows.

"This building is beautiful," I complimented.

"Oh, thank you, dear. You should have seen what a tacky disaster this place was when we bought it back in the eighties."

We strode through a series of rooms, each elegantly furnished and decorated, before reaching the back of the well-appointed mansion. Darcy opened twin French doors that led us outside to a patio that overlooked their grapevines. The patio was quaint and intimate with half a dozen patio tables and matching chairs. Like Lark Estates, the vineyard was still mostly sleeping, but I imagined in early and late summer the views were magnificent.

Darcy disappeared behind a formal bar—a massive upgrade compared to the upright wine barrels Natalie used at the barn—and retrieved two clean wine glasses and a corkscrew.

"This is very impressive, Darcy," I remarked. The compliments kept falling from my mouth.

The woman smiled, pleased by my praise. "Have a seat," she said, gesturing to one of the empty patio tables.

"Hey, Dee?" I heard a robust male voice call from inside the house.

"Out here, Bruce," Darcy returned.

The French doors swung open again and an older man—or at least visibly older than Darcy—walked outside. He wore a light blue dress shirt and long, khaki-colored cargo shorts.

"Have you seen my readers?" The man paused when he realized his wife wasn't alone. "I'm sorry. I didn't know we had visitors."

"Bruce, this is our new neighbor," Darcy introduced. "June just bought Lark Estates."

The man's face lit up with recognition. "Oh! Welcome to the neighborhood."

I inclined my head. "Thanks."

Darcy produced a third wine glass. "June and I were just about to break into the wine she brought. Will you be joining us?"

Bruce glanced at his wristwatch. It was gold and oversized, and it might have cost more than my car. "I've got time," he decided. "Why the hell not."

Bruce sat down in the empty chair beside me. He was a handsome, albeit older man. His face was unseasonably tanned, which contrasted with a thick shock of silver hair. It made me wonder if that's how they'd named their vineyard.

He smiled as Darcy set out the empty glasses in front of us and proceeded to fill each one. "So you're the new owner of Lark Estates," he observed.

I could read between the lines. I didn't look the part.

"Yep," I said, working hard to contain feelings of anxiety and inadequacy.

"How much did you end up paying for the place?" he asked. "I put in an offer, but I guess it wasn't good enough."

"Oh hush, Bruce," Darcy admonished. She settled into her own chair. "This isn't a business meeting. This is neighbors getting to know each other."

Bruce held up his hand in retreat. "Okay, okay," he conceded.

"So how are you liking things?" Darcy pressed. "Are you getting along with everyone?"

By *everyone*, I assumed she meant my vineyard staff. I hadn't ventured out to meet the other neighbors yet.

"Everything has been great so far," I said. I could be honest with my best friend, but I was more guarded with the Jeffersons. "Rolando and everyone have been great. I really lucked out with inheriting that staff."

Bruce held onto the base of his wine glass and agitated the liquid inside. "Rolando Santiago is a legend," he openly admired. "You won't find a more respected winemaker in the region."

I smiled at the kind words, simultaneously pleased and proud.

"The daughter though." Darcy's voice lowered as if she worried someone might overhear us. "She's a bit of a wild card."

My smile flattened. "Lucia is very hardworking." I found myself defending my assistant winemaker. "I've only been impressed by her passion and dedication."

"Oh, of course," Darcy hastily corrected. "They're all very hardworking. None of this would be possible without them."

I took a measured sip of my wine as I considered Darcy Jefferson's words. Who exactly was the *they* and *them* to whom she was referring?

"I'm glad you stopped by, June," Bruce vocalized, breaking into my thoughts. "It's always good to be friendly with your neighbors, especially in our business." He continued to swirl the wine I had brought. "Not everyone feels this way, but I consider us colleagues, not competition. We little guys have to stick together."

"And gals," Darcy interjected.

Bruce chuckled. "Right. We little guys *and* gals have to stick together against the Trader Joe's and Costco's of the world."

"Hey, do you know what they say about how to make a small fortune?" Darcy asked, her blue eyes twinkling. "Start with a large one!"

Bruce held up his wine glass to the late morning sunlight and laughed. "We might lose all our money, but at least we can drink the wine!"

+ + +

I didn't stay long at the Jeffersons' property. After I finished my glass of wine, I begged off with the excuse that I needed to get back to work: there was always work to be done. When I returned to the vineyard, everyone was away, busy with their own individual tasks. I could have poked around the property to find Lucia, but I settled for helping Natalie finish setting up the bar area for that afternoon's tastings and tours.

I found myself frowning at our low-budget setup. I hadn't previously found fault with the converted wine barrel furniture, but after seeing the Jeffersons' visitor area, I began to feel a little underwhelmed.

"If we had all the money in the world," I proposed, "what would you like this place to look like?"

Natalie cleaned a set of wine glasses to remove fingerprints before placing them on the table reserved for tours. "Do we have all the money in the world?" she posed.

I chewed on my lower lip. "No."

"Then don't worry about it, June," she placated.

"What do you think about the Jeffersons next door?" I couldn't help asking.

Natalie continued to clean. "I don't think about them at all."

That was all the answer I required. "O-okay."

She paused long enough to look up. "Why do you ask?"

"I don't know." I floundered for a response. "I just got a weird vibe from them."

"Xenophobic?"

I cleared my throat, not expecting her to be so direct. "Yeah. That."

Natalie made an approving noise. "There's definitely an Us versus Them mentality between ownership and staff around these parts," she revealed. "I try to stay out of it; I suggest you do, too."

I nodded sagely and let her words of wisdom sink in.

I stopped fixating on our peculiar neighbors when the barn door opened and Rolando stepped inside. He removed his wide-brimmed hat and wiped at his forehead with the back of his hand. "It's getting warm out there. If this heat keeps up, we might have an early *veraison*."

Natalie turned to me. "That's when the grapes turn red."

"Thanks," I smiled tightly. I hoped there would come a day— soon—when I'd no longer need these little educational asides.

"Will we see you tonight?" Rolando asked me.

"What's tonight?"

"The bud break party," he said. "Didn't Lucia tell you?"

I tried not to frown. "No. But I was visiting with the Jeffersons this morning. I'm sure it wasn't an intentional snub."

Rolando smiled gently. "You don't have to make excuses for her, June. I know how she can be. I love her, naturally, but she's a stubborn old mule."

I couldn't help smiling at the description.

"Come over tonight," he implored. "We'll celebrate the vines, and us, making it through another winter. There's a big bonfire, food, and music. We'll burn the old wood that didn't survive the season or that's no longer producing fruit."

"That sounds like fun." I hesitated despite my eager words. "Are you sure you want me there? In my experience, office parties are less fun when the boss is there."

This wasn't your typical work place, and I definitely didn't feel like a boss, but Rolando would know what I meant.

"I insist," he said with an encouraging smile. "And I can guarantee you that no one will be on their best behavior just because you're there."

His assurances made me a little more confident about the invitation. I nodded my head agreeably. "Okay. I'll try to make it. Can I bring anything?"

"No. We'll have plenty of food. Lucia's aunt, my sister Clara, has been making tamales all day for the occasion."

I looked to Natalie. "Are you going?"

"Not this time, no," she said, looking sorry. "I already committed to babysitting my grandbabies tonight. You should definitely go though. It's fun."

I nodded my head. "Yeah, okay."

"You're supposed to act surprised, by the way," Natalie said. She stuck out her lip in an exaggerated pout.

I furrowed my eyebrows. "About what?"

"That I'm old enough to be a grandma!"

CHAPTER EIGHT

April in Calistoga was mild, with sunny, typically rainless days that reached 70 degrees and evenings that dropped to 50 or 40 degrees. Anything cooler would have damaged the fragile first signs of life on the vineyard. San Francisco was famously cold, so I had plenty of clothes suitable for the evening's lower temperature, but that didn't mean I knew what to wear.

Owning a vineyard might have sounded fancy, but the day-to-day uniform was far from glamorous. I typically wore jeans, heavy work boots, and durable tops like everyone else on the property. But since this was a party, would people be more dressed up than usual? I didn't want to offend Ronaldo and the others by looking too casual, but I also didn't want to stick out more than I already did by overdressing.

I eyeballed the clothes in my closet. Nothing in my wardrobe said 'bud breaking party.' After much deliberation, I eventually settled on a patterned sundress, a jean jacket, and ballet flats.

I grabbed a bottle of reposado from my limited alcohol collection before leaving the house that evening. It wasn't the fanciest tequila, but it was far superior to the kind of gasoline I'd consumed as a college student. Alex and I had bought the bottle a few years back on vacation in Mexico. Neither of us were big tequila fans, however, so the bottle had gathered dust in a cabinet of our San Francisco condo.

Just beyond my own property line, Rolando's house looked out of place on a Napa Valley vineyard. The dark stained, hand-hewn logs would have fit in with a thickly wooded forest farther north, but it contrasted deeply on a semi-arid landscape that favored updated, luxury designs. The dark stain gave the home a kind of gingerbread essence, adding to its already picturesque feel. The home was charming—upkept and tidy—a far cry from the drafty farmhouse I currently inhabited.

The front yard was dotted with small fruit trees, still dormant despite the new growth springing up elsewhere on the vineyard. Rolando had his own vines—a few rows of woody canes similar to those on the main property. I was curious what he did with the fruit he grew on his land, but wondered about the etiquette of the question. Could you ask a man what he did with his grapes?

Rolando answered the door. His warm, genuine smile greeted me and caused some of my earlier anxiety to subside. Most of the vineyard staff unintentionally made me feel inadequate and unqualified—because I was—but Rolando's continued kindness put me more at ease.

"Come on in, June."

"Something smells amazing," I complimented.

"That would be my sister Clara's cooking. She's quite talented in the kitchen." He chuckled pleasantly and rubbed his palm across his slightly protruding stomach. "Which may or may not be a good thing."

I remembered I hadn't arrived empty handed. "I brought alcohol. I don't know if it's any good," I apologized.

Rolando accepted the gift and inspected the amber-colored liquid in the squat bottle. "I'm sure we'll make good use of this tonight. Thank you for the gift."

I flattened my palms along the skirt of my dress. "No, thank *you* for the invitation. I'm really grateful to have been included."

Rolando inclined his head. I thought we might get stuck in the front foyer thanking each other for the rest of the evening, but he turned on his heel and gestured for me to follow him deeper into the house.

We walked through the living room and the attached dining room. I passed several hanging framed photographs that made me want to pause and reflect, but I continued to follow Rolando to the back of the house. The mouth-watering scents intensified as we entered the back kitchen. The kitchen, like in so many other homes, was the center of activities. Everyone had gathered in the room, despite its modest size.

I spied Oscar and Carlos right away, each with an attractive woman on their respective hips. The only other person in the room was an older woman, busy at the electric stovetop, whom I assumed was Rolando's sister, Clara.

Carlos was the first to greet me. "Eh, it's *Jefa*!" His tone was approving as if no one had expected me to actually show up.

I lingered in the kitchen doorway with a raised hand. "Hey, everyone. Thanks for having me."

Rolando held out the tequila bottle. "Look what June brought."

A chorus of approving noises filled the small kitchen, and I found myself growing embarrassed by the attention.

Carlos looked comfortable digging through the cabinets and drawers of a kitchen that didn't belong to him. "We should do a toast," he suggested. "Clara, where's the shot glasses?"

I gave a sideways glance to the short, round woman. She may have been a few years older than her brother, but I'd never been good at that type of thing. She wore her dark hair in a short bob that framed a strong jawline and dark, serious eyes. She rattled off a few phrases in Spanish, which I had no hope of decoding.

Carlos understood the directions, however, and opened a cabinet closer to the double basin sink. "Alright!" he cheered. He set up the miniature glasses on the kitchen island. "Is this everyone?" he asked.

Oscar scanned the room. "Where's Lucia?"

Aunt Clara tilted her head to the ceiling and hollered: "Lucia Maria Santiago!"

Noisy feet tumbled down a wooden staircase. Lucia appeared, looking cross and hurried. She still wore her hair in its signature braid, but she'd changed out of her work clothes for a pair of dark jeans and a fitted long-sleeved t-shirt. Her stampede faltered when she noticed me in the kitchen. Her features briefly showed confusion until her previous sour look reappeared.

I was too distracted by her reaction to realize that someone had passed me a shot glass. "Oh, I-I don't," came my weak protest.

Carlos flung his arm around my shoulders. "You do tonight, *Jefa*."

I looked around the small kitchen and at the half a dozen smiling, expectant faces—well, mostly smiling. I could feel the heat of Lucia's scowl even from across the room.

"*Salud?*" I offered up.

Everyone raised their miniature glasses and repeated the sentiment.

I brought the glass to my lips and took a tentative sip. While the others had tossed back their shots in a single, fluid motion, I was content to take multiple, conservative sips. I was relieved when Rolando resealed the bottle rather than allowing Carlos to set up a second round.

A tall, silver pot sat on the largest burner. Twisting wisps of steam filtered up from the oversized container. Clara used a crocheted potholder to lift the silver lid. A cloud of steam mushroomed out of the pot. She fished out empty corn husks with a set of tongs before reaching the tidy cluster of tamales at the center of the pot.

Oscar rubbed his hands together. "Clara, you've outdone yourself again."

"I don't want any leftovers," Clara warned, "so I hope everyone brought their appetite."

I grabbed at my abdomen when my stomach loudly growled. Instead of teasing me for the obvious noise, Aunt Clara rewarded my hunger with the same kind smile I'd seen so many times on her brother's face. If Lucia had inherited anything from her father's side of the family, it hadn't been that gentle, accommodating smile. Her dark eyes narrowed in my direction.

"*Jefa*, you should go first," Carlos grinned. "You might starve otherwise."

I held my hands up. "Oh, no. Clara—you worked so hard. You should go first."

"No, no," she declined. "Guests first."

"I really insisted," I demurred.

"Oh for Christs' sake," Lucia interjected in a loud, booming voice. "She's not Our Lady of Guadalupe. Somebody *go*."

I bristled at Lucia's volume and tone, but grabbed the long tongs from the stovetop. I carefully fished one of the delicate tamales out of the silver pot and set it in the center of my plate.

Aunt Clara clucked her tongue. "More! *Come algo, calaca.*"

I knew very little Spanish, but I suspected Aunt Clara was like so many maternal or grandmotherly types: *Eat more, you're too skinny*. I helped myself to a second tamale, which seemed to give Aunt Clara great satisfaction. I spooned a rich reddish-brown sauce over the tamales and took my plate to the dining room table.

Once everyone had served themselves, we took our seats around the long, wooden dining room table. Aunt Clara sat beside me. The woman who had clung to Oscar's arm, presumably his wife, sat on my other side. Seated directly across from me, Lucia dug into her tamales without ever looking up in my direction.

"*Mija!*" Aunt Clara sharply chastised. "Not until we pray."

Lucia paused, mouth open, a square bite of tamale dangling from her fork. I heard her quiet grunt before she set her utensil on her plate and bowed her head.

Clara grabbed my hand and Oscar's partner held the other. I didn't consider myself religious or even mildly spiritual, but I also wasn't in position to protest the pre-dinner prayer. Succumbing to the moment, I similarly bowed my head.

Aunt Clara's version of grace was a mixture of Spanish and English. I waited with head bowed and eyes closed as she asked for blessings for those seated around the table and for the land and for our meal to be similarly blessed. She squeezed my hand with surprising strength.

"And we ask, Lord, that you watch over our new friend, June," she continued. "And that she find peace and comfort in her new surroundings." The touched smile on my lips stalled when Aunt Clara concluded the blessing. "And we ask that you provide a place at your Holy Table for Alex—taken away from this world before her time. We ask for the gift of forgiveness and understanding as we try to make sense of her death. We ask this in the name of your son, Jesus, through whom all good things come. Amen."

The others at the dinner table repeated the prayer's closing: "Amen."

Despite the delicious-smelling food growing cooler on my plate, I was too stunned by the closing of Clara's prayer to take my first bite. All around me, the other dinner guests dug into their meal. Utensils scraped across dinner plates, more food was passed around the table, and everyone praised Clara for a well-executed meal.

I stared at my glass of ice water and watched a single drop of condensation stream down the cup's exterior. I swallowed hard and worked the muscles in my throat to keep my emotions in check. Most of all, I avoided looking at the woman seated directly across from me—the only person on the farm who knew the real reason why no one had ever met Alex.

I couldn't help but feel like everyone at the table regarded me with new eyes. That wasn't necessarily a good thing though. I didn't want them to feel sorry for me. I didn't want to be pitied. I wanted them to respect me.

I felt a soft touch to my elbow. "Eat up, June!" Aunt Clara encouraged me. "Don't let it get cold!"

I shoved down complicated emotions and tried to snap out of my funk. I focused on the steaming food on my plate and cut into my first bite. Chairs and place settings had been assembled for eight, but it was clear that the table was really only intended for six people. My elbow frequently bumped into Oscar's wife's each time I used my knife to cut into the masa, chicken, and root vegetable filling. As I looked around at the assembled group, I noticed I had been the only one so modest with my plate. Everyone else—even the women—had helped themselves to at least three tamales.

"Clara, these are amazing," I spoke in earnest.

My praise brought a pleased smile to Aunt Clara's mouth. "Do you cook?"

"I love to cook," I admitted, "but I haven't done much lately."

"Is my brother working you too hard?" she pressed. "You can always tell him no."

"No, no. I *want* to work," I insisted. "I want to learn everything they're willing to teach me."

Clara patted the top of my hand. Her skin was warm, like proofing bread dough. "You can help me make the tamales next time. It's more fun that way. We can gossip about the boys."

I heard a disgruntled noise across the table. "You've never offered to let me help with the tamales," Lucia openly complained.

"You've never shown any interest," her aunt calmly returned.

Lucia grumbled under her breath. The words were indistinguishable, but I sensed they were probably about me.

When the last of the food had been eaten, I moved to help clear people's plates. Clara stopped me before I could take away anyone's place setting. "No, no. You go outside with the others."

"But you've been cooking all day," I protested.

"Next time," she promised. "Go outside now. You won't want to miss the big fire."

The others had already filed outside. I lingered a little longer to help Clara with the dishes, despite her insisting otherwise, before grabbing my jean jacket and going outside as well.

I walked away from the warmth and good scents of Rolando's home to the oversized bonfire several yards away. The fire burned large and bright, cutting through the twilight that had fallen during dinner. The fire aggressively snapped and crackled from the dry wood that served as its fuel. A plume of ash launched into the sky before returning to earth every time one of the boys tossed an awkward shaped log into the fire.

Everyone seemed to have coupled up around the blaze. Oscar and Carlos each held their respective partners close as they gazed into the flames. I looked around, but Rolando wasn't in sight. I considered that he might have gone inside to help his sister clean up while the younger people played with the fire.

Not wanting to stand by myself, but also not wanting to be a third wheel, I stopped and stood a few feet from Lucia.

"So you guys do this every year?" I asked conversationally.

I wanted to crack her code. I didn't need us to be best friends, but I was hoping I could move the needle from outright hostility to her tolerating me.

"Yeah," she nodded. She hugged her arms around her torso. "We do a bigger harvest party with all of the part-time workers at the end of growing season, too."

I watched Lucia in profile while the bonfire held her attention. I was still too intimidated by her most days to really inspect her features. My friend Lily, who had always been more brave, hadn't had the same hang-up about unabashedly staring before deciding that my assistant winemaker was, in fact, hot.

I didn't think Lucia wore makeup, but her skin was visibly flawless. Her dark eyes were framed by expressive eyebrows and the dramatic sweep of lush eyelashes. Her face was narrow, almost pinched in its seriousness with defined cheekbones positioned high on her face. Her head was tilted back, her chin proud and slightly raised. My eyes swept down her long, elegant neck to the collar of her jacket.

Lucia stirred beside me. "I'm sorry if things are weird now," she started to apologize. "I ... it wasn't my secret to share."

"It's not a secret," I corrected, "but you're right. It wasn't yours to tell."

I couldn't help my feelings of betrayal. I hadn't explicitly told her not to tell the others about Alex's death, but I also hadn't expected her to share such delicate information without my knowledge.

Lucia's eyes dropped in shame. "I've never been a gossip. I don't know why I told them."

I chewed on my lower lip and stared into the hottest part of the fire. "Is it really so terrible that I'm the one who bought this place?"

Lucia didn't immediately reply, but I wasn't sure if I expected a real answer.

I breathed out sharply. "I'm going to get going."

Lucia hollowed out her already thin cheeks and silently nodded.

I circled the bonfire in search of the party's hosts. Rolando and Clare were just joining the fire as I came upon them.

"Thank you for a wonderful evening," I praised, forcing a cheerful tone to my voice. "I'm going to head out."

Carlos overheard my words of parting. "Leaving so soon, *Jefa*? You'll miss Oscar getting drunk." His grin looked more mischievous in the flickering light of the bonfire. "It's like seeing an asteroid or a shooting star."

A new voice, this one feminine, entered the conversation. "It really is a once-in-a-lifetime experience." Lucia stepped closer. I hadn't seen or heard her follow me.

"Oh, I don't want to overstay my welcome," I begged off. "But thank you for your hospitality."

"Lucia, walk June back to the farmhouse," Rolando instructed.

"Me?" Lucia complained. "Why me?"

"Because you know this property better than myself," he said.

"I'm really okay on my own," I insisted. "I only had a little tequila."

"I'm not worried about your alcohol tolerance," Rolando clarified. I'm worried about mountain lions."

"Mountain lions?" My voice practically squeaked.

I heard Lucia's snarl, nearly a kind of lioness herself. "Okay, fine. I'll take her home."

Lucia began to stalk away with her shoulders slumped forward and her head tilted down. "Come on," she grumbled.

The sky was inky blue and starless. Not even the moon had bothered to come out that night. I had no flashlight, not even my cellphone to help guide my way. Privately I was grateful Rolando had compelled his daughter to walk me home. Physically though, I was struggling to keep up.

I tried to pick my way across the rough terrain. The walk to Rolando's house hadn't been half as challenging, but I'd also had sunlight and my anxiety to distract me. Roots and ruts and the hard edge of dug up earth challenged every step. I had to focus hard to avoid tripping.

Lucia walked too quickly for my cautious pace. I was typically too proud to admit weakness, but the threat of mountain lions overcame my ego. I would have told her to go home and leave me—that I'd eventually find my way back—but I also didn't want to be the top news story on the local news that night: "*Bay area woman mauled in mountain lion attack.*"

"Lucia?" I called out. "Can we go a little slower? It's darker than I thought."

Lucia stopped and turned to face me. She silently waited for me with her hands on her hips. When I reached her side, she looped her arm through mine like one might when ushering an elderly person across a busy intersection. I could have taken offense at the geriatric gesture, but I was too mindful of her sudden proximity to really protest. It wasn't as intimate as if she'd been holding my hand, but it did force us bodily close—closer than we'd been with each other so far.

Despite Lucia's assistance, I still managed to trip across the uneven terrain. My toes seemed to catch on every exposed root and rut in the hard-packed earth. "Couldn't we have taken the road?" I openly complained.

"It's a shortcut," she claimed.

"It might be shorter, but my feet can't tell the difference."

The thin leather of my shoes offered no protection. I'd jammed my toes so many times I wouldn't have been surprised if my toenails were black and blue afterwards.

"Who wears ballet flats in spring?" she wondered aloud.

"My boots would have clashed with my dress," I offered weakly.

Lucia snorted, but thankfully didn't continue to critique me and my unseasonable wardrobe.

I'd remembered to keep a few lights on in the farmhouse, and its illuminated windows beckoned me like a lighthouse to a lost sailor. I breathed a little easier when the ground became more tame as well.

"I've got it now," I assured her.

"Nope," Lucia resisted. "Not until we're on the front porch."

Her hand seemed to tightened around my bicep even more. It was part stubborn, but also a little chivalrous I thought. True to her word, she only released her vice-like grip when we reached the short set of stairs that led to the wraparound porch.

I released a thankful sigh when we made it to the porch. It felt like being back on solid land after months of being adrift at sea. "Thanks for walking me back."

Lucia shoved her hands into her jacket pockets. "It's no big deal."

I furrowed my eyebrows as a thought settled in. "Will you be okay getting back to your dad's?"

"Yeah," she nodded. "You just have to be scarier than the mountain lions."

"They don't stand a chance," I joked.

Lucia wet her lips. "You think I'm scary?"

"Intimidating," I corrected.

Lucia's features pinched with contemplation. I thought she might press me for more information, but she changed the subject instead: "How do you like living in the farmhouse?"

I looked up to the faded beadboard that covered the front porch. "It's a little rough around the edges," I pronounced, "but I'm dealing."

"No granite countertops or stainless steel appliances; it's a wonder you're still alive," she said drolly. "Still, at least you're not under the same roof as your dad and nosey aunt."

"Why didn't you move in here when it was empty?" I wondered.

"I'm not here full time," she explained. "When it's winter in the valley, I'm usually someplace warmer that still has grapes. Australia. Chile," she listed.

"Wow," I said, genuinely impressed. "That's got to be exciting."

She curled her lip. "Eh, it's no big deal. It's not like I'm this jet-setting Instagram influencer. I work in the vineyards in exchange for room and board. I soak up as much as I can from each of the winemakers and bring it back here."

I vaguely remembered Rolando's surprise that she was 'back.' I hadn't thought to consider from where she'd been back.

"So, I'll see you tomorrow?" The question felt dumb on my lips. I coughed in an attempt to cover my awkwardness.

Her head tilted to one side. "Yeah. I'll be there."

My stupidity continued: "Cool. Me, too."

"Cool."

Lucia raised a silent hand in parting before turning in the direction from which we'd just come. I felt compelled—obligated—to watch her retreating form on the darkened horizon. I was just making sure she was safe, I told myself. I stayed on the front porch until I could no longer see her.

I stared out at the horizon and reflected on my complicated evening. Everyone knew that Alex was dead. There'd be no need to make up new excuses for her continued absence. I would have to overcome the sting of Lucia telling the others, but in a strange way, I could have felt indebted for her helping me avoid that awkwardness.

I thought more on the irritable assistant winemaker. Out of everyone on the vineyard, she alone continued to be the final holdout—the one person still plainly annoyed by my existence. Lucia might not have been ready to tolerate me yet, but after that night I felt the needle begin to move.

CHAPTER NINE

Just beyond the tasting barn was one of the more comfortable and welcoming spaces on the vineyard. When the weather allowed, we set up patio furniture on a relatively flat patch of grass with wooden tables covered by canvas umbrellas to provide shelter from the sun or the rain. It was a slow day on the farm with no tastings scheduled and no real pressing work to be done, so I'd decided to give myself the day off to sit in the sun and read a book. Gato sunned himself nearby, not close enough that I could ever pet him, but in the vicinity to keep an eye on things. Ever since I'd provided him with shelter that one stormy night, he'd been hanging around a little more frequently. He currently sprawled across the hot pavement with his skinny tail flicking back and forth.

It still wasn't quite hot enough to call the season summer, but as long as I was in the sunshine, I was comfortable in a tank top and shorts. The vines were growing greener and larger every day; soon enough the small, blooming flowers would become small, green grapes.

I opened my novel, but I didn't get very far. The sound of a car's engine pulled my attention away from the words on the page. A vintage truck, the body a deep green color, came to a stop a few yards away from where I sat. Unlike a more modern vehicle, this truck rode closer to the ground. I didn't know much about old cars, but the radial whitewall tires and the rounded curves of the truck's body looked straight out of a classic movie. The vehicle was in remarkable shape for its age. The exterior appeared as pristine as it probably had the day it rolled off the factory floor, maybe sixty or even seventy years earlier.

I peered over the top of my sunglasses as the driver's side door opened and Lucia unexpectedly climbed out. Her hair was braided like usual, but instead of her typical work uniform, she wore a sleeveless t-shirt, cutoff jean shorts, and flip-flops.

"Cool car," I greeted.

"Thanks," she returned. "I just got it out of storage for the season." She stood before me and rubbed at the back of her neck. The movement drew my attention to her bare arm and the thinly muscled bicep. "Mind if I use the hoses in the barn to wash my truck?" she asked. "I would do it in town, but it'll only get dirty again by the time I drive it back to the farm."

She looked uncharacteristically sheepish, almost embarrassed by the request.

"Oh, of course!" I enthused. "Go right ahead."

She nodded curtly, still looking uncommonly flustered. I imagined it was humbling or at least annoying that she'd asked me for permission.

Lucia disappeared inside of the barn and I returned my focus to my novel. I had just begun to get lost to the book's setting and introduction of central characters when more noises pulled my attention away from the printed pages. Lucia exited the barn with a black rubber hose hoisted over one shoulder. She carried a five-gallon bucket in her other hand. I paused my reading and watched her fill the bucket from the hose. Foamy soap suds peeked over the bucket's top rim.

She turned the hose's nozzle onto her truck and sprayed down the deep green truck. It hadn't looked dirty to begin with, but I suspected she was just as much of a perfectionist about her vehicle's appearance as she was about making wine.

When the truck was glistening from the first rinse, she turned off the hose and set it to the side. Bending over, she dunked an oversized sponge into the soapy bucket. The sponge connected with the hood of her trunk with a wet, slapping sound. The suds coated her arm, up to her elbow.

Lucia focused on cleaning the truck's exterior with her typical intensity. I watched the soapy sponge reach every inch of the truck's body. Her t-shirt darkened in spots from stray water or soap. It wasn't exactly a wet t-shirt contest, but I couldn't help noticing how the t-shirt material clung to her torso like a second skin. She normally wore button-up shirts that weren't necessarily ill-fitting, but this was the slimmest I'd seen of her silhouette.

It felt strange to relax and read while Lucia worked right in front of me. I pushed my sunglasses up to my forehead. "Do you need any help?"

I didn't expect her to accept my offer, but it felt like the right thing to do.

Lucia wiped at her forehead with the back of her hand. The hair near her temples had curled from the day's relative humidity. Flimsy soap suds clung to the wispy strands. "If you want."

It wasn't exactly a yes, but it wasn't an outright refusal either.

I didn't particularly *want* to wash her truck, but I literally jumped at the neutral response, eager for another opportunity to chip away at Lucia's rigid exterior.

I hopped out of my lawn chair. "What can I do?"

"How about the rims?" she suggested.

She reached into the soapy bucket and produced a small scrubbing brush. It looked exactly like the brush she'd given me only a few days prior to eliminate the 'wine diamonds' from the fermentation tanks.

I shook my head in disbelief. "You're kidding, right?"

Lucia's mouth curved up to form a sheepish grin. "It gets the job done."

I snatched the scrub brush out of her outstretched hand and resisted the childish urge to stick out my tongue at her.

Lucia returned to cleaning the headlights and the truck's front grill. I crouched down to wheel level and began to polish the solid silver rims. Like the rest of the vehicle, they didn't look dirty, but I was willing to put in a little unnecessary work to stay on Lucia's good side.

"Thanks for the help," Lucia said after a while.

"You're welcome," I cheerfully returned.

Lucia paused her scrubbing, and I lifted my eyes when I heard her tired breath. She tugged at the lower hem of her t-shirt and lifted the bottom material up her torso to wipe at her damp forehead. I could see her dark blue sports bra and the modest cleavage of well-proportioned breasts. Above the loose waistline of her jean shorts, her stomach was flat with just the hint of a feminine abdomen. I quickly averted my eyes when she returned the t-shirt to its proper place. I hadn't intended on staring for so long and hoped she hadn't caught me gawking.

My focus temporarily returned to scrubbing the already gleaming silver rims, but it didn't take long for me to glance again in her direction. Her legs had gotten wet from the sudsy water as she cleaned. Rivulets dribbled down her bare, bronzed skin.

"Let me know if I get you wet."

I looked up sharply at her words. It took me a long, panicked moment to realize she meant the water from her sponge and not … something else.

"Oh, uh, sure. Y-you're fine," I stumbled.

Lucia returned her attention to cleaning the front of the truck, but I swore I could see a ghost of a smile painted on her lips.

I stood and stretched out the stiffness in my knees and legs. "So I was thinking," I began, "we need to step up how many tastings and tours we're doing every week. I'm going to manage our social media accounts from now on to get new traffic to the website, which I'm also going to be updating."

I might not have known anything about making wine, but I did know a lot about marketing and public relations.

"We have social media accounts?" she questioned.

"See? That's the problem right there," I countered. "Why would someone buy our wine and not a bottle that's ten dollars cheaper?"

Lucia stood a little straighter. "Because our wine is better?"

"I agree with you. But how are they going to know that unless we get our product in their glass?" I posed. "We need partnerships with local restauranteurs. We need to bring more traffic to the vineyard. Word of mouth, social media buzz—that's what we should be focusing on."

"I'm pretty sure we should be focused on growing grapes," she snorted.

"I'm also looking into what it might involve to host functions on the vineyard," I said, ignoring her words. "We can probably increase our revenue significantly if we start hosting weddings."

Lucia scrubbed hard at what seemed to be a particularly stubborn spot. "We're a vineyard," she grunted, "not a party place."

An urgent shout interrupted our conversation before it could take a turn from civil to hostile: "Coming through!"

Rolando, Oscar, and Carlos sped past us. The three men seemed to be collectively laboring.

Lucia dropped her sponge into the soapy bucket. "What happened?"

"Oscar's wedding ring got snagged on the rototiller," Carlos called out as they passed us. "Ripped his finger right off."

Lucia and I hustled after the three men as they entered the tasting barn. Rolando laid Oscar's slumped body onto the picnic table as if it was a hospital gurney. Carlos had said Oscar lost a finger, but it seemed more serious than that. Oscar's normally docile features strained under the shock and pain.

I was too stunned by the sight of so much blood to do much of anything. Luckily, Lucia and Rolando weren't similarly paralyzed by the scene.

"Carlos," Lucia ordered as she tended to Oscar's blood-stained hand, "run to the house and get my Aunt Clara."

Carlos nodded before sprinting back outside.

I hovered a few feet from the picnic table. "Why isn't anyone calling 911?"

Lucia glanced briefly in my direction. "Oscar doesn't have health insurance. Ice," she barked out. "We need ice."

"Ice," I repeated, almost in a trance. "I can get ice."

I turned away from the graphic scene and hurried out the barn door. My lungs were nearly bursting by the time I reached the farmhouse. I threw open the front door and raced to the kitchen.

"Ice," I chanted, adrenaline pumping through my core. "Oscar needs ice."

I ripped open the freezer door and grabbed everything in view: ice cube trays, bags of frozen vegetables, and reusable ice packs intended for sore muscles. With my arms full of frozen items, I tripped out of the house and back in the direction of the barn.

Aunt Clara and Carlos had arrived to the scene by the time I returned. My arms and chest felt numb from either the icepacks or the intensity of the moment—I didn't know which.

Lucia held onto Oscar's good hand while Clara bent close to the injured one. Oscar was quiet, but he squirmed uncomfortably on top of the picnic table. His face looked sweaty and pale.

"Is she a doctor?" I wondered aloud.

Lucia noticed my return. "No. But she's good with a needle and thread."

"I've got ice," I announced.

Carlos approached me with a bounce in his step. He dug into the pockets of his work pants and fished out a long, slim object. My mouth went dry and my stomach lurched when I realized what it was—Oscar's ring finger.

"Keep it cool," he told me.

I gulped down giant mouthfuls of air to keep that morning's breakfast from making a repeat appearance.

I found a clean-enough looking bowl near the bar area and dumped the ice cubes from their plastic trays inside. I gagged again when I placed Oscar's finger on top of the ice cube mound. My mind went to someplace morbid and inappropriate as I stared down at the dismembered digit. The only thing missing were lemon slices and cocktail sauce. I was never going to eat seafood again, I lamented.

I brought the bowl back to the picnic table. "Here," I said, still choking back the bile.

Lucia barely looked in my direction; she took the bowl from me. "Thanks."

I took a few steps backwards so as to not crowd Aunt Clara and her work. Her features were serious, but unaffected as she threaded a wide sewing needle with dark, thick thread.

I covered my hand over my mouth and stifled a silent scream. "I'm sorry," I mumbled out a hasty apology. "I can't."

I sucked in great mouthfuls of cool, cleansing air once I stumbled outside. I put more distance between myself and the barn before settling on my knees in the grass. I closed my eyes when the screaming began. I could have kept running until I could no longer hear Oscar's audible struggle, but I remained in the lawn just beyond the barn. It was bad enough that I couldn't stomach being in the same room; it would have been a greater dishonor if I ran away entirely.

Oscar's cries eventually went silent, and I hoped for the best. The barn door opened and Lucia, still in her cutoff jeans and sleeveless shirt stepped outside.

"Is he going to be okay?" I asked.

"Aunt Clara is handling it," she said vaguely. I couldn't help but notice the dark crimson splotches on the t-shirt's grey material.

"That was ... that was..." I didn't have the right words.

"Intense," Lucia finished for me. She sat down in the grass next to me and kicked off her flip-flops.

I shifted from my knees to my backside on the thick grass. "Do *you* have health insurance?"

Lucia nodded, looking thoughtful. "My whole family does, but we're the exception to the rule."

"But why not Oscar, and I'm assuming Carlos?" I wondered. "Were the Mitchells really cheap or something?"

"It's more systemic than that, I'm afraid," Lucia said grimly. "Only about two-thirds of Napa Valley grape growers provide health insurance for their fulltime employees. And only about twelve percent offer their seasonal employees any assistance."

"I had no idea," I marveled. "I just assumed you all had health benefits."

"You're new," she remarked with a casual shrug, "how could you have known? Priority for the farmworker is survival, not health," she said. "Insurance is expensive, and when you're at the doctor, you're not at work. Most hourly workers can't afford those wage losses."

I ran my fingers through the long grass, feeling particularly helpless. "I wish I could do more," I opined. "But it's not like I'm independently wealthy. My entire nest egg is invested in this property."

Despite the sunny skies, a cloud seemed to settle over Lucia's features. "People are an investment too, *Jefa*."

CHAPTER TEN

A full, fat moon illuminated the landscape far from the farmhouse's central location. I'd only been to the edge of the property once—with Belinda the realtor, and it had been during daylight hours—but the presence of hot springs on the property had tempted me ever since. After the harrowing activities of the day, I'd uncorked a bottle of wine and had traversed the property in search of the fabled hot springs pools. I parked my car as close as the gravel roadway allowed and carefully picked my way across uneven earth.

I pulled off my sweatpants and my zip-up sweatshirt and carefully folded them on a nearby rock. I poured a generous amount of wine into a pint glass and set it on the ground, within reach of the hot springs pool I'd decided on. The chosen crater was particularly well suited; it almost resembled a hot tub with its steaming aquamarine water and slightly raised edges. I dipped my fingers into the water to test its temperature. Finding it hot, but not scalding, I climbed over the slightly elevated ridge and eased into the mineral spring.

I scanned my immediate surroundings. The landscape was relatively open with a few rock outcroppings and some large, gnarled oak trees farther off in the distance. The vineyard's property was relatively isolated, but the hot springs were located even farther from civilization. With a final look around me, I reached for the knot that secured my bikini top at the nape of my neck. I worked the material loose and unfastened the hook at the center of my back. I was no exhibitionist or nudist, but I felt safe to strip away all of my layers— literal and figurative—to enjoy my late evening soak. I lifted my hips and backside just enough to wiggle out of my bikini bottoms. I laid the whole beach ensemble over the edge of the elevated ridge, out of the way but still within reach.

I carefully lowered myself into the natural mineral water, mindful of temperature and not really knowing the small pool's depth. It took my body only a moment to adjust to the heat. It was a natural-occurring hot spring, not manufactured; my feet passed along gritty clay and small, smooth pebbles on the pool's floor. I found a relatively rounded corner to lean against. I sank a little deeper into the water to let the restorative water cover my shoulders like a warm blanket. The water didn't bubble like a hot tub with jets, but wispy strands of steam twisted up and into the night sky.

I stretched to collect my wine-filled pint glass. I took a sip and swirled the liquid around in my mouth before swallowing. I'd purchased a bottle of our 2018 cabernet just for the evening. It was a good red wine: spicy with a hint of blackberry. I set the glass back on the ground to let the cabernet breathe like Natalie had once instructed.

I shut my eyes and released a long breath. With each deep breath and exhale, I let the stress of the unknown and the anxiety that came with that disequilibrium begin to fade. I dipped my hands beneath the water's surface and lazily stroked my fingers across my naked breasts. The tip of my middle finger traveled in a slow, horizontal line to stimulate my right nipple. I hadn't been able to get any kind of release since Alex's death. My body was ready for orgasms, but my brain apparently wouldn't allow it to happen. I could become aroused, aching really, but some kind of barrier was preventing me from truly letting go.

I passed the fingers of my right hand back and forth in an unhurried motion. I had no place to be; I could take my time. I could tease myself, bring myself to the edge, back off, and then start again. When I moved my hands lower to stroke my abdomen, anticipating what would follow, an involuntary sharp breath escaped my slightly parted lips.

An unamused feminine voice cut through the darkness and interrupted both my thoughts and my activities: "Wow. You're really taking everything over."

My eyes popped open and my hands stilled beneath the water at the sound. Lucia stood in her work denim, a few yards from my location, with a bath towel flung over her shoulder. I had no idea from where she'd come, how long she'd been standing there, or how much she'd seen.

I struggled to sit upright, but not so much that my breasts might appear above the water's surface. I didn't need to justify my presence—the hot springs were well within the boundaries of my property—but I continued to feel like a trespasser on my own land.

"Oh, I, uh … the realtor, Belinda, she said—."

Lucia cut me off: "Do you mind?"

I had no idea what she was asking, but I hastily averted my eyes when I noticed her hands go to the buttons of her denim shirt and she began to undress. A wave of heat rushed over me that I couldn't blame on the hot water.

I only looked up when I heard the sound of splashing, displaced water. I caught a flash of naked flesh before I furiously cast my eyes back to the water's surface. Lucia had to have noticed my clothes scattered on adjacent rocks; why was she climbing into the water with me, and why was she also naked? I wanted to voice a protest, but I also didn't want to make a big deal about us sharing the space.

I continued to train my eyes on the water's shimmery surface. I only braved a glance in Lucia's direction when I heard her loud, satisfied sigh.

"God, what a day."

Her face was tilted towards the sky and her eyes were closed, so I didn't take her statement as an invitation to talk. I reflexively reached for my wine glass but discovered I couldn't retrieve it without exposing my body. Having moved from my original spot to make room for Lucia, my wine was just beyond my outstretched fingers. I would have to stand or at least lean over the edge of the rocky ridge to retrieve my drink.

I had nearly made peace with sobriety when I heard Lucia's disgruntled noise. She shifted in the space beside me. Her left arm draped across her naked breasts and she stood from the hot pool. I hastily looked away; I cast my gaze to the water directly in front of me, despite a curious, more carnal urge to openly inspect her naked figure.

"Here."

The single word pulled my attention away from the water's surface. Lucia had returned to her seated position, the shape of her body once again obscured beneath the steaming water. She held my pint glass in front of me.

"Thanks."

I took the proffered glass, mindful not to splash any water into the cup and careful not to inadvertently touch her hand. I didn't want to ruin the wine with mineral water, but I didn't know why I so purposefully avoided grazing her fingers. I clutched the glass in both hands to make sure it didn't slip from my grip. I wasn't normally so uncoordinated, but I seemed to become all thumbs around her.

"You shouldn't drink wine from that kind of glass," she said. Even though she had spoken to me, she didn't look in my direction. Her eyes remained closed and her face was neutral.

"No?" I naively asked.

"You're dumbing down the wine. Wine glasses are shaped like that on purpose."

"Oh. Sorry."

I knew my chosen words were an odd choice, but I didn't know how else to respond. My impulse was to fill the silence with banal conversation, maybe quiz her about stemware, but Lucia's body language continued to relay to me that she wasn't interested.

While I slowly sipped wine from my inferior glassware, Lucia took a quick swig of water from a clear plastic bottle. She pressed the presumably chilled bottle against her forehead. The humidity had caused her normally stick-straight hair to slightly curl around the perimeter of her face. Her hair was still wrangled into a thick braid down the center of her back. It made me wonder if she ever wore her hair in a different style. She'd thrown the thick braid over one of her shoulders to avoid the ends from getting wet.

Her rounded shoulders poked above the water's surface. I could see a small mark on the shoulder closest to me. The area was a shade darker than the surrounding skin. It looked more like a birthmark instead of a scar. Beneath the mineral water, the fingers on my right hand twitched. I wondered what the mark felt like. I found myself wanting to run the pad of my thumb across her shoulder. Would the skin be smooth? Would the birthmark feel raised?

Lucia's dark eyes swept in my direction. "Are you okay?"

I swallowed, worried she'd caught my prolonged stare. "Uh huh."

She leaned in my direction as if to get a better look. "No, for real. You're looking really flushed."

The heat had seemed to elevate in the last few minutes, but I contributed the change in temperature to our mutual nakedness and my neglected libido.

"I'm fine." I ran a self-conscious hand across my forehead. My skin *did* feel warmer than usual. "The water's just hot."

"How much have you had to drink?"

I looked down to my pint glass as if the cup offered the answers. "Not a lot."

"Hot water and alcohol don't mix," she warned. "It opens up your blood vessels and messes with your body's natural ability to regulate temperature."

"I'm fine," I continued to resist. I flicked my hand to dislodge water droplets from my fingers.

"No, you're not. Come on," she said grimly. "We need to get you out of the water and cool down your core body temperature."

I opened and closed my mouth. "But I'm … I'm naked."

"I really don't care."

Lucia stood from the hot springs pool in a fluid, but urgent motion. I tried to not openly gawk at her nakedness, but she practically towered over me. I watched a long, single water droplet spill over her collarbone, travel between the valley of her breasts, pick up momentum down the flat plane of her stomach, and collect in the shallow indentation of her bellybutton.

I didn't have long to admire her lean, but feminine form. Despite my earlier complaints, Lucia bent and hooked her arms beneath my armpits. I was too startled by her modest breasts being thrust in my face to resist her tugging me to my feet. With her assistance, I managed to stand up from the steaming water.

The arms hooked beneath my armpits lowered once I made it to my feet. Without Lucia to ground me, my knees buckled and the world began to spin. I shut my eyes and reached for something— anything—to keep myself steady, but I only found air.

A solid arm went around my waist, and I heard Lucia's voice close to my ear: "I've got you."

My legs felt like rubber as Lucia helped me climb out of the hot springs pool. My lower limbs wobbled unsteadily like a baby giraffe just learning to walk. Only Lucia's arm around my waist kept me from collapsing. Whatever was happening to my body and brain had snuck up on me; I had been fine one moment and then completely useless the next. The only good thing about the dizzy, nauseous, sweaty feeling was it distracted me from embarrassment.

Lucia grabbed the bath towel intended for herself and laid it across a relatively flat stretch of land. The task was doubly hard as she only had one free hand. I hung my head while she prepared the area; I was so unprepared, I hadn't even thought to bring a towel with me.

I stumbled onto my hands and knees on top of the bath towel. Sharp-edged rocks pressed into my palms and kneecaps through the thin material, but I was too focused on not regurgitating my dinner to vocalize a complaint.

"Lay on your back," Lucia instructed.

All of my previous resistance crumbled away; she could have convinced me to eat dirt. With her continued assistance, I managed to roll onto my back. I filled my lungs with cool, night air as some of the previous nausea faded.

Lucia kneeled beside me. "Drink some water."

She handed me her half-filled plastic bottle, and I drank in large, greedy gulps. The water wasn't freezing, but it was cold enough to be exactly what my body needed.

"Not too much," she corrected.

I immediately stopped drinking as if we were playing a game of Red Light-Green Light.

Lucia re-capped the plastic bottle and pressed it to my forehead. My hands replaced hers, and I held the chilled bottle to my skin.

"The nape of your neck, too," she told me.

The bottle felt good against my burning forehead, but I did as she instructed and relocated the makeshift cold compress to the place where my neck met the bottom of my skull. Despite our mutual nakedness, there was nothing erotic or sexy about the scenario. It was like being naked in front of a doctor. Lucia wasn't trying to seduce me; she was making sure I didn't pass out from heat stroke.

Lucia's dark eyes regarded me with clear concern. "Better?"

"Mmhm," I confirmed.

Lucia, still kneeling in the space beside me, settled back on her calves. I heard her sigh. It wasn't an impatient noise; it sounded happy or content. "The stars are really impressive on this side of the property," she thought aloud. "I bet you can't even see the stars in San Francisco."

I took that moment to stare up into the sky. Dusk had turned to night. The evening sky was bright with twinkling stars and the illuminated swirls of distant galaxies. She was right; the stars were never very visible in the city with the exception of a few of the closer, larger looking ones. Logically, I knew it was the same sky, but the view couldn't have been more different.

"Do you miss it?" she asked.

I would have been content to cool down and recover in silence, but this was the most Lucia had ever spoken to me. Well—minus the moments when I was epically screwing up in the winery.

"I miss my friends," I verbalized. "But it's probably for the best that I left. Even if I'd stayed in San Francisco, I think I'd still be sad and lonely."

The honesty and vulnerability of my statement surprised me. But I was naked, and I'd nearly passed out only moments before. There was really nothing left to hide.

Once the world stopped spinning and my surroundings started to come back into focus, my self-consciousness about my nakedness returned. I worried about sitting up in case the nausea returned, but I desperately needed my clothes.

"Do you think … could you possibly get me my clothes?" came my meek question.

Lucia didn't confirm or deny my request, but she stood up and walked in the direction of the hot springs pool. I was fairly confident she wasn't going to leave me to fend for myself, or worse yet, run away with my clothes, but I watched her just in case. In her absence, I gingerly sat up. I sucked in more night air and willed my body not to fail me again.

She returned to my side a few moments later with my flip-flops and the pile of my carefully folded clothes. She had redressed in grey joggers and her denim shirt, but she hadn't bothered with the buttons in the front. The front panels of her shirt covered her bra-less breasts.

She set the clothes beside me. "Do you need help?"

I didn't see my bikini amongst the pile; it was probably still flung over the side of the hot springs pool. I reached for my zip-up sweatshirt. "No. I-I've got it."

I managed to push my still damp arms through the arm holes of the cotton top. My fingers shook, but I was able to latch the two sides of the zipper together and pull the metal zipper tab up to my chin. I looked next to my sweatpants. What would be least embarrassing? Could I shimmy into them while I sat? Would I look like a fish out of water, flopping around on the ground? The alternative was equally dubious. Was I even capable of standing up on my own?

My hesitation drew an impatient huff from Lucia.

"God, you're stubborn."

I looked to her just in time to see her snatch my sweatpants from the ground. I reached helplessly for my final article of clothing. "I can do it," I weakly protested.

She rolled up the legs of the sweatpants as if they were pantyhose. "Right leg," she ordered.

I sheepishly complied and lifted my right foot in the air. My lower body was still wet from the hot springs, so the material got stuck several times as she pulled the pant leg up my right leg. The left leg followed. It made me feel like a child being shoved into snowpants.

"Lift your ass," she grunted next.

This was the part I had been dreading. I planted my feet in the ground and lifted my backside off the ground. I shut my eyes to keep the embarrassment to a minimum. I might have died where I sat if I'd had to watch Lucia pull the waistband over my exposed sex.

I settled back down on the towel when I felt the elastic band settle around my midsection. "Thank you," I mumbled my appreciation.

Lucia stood and began to button up the front of her shirt. She scanned the surrounding landscape. "Where are your car keys?"

"I'm really fine," I continued to insist. I still wasn't confident I could stand on my own, but I didn't want to admit that to her.

She flashed me an impatient look.

"I left them in my car," I sighed in defeat.

Lucia crouched beside me. "Put your arm around my shoulder," she instructed. "It's time to stand up."

I did as she told me. Lucia began to stand, and my body raised with hers. Her core strength was a surprise. She hardly looked capable of deadlifting my weight, but she hefted me to my feet with seemingly little effort.

"Wine barrels weigh a lot more than you," she pronounced as if reading my mind.

Her arm tightened around my waist, and we began a slow shuffle in the direction of my parked car.

"Small steps," she told me. "Don't get cocky."

I focused on my feet and each careful step. My legs felt significantly more stable than before, but my shoes made the trip precarious. The flip-flops had been a terrible choice; I routinely stumbled in the shoes even on a good day.

"Is this a good pace for you?" she asked.

"Uh huh," I confirmed.

We fell into a silent and easy cadence, like the participants of a three-legged race. When I was no longer concerned about tripping out of my flip-flops, my attention drifted to the solid arm around my midsection. With my arm flung over her shoulders and her arm circling my waist, it was the closest anyone had been since Alex's death. I had held onto Lucia's elbow when she'd guided me back from her dad's house after the bud break party, but we hadn't been draped over each other.

The air temperature had noticeably dropped once I was no longer in danger of heat stroke, but Lucia's body was warm where it pressed against me. Over the scent of earth and the lingering minerals from the hot springs, I could smell the flowery detergent buried in the fabric of her denim shirt and the faint salty scent of sweat. The combination was strangely familiar and comforting.

When we finally reached my abandoned car, Lucia opened the passenger side door and helped me ease into the front seat. She shut the door behind me and rounded the front of the car to get behind the steering wheel. She found my keys in the center cupholder and started up the car. The digital clock on the dashboard illuminated with the start and indicated the late hour. I hadn't realized so much time had passed since arriving at the mineral pools. I felt even more guilty for having monopolized Lucia's night.

I licked at dry lips. "I'm sorry," I croaked out.

I heard her turn toward me, but I refused to look in her direction. "For what?"

"I'm such a nuisance," I sighed. "You wanted to relax tonight, not babysit me."

"It was an honest mistake," she dismissed as we began to drive. "You didn't know that would happen."

"There's a lot I don't know," I openly bemoaned. I thought about the accident with the wine sediment.

"You shouldn't be so hard on yourself, June. Leave that to me."

I twisted my head to finally regard her. "Did you just try to make a joke?"

She shrugged beneath her denim shirt.

We drove the rest of the way in silence from the hot springs back to the farmhouse. Lucia parked out front and turned off the car. She nodded towards the front porch. "Do you need help getting inside?"

"No," I refused. "I'm feeling much better. I've got it from here."

Lucia nodded, finally satisfied that I was no longer being stubborn.

I climbed out of the passenger side door while she removed herself from behind the steering wheel. We met in front of the car's headlights where she returned my keys.

Lucia shoved her hands into the deep pockets of her sweatpants. "My aunt thinks you're lonely … living in this big house all by yourself."

"You guys talk about me?" I frowned and tried not to feel judged. First the reveal about Alex's death, and now this?

"My aunt is a busybody," she explained away. "She also suggested that I should move in here to keep you company."

"She did?" My stomach twisted at the suggestion, but I didn't know why. "Wh-what did you tell her?"

"That if she was so worried," she snorted, "*she* should come live with you."

I tried to imagine what cohabitation with Lucia might look like. I'd never lived with someone who wasn't my partner. Actually, with the exception of my immediate family, I'd never lived with anyone who hadn't been Alex. As much as I might have appreciated the company, I couldn't picture the brusque assistant winemaker making popcorn with me and watching rom-coms on the couch. I couldn't imagine sharing cleaning duties or making dinner together. I decided she would probably keep to herself, locked away in her bedroom. I knew from experience that it could feel even more lonely when you knew that someone was just in the next room, but was actively ignoring you.

"I couldn't handle living with my parents again," I thought out loud.

"I don't see why not," Lucia countered. "Free rent. Free food. What's not to love?"

I wrinkled my nose. "You really don't want a place of your own?"

"What for?" she said with a shrug. "I'm not here half of the time anyways," she reminded me. "I get to squirrel away my money and save for what I really want."

"Which is?" I asked.

"My own vineyard, obviously. I don't have a degree in business or viticulture," she continued, "but I've paid my dues. I want to go from being the person who picks the grapes to the person who owns them."

It was a noble speech. I'd never seen her express herself with such passion.

"Why not start your own label?" I asked.

She shook her head. "This is Napa, not Silicon Valley. Even if I could convince a grower to sell me their excess fruit, that's no way to make a living. There's no start-up companies in wine."

I nodded although I still didn't really understand.

I curled my fingers around the keys in my hand. "Thank you for your help tonight."

"It's no big deal," she dismissed. "I'm glad you're feeling better."

It was the second occasion that she'd walked me back to the farmhouse. Each time had felt awkward like the conclusion of a terrible first date. I was certain when my brain allowed me to revisit the night's events that I'd be dead from embarrassment.

"Drink more water before you go to bed, okay?" she urged.

"I will," I promised.

"Get some sleep, June," she told me as she began to walk away. "I'm still not planning on taking it easy on you in the morning."

CHAPTER ELEVEN

Outside of my bedroom window, the sun had yet to rise. Inside, my morning alarm wouldn't go off for another hour. The bedframe creaked as I tried to get comfortable on the lumpy mattress. I flexed my hips and stretched out my lower back. After returning from my ill-fated visit to the property's hot springs, I'd consumed about a gallon of water before going to bed. An urgent bladder hadn't woken me up early, however. Instead, my unsatisfied libido called for attention.

Lucia had interrupted my solo activities, and then there had been the humiliation of nearly passing out from alcohol and too much heat. But even that horrific ordeal hadn't silenced the reality that my body still desired some kind of release.

I slid my right hand beneath the elastic waistband of my cotton joggers. The tip of my middle finger reflexively sought out my slightly protruding clit. My fingers slid through closely cropped curls. I ghosted my fingertips across my skin, but with no real urgency. I imagined sleepy nerve endings coming alive and my body's blood rushing to my nether regions as everything below my bellybutton grew increasingly warm.

I closed my eyes and tried to clear my brain of all thoughts and outside distractions. I didn't want to think about anything or anyone—just the growing heat between my legs. I lightly traced the contours of my outer lips; I imagined my skin swelling beneath my fingertips and becoming more flushed. I pressed my backside more deeply into the mattress as the tingling increased and my breath became more labored.

Outside, something emitted a long, single, shrill chirp. My fingers stilled. Was it a bird? Its call wasn't familiar, not that I knew much about ornithology. It sounded like an obnoxious alarm instead of a cheerful, morning song. The sun wasn't awake yet, so why was this bird?

My top row of teeth sank into my lower lip as I struggled to refocus. I pinched a braless nipple through my t-shirt, coaxing it to full attention.

A second bird noise pulled my attention to my closed bedroom window. It was a chirp, not a more robust honk, so I imagined a small bird instead of a goose or a duck. The irregular rhythm—the space between each isolated chirp—reminded me of a smoke alarm with a low battery. Nothing had annoyed Alex more than having to stalk around our condo in search of the smoke alarm responsible for the single, irregular tone. We could be in the middle of a meal or a favorite movie or even sex—all would be abandoned so she could identify the culprit.

I tried to bring my attention back to the accumulating dampness beneath my pajama bottoms, but I found myself waiting for the bird's next chirp instead. I sighed and made a disgruntled noise. This wasn't going to happen. My brain and my body refused to sync up. My body wanted an orgasm, but my brain continued to hold out.

I sat up and threw off the top blankets. I hopped out of bed and stomped out of the room. I could no longer hear the chirping bird, but I still made my way to the front door and stormed outside. I tumbled, barefoot, down the front porch steps and onto the lawn. The grass was damp and cool against my bare ankles from morning dew. I rounded the house in search of my bedroom window and the source of the distracting noise.

A large boulder poked out of the earth a few feet from the house. The sun had yet to rise, and I hadn't bothered to bring a flashlight or my cellphone, but the sky had lightened just enough that I could make out the small, silhouette of something perched on top of the rock. I kept my distance in case I was wrong and it wasn't a bird. It obviously wasn't a mountain lion, but it could have been any kind of small vermin. I'd been annoyed to be denied an orgasm, but I certainly didn't want to start my day being attacked by a rat or a gopher.

"Go away!" I hissed. I waved my arms above my head, hoping to startle the animal and make it fly or scamper away. "Go on—git!"

"June?" I heard a voice. "Is that you?"

I hastily turned on my heels at the sound of my name. Lucia stood nearby on the gravel roadway, dressed in her typical work uniform of chambray shirt and dark blue jeans.

"What are you doing?" she questioned. She spoke slowly and carefully as if trying to coax a potential jumper off of a ledge.

I gestured wildly in the direction of the boulder, which now appeared to only be a rock. Whatever had been perched on top of the large stone was no longer there. "I was trying to sleep," I lied. "But a bird was making the most obnoxious noise outside of my window."

"It was probably a horned lark," she described.

"So?" Impatience crept into my tone.

"They're the namesake of the property," she said. "Lark Estates?"

"I get it. But why does it have to be so loud?" I huffed.

Lucia cocked her head to the side. "Are you okay?"

"I'm great," I snapped. I couldn't very well tell her that I was sexually frustrated, and that a harmless bird was the reason I'd been denied an orgasm.

Lucia looked unconvinced, but also mildly amused. *Awesome*, I privately lamented. Something else to tease me about. The out-of-her-element vineyard owner who yelled at birds in the pre-dawn hours.

"Why are *you* up?" I questioned.

Lucia nodded in the direction of the barn. "Going to work."

I didn't know the exact time, but it was earlier than our typical six o'clock start. I wanted to point that out, but a brisk breeze swirled around me, disturbing old sticks and dead leaves. I hugged my arms around my torso, acutely aware that my t-shirt was thin and that I wore no bra.

"I'll see you later," I grunted.

Lucia shrugged, unbothered by my abrupt dismissal. "Okay, *Jefa*. Whatever you say."

When I returned inside, I didn't attempt to resume my solo activities; that moment had passed. I did somehow manage to fall back asleep, however. I slept so hard, in fact, I must have turned off my alarm and gone back to sleep again. I woke up a few hours later to a pounding sound. At first I thought the pounding was in my head, the product of dehydration, until I realized the noise was coming from outside. I climbed out of bed and followed the noise until it took me to the front of the farmhouse. I pulled on a jacket that was hanging in the front foyer and stepped outside.

"Morning," I grunted in greeting. I pulled the jacket tighter around my pajamas even though the woman working on my front porch had seen me in far less the previous evening. There was a slight chill in the air, but the day had potential once the mid-day sunshine burned away the valley's fog.

Lucia was on her hands and knees at the bottom of my porch. She held a hammer in one hand and a long nail in the other. "Morning," she returned. "How are you feeling?"

"Good," I decided. "Embarrassed."

I blinked a few times as my brain played catch up. Lucia was fixing the bottom step of my broken porch. She'd removed the formerly rotten board with a brand new wooden plank.

"Oscar is home today, still healing up," she said. She pounded a final nail into the bottom step with two expert swings of her hammer. "I told him to take it easy for a few more days, if that's okay with you?"

I was too stunned by her considerate gesture to respond. I mustered enough awareness to nod.

Lucia stood and brushed at the knees of her jeans. They'd collected dirt and Calistoga moon dust. "I'll be back later to paint the steps," she informed me. "Any special color requests?"

"Oh, uh, no. Whatever you think is good."

"Careful," she said, nearly smiling. "You might wake up tomorrow to a Pepto-Bismol colored porch."

I barked out a laugh when my words continued to fail me.

Lucia glanced in the direction of the barn and stood with her hands on her hips. She continued to speak to me, but I quickly lost focus on whatever she was talking about—something about flowering buds and soil management. I tried not to overtly stare, but she'd worked up a light sweat during her morning activities. Beads of perspiration collected in the hollow of her throat. My gaze traveled lower to the top of her denim shirt. She typically wore the work shirt with the first two buttons unfastened. That morning, however, a third button was undone. It didn't feel flirtatious, but rather the result of a button having worked its way loose while she labored.

I could see more of the top of her breasts than she'd probably intended, but I didn't want to embarrass her by pointing it out. I'd seen her entirely naked the night before, but something about this unintentional view was far more erotic. Poking above the beige-colored fabric of a practical bra, the skin looked soft, spherical, and a few shades paler than her hands and arms despite her daily ritual of high SPF sunscreen. I forced myself to look away when my eyes lingered just a little too long.

"I'm sorry I overslept," I blurted out. I hadn't looked at a clock recently, but the sun's position in the sky indicated I was late for work.

"It's okay," she allowed. "You had a pretty long day yesterday."

"Yeah," I roughly agreed. My eyes drifted back to her open shirt.

A cheerful whistle, almost bird-like, had me casting my eyes away from Lucia's exposed breasts and down to the newly fixed porch steps.

"Morning, *Jefa!*" Carlos cheerfully greeted. He walked along the gravel road with a shovel slung over his shoulder.

"Morning, Carlos," I mumbled in return.

"Hey, Lucia. Your tit's hanging out," Carlos informed my assistant winemaker. His words weren't teasing or licentious—just matter of fact.

Lucia cursed under her breath and hastily rebuttoned the front of her shirt, this time all the way to the very top. I felt the heat of her accusatory glare as if it had been my fault her buttons had given up on the job. I knew I should have said something though—like it was girl code to tell someone when their skirt was tucked into their nylons or like having an extra tampon in your purse for someone in need.

I swallowed hard and attempted a shaky smile. "I guess I'm getting a Pepto-Bismol porch?"

After my late start that morning, I spent the remainder of the work day with Natalie in the tasting barn. In addition to our usual tastings and tours, a small party had reserved a corner of the barn for a private function. I hadn't looked closely at the reservation details, but the multicolored balloons strung on tables and chairs suggested it might be a birthday party. While I had slept in, Natalie had been busy setting up the separate area for our guests. Long tables with organic-looking tablecloths and season-appropriate centerpieces enhanced what was typically a barren area in the barn. It was a marvel what Natalie was able to do with a tight budget. The transformation was even more miraculous armed with the knowledge that the same area had basically been an operating room for Oscar's ring finger the previous day.

I assisted Natalie at the bar, filling up guests' empty wine glasses and reciting my rehearsed script about that day's available wines. In between serving drinks and credit card transactions, my attention wandered to the small group of mixed couples at the birthday celebration. I tried not to roll my eyes at the twenty-somethings with their cellphones and floppy wide-brimmed hats and the clinking glassware and multiple social media posts that would no doubt follow. I should have been excited about the party and the potential of Lark Estates being tagged in their posts. Maybe Lucia's cynicism was starting to rub off on me.

I heard a sharp gasp and expected the worst—broken glasses or spilled wine at least. But instead of another disaster, I spied a young man on one knee and a surprised woman standing before him. A proffered diamond ring glimmered in the early afternoon sunlight. The woman's manicured hands covered her mouth, but I could see the enthusiastic bob of her head as she accepted his proposal.

"How original," I heard Natalie's snort.

I watched the young man leap to his feet and envelope his bride-to-be in a massive hug. In his excitement, he lifted her off of the ground before returning her to earth.

"I think it's kind of sweet," I countered.

"Let's talk again after your hundredth secret proposal," Natalie mused.

I turned away from the celebrating couple and their friends. "I miss it," I said wistfully. "Being part of a couple. Being in love."

"Call me a cynic, but I like not fighting over the TV remote," Natalie remarked. "I watch what I want, when I want."

"But doesn't it ever get lonely?" I posed. "Don't you want someone to cuddle with when you're watching TV?"

"That's why God made cats and quilts," she said pragmatically.

I gave the young couple one last look. "I don't know, Nat. Nothing against pets, but there's some things you can't do with a cat."

I heard Natalie's chuckle. "And that's why God made vibrators."

+ + +

"Morning!"

I walked into the tasting barn the following morning with a bounce in my step and a cheerful lilt to my voice. I'd been pleasantly surprised to discover a fresh coat of paint—white, not violently bright pink—on my front porch steps when I'd left the house for work. It was a small gesture, but an important one. Despite the awkwardness of the past few days, maybe Lucia and I were finally getting along.

Rolando was absent, but Carlos, Oscar, and Lucia sat at the picnic table with their ritual cups of coffee. I was surprised to see Oscar back so soon, but I was mindful of what Lucia had told me about hourly-wage workers. The more time spent at home, the less his take-home pay would be.

I approached the employee breakfast table and rubbed my hands together. "What's on the agenda this morning?"

Lucia stood, not giving me the opportunity to join them at the table. "It's your lucky day; you get the day off."

I stared after them as Carlos and Oscar also stood from the table and finished the last of their respective coffees. "There's nothing to do today?" I questioned.

"We have to run into town," Oscar explained in his soft timbre.

"I could come," I readily offered. "Do you need an extra set of hands?"

"*No.*" Lucia's refusal was immediate, almost desperate, I thought. "There's no more room in the truck."

Carlos offered me the friendliest smile of the three. "Take a load off, *Jefa.*" He clapped the top of my shoulder as he walked by. "We've got this."

I watched out the windows of the tasting barn as Lucia, Oscar, and Carlos piled into an older pickup truck parked out front. The vehicle wasn't Lucia's antique truck, so I imagined it belonged to either Carlos or Oscar.

"Where are those three off to?" Natalie appeared at my side and looked out the window with me. I hadn't realized she would be at the barn so early; we must have had several tastings scheduled for the day or an upcoming private event to plan.

I stared after the tan and brown truck's retreating taillights and struggled not to feel left out. "Oscar said they had to go into town."

"Looks like trouble to me," Natalie observed.

I turned to her, not really understanding. She handed me a stiff, slim piece of paper.

"What's this?" I questioned. The flier was in Spanish, and unfamiliar words like *gremio* and *huelga* and *trabajo* joined others like *el vinedo* and *vino*. The outline of a black hawk or tribal looking bird was centered on the sheet of paper.

"I found it on top of a garbage bag when I was emptying the trash," she said. "Looks like some kind of rally or mass meeting is happening in town today."

"A meeting?" I continued to stare at the piece of paper as if it might magically translate itself. "About what?"

"You might want to see for yourself."

I sat in my car in the parking lot of an elementary school just outside of downtown Calistoga. I'd entered the address listed from the flier into my car's GPS and had followed its instructions, but I didn't understand the significance of the location or why Lucia and the others would have come there.

I watched a steady stream of people walking from the parking lot to a detached building with the word 'cafeteria' posted on its exterior. I was curious about the trip and their need for subterfuge. Natalie had convinced me it would be in my best interest to see what was going on, but I couldn't help feeling like a busybody, and like this wasn't any of my business.

Despite lingering doubts about being nosy or intrusive, I got out of my car and followed a few others in the direction of the school cafeteria. I stepped through the open double doors with an anxious knot in my stomach. I stayed in the doorway and let my eyes adjust to the lack of natural light inside. I still didn't know what was going on; I didn't know what I'd walked into.

The air was sticky and smelled like maple syrup and Elmer's glue. If this was really an active school cafeteria, the lunch tables had been removed and metal folding chairs had been set up in long, neat rows, all facing a slightly elevated platform. I spotted a few familiar figures on the makeshift stage—over half of my full-time staff—Carlos, Oscar, and Lucia. The three were huddled together, conferring with each other before the start of whatever this was.

The room was busy with people, but no one acknowledged my arrival. The aging cafeteria had poor ventilation; most of those seated fanned at their faces with the same flyer Natalie had found. I stood at the back of the room with a few others and avoided making eye contact. It didn't matter though; no one beyond my own employees would have known who I was. And they were all busy at the front of the room, calling the seemingly clandestine meeting to order.

Carlos stuck two fingers into his mouth. A shrill whistle followed, compelling the others in the room to table their private conversations and find someplace to sit. There was no microphone or PA system at the podium where my assistant winemaker stood. I hovered unobtrusively in the back of the room, far enough away that I hoped Lucia wouldn't spot me, but close enough to hear her words to the assembled crowd.

"Thank you all for coming today. My name is Lucia Maria Santiago," she started, "and I have the privilege of being assistant winemaker at Lark Estates. I know many of you are unsalaried and took time off without pay to be here, so I won't waste your time. We all know why we're here and what's at stake. For too long in this country," she continued, her voice somber, but intense, "we've had to endure the glorification of White European wine history. The Anglo community dismisses the brutal history of colonization of indigenous land for wine growing and other wine business activities."

Lucia paused as if expecting some kind of reaction to her opening words. But those seated in their metal folding chairs remained impassive. Even from where I stood, I could see the uncertainty pass across her features.

"My grandparents crossed the border from Mexico in the early 1940s," she began again. "They, like many of your own ancestors, came to California through the Bracero program when America was desperate for laborers to help with farming shortages during World

War II. My father was born here. He started as a teenager, cleaning conveyor belts and grape destemming machines. He worked his way up to pruning vines in spring and picking berries in the fall. But the ultimate goal, to work for himself, to own his own vineyard, has consistently been out of reach."

Lucia continued to speak in a loud, clear voice. The growing intensity in her features and posture was visible even from the back of the room. The longer she spoke, the more agitated she became.

"No bank will take a chance on him. No vintner with land for sale will seriously consider his offers, despite him having over forty years of experience."

I leaned against the back wall as if it could better hide me. I tugged on my baseball cap and pulled it lower to obscure my face. No one in the room besides the three people on stage would know who I was, but I still felt the need to hide my identity. I was the enemy. I was the Bad Guy—an inexperienced vineyard owner in a room full of people who'd been refused the same chance.

"Ninety-five percent of farm workers in the valley are originally from Mexico," Lucia continued, "and yet few of us are represented in the tasting rooms." She paused and took her time to scan the assembled crowd. "It's time we change that."

I could feel the energy in the room start to shift. The audience, most of whom had begun as casual or curious observers, sat a little more erect in their metal folding chairs. I watched the room collectively lean forward, eager for Lucia's next words.

"I can't promise that change will come soon or without struggle," she noted. "We need to work together—everyone from the winemakers to the kids in the wine cellars—if we want to stand a chance against the conglomerates and the banks. That's the only way this thing will work; they can't replace us all."

The gymnasium erupted into cheers. Several people rose to their feet while others whistled or stamped their feet. I couldn't blame them. She'd had a slow start, but standing at the front of the room, Lucia was oddly motivational.

It took a while for the group to quiet enough that Lucia could speak and be heard again. She was patient, however, and seemed to drink in the collective reaction. She concluded her inspirational words with pragmatic next steps. To start locally in Calistoga before branching out to St. Helena, Yountville, or Napa. To take on the boutique wineries and tasting rooms first and then to organize workers at the larger wine producers. Avoiding scabs crossing the picket line would be the biggest challenge if the owners refused to recognize their efforts. They would need to canvas the places where migrant farmers traditionally found work during peak harvest times. They would aim small before turning into a mass movement.

A few more individuals whom I didn't recognize took the stage before the meeting came to a close, but none of them were able to garner the same enthusiasm as Lucia had. At the meeting's conclusion, I waited at the back of the cafeteria as most of the crowd filed out. I watched Lucia speak and shake hands with the final few people in the meeting. Oscar and Carlos had started to break down the room while she networked. Oscar had found a push broom and Carlos had begun folding up the metal chairs. I pulled the brim of my baseball cap lower and walked in their direction. I kept my distance at first and helped with the metal folding chairs at the edge of the room before daring to move closer.

Carlos and I were soon working in tandem, shoulder-to-shoulder. I handed him the folded up chairs while he stacked them in a tidy row. I kept expecting him to notice me, but he was too focused on the chairs to ever really look at my face.

"Thanks for the help," he said to me when the job was done.

"No problem."

The familiar sound of my voice had him freezing in place. He stared at me, a look of confusion and shock splayed across his features.

I couldn't help my sheepish smile. "Hey."

Carlos' eyes never left mine. I watched his mouth slowly open to begin to shape words. "Lucia!" he called out.

His volume made me flinch. I heard Lucia's voice, somewhere in the room. "What?"

Carlos didn't respond with words. He only pointed at me.

Lucia stormed across the cafeteria. "What are you doing here?" Her tone was heated and her dark eyes flashed with anger.

It was like I'd been playing a game of hide and seek, and I'd suddenly been discovered. I sputtered out a few syllables, but I couldn't find my words. "I … I …"

Lucia grabbed onto my elbow and spun me towards the exit. "You need to leave," she practically growled. "You don't belong here."

"Is this why you fixed my porch?" I had no idea, after everything I'd witnessed, why that thought popped into my brain.

"I fixed your porch because it was a damn eyesore," she shot back.

I didn't know what compelled me, but I stood my ground, digging in my heels, instead of letting her shove me out of the building. "Are you going to unionize the Valley?"

The fingers at my elbow loosened and then finally fell away. Lucia roughly rubbed her hands over her face.

"Fire me," she mumbled.

I blinked, not expecting her words. "What?"

"My dad knows nothing about this. And Carlos and Oscar are only here to support me. Don't take this out on them," she implored. "If you have to punish someone, punish me."

"Why would I punish you?"

"Union is a dirty word around here," she said simply. "I get it if you have to make an example of me."

"I'm not ..." I shook my head. "I'm not going to fire you."

"Why not?" she challenged.

"You made a lot of sense up there," I said, gesturing to the now-empty stage. "Honestly, I had no idea there was such disparity. You've ... you've opened my eyes about a lot of things."

Lucia carefully regarded me. She wet her lips and seemed to be considering her next words. She might have been contemplating if she could trust me as well. "Do you know how Napa got its name?"

"Was there a Mr. Napa?" I guessed.

Lucia shook her head. "No. It's Yukian for 'plenty.'"

"Don't judge me," I felt myself wincing from ignorance, "but what's Yukian?"

"It's okay," she allowed. "It's an extinct language. The Wappo tribe—they were here in the 1700s before the Spanish took over—they named the region. The Franciscan padres who established the Spanish missions were the region's first winemakers, but it was indigenous people who did the actual work. They were the ones planting and tending to the vines, harvesting the grapes and making the wine. And yet they weren't allowed to have even a taste of the fruits of their labor."

I remembered the opening of her speech: the glorification of White European history.

She twisted her wide-brimmed hat in her hands, turning it into a tight coil. "Today, it's corporations like Coca Cola or Seagram's or, hell," she snorted with disdain, "John Hancock Insurance buying up the vineyards. They could care less about the wine they make or the people who do the work. They only care about quarterly reports and shareholder profit margins."

"How can I help?"

Lucia inspected me with justified skepticism. Technically, I was a vineyard owner. I was supposed to be an enemy to her cause. "Really?"

"Really," I confirmed.

"You could start with Lark Estates," she said. "Insurance for full-time employees would be a good first step. Come harvest time, we'll take on part-time migrant farmers, most of them from Mexico. They deserve a fair wage and benefits, too."

An uneasy feeling settled in my stomach. All of that sounded expensive. But I couldn't say no after Lucia had told me what I could do to make a difference. I couldn't take back my offer to help.

I found myself nodding, agreeing to her suggestion. I choked on the next word: "Done."

+ + +

"You did *what?!*"

I winced at my friend Lily's volume and tone. Her number had been my first phone call when I'd returned to the vineyard.

"Junie, Junie, Junie," she sighed into the phone. "You can't throw away your money just because this girl is hot."

I bristled at the suggestion. "I'm not doing this because of that."

"Ohhhh." She drew out the word. "So you agree? You think she's hot?"

"Can I afford this or not?" I was desperate to keep us on topic. "My employees ..." I trailed off. It still felt unnatural to call anything in this wine world *mine*. I'd continually referred to the vineyard as *the* vineyard, not mine. I hadn't earned that possessive pronoun yet. "Not all of them have health insurance," I finished. "Can I make that happen?"

"I've been wanting to talk to you," my friend interjected. "This is a lot more than a traditional business, June. I really think you need an accountant who specializes in vineyards or farms."

"You're probably right," I conceded, "but until I can find one, could you look into it for me?"

Lily continued to hesitate. "Alex really went for broke with this business plan. All of your cash——."

I interrupted her. "I know. It all went to the down payment."

"You really need more consistent revenue," she told me. "You're spending money consistently, but not really making any. I'm guessing that doesn't happen until after harvest?"

I exhaled loudly into the phone and tugged at my hair. "God, I don't know. I don't know anything about any of this, Lily."

My friend, perhaps sensing I was about to spiral out of control, offered me encouraging words. "I'll look into the health care situation. We'll take it one step at a time, one project at a time, okay?"

I choked down the nervous breakdown that threatened to make me unravel. "Alex would never do this," I impulsively blurted out, "but it's the right thing to do."

I heard Lily's pregnant pause. I wasn't sure why I'd felt compelled to make the distinction. "I'm sure it is," she said carefully. "Listen: let me do a little creative number crunching, and I'll see what you can offer without bankrupting yourself. I'll get back to you soon."

CHAPTER TWELVE

Growing up, I'd never really liked the month of June. I'd endured too many juvenile reminders that my name was also June—as if it was something I was supposed to be embarrassed about. Luckily the school year came to a close early enough in the month that the playground teasing was always short lived. As an adult, June meant Pride Month, and having lived in San Francisco for close to a decade and a half, Alex and I had taken full advantage of the city's many festivals and Pride-related activities over the years.

I'd just graduated college when Alex and I had attended our very first San Francisco Pride. It was late June of 2003, not long after *Lawrence vs. Texas* had been decided. We didn't live in the city yet, but we'd made the trip, almost like a pilgrimage to Mecca. I'd never felt so excited and encouraged and supported while watching the brightly colored floats traverse through the Castro neighborhood and the liberating feeling of openly holding Alex's hand the entire weekend. We'd decided right there that we were going to move to San Francisco and never leave.

My phone had been buzzing all morning with probing texts from my best friend Lily about if I was going to escape from the vineyard long enough to go to the weekend parade in San Francisco. I had no idea if Napa held any Pride-month events, but I was certain they paled in comparison to San Francisco's usual festivities. I still was undecided, however. It would be my first Pride without Alex. Would I be able to handle all of those old memories, surrounded by so many other happy queer couples?

"Do you want to do this today or do you have somewhere else to be?"

Lucia's impatient tone snapped me back to the vineyard. Bright green leaves glistened on the vine with early morning moisture, and my work boots sunk into the soft earth.

I hastily silenced my phone and shoved it into the back pocket of my jeans. "I'm here," I insisted. "I'm listening."

Lucia sighed and began again. "This month is all about canopy management."

"Right," I said brightly, "managing the canopy."

Beneath her wide-brimmed canvas hat, I saw Lucia roll her eyes. "We trim away the branches or shoots that don't need to be there. If we just let it grow wild, not only would it shield and obscure this cluster," she said, gingerly cradling a tight bunch of immature berries, "but it would also be a hog and try to develop its own cluster."

"But isn't that ideal?" I posed. "More grapes?"

Lucia shook her head. "We're interested in quality, not quantity. Right now the vines are building leaf material to be able to photosynthesize, to be able to produce sugar in the fruit, but that's still about two months down the line. Managing the canopy allows more air into the vine and, even more importantly, gets more sunlight onto the morning side of the fruit."

I stared out at all of the acreage that surrounded us. Seven acres of pruning and trimming cabernet grape vines. The number didn't seem that impressive, but actually standing amongst the rows and rows and rows of vines made it feel impossible and not a little overwhelming. I imagined us toiling under the hot summer sun from morning until night. "All of this by hand?"

"Uh huh," she confirmed. "Each vine will get touched at least a dozen and a half times between pruning, tying up, shoot repositioning, thinning fruit, and cleaning off growth at the bottom of the vine."

Lucky vines, I silently mused. I hadn't been touched in months.

"It's not so bad, really," she noted. "In fact, because Calistoga has the highest percentage of volcanic soils, that means less green growth and more concentration within the berries. Different climates affect the sweetness of the berry. The Valley is perfect for making wine grapes. Hot days provide color and big berry flavor. Cool nights maintain good acid balance and retention."

Lucia began to walk down one of the rows of manicured vines, so I followed closely behind. "Right now we've got bloom and continuing growth," she said, "and then around late June, early July, the vines will flip an internal switch and will devote all their energies to ripen the fruit. And at that point," she stated, "the fruit gets soft and starts to get sweet. The red grapes develop their color, and within a few months we'll be ready to harvest."

"*Veraison?*" I guessed.

Lucia's normally stoic features took on a surprised look. "Yeah."

I couldn't hide my pleased grin. "I've been paying attention."

Lucia regarded me, almost as if seeing me for the first time. "Cool," she settled on. "I'm probably going to regret this," she said, more to herself than to me, "but here you go."

She extended her right hand and the pair of metal gardening shears she'd been holding.

My eyes widened as I excepted the tool. "Really?"

"Just don't cut off any fingers," she told me, lips quirking up. "Aunt Clara only fixes one finger per growing season. I think it's in her contract."

"You don't think she'd make an exception for me?" I couldn't help teasing.

Lucia's laugh sounded more like a snort. "Let's not press your luck, *Jefa.*"

I wasn't entirely confident what I was supposed to do, but as long as I didn't cut away anything that looked too large and healthy, I figured I would be fine. Lucia trimmed and pruned by herself in the next row over. She had either had enough of me or she trusted me not to screw up too epically. We worked in silence under the strong morning sun. I was thankful I'd followed her advice about wearing an oversized hat to work in the fields. And ever since my hot springs debacle, my water bottle was never far away.

"Your phone was really blowing up earlier," Lucia observed from her adjacent row. "Is everything okay?"

"Yeah. Everything's fine," I said. I started to snip away at small, curling vine tendrils that lagged behind the other new growth. "My friend Lily—you met her at that bar in Guerneville," I recalled, "she's been bugging me to come back to San Francisco for the Pride parade."

Lucia made a noncommittal noise. "You should go."

I looked down my single vineyard row. I knew it had an actual end, but from where I stood it seemed to go on forever. "I'm not sure I'll have time. Have you ever been?" I asked conversationally.

"No," came her one-worded response.

"Does your dad know?" I stopped trimming long enough to glance in her direction. I could just make out her silhouette through the bright green growth.

Lucia didn't look away from her work. "Know what?"

"That ... that you're ..." I rolled the words around on my tongue as if determining which I liked best. I had assumed Lucia's sexuality based only on a single appearance in Guerneville. It was an unfair assumption, however. Maybe she just liked that particular bar.

Lucia saved me the embarrassment by finishing my question. "That I'm gay?" She continued to snip and cut and prune the vines, never losing concentration. "I'm a grown woman, June. I don't need my father's permission."

She hadn't directly answered the question, yet her response had me ducking my head in shame.

I didn't dare look back in her direction, but the metallic snip of her shears stopped, and I heard her frustrated sigh.

"Yeah. He knows. But he's never thrown me a parade or a party, you know?" The snipping sounds resumed as she went back to work. "Not like it matters. I'm never in one place long enough. I'm much better as cultivating wines than relationships."

She hadn't asked about me, but I didn't let it bother me. Lucia had never showed any interest in my life except when she'd believed I was being unfaithful to Alex.

"I Came Out to my parents in college, not long after I met Alex," I offered up.

I started to pick up the pace as I gained more confidence in which shoots should stay or go, but I was still no match for how quickly Lucia could go.

"So Alex was your first girlfriend?" she asked.

I chewed on the inside of my mouth. "Alex was my first a lot of things."

"That's wild."

I could feel my defense mechanism start to kick in and prickle up my spine. The fact that Alex had been the only woman I'd ever slept with had been a favorite topic of conversation among our mutual friends. I'd heard just about every taunt over the years—how could I know if I was really gay or just simply gay for Alex if I'd only ever had sex with her?

"I can't imagine being with the same person for so long," Lucia remarked. "That's really commendable—like, seriously goal worthy."

I hadn't expected the compliment, and especially not from Lucia of all people.

"Oh, uh. Thanks."

My shears continued to snip away at small, struggling new growth and thin, woody branches that hadn't survived the winter. I should have been focused entirely on the task Lucia had entrusted me with, but my attention periodically strayed through the tall, bushy vine that separated our work. Lucia's back was to me. The heat of the day had caused perspiration to accumulate in the small of her back, penetrating through her work shirt. Her work ethic was admirable. She worked so hard, all of the time. I still didn't know her very well, and yet I couldn't imagine her doing anything else. Picturing her in an air conditioned cubicle was nearly laughable.

My metal snips cut through something that felt different from everything else I'd been trimming. I froze when I realized what I'd done. I hadn't cut back a piece of dead wood; I'd cut the irrigation line attached to the vine. My body temperature spiked. I felt hot all over as if I was back in those hot springs. I stared down at the severed irrigation line. Part of me was tempted to ignore my mistake and continue pruning as if nothing had happened. But I knew myself too well; if I didn't say something, my anxiety and guilt would never go away.

"Uh … Lucia?" I called out.

She didn't seem to hear my initial attempt to get her attention. Her focus was entirely on the vines in front of her as she expertly clipped and snipped and used plastic ties to rearrange the vine's new growth.

I refastened the plastic hook that closed my pruning shears as if activating the safety of a handgun. My feet were slow as I trudged to the next row where she continued to work.

"Lucia?" I called again.

She grunted, but didn't look in my direction.

"I made a mistake."

Those words caught her attention. She stopped her own work and pushed her wide-brimmed hat up her forehead. She wiped at the newly exposed skin with the back of her hand. "What's wrong?"

"I, uh, you should come see."

Lucia looked annoyed that I'd interrupted her, but she followed me back to the place where I'd previously been. When we reached the spot where I'd unintentionally separated the vine from its water source, I felt my own water source trigger. My eyes welled up with embarrassed, guilty tears. I couldn't speak, so I simply pointed.

Lucia removed her hat and bent closer to the vine to inspect. "God damn it," I heard her quietly mutter.

The tears that I'd barely been holding back began to stream down my cheeks. "I-I'm sorry," I mumbled. "It was an accident."

Lucia righted herself. She turned to face me and I braced myself. But instead of anger or frustration, her face only showed concern. "Why are you crying?"

I choked on my tears. "I-I ruined it."

"You didn't ruin anything," she said matter-of-factly. "It's a quick fix. I just have to cut away some of the old irrigation tubing and connect it to new material."

"R-really?" I couldn't get my bottom lip to stop quivering.

"Really," she assured me. "I don't think there's any leftover tubing in storage—or at least nothing that isn't cracked or dried up—but I'm due to the hardware store anyway. Do you want to come with?"

I sniffled loudly and wiped at my cheeks. I didn't trust my voice yet, so I nodded instead.

"Let me tell my dad we're going into town," she said. "I'll meet you by your car, okay?"

"O-Okay," I managed to agree.

I took a deep breath and slowly exhaled. I'd been so worried, practically expecting Lucia's anger, that I hadn't been prepared for this softer, accommodating version of the assistant winemaker. I grabbed my tools and water bottle and walked back to the farmhouse. I dropped off my gear on the front porch and grabbed my purse and car keys from inside.

Lucia hadn't arrived yet, but I slid behind the steering wheel of my car and flipped the visor down to inspect my reflection. I'd long ago stopped wearing makeup to work on the farm, so my tears hadn't upset any eye makeup. My eyes did look more red than usual and my cheeks were a little flushed, but otherwise I looked okay.

I snapped the visor back into its original position when the passenger side door opened and Lucia slid inside. She looked around the interior of my compact car. I kept the car's interior meticulously clean, so there was no fast food wrappers or other garbage for her to comment on. Even though she hadn't scolded me for cutting the irrigation drip line, I found myself almost anticipating her next critical words.

I started up the car and shifted it to drive. I wasn't sure where the Calistoga hardware store was located, but I knew the way to downtown and assumed Lucia would give me directions when we got closer. Lucia made herself more comfortable in the passenger seat. She took it upon herself to find a suitable radio station. Then she used the levers beneath the seat to tilt the passenger seat farther back until she could stretch out her legs. She hadn't commented on my water works, and I was content to not bring them up again either.

She'd exchanged her wide-brimmed hat for a pair of aviator sunglasses. She leaned far back in the seat and crossed one leg over the other. Her fingertips tapped against her kneecap in time with the song on the radio. Her head was almost always covered by her field hat when we were outside in the sun. I took the time to appreciate how the sun reflected off of her dark, braided hair.

"I was helping my dad on the vineyard this one time," she spoke up. "I must have been in my early teens—too early to have a driver's license at least," she reflected. "I was always looking for ways to prove myself or impress him so he'd trust me with more responsibilities. I noticed that the gas gauge on the tractor was getting low, so I took it upon myself to fill up the tank without him needing to ask. I didn't realize there was a difference between fuel types, and I filled up the tank with the can I'd seen him use a million times on the old riding lawn mower. It was an oil and gas mixture when the tractor took regular unleaded gas."

"Oh no," I quietly murmured.

"The next time someone went to use the tractor, the engine totally seized. I can still remember all of that smoke pouring out of the exhaust pipes. It was practically blue," she chuckled, remembering. "My dad got so mad when he thought one of the other workers had messed up the tractor."

"Rolando got mad?" I interrupted her story. "I can't imagine him ever losing his temper."

"He's usually a cool customer," Lucia confirmed, "but he has his moments, too. I knew I was in big trouble, but I didn't want someone else to take the fall for my mistake."

"So you told him it was you?"

"Not right away. I'm no angel," she said. "But at dinner that night, yeah."

"What did he do?"

"I was expecting the worst," she admitted, "but he was more impressed that I'd eventually fessed up. It made it a lot easier to make mistakes later, knowing he wasn't going to chew me out."

I kept my eyes on the highway. "Are you telling me this because I cried back there?"

Lucia cleared her throat, perhaps not expecting me to be so direct. "I know I'm a little rough around the edges. But I never want to make you cry."

"That really had nothing to do with you," I assured her. "I-I'm wound pretty tight. I take myself too seriously; I want things to be perfect. And when they're not," I shrugged, "I kind of fall apart."

Lucia twisted in her seat to appraise me. "That's some pretty insightful self-awareness."

"Do I keep going straight on this road?" I deflected.

It felt good to be able to open up with someone, but that didn't mean I was ready to divulge everything to this woman.

"Oh, uh, yeah," she said, returning to face forward in her seat. "Just a little longer on here and then go right at the next stop sign. The hardware store will be on the left a few blocks down the main street."

Lucia provided me with additional directions once we reached Calistoga's city limits. I found a parking spot close to the hardware store. I locked my vehicle, but paused outside.

"Is everything we need going to fit in my car? Should we have taken your truck instead?"

"Hell, no," Lucia snorted. "I'm not going to risk scratching up my baby hauling stuff around."

I gave her a perplexed look. "Then why do you drive a truck?"

She flashed me a quick grin, nearly mischievous. "Because I look good in it."

I hadn't really seen her drive the truck, but I'd seen how good she looked *washing* the vehicle, so I trusted the truth in her words.

We walked the short distance to the hardware store. The not unpleasant scent of motor oil and topsoil perfumed the air as we stepped through the front door. A small bell above the entrance announced our presence. The store was small, but the high ceilings gave the impression of something more grand. I was happy to discover that the store was locally owned rather than being a big chain. The usual products one might expect to find in a hardware store filled the tidy shelves that ran throughout the shop. I noticed a heavier influence of gardening supplies toward the front of the store which was appropriate for the agricultural community.

A tall thin man, his hair grey and thinning, sat behind the front counter. He stood up with our arrival. It was a good thing the ceilings were so high or else the man might have had to stoop while at work. The man's advanced age made me reflexively think of Alex. I didn't think she was ageist or classist, but she wrinkled her nose at senior citizens in the workforce. I would gently remind her that not everyone was fortunate enough to have a pension or 401k or that maybe they just *liked* to work. Alex would call me naïve and scoff at what she assumed to be the individual's lack of retirement plan. "*That will never be me,*" she'd boldly declare.

A dark thought crossed my thoughts: *No. That would never be her.*

Lucia's voice, more jovial than I'd ever heard her, pulled me back to the Calistoga hardware store. "Hey, Jim. My dad said the stuff he ordered came in?"

The grey-haired man in the red cloth vest nodded. "It's in the back. Give me a second and I'll bring it right up."

"Thanks," Lucia approved. "And while you're it, can you rustle up some irrigation tubing?" She pulled a small piece of the plastic tubing out of her back pocket. "Here's the gauge I need. Let's go with five feet." She looked once in my direction and flashed an easy smile. "Just in case we have another accident."

The man—Jim—took the slender black tubing and rolled it between his fingers. "You got it."

Jim abandoned his station behind the front counter and disappeared to the back of the store.

I didn't need to buy anything, but I strolled down the shop's aisles and inspected the goods on display. I stopped periodically to closely regard one tool or another and used that opportunity to observe Lucia over the top of the store's short aisles. I regarded her profile, my long stare unnoticed. Her squared jaw exuded understated confidence. Her nose was long and almost hawkish, but the sharp features fit her personality. She'd taken off her aviators, which now hung from the front of her button-up shirt by one of the stems. The extra weight caused her shirt to drop a little lower on her chest. It was only a modest amount of cleavage, but I still found my attention being drawn to the view.

In Jim's continued absence, Lucia leaned against the checkout station. She drummed her fingers against the countertop while she waited. They were smudged with dirt from the day's work. Her fingers were long and tapered, capped by blunt nails that she never let grow out. She'd rolled up the sleeves of her denim shirt to her elbows. Her forearms were slender, but solid. Endless pruning had produced thinly corded muscles.

I had never really been attracted to specific female body parts—well, besides the obvious ones—but I felt my attention constantly drawn to Lucia's wrists, her strong-looking forearms, and the suggestion of a collarbone that routinely made an appearance at the open collar of her button-up shirts. With her long hair, Lucia wasn't exactly androgynous, but the pendulum swung more to the masculine side than previous women whom I'd found attractive.

I paused and licked my lips at the observation: *Was I attracted to Lucia?* Was I actively crushing on the obstinate woman who had been so quick to display her displeasure towards me?

The bell above the hardware store chimed with the arrival of another patron. I swung my attention to the doorway and instantly recognized the newcomer as Bruce Jefferson; he and his wife Darcy owned the adjacent boutique vineyard. I hadn't seen either of them since their original welcoming me to the neighborhood.

I opened my mouth and raised my hand to say hello, but I cut off the gesture when I heard his accusatory tone.

"*You,*" he growled.

The one-worded accusation wasn't aimed at me; it was intended for Lucia. I wasn't sure he'd even noticed me in the store. Bruce stalked closer to Lucia and the cash register. He waggled a beefy finger in her direction. "I know what you're trying to do."

Lucia calmly righted herself. She straightened her shoulders and stood erect. "Hello, Bruce," she said. "It's good to see you."

"As if I don't have enough to deal with, competing with the Trader Joe's of the world," he bitterly complained, "Now I've got to worry about my seasonal help walking out on me."

"Pay them what they're worth, and you'll have nothing to worry about." Lucia's calm, even tone was at odds with the aggressive bite to Bruce's words.

"Who do you think you are," he growled, "goddamn Caesar Chavez?"

Lucia's eyes narrowed and darkened. "No," she spat out. "Dolores Huerta."

I quickly made my way across the store to intervene. I had no idea what I could do to keep their interaction from escalating, but I needed to do *something*.

"Hi, Bruce," I greeted in a cheerful tone. "It's been a while."

Bruce turned in my direction. "Did you know she's trying to unionize the seasonal vineyard workers?"

I nodded, slowly. Bruce's anger continued to elevate, and I worried what might happen in the little store if he truly exploded.

Lucia stood beside me and folded her arms across her chest. "It's the right thing to do, Bruce. If you can't pay your workers a living wage and provide them with adequate benefits, then maybe you shouldn't be in business."

I visibly winced, anticipating that Lucia's declaration was only going to make Bruce angrier. I looked in the direction of the back of the store. *Where was Jim? What was taking him so long?*

Bruce stared at Lucia, almost in disbelief, before turning back to me. He shook a raised finger in my direction. "You need to get your girl in line before she gets herself in trouble."

Now it was Lucia's turn to grow angry: "I'm nobody's girl," she hissed.

"We should ... we should be going." I reached for Lucia's arm, but she refused to be corralled. She blindly swatted my hand away. Unblinking, she continued to glare at Bruce. "Not until we get what we came for."

Thankfully, Jim returned from the back of the store with a pile of boxes stacked on top of a dolly. "This should be everything," he cheerfully announced, fully unaware of the throwdown about to happen at the front of his store. "Oh hey, Bruce," he greeted when he finally spotted the other man. "What can I get for you today?"

With Jim's appearance, some of the intensity left Bruce's features. "You should finish with these two ladies first. I'll wait."

It was a long, awkward moment between paying for our order and wheeling the supplies outside. Lucia continued to silently fume as she unlocked the boxes into the truck of my car.

"I'm sorry," I announced.

My words and apology finally snapped Lucia from her angry fog. "What? Sorry? For what?"

"I'm sorry Bruce spoke to you like that. And I'm sorry I didn't speak up more to support you."

Lucia continued to look perplexed. "You don't have to apologize for that guy being an ass. I'm a big girl. I can handle myself."

"I know you're totally capable," I agreed, "but I still feel bad. Bruce owns a vineyard, just like me. It makes me feel like an asshole, too."

"You're not like them, June."

I licked my lips. "I'm-I'm not?"

Lucia put the last of the supplies into the trunk of my car and closed the lid. She wiped her hands against the tops of her thighs as if her hands had gotten dirty from the task. "You're not just in it for the money."

"I'm not?" I apparently didn't know any other words.

Lucia's mouth tugged up at its corners. "You wouldn't be trying half as hard on the farm if you were."

I still didn't understand her logic or reasoning, but I was privately pleased that she didn't lump Bruce Jefferson and me into the same category.

"Come on," Lucia urged. "We've got some thirsty vines to tend to."

+ + +

I stood in front of the microwave in the vineyard office later that evening. I still didn't have internet in the farmhouse, so I'd started streaming movies after dinner in the tasting barn. The isolated back office was nowhere near as comfortable as my living room, but the movies were a distraction from being alone and bored in the farmhouse when the workday had come to an end.

I hadn't set a timer on my microwave popcorn. I listened for the sustained pauses in between the final popping kernels to find the sweet spot between underdone and burnt. As the moments between each pop became more pronounced, I took note of another sound. In between the familiar snap of the final kernels popping, I heard undistinguishable, muffled noise come from beneath me. I discerned no voices, only the barely audible sounds of what sounded like heavy objects being moved around.

I wasn't the kind of person to reach for a weapon whenever I heard something unexpected. Alex had slept with a baseball bat under our bed, but beyond that—and the knives already in the kitchen—we'd never kept any self-defense items in our condo. I didn't think we were being robbed—the parking lot was empty, and I hadn't seen any unexplainable lights, but I was concerned. I didn't know the age of the tasting barn or wine cellar below to worry about a structural collapse or if an animal too large for Gato to take care of had wandered into the building. I turned off the microwave and left the finished popcorn bag inside. I grabbed my phone, if only for its flashlight function, or to call Rolando if I found something problematic in the wine cellar.

The entrance to the underground wine caves were through the production side of the tasting barn. It was the only way into the root cellar from inside of the barn, but for safety, a second entrance popped out elsewhere on the property like an emergency exit if the primary entrance became blocked.

I kept my steps light as I traveled down the built-in brick steps. The overhead lights in the stairwell weren't overly bright compared to the lights in the tasting room, but they offered enough illumination that I didn't need to use my cellphone's flashlight to avoid tripping over my feet.

The noises became louder and more pronounced the closer I came to the subterranean space where the wine casks were located. I still heard no voices, but the shuffling and moving of solid objects became more obvious. Maybe someone really was trying to rob us, I briefly considered. I looked down at my phone and frowned at the lack of connectivity. The wine cellar was a dead zone. Even if I'd wanted to call Rolando or even the police, I would need to be above ground to have a signal.

I started to regret not bringing anything with me for self-defense, but it wasn't like the winery's office was stocked with weapons. What was I going to do? Staple an intruder to death?

I stooped and retrieved a loose chunk of brick from the ground. I couldn't imagine myself actually hitting someone with the object or causing serious harm, but its dense weight was oddly comforting in my hand. My body went rigid and I held the brick high over my head as I crept closer to the sounds' origins. I had only to round another corner and I would be in the room with the oldest, most established wine casks.

I held my breath as I turned the corner.

The lights were slightly brighter in the wine aging room. I didn't immediately notice anyone or any obvious vermin, but I remained quiet and alert.

Another sound, like solid metal being dragged across concrete, filled up the small space. A figure, narrowly built and dressed in denim, came into view. My body released its earlier tension and I lowered the arm that had held the piece of red brick above my head.

"Lucia," I breathed out. "What are you doing down here?"

The assistant winemaker was unaffected by my entrance. I would have expected her to at least look a little surprised, but her features were unmoved and she hadn't jumped at the sound of my voice.

"Hey," she smoothly returned. "I'm working on my blends."

Her brow furrowed in concentration as she attempted to drag a metal shelving unit across the wine storage floor. The tip of her tongue poked out from between her lips and quiet but discernable grunts followed with each tug and pull of the shelves.

"It's late," I couldn't help pointing out.

I knew she arrived on site even earlier than me. And now here she was at night. Was she ever not working?

Lucia stood and wiped at her forehead. The wine cellar was several degrees cooler than above ground, but who knew how long she'd been struggling with the heavy shelves. "This is the only time I have to do my mad scientist routine," she noted. "I'm working on my dad's wines during the day."

She gave me a curious look when I strode purposefully to stand beside her. "What are you doing?"

"Helping." I bent at the knees and grabbed one of the metal poles that held up the shelving. "On three."

Lucia looked like she might protest the extra set of hands, but she dug in beside me. Her fingers wrapped around another of the vertical poles.

"One," I started the count. "Two. Three."

At the signal, we both began to tug at the oversized, stubborn shelving. Our quiet grunts and growls of exertion echoed in the cavernous room. The unit initially resisted our joint efforts, but just when I thought it might never move, it began to budge. It wobbled at first like it might topple over, but then it righted itself and began to move. Lucia and I continued to pull and tug; little by little, the heavy shelves scooted across the cellar floor in short but progressively longer bursts.

When we'd successfully relocated the unit to the other side of the room, Lucia released her grip on the metal shelves. "That's good," she approved. She gave me a sideways glance. "Thanks."

"No problem." I rubbed my hands together. My palms felt gritty and had become slightly covered in rust from the old metal. "What are the shelves for?"

"I'm prepping a new area of the cellar. Those barrels my dad promised me are going to go right here."

She stood back and inspected her handiwork.

"The fruit you get for babysitting me," I observed.

Lucia cleared her throat. "Right." She looked back in my direction. "What are *you* doing here so late? And what's up with the outfit?"

I looked down at my ensemble. Carlos was still tinkering with the washing machine in the farmhouse, and I hadn't had the time or energy to go into town to do laundry with any kind of regularity. I was starting to run out of clean clothes. I'd had to dig deep into my packing boxes to find the fuzzy sleep pants. They'd shrunk over the years during previous washings and the once-vibrant colors were a little faded. Red hearts and green dinosaurs covered the patterned fabric.

I tugged at one of the legs self-consciously. I was definitely dressed down, but I needed no reminder that she had seen me in less—far less.

"I was going to stream a movie in the office. There's no internet in the farmhouse yet."

"That's rough," Lucia observed.

"Yeah," I confirmed.

"Do you have time to check out this blend I've been working on?" she prompted. "It's got a nose that'll blow your wig off."

I had no idea what half of those words meant, but I was curious to learn what kinds of projects Lucia worked on after hours. My popcorn could wait.

Lucia stood next to one of the French oak barrels and removed the plug—the bung—from its top. Next came the wine thief—the foot-long glass apparatus that looked like a turkey baster. She dipped the wine thief through the cask's open hole and removed a long pull of red wine. Small wine glasses, almost the shape and size of a brandy snifter, came next. She poured equal amounts of the red blend into the cups.

"Do I have to wait to drink this?" I asked when she handed me the small glass. I didn't want to look like a Neanderthal and toss back the liquid like it was a shot of hard liquor.

"Not when it's straight out of the barrel," she said. "You only need to decant something if it's been sitting in a bottle."

"What's the purpose of decanting? Should all wine be decanted?" I frowned at the question. "Is that even a word?"

"Not really. Ninety-nine percent of wine is meant to be consumed immediately," she told me. "Decanting oxidizes the wine—lets it breathe a little outside of the bottle—which reduces acids and tannins. Essentially, it makes the wine taste smoother," she summarized. "It's a great trick to improve the taste of young wines or affordable wines."

I held onto the base of my wine glass and swirled around the red liquid like I'd seen done in the movies. I had no idea what I was doing though. When I'd gotten my first apartment with Alex, we'd hosted a wine-tasting party for our friends. Neither of us had had any money, but we'd wanted to seem grown-up. To be an adult meant the cheap beer had been replaced with cheap wine and hunks of discount-market cheese. It was embarrassing to think about now—nothing but screw-top bottles with animals on the labels.

I brought the glass up to my nose and breathed in. Lucia had promised the wine would blow off my wig, but luckily my hair remained connected to my scalp.

"Why am I smelling this?" I wasn't ashamed to ask.

"You're checking out the wine's bouquet. About eighty percent of how something tastes actually comes from its aroma."

I lifted the small glass under my nostrils again. "So that's the nose?"

"Uh huh." Lucia watched me with interest. "What do you smell?"

"It's almost like …" I smelled the inside of the glass again. "Chocolate?" I guessed.

Lucia grinned like a proud parent. "Totally." She brought her own miniature glass to her nose. "Can you detect the black currant, too?"

"I have no idea what that smells like," I revealed.

"That's okay," she allowed. "You're a work in progress."

"Can I drink it now?" I posed.

Lucia chuckled. "Sure. Go ahead."

I took a small sip at first, dainty and experimental. I glanced to see Lucia's progress. She'd drained the contents of her glass already, so I felt confident to finish mine as well.

"I like it," I approved. I smacked my lips, but didn't elaborate. I wished I knew the lingo so I could say more, but I was still such a novice.

Lucia held up her empty glass to the overhead lights as if to inspect the residue. "Cabernets are like the John Wayne of the red wine world. It practically swaggers in the glass."

"And that's a good thing?" I hesitated to venture.

"Totally. I'm not interested in the easy reds. Not the fruit-forward reds that dominate wine lists because they don't do anything risky or brave." Her eyes took on an intense, but faraway look. "I want to make a red that will make you take notice. I want it to be life changing. I want it to make your knees buckle." She looked in my direction as if remembering my presence. "N-not you specifically," she was quick to clarify. "The consumer."

Lucia appeared moderately embarrassed by her small speech. I didn't want to prologue her discomfort, so I set my empty wine glass on one of the French oak barrels. "Thanks for the sneak preview," I approved. "My wig has been officially blown."

Lucia retrieved my discarded glass. She held both of the miniature cups close to her chest. "Are you still planning on watching a movie upstairs?"

The cellar contained no windows, but I could sense that it was late. I glanced down at my phone which I'd continued to hold on to this entire time. More time had passed than I'd intended when I'd initially sought out the source of the mysterious basement noises.

"Probably not," I decided. "I should get to bed at a decent hour tonight. My boss works me pretty hard; doesn't take it easy on me."

"Sounds like a real ball buster," Lucia noted, playing along.

I couldn't help the smile that crept to my lips. "I don't know. She's not so bad once you get to know her."

veraison

CHAPTER THIRTEEN

I alternated my attention between my book and the trashy talk show on the television. The sound was muted and there was no closed captioning, but I'd deerned from the action on the screen that two women were fighting over a man. The talk show host had to periodically separate the women as the tension on the stage escalated from yelling to hairpulling.

The Calistoga Laundromat was empty that day. I could have changed the channel if I wanted to, but there was something oddly comforting and mundane about the cheaply produced television program. It was so pedestrian and normal—like the laundromat itself—worlds away from the rarified experience of vineyard life.

I looked away from the grainy television set when the bell above the laundromat's entrance jingled with a new patron. The woman who walked through the door paused when she saw me occupying one of the laundromat's hard plastic chairs.

Lucia's expression turned from surprise to disinterest in seconds. "Hey," she grunted. She shifted the canvas bag flung over her shoulder.

I sat to attention, mildly embarrassed by my location and choice of television program. "Hey."

She walked past me in favor of one of the unoccupied front-loading washers. She inelegantly emptied the full contents of her laundry bag into one of the larger machines, not bothering to sort the clothes into separate loads. She rummaged in her jean pockets for a few quarters and pumped them into the machine.

When her hands curled around the bottom of her t-shirt and she began to tug the clothing up her torso and off her body, I hastily returned my eyes to the fine print of my book. Even over the continuous drone of running washers and dryers, I heard the metallic bite of a zipper being undone, denim being pushed aside and then being unceremoniously thrown into the open washer door.

I didn't dare look again in her direction even when she spoke to me: "What are you reading?"

"A book."

"I can see that. About what?"

I glanced once at the book's hardcover and title. "*The Business of Wine*. It's actually really good," I noted. "I'm learning a lot. Like, how does a boutique winery like ours sell to a consumer who has never visited the winery or tasted the wine? Forget about direct to consumer wine clubs. We need to think bigger: digital native vertical brands."

I heard Lucia's snort. At the sound, my eyes inadvertently flicked in her direction. She no longer stood, but rather sat perched on an unoccupied dryer.

The edge of my mouth lilted up. "What are you wearing?"

Lucia looked down at her unorthodox outfit. "A bathing suit."

Hidden beneath the t-shirt and jeans that she'd dumped into the washing machine was a dark blue one-piece bathing suit. It looked old and ill-fitting, practically hanging off her narrow build.

"I can see that," I drolly responded. "But why?"

Lucia shrugged in her maddeningly nonchalant way. "It's laundry day."

I rolled my eyes and returned my attention to my book—or at least I *tried* to focus on the small, printed letters—instead of being drawn to Lucia's exposed legs which she kicked back and forth as if she sat at the edge of a swimming pool instead of a laundry machine.

"I take it there's no laundry in the farmhouse?" she asked.

I wanted to retort with something smart or sarcastic—*no, I just like hanging out at laundromats*—but I bit back the caustic response.

"There is, but I can't seem to get the washer to work. It looks like it's hooked up to water, but when I turn it on, nothing happens."

"You should ask Carlos to take a look," she proposed.

I shrugged noncommittally. "He's a pretty busy guy. I don't mind roughing it for a little longer. What about you?" I asked. "Doesn't your dad have a washing machine?"

Lucia scratched at the back of her neck. "Yeah, but I'm banned from using it. My aunt doesn't like that I don't separate my lights and my darks."

"Couldn't you just separate your lights and darks?" I said pragmatically.

Lucia shrugged again. "I don't mind this; it gets me out of the house." She nodded at the book still clutched in my hands. "What else are you learning from your book?" she asked.

I looked down again at the book's nondescript cover. "That the tasting room is the key to building a long-term relationship with the customer. When they have a positive tasting room experience, they buy our wine."

"You don't need to read a book to know that," Lucia challenged.

I sat up a little straighter in my hardbacked plastic chair. "Well, did you know that Millennials are the first generation open to not just receiving ads, but also to engage and share them?" I posed. "Brands can be scaled quickly but still maintain a one-to-one connection that delivers an elevated customer experience."

"Do you want to come over tonight for a movie?" Lucia suddenly asked. "You know, so you don't have to hang out at the barn all night?"

"Oh, I ..." The invitation was unexpected, and I didn't immediately respond.

Lucia took my hesitation as rejection. "Or not, if you have other plans, that's fine."

"I don't—I don't have other plans," I quickly corrected. "Yeah. A movie sounds great."

Lucia bobbed her head. "Cool."

"Should I bring anything?" I asked.

Lucia offered me a rare, lopsided grin. "Got any more popcorn?"

A few loads of laundry later, and I was nearly out the farmhouse's front door with a packet of microwave popcorn secured in my purse. I paused my hurried exit, however, when my cellphone rang. For a second I considered it might be Lucia, calling off movie night, until I realized she didn't have my number. I stood in the front entrance and dug through my purse to find the jangling phone. My friend Lily's name and number lit up my cellphone screen. We hadn't spoken much since I'd rejected her continued pleas that I come to San Francisco Pride.

In my defense, however, work was really starting to pick up on the vineyard. With *veraison* probably only a few days away, we continued to trim and tie back the vineyard canopy. Guest traffic had similarly increased on the property as vacation season came upon us and the area bloomed more vibrantly than in the weeks before.

"Hey," I breathed into the receiver. "What's up?" I pressed the phone between my ear and my shoulder as I searched through my purse for my elusive car keys.

"Nothing—just calling to check in," my friend replied. "I haven't heard from you in a while."

"Things are good," I said without going into much detail. "At least better than when I first got here."

"Feeling a little less like a fish out of water?"

"I'm definitely not swimming laps," I said, going along with her analogy, "but I'm not drowning anymore."

"That's good to hear," Lily approved. "Want to check out the local talent in Guerneville tonight? Or I could come to you?" she offered. "I still need a private tour of your new digs."

I chewed on my lower lip. "I'm sorry, Lil. I would, but I already have plans tonight."

"Don't apologize. That's good!" she eagerly approved. "I'm glad you're getting out."

"Yeah," I concurred. "Lucia invited me over to watch a movie."

I idly ran my thumbnail across a deep groove in the worn doorframe. I didn't want to make a big deal about the evening, but I was kind of feeling like the most popular girl in school had asked me to hang out with her.

"Lucia," Lily echoed the name. "As in Lucia from your work? The same Lucia who hates your guts and resents that you bought the vineyard?"

I winced at the description. "That would be the one."

"That doesn't sound like she hates your guts," my friend observed.

"No. Not anymore," I admitted. "I don't want to jinx it, but we're actually getting along pretty well these days."

"How well?" Lily pressed. "Like, is this a date?"

"Absolutely not," I immediately rejected.

"How do you know?"

"There's nothing happening," I denied. "It's just a movie at her dad's house. She was probably feeling sorry for me, and it's a pity invite," I reflected. "I don't know why, but I'm *so awkward* around her. She probably thinks I'm an idiot; I fall all over myself and make such stupid mistakes."

"Because you're crushing on her?" Lily guessed.

"I am not!" I practically squeaked.

"You're not a nun, June. You're allowed to crush on pretty girls. Hot, brooding, mysterious girls," she unnecessarily added.

I swallowed. "But Alex—."

"Isn't here anymore," Lily gently interrupted my protest. "And you know she would want you to be happy, Junie."

"It's too soon," I dismissed out of hand. Her suggestion that this was a date was ridiculous anyway. Lucia barely tolerated me.

"There's no timetable for grief, sweetie."

After a promise that we would hang out soon, I hung up with Lily and hustled outside to my parked car. Lucia had asked me to drop by around 8:00 p.m. that night, and I didn't want to be late for something that was definitely not a date.

I had mountain lions on my mind when I drove to the house Lucia shared with her father and her aunt. I was able-bodied, and the distance between the two homes was minimal, but I had no desire to meet up with a wild animal either coming to or from Lucia's house that night. Concerns of being mauled by a wild animal competed for attention with my curiosity about what had led to Lucia inviting me over in the first place. Did she feel sorry for me, relegated to eating microwave popcorn in the vineyard office in my free time? Was she actually starting to warm up to me? Would this be the start of a friendship beyond working hours? I didn't want to overanalyze the unexpected invitation, but it was in my nature to overthink things to death.

A pleasant wood-burning scent filled the air as I climbed out of my parked car. A thin plume of grey smoke drifted out of the Santigos' chimney. I climbed the three steps to the welcoming, wrap-around porch and knocked on the solid wooden door.

The front door flung open with Lucia on the other side.

"Hey," she greeted.

"Hey," I returned, a little taken aback by how quickly she'd answered the door. The immediacy made me wonder if Lucia had been waiting, watching out the front-facing windows, for my arrival. Lily's phone call had made me a little late, but not so late that she would have worried I'd flaked on our plans.

Her gaze perceptively scanned down my body. "No dinosaurs tonight?"

Her quip brought a smile to my lips, my nerves momentarily forgotten. I'd worn skinny jeans and a loose sweater—relaxed, but definitely not pajamas. "No. The dinosaurs are back in their packing box where they belong."

Like myself, Lucia had changed out of her work clothes, but her chosen outfit was curiously similar to what she typically wore on the vineyard each day. The denim shirt had been exchanged for a dark blue button-up flannel shirt whose sleeves she'd rolled up to her elbows. Her black skinny jeans were a little more fitted than the denim she usually wore to work. She looked good, I decided. Comfortable. Confident.

"Too bad," Lucia mused. She opened the door wider. "Come on in."

The temperatures had started to dip outside with the late hour, but it was cozy inside of the Santiago home. Despite the summer month on the calendar, Napa County nights could get cold; a fire crackled in the living room's open fireplace, filling the air with its warm and welcoming aroma.

The house was eerily quiet with the exception of the burning fire. "Where's Rolando and Clara tonight?" I asked.

"My dad is playing poker with a group of old timers," she said. "A bunch of winemakers from the region get together every month."

"And your aunt?"

"I told her I had someone coming over tonight, so she's making herself scarce."

I hummed at the admission. I found it curious she hadn't simply told her aunt that *I* was coming over, but rather *someone*. I didn't know how to feel about it. Did she not want her family to know we were hanging out? Was there some kind of unwritten rule in the wine world about employees and vineyard owners not hanging out?

"Do you want something to drink?" Lucia offered. Her question stopped my insecure musings.

I'd contemplated bringing a bottle of wine with me, but I assumed that anything I brought over would be inferior to whatever Lucia was used to drinking.

"I don't know," I said, following her back to the kitchen. "Have anything that'll blow my nose off?"

Lucia's mouth twisted into a smirk. "The *nose* on the wine will blow your *wig* off," she corrected.

"Why do you all talk like that?" I wondered aloud. "All of those made up words like 'mouthfeel' and 'bouquet.' It makes us mere mortals feel bad."

"You didn't have industry jargon where you used to work?" She tilted her head to the side. "What *were* you doing before this?"

She looked like she hadn't considered the question before.

"Sitting behind a desk in a San Francisco high rise."

"Let me guess." Lucia tapped her fingers to her lips. The action brought my attention to her mouth. She had a wide mouth, with not overly plump lips, but her lower lip was noticeably more full than her upper lip. It made her appear as if she was constantly pouting. "Something in the non-profit world."

Her guess was curious. "What makes you say that?"

"You seem like the do-gooder type," she shrugged. She opened up a cabinet door and pulled out two wine glasses. "Like you believe that people naturally want to do what's right."

"I suppose that's not the worst thing I've been called," I decided. "But no. I didn't work for a non-profit. I did marketing for a big advertising firm. I was the creative director, in fact." I let myself brag a little.

"Huh," she clucked. "I wouldn't have guessed that."

My insecurities prickled. "Why not?"

"I don't know. It seems like a cut-throat, competitive world. But maybe that's just in the movies."

"I'm not … I'm not normally so weak," my voice wobbled.

Lucia grimaced. "Shit. I didn't mean to offend you. I'm sure you were terrific at what you did. You're, like, really creative," she said in earnest. "I can tell."

I cleared my throat and swallowed down a wave of complicated emotions. "So, what pairs well with popcorn?"

Lucia looked relieved by the change in subject. "Chardonnay or pinot grigio—something buttery."

I leaned against the kitchen island while Lucia busied herself with the popcorn and finding a big enough bowl. "Why do we only make cabs?" I wondered aloud.

"Because we only grow cabernet grapes?" she countered.

I rolled my eyes. "Yeah, but we replant new vines every year. Why not diversify?"

"You're thinking like a hedge-fund investor," she said with a shake of her head. "We do one thing very well. In fact, I'd argue we do it better than anyone else in the valley. Besides," she continued, "white wines are easy. They're for bridal showers and girls' only weekends."

"And microwave popcorn," I added.

My words pulled a rare smile to Lucia's lips. "That, too."

A strange sensation tickled down my spine at the sight of Lucia's toothy grin. It started in the center of my back and traveled down my tailbone.

"I'll have to set up a vertical tasting for you one of these days," she offered. "You try the same kind of wine, like a cabernet sauvignon, but from multiple vintages."

"Vintages," I echoed. "That means different harvest years, right?"

"Look at you," Lucia seemed to tease. "You're starting to sound like one of us."

I didn't think I would ever feel totally at ease or like I belonged in this world, but I didn't want to sour Lucia's good mood with my lingering discomfort.

We left the kitchen with our glasses of chardonnay and an oversized bowl of freshly popped microwave popcorn. Rolando's living room was large, but cozy. A patterned area rug covered much of the dark wood flooring. A crocheted afghan hung off the back of a cloth upholstered couch. Decorative lamps sat atop end tables and threw light into the otherwise darkened room. The fire in the fireplace continued to appealingly pop and crackle. I spied a series of framed photographs set up on the mantle. My curiosity compelled me to take a closer look, but I'd only been invited over for a movie, not a window into Lucia Santiago's life.

I set my glass on a coaster on the coffee table and occupied the couch while Lucia grabbed multiple remotes and fiddled with the television's settings.

"What are you in the mood for tonight?" she asked. "A comedy? Action? Romance?"

Was that a line? I wondered.

"I'm not picky," I said.

"Horror?" she seemed to challenge. "Or will that give you nightmares for weeks?"

"I can handle it if you can," I tossed back.

One of my first dates with Alex had been to a foreign film at a small independent movie theater close to campus. I'd been surprised when she'd proposed going to a film with subtitles. I learned later in our relationship that the choice had been purposeful; she'd wanted me to believe that she was sophisticated and cultured. Her humble upbringing had long been a source of discomfort for her. Having grown up in rural Iowa, she navigated the West Coast with a chip on her shoulder. She wanted people to find her impressive. As an adult she sought out the latest technology, the fanciest finishes, the highest level of luxury. Part of her decision to purchase a vineyard, despite neither of us having any previous experience or even interest in viticulture, was probably rooted in that inferiority complex.

Lucia queued up a movie and sat in a recliner on one side of the room instead of the vacant spot beside me on the couch. The distance between us brought a frown to my face. The couch was big enough for at least three people. She had been the one to invite me over; did she not feel comfortable sitting next to me? I'd thought we were beyond all of that.

"You're not going to make me eat this popcorn all by myself, are you?" I didn't exactly pout, but I made my disapproval apparent.

"Oh, uh, sorry," she sputtered out an apology. "Yeah, I'll have some."

She hopped up from the recliner, and for a moment I thought she might return to the kitchen to get a separate bowl for herself. But instead of evenly dividing the popcorn between us, she flopped down next to me on the couch. She'd gone from sitting on the other side of the room to sitting so close that her thigh periodically pressed against mine. The distance between us had made me uncomfortable, but her extreme and sudden proximity was similarly alarming. I tried to put a little more space between us, but the stiff armrest to my side made that nearly impossible.

Lucia grabbed the popcorn bowl and set it in her lap. She used her hand like a skill crane to collect an overly large handful of popcorn before shoving the buttery snack into her mouth. Most of the popcorn made it to her mouth, but a few scattered pieces tumbled down the front of her shirt.

Not thinking, I plucked one of the runaway pieces from her chest and popped it into my mouth.

Lucia paused her aggressive snacking long enough to stare. "There's plenty in the bowl."

I felt the slight blush of embarrassment color my cheeks. I mumbled out a weak excuse. "I didn't want the butter to stain your shirt."

"Oh. Thanks," she returned. She brushed her hands down the front of her shirt, dislodging any remaining popped kernels. "It won't be laundry day again for a while."

"Your aunt really banned you from doing laundry at home?" I mused.

Lucia nodded and grabbed another handful of popcorn. "Apparently my clothes get too dirty for her washing machine or something. So she makes me take them into town to ruin the Laundromat's machines instead."

I watched her inelegantly shovel another pile of popcorn into her mouth.

"I can't imagine why she'd ever think that," I slyly replied.

Lucia shot a quick look in my direction. "Are you teasing me, *Jefa*?"

I held up my hands and smiled. "I would never."

She licked at her lips, now covered in salt and butter from the popcorn. It made me wonder if she ate everything with such enthusiasm. I pressed my thighs together as an unexpected heat radiated from my core. I prayed that the movement went unnoticed.

Lucia started the movie, but I missed the film's title and opening credits. I'd become too distracted by the oblivious woman sitting too close to me for anything playing across the TV screen to register with me. With the pretense of needing to sit close enough so we could both reach the popcorn, Lucia's thigh remained pressed against mine. The pressure varied from a solid presence to barely there; each time she shifted on the couch, causing her leg to move slightly away from mine, I found myself missing the press of her body.

Lucia sat with one arm cradled around the oversized popcorn bowl as if holding onto a swaddled infant. She no longer shoveled handfuls of popcorn into her open mouth. She plucked individual pieces from the top of the pile. When she lifted the popcorn close enough to her mouth, her tongue popped out to receive the snack from her fingertips. Her tongue undulated, almost coaxing each popcorn piece into her mouth. From time to time she flicked the tip of her tongue against her fingertips, erasing any buttery or salty residue.

"You should really watch this part."

I blinked hard, suddenly aware of how long I'd been staring at her fingers, tongue, and mouth. I returned my attention to the television. "Am I missing out on important plot points?" I deflected. "Will I be lost later in the movie?"

"No," she countered, "but if you don't get each character's backstory, you won't care when they inevitably die."

I sat up a little straighter. "I didn't realize there were rules."

"Horror films are nothing but rules."

"I thought these movies were just blonde chicks running away from masked guys with chainsaws."

"Oh, it's a very sophisticated genre." Lucia tossed a few more popped kernels into her mouth. "This chick dies first."

"Spoilers!" I protested.

"It's not spoilers," she insisted. "The useless, sexually promiscuous girl always dies first."

"Oh, right. Your rules."

"They're not *my* rules," she rejected. "Everybody knows you don't have sex in a scary movie unless you want to die."

"Who makes these movies?" I scoffed. "The purity police?"

I blindly reached for a handful of popcorn, determined to pay more attention to the developing action on the TV rather than the curious woman who sat with her thigh pressed against mine. My fingers sifted through the buttery, popped kernels, but then bumped against a new texture, something solid and warm.

Lucia jerked her hand out of the popcorn bowl, nearly spilling its contents. "Sorry," she mumbled.

I hated this teenaged awkwardness that made us so stiff and uncomfortable around each other. If my friend Lily had been sitting next to me, she would have been draped across me without issue or apology. But Lucia and I weren't friends who had known each other since college. I didn't know what to label us. I had been emphatic with Lily about this not being a date, but sitting on this couch brought me back to my teenaged years and darkened movie theaters when I could only focus on the person seated beside me.

I tried to pay better attention to the film. The movie's central female character was searching through a bathroom medicine cabinet. When she shut the mirrored door, a second unexpected actor was standing directly behind her. My body twitched from the cliché jump scare.

I heard Lucia's quiet chuckle. "You okay over there?"

"Yes," I huffed, embarrassed by my body's involuntary reaction.

I looked down when I felt the brief touch of fingers against my lower thigh. Lucia patted the space just above my knee. It wasn't an intimate touch, but something akin to coddling a frightened child. "I can turn it to something else."

"I'm fine," I stubbornly insisted.

"Okay," she said, still sounding like a parent appeasing a child.

I didn't hyper-focus on her mildly patronizing tone, however. My attention stayed on her hand, which unexpectedly continued to linger on my knee. I breathed out through my nose when she passed the pad of her thumb across my covered kneecap.

A door slammed somewhere inside the house. Lucia flinched and jerked her hand away from my leg.

"*Lo siento!*" a female voice called out.

Lucia's features soured and she turned around on the couch. She spoke in rapid Spanish, too quickly for me to decipher even one word.

The floorboards creaked and Lucia's aunt rambled into the living room. Clara responded to Lucia's sharp tone with her own rapid-fire Spanish. Her words stopped, however, when she spotted me on the couch.

"Oh! Why didn't you tell me June was coming over?" She didn't wait for Lucia's answer. "I thought maybe you were on a date," she said with a censuring clucking noise. "Too much for me to hope, I guess."

Aunt Clara confiscated the popcorn bowl from Lucia. "Scooch over," she commanded.

It took a long moment of stunned confusion before both Lucia and I separated for opposite ends of the couch while Clara made herself comfortable in the new space between us.

Aunt Clara grabbed a handful of popcorn from the bowl. "What are we watching?"

"It's a scary movie," Lucia mumbled. "You won't like it."

"Scary?" her aunt echoed. "But you scare so easily, *mija*. Remember when you refused to sleep by yourself for weeks after you watched that movie with the clown?"

"*It*?" I took a guess.

"*Killer Klowns from Outer Space*," Lucia grumbled.

I stifled my laughter at her expense.

Aunt Clara monopolized the popcorn and peppered Lucia with more questions throughout the second half of the film. Her periodic gasps brought an amused smile to my lips and helped defuse my own fright. I had no choice but to actually pay attention to the rest of the movie. I hugged one of the couch's decorative pillows against my chest and hid my eyes whenever a particularly tense or gruesome scene played out on the television. At least with her aunt positioned between us, Lucia could no longer observe how I squirmed uncomfortably as the gory plot unfolded.

The lead female actor tiptoed through a dark and sinister-looking basement, guided only by the failing illumination of a flickering flashlight. A mass murderer, who had already mowed through all of her friends, was hiding somewhere in the house. I clutched the decorative pillow tightly, fully prepared to hide my face when the killer inevitably jumped out. But instead of the shriek of chainsaws or of young women screaming, a loud noise—a deep, rattling snore—filled up the space beside me.

My heart leapt in my throat and I swiveled my head in the direction of the sound. Aunt Clara's head had fallen forward in sleep so her chin lightly touched her chest. The popcorn bowl was empty and it tumbled harmlessly to the carpeted floor.

I heard Lucia's heavy sigh. "I guess movie night is over."

CHAPTER FOURTEEN

I woke up early the following morning without the assistance of a chirping lark or my cellphone's alarm. I hadn't exactly experienced a restful or easy night's sleep, however, as my brain continually replayed the Greatest Hits from my movie night with Lucia. Despite my best efforts, I hadn't been able to dismiss the memory of her hand ghosting over my knee just moments before her aunt had interrupted us.

Instead of tossing and turning from either denied rest or maybe even an orgasm, I got out of bed and tackled the limited contents of my refrigerator and pantry. I didn't have many hobbies, but I did love to cook. When everything else was chaos, focusing on the details of a challenging recipe or measuring out precise ingredients tended to distract me from anything that plagued my thoughts.

I spent the early hours baking miniature desserts and assembling bite-sized appetizers. The culinary distraction worked; by the time the workday rolled around, I felt like I'd achieved the mental reset I'd desired. I had no intention of eating everything I'd made, so I packed up all of the mini cheesecakes, tiny quiches, and savory puff pastry bites into plastic containers to share with my staff and vineyard guests.

No one else was in the barn yet when I arrived, so I took it upon myself to set up a small plate of snacks for Rolando, Carlos, Oscar, and Lucia to taste test while they had their morning coffee. I started up the coffeemaker and settled at the staff picnic table, eager for the first employee to arrive.

I didn't have to wait long before the main barn door slid open. Lucia strode inside, work hat in hand. Despite the hard labor required on the farm, she never looked sloppy or dirty. Her hair was tightly braided down the center of her back, the collars of her shirts were always crisply pressed. Her jeans were never stained with either wine residue, clay, or dirt. I had the strangest urge when I watched her cross the barn to join me. I wanted to hug her. I wanted to grab her hand and show her what I'd accomplished that morning.

"What's all of this?" Lucia asked, noticing the serving trays piled with miniature foods.

I stood from the picnic table and gazed fondly at my handiwork.

"Food for this afternoon's tasting," I said, feeling particularly pleased with myself. "I thought it might be nice if our customers had something to chew on besides tannins."

"You made all of this?"

"Uh huh," I confirmed. "I woke up this morning feeling particularly inspired."

Lucia didn't notice my adoring gazing. Her focus was on the food spread out on the picnic table. "This is really great, June, but we can't serve any of this."

I felt my mouth go dry. "What? Why not?"

"We don't have a food license. Someone could sue us if they got sick or, God forbid, they had an allergic reaction," she said. "I'm not saying it's not a good idea," she qualified, "but there are rules and laws about these kinds of things."

My chin began to tremble. *Why couldn't I get anything right?*

"Don't cry," Lucia nearly barked. "This isn't a mistake, okay?" she fervidly insisted. "You didn't do anything wrong. You didn't know any better."

Her elevated volume and urgency temporarily scared my tear ducts into obeying her when they'd ignored my own wishes so many times before. "I just wanted to help," I said, feeling defeated. "I just want to be useful."

"I know you do. And we'll find you something, I promise. But for the time being," she said with a small, encouraging smile, "pump the breaks on the culinary skills."

"O-okay," I conceded.

Lucia grabbed one of the mini quiches and popped it into her mouth. "It's really good," she said around her mouthful. "Maybe I'll eat them all myself."

I sniffled loudly, but didn't respond to her obvious attempt to cheer me up.

"Have you noticed the vines today?" she asked.

"No," I said dully. "Are they all dead?"

Lucia's lips quirked into an amused smile. "Come on, Little Miss Grumpy Pants."

When she took my hand in hers, I had no choice but to follow her outside.

My brain was still hyper-focused on Lucia's sturdy fingers intertwined with mine as she pulled me across the property to the nearest row of vines. Maybe she'd been experiencing some of those same strange urges as myself.

"Ta-da!" she announced, dropping my hand.

I peered at the vines, not sure what I was supposed to be seeing or noticing. "I don't see anything."

"Look closer," she urged.

I stepped a few feet closer to the vines. The sun was still low with the early morning hour. A light dew peppered the green vines, making them almost sparkle. The leaves on the vines had darkened over the past few weeks from a light yellow-green to a deeper and more robust color palate. Nestled among the dark green vines and carefully constructed leaf canopy, tight bunches of purple grapes sunned themselves in the early morning sunshine.

A quiet gasp tumbled out of my mouth. "*Veraison.*"

"Here. Come check this out," she urged.

We stepped closer until we stood in front of one of the large, reddish-purple bunches. Lucia popped a few berries from their cluster and held them in the palm of her hand as if they were precious gemstones.

"The vines have stopped growing new leaves and extending their shoots," she said. Her quiet tone drew me closer in. "Now they're devoting all their energy to ripening the grapes. It's a simple, but kind of magical thing."

She handed me one of the grapes before peeling the skin off of another to reveal its seeds and still-green interior. "Glucose and fructose are starting to get manufactured in the berry. The darker the berry, the sweeter the fruit. It's decreasing the acid and increasing the sugar. We're seeking out the sweet spot between the two before its time to harvest."

I stared down at the single berry in the palm of my hand. "So much trouble for something so simple," I mused.

I recalled one of Rolando's early speeches to me when I'd felt entirely out of my element: *It's easy to get caught up in the romance of wine making. But growing grapes and making wine is just a farm.*

Lucia had intended on distracting me from yet another of my missteps. It had been a good effort—she'd nearly succeeded—but I was still feeling morose.

+ + +

The warm, mid-summer days were getting longer, pushing sunset a few hours after the workday was over. I'd been going to bed earlier over the past few months knowing that my alarm would go off well before I'd normally be getting up if I had stayed in San Francisco. Either my body was getting used to the new schedule or the rigors of working on the vineyard were starting to lessen; regardless, when my typical bedtime rolled around later that evening, I found myself with extra energy instead of seeking the mattress of my downstairs bedroom.

Beyond the neat rows of cabernet sauvignon vines, the property transformed to gently rolling hills, long green grass, and tall gnarled oak trees—the slightly elevated vista that Belinda, the realtor, had once referred to as my million-dollar view. The sun was still at least an hour from setting, but I had no other place to be.

"You would have hated this," I spoke into the universe.

Alex had had an appreciation for beautiful things, but she'd been a city girl to her core. When she had proposed we buy a vineyard in the country, I'd honestly been shocked.

I turned when I heard someone clear their throat followed by the sound of boots crunching against gravel. Lucia, still in her work clothes from the day, stood a few yards away.

"Hey," she greeted. "Looks like you had the same idea as me."

I smiled in her direction, but I had no words for her.

She gestured to the open space beside me. "Mind if I ... ?"

"Go ahead," I allowed. "There's plenty of sunset to go around."

Lucia dropped a canvas bag onto the hard earth and sat down beside me. She didn't immediately fill the silence with forced conversation, for which I was thankful. We stared out in silence at the purple, pink, and orange sky.

I heaved a giant sigh. *What am I doing here?*

"That was a pretty big breath," Lucia observed.

"I'm sorry," I apologized in haste. "I'm probably ruining this for you."

I shifted on the ground with every intention of standing up until strong fingers around my wrist anchored me in place.

"Don't go."

I looked down at where her skin met mine. "Oh. Uh, okay."

Lucia dropped her hand and cast her eyes away, as if embarrassed by the familiar touch. "Want some wine?" she asked, still not looking in my direction.

I licked my lips. "Sure."

She leaned away momentarily and pulled a bottle of unlabeled wine out of her backpack. Moments later, she produced two red solo cups from the same bag. I watched while she removed the cork and poured a few ounces of wine into each of the cups.

"You came prepared," I observed.

Lucia focused on the equal pours. "Never know when you might need to share a bottle of wine with a pretty girl."

I didn't take her comment seriously, but I accepted one of the red party cups. "So fancy," I lightly teased.

Despite the fact that we were drinking out of plastic cups, I still dipped my nose into the glass and inhaled. The aroma was distinct and a little confusing.

"Bell pepper?"

Lucia raised an eyebrow. "Good nose."

I pressed my nose deeper into the cup. "It's ..." I took another sniff. "Spicy?"

"It's cab franc," Lucia explained. "My dad's been growing them since he and my mom moved onto the property. Cab franc is the wild child of red varietals. It's the go-to blending grape."

I couldn't get a closer look at its body or color because of the frat party vessel, but I took a good sized sip and swirled the liquid around in my mouth. "Strawberry. Plum." I spoke without much deliberation. "And a little spice."

"You're getting good at this," Lucia observed. The approval was obvious in her warm tone. "Did you know some tasters are naturally more sensitive than others?"

I shook my head.

"And women," she continued, "are over two times more likely to be hypersensitive tasters. They could have more than *thirty* tastebuds in the space no bigger than a hole-punch hole."

"So you're saying that women have better taste than men," I quipped.

She smiled and spoke into her plastic cup. "Obviously."

"Do you want to come over for dinner tonight?" I asked.

My question seemed to surprise her; to be honest, it surprised myself as well. I watched her eyebrows creep up her serious forehead while her dark eyes perceptively widened.

"It's no big deal," I said with practiced nonchalance. "I love to cook, and I haven't been able to cook for someone else since moving here," I explained. "My friends are all in the Bay Area, so I can't just invite them over without it becoming a big production. Plus, I have all of this food that's just been sitting in the refrigerator, and it'll probably go if I don't do something with it soon."

"So really I'd be doing *you* a favor," she seemed to tease.

"Exactly," I agreed. "Come eat my food."

Lucia's mouth twisted. "I don't know," she seemed to consider. "My aunt is making tortilla soup tonight, and it's one of my favorites."

My previous excitement drained from my body. "Oh, okay. Some other time then." I swallowed down the inconvenient emotions of disappointment and embarrassment as I scrambled to my feet. "I'll see you tomorrow."

I began a quick march in the direction of the farmhouse. I felt ridiculous—like I couldn't flee the scene quickly enough. I didn't know why I was so upset though. She had other plans; it wasn't the end of the world.

I heard a quiet curse word and then the sound of heavy boots striking against solid earth.

"June. Hold up."

I was too inside of my head to really register the plea for me to wait. Lucia eventually caught up with my hasty retreat.

"I'm sorry," she breathed out. "I'm so bad at this."

"This?" I questioned.

She held out her hands at her side. "I don't know—friendly banter? I got carried away. I took it too far. My aunt doesn't make tortilla soup in summer."

"So ... you *don't* have dinner plans tonight?" I carefully asked.

Lucia shook her head, making her dark braid whip around her face. "Unless you count a bowl of cereal a plan." Her smile was crooked and hopeful. "Can I still come over?"

Lucia nudged a ceramic bowl with her sock-covered toe. The container made a quiet scraping noise against the kitchen's linoleum floor. "You have a cat or something?" She looked around the otherwise empty space as if expecting a ball of energized fur to appear.

"No. It's for Gato," I said as I straightened up the kitchen area. I hadn't expected entertaining that night, but luckily I typically kept the farmhouse relatively tidy. "He comes by sometimes."

"So I'm not the only one you've lured here with the promise of food?" She smiled, showing off surprisingly deep-set dimples.

"I didn't lure you," I scoffed.

"Uh huh. I'm on to you, *Jefa*."

"Wash your hands and help me set the table," I said, quick to divert the subject.

I had no nefarious reasons for inviting Lucia over, I told myself. I was just feeding a hungry co-worker. So what if she was easy on the eyes?

I hadn't anticipated inviting anyone over for dinner that night, so I didn't have anything prepped. It was already relatively late, so I didn't want to make her wait too much longer before eating. I scanned the refrigerator's limited offerings before my thoughts harkened back to the cab franc in her canvas backpack.

"How about stuffed bell peppers and wild rice?" I proposed.

"Sounds good to me."

I visibly jerked at the sound of her voice. I hadn't noticed Lucia had crept perceptively closer.

"You're so quiet," I complained. "You're like a ninja or a cat."

She licked her lips, her tongue appearing between plush parted lips. "Do I make you nervous?"

"No," I stubbornly refused. I retrieved what food I needed before shutting the refrigerator door with my hip. "I think you try to scare me on purpose."

"You're so jumpy, June." She laughed at the alliteration. "Jumpy June. Maybe I'll call you JJ for short."

"It's better than *Jefa*," I opined.

"You don't like that?"

"I'm not ..." I waved my hands in frustration. "The boss. I haven't earned that. I still have no idea what I'm doing."

Lucia didn't defend me or double-down on my observations. Instead, she raised the non-descript wine bottle from earlier. "More wine?" she offered.

I nodded and sighed. "Please."

It didn't take much work to prepare the stuffed peppers. The rice cooked up quickly. I only had to clean out the insides of the twin-sized peppers to remove the seeds and membranes before stuffing them with black beans and wild rice.

Lucia leaned against the kitchen counter and tried to stay out of my way. She silently sipped from her wine glass while she watched me assemble dinner. "Where'd you learn to cook?" she asked.

"TV?" I shrugged. "In one of our first apartments, we didn't have money for cable, but we discovered if we plugged a co-axle into the wall we got exactly three channels: The Golf Channel, Food Network, and Bravo."

"Sounds like the queer trifecta," Lucia joked.

The stuffed peppers cooked up quickly. I charged Lucia with setting the kitchen table, and soon we were seated with full plates and wine glasses. Lucia ate the meal, nearly without breathing. She aggressively cut into the pepper, beans, and rice. I was hungry, but it was almost more fun watching her ravenous appetite.

I swirled Lucia's cab franc around in its proper glass. "This is a really good wine," I noted. "Do you sell it?"

"Nah," she said, pausing her digestive pace long enough to address me. "The family just gives it out as presents."

"That's an awfully nice present."

"It's not all about making money," she philosophized.

"Alex would have enthusiastically disagreed with you," I said. "With her it was always make money, save money, so we could retire early. Owning a vineyard was her grand retirement plan."

"She thought owning a vineyard would be easy?" Lucia almost sounded offended.

"I think she definitely underestimated all of this," I said wistfully, running my fingertips along the rim of my wine glass. "But Alex was a risktaker. She's the one who left her hometown and came to California with whatever could fit into the back of her Civic. I've never done anything remotely brave," I considered. "I went to college close to home and never really left."

"You came out here," Lucia pointed out. "You're trying something totally new. That seems pretty brave to me."

I shook my head. "What I'm doing right now isn't brave; it's a necessity. Alex sunk all of our money into this winery. It's not like I have a choice."

"You could always sell," Lucia innocently replied.

"At a loss, probably," I said with a sigh. "I don't think Alex got a very good deal. She was so gung-ho about this plan, she didn't seem to care about the price tag."

"But you wanted the land, too?"

I shrugged, noncommittally. "We fought about it. I was happy with our life in the city. I loved my job, our friends, going to Chinatown for dim sum. But it wasn't enough for her—which made me feel like I wasn't enough."

I looked down at my hands. I'd manhandled my wine glass; the formerly crystal clear bowl was smudged with my fingerprints. "This wine is like a truth serum," I said with a rueful laugh. "You should put a warning on the label."

"Do you want more?" she offered, holding up the bottle.

I nodded and lifted my glass to her. Lucia wrapped her hand around my fingers where I held onto the wine glass. The rational part of my brain decided the touch was only to stabilize my glass while she gave me a refill. But the alcohol had made the rational part of my brain lazy and inattentive. Another part of my brain—something more primal and carnal—threatened to take over.

But before I could do anything about the hand lightly touching my own, it was gone.

After the food on our plates had been eaten and the last of Lucia's family wine had been consumed, I cleared the place settings and quickly washed our dishes. Lucia offered her help, but I sent her to wait in the other room while I finished up. I selected an unopened bottle of wine and brought it to the living room for Lucia's approval. It might have been presumptuous to assume she wanted to keep hanging out, but I found myself not wanting to say goodnight just yet.

Lucia stood in front of the wood burning fireplace in the living room. She picked up the solo framed photograph that sat alone on the mantle. I hadn't bothered to set out too many personal belongings or knickknacks throughout the farmhouse with the exception of that photo.

"Alex?" she guessed.

I nodded. I wrapped my arms around my torso to keep from snatching the photo from her hands.

"She's got a nice smile," Lucia remarked. She continued to scrutinize the framed image. "I bet you guys laughed a lot."

"All the time," I confirmed. I couldn't help myself; I smiled of my own volition.

Lucia returned the photograph to its original position above the fireplace. "I don't think I'm very funny."

The comment struck me as odd. Was she comparing herself to Alex? Had this become some kind of competition that Lucia believed she was losing?

"You two are very different," I stated carefully.

"Too different?" she posed.

I paused and licked my lips. "Too different for what?"

"Would I ... would I ever be your type? If you saw me in a bar— would you ever come up to me?"

"Never."

The wounded look in her dark eyes was palpable.

I took a breath, readying myself for what I was about to admit. "I wouldn't be brave enough. I'd stare at you from the other side of the room and hope you didn't notice me pining away."

A slow smile appeared on Lucia's features. It started in the left corner of her mouth, her lips curving up just barely until the cocky grin eventually took over her features entirely.

"Hold still. You've got an eyelash."

My eyes nearly crossed watching Lucia's hand approach my face. A look of concentration crossed her features as she focused on retrieving the defiant eyelash that clung to my cheek. Her fingertips were light, but sure, as she captured the dark lash between her thumb and forefinger.

"Make a wish," she told me.

My attention drifted from her solemn face down to her offered fingers. A single black eyelash clung to the tip of her pointer finger. I leaned closer, pursed my lips, and blew. The eyelash scattered to an unknown destination.

"What'd you wish for?" Lucia's voice was quiet. If the music playing in the background had been any louder, I might have missed her question altogether.

"I'm not allowed to tell you that."

"No?"

I shook my head, just barely. "If I tell you, it won't come true. That's the rule."

Lucia didn't seem to hear me. "I know what I would have wished for."

My eyes fluttered shut when her thumb passed over my cheekbone again. I exhaled deeply, but my eyes remained closed. I wasn't brave enough to open my eyes. I wasn't prepared for the look of longing I'd see in her gaze. And even without looking in a mirror, I suspected I might find the same hunger reflected in mine.

I sensed her moving closer. My breath escaped in a short burst.

I stiffened when I felt the first, tentative brush of her lips against mine. Her mouth was warm. I could taste the sweetness of our dinner's wine on her lips. I still couldn't open my eyes, even when her hand rose to cup the side of my face.

"Is this okay?" she roughly whispered.

I nodded; I didn't trust my voice. My head bobbed in small, jerky motions.

My eyes still closed, I felt her nose slide against mine until our mouths connected again, this time with more confidence.

Lucia was kissing me. And I was kissing her back.

"I've been thinking about doing that ever since that night I found you in the hot springs," she breathed into me. "I could have watched you masturbate all night."

"Y-you knew what I was doing?" I stammered.

She nuzzled her nose against the shell of my ear. "Mmhm."

"Why did you stop me?" I thought back to how she'd announced her presence, interrupting my early solo activities.

"Maybe I wanted to help out."

"Oh God," I groaned.

"Where's your bedroom?" she asked into my mouth. I didn't think she was asking for a tour.

"Down the hall."

She took the information as an invitation. She left me, without another word or another look, and traveled down the short hallway that led from the living room to my bedroom. I stared at her retreating form until it disappeared behind my bedroom door.

I heard her voice call to me: "Are you coming, June?"

It had been a while, but maybe I would be tonight.

I slowly padded down the hallway. My feet were loud on the floorboards, but no louder than my heart inside my chest. When I entered the room, Lucia was sitting on my mattress. I hadn't bothered to make my bed that morning; I hadn't expected the dinner guest. At least all of my dirty clothes were in the hamper.

Lucia patted the empty space beside her. "Come here."

My feet were more courageous than the rest of me. I walked toward her and gingerly sat down on the mattress beside her, as if I doubted the bed could manage our combined weight.

"You have a nice bed," she complimented.

"The furniture came with the house."

"That's a nice perk," she observed.

"Uh huh." I cleared my throat to dislodge the frog that had taken up residency. "It's been a while," I warned with some hesitation.

"Since?"

"Since …" I couldn't believe she was going to make me say it.

"Are you nervous you've forgotten how to have sex?" she asked. I would have expected there to be at least a little teasing lilt to her voice, but she spoke with only genuine concern.

"Not so much forgotten," I eased into my confession, "but I've only ever had sex with one woman."

Lucia's lips parted, not quite to the point of her mouth hanging open, but almost as if the revelation had never occurred to her until then.

I twisted at my fingers. "I know what Alex liked. But what if I don't know how to make anyone else feel good?"

Again, Lucia showed no signs that she was taking this any less seriously than me. "Do you make *yourself* feel good?"

Her question was unexpected and brought a blush to my cheeks. "Oh, well, I-I manage to do *that* just fine. But that's different."

"Why?"

I found her question to be ridiculous and not a little bit frustrating. *Was she being serious?* "Y-you know why. When you-you masturbate," I couldn't help my stutter, "you can *feel* when you're doing something right."

Her eyes narrowed in contemplation. "And you can't tell on another person? You can't tell when someone's nipples are hard? You can't hear when their breath becomes more labored? You can't feel another woman's wetness?"

I didn't know quite what to say.

Lucia leaned closer. She carefully brushed my loose hair away from my shoulder. "I know I'm not a great talker, but I can be vocal for you." My eyes shut tight when her fingers tickled over the side of my neck. Her voice dropped to a murmur. "I'll let you know how you're doing."

I stood up abruptly from the mattress, my legs propelling me off the bed like a rocket ship into space. "I have to pee," I announced.

Lucia's mouth tugged up on one side. "Okay." She scooted back on the mattress until she was leaning against the headboard. She folded her arms behind her head and proceeded to get even more comfortable. "I'll just be here."

I escaped to the bathroom attached to the bedroom and rushed to shut the door behind me. I fled with alacrity, not because of an urgency in my bladder, but because of the tightness in my chest and the heaviness in my heart. I turned on the overhead light and stared at my reflection in the mirror above the bathroom sink.

Was I actually going to do this? Was I ready to move on from Alex? Was I going to have sex with Lucia?

After a long moment, I turned away from my uneasy reflection and left the bathroom. The bedroom was dark when I returned. My eyes still needed to adjust to the lack of light, but I could just make out Lucia's reclined figure on the bed. My bare feet discovered clothing on the floor that hadn't been there before. A knot formed in my throat when I realized they were the clothes Lucia had been wearing earlier. The realization nearly had me scampering back to the bathroom, but I somehow managed to take another step forward.

I opened my mouth to apologize for the brief interlude—my momentary panic attack—until I heard an unmistakable sound.

Snoring.

Lucia had fallen asleep.

I approached the bed, but kept my feet light so the noisy floorboards wouldn't disturb her. She lay on her side, beneath the comforter, with her hands folded beneath her head. I wiggled out of my jeans and let them fall to the floor. I was too old to be sleeping in the clothes I'd worn that evening, but I also couldn't risk waking Lucia up by digging around in my closet for pajamas.

I pulled the covers back, just enough so I could get into bed, but I let my eyes linger on her sleeping form. Like myself, she'd taken off most of her clothes, but her undergarments remained. I'd seen her completely naked when she'd rescued me from alcohol and the natural hot springs, but at the time I'd been gasping for cool air and willing the world to stop spinning.

Her most intimate places were covered in cotton and lace, but that didn't diminish the erotic sight. I admired her form for a long moment, taking in the slight curves of her body and silently appreciating the rise and fall of her chest. Her bra-encased breasts filled the cups of the plain cotton bra with each deep inhalation. The rhythmic inhale and exhale was mesmerizing, like the golden pendulum of a hypnotist.

Guilty that I'd stared for so long, I pulled the blankets back into place. The brass bedframe was silent when I was its only bedfellow, but it squeaked and complained when I attempted to quietly slip into bed. My body stilled and went rigid while I waited to see if Lucia would wake up. The light snoring paused, but her eyes remained shuttered.

If I had been bolder, I might have used my mouth to gently rouse her from sleep. Her physique was lean and strong, but I suspected her skin would be soft. We'd hardly been drinking, but early wake up calls on the farm paired with long, physical days resulted in early bed times. I didn't allow myself to be offended that she'd fallen asleep. Instead, I took it as a sign from the universe that I was moving too fast with this woman.

+ + +

I hadn't unpacked the moving box yet, but I knew its contents even without the permanent marker wording on the outside of the box. I retrieved a box cutter from the kitchen junk drawer and sliced through the clear packing tape that held the box's top sealed shut. I dug past the carefully wrapped knick-knacks until I found the smaller, rectangular shoebox at the bottom of the moving box. I'd wanted to throw away the shoebox and its contents long ago as if its disposal would absolve me of lingering guilt. But, masochistically, I'd kept the evidence of my shame and remorse.

I lifted my head at a quiet noise. I peered up at the wall as if expecting to be able to decipher if Lucia had woken up in the next room or if the aging farmhouse was creaking and groaning on its own. I continued to wait until I could be sure I was still the only person awake.

The shoebox itself brought on a flood of memories. Alex had been so excited about the purchase that she hadn't been able to wait until my actual birthday to gift the present to me. She hadn't even bothered to wrap it.

"Running shoes," I'd said with little emotion.

I hadn't been expecting a specific present for my birthday, but I certainly hadn't expected the gift of exercise.

"Are you calling me fat?" I'd deadpanned. I wasn't as skinny as when we'd first met, but then again—who was? People tended to put on a few pounds when they were happily coupled up.

"I don't think you're fat," she'd promised. "But I know you've been looking for something we could do together."

I'd wrinkled my nose at the suggestion. "Yeah, but I meant a ceramics class or maybe even ballroom dancing."

Alex had been disappointed I wasn't more enchanted with the idea of us going on runs together. "You hate it. I'll take them back."

I'd grabbed the damn shoebox and had clutched it close to my chest like I was protecting precious jewels. "Don't you dare."

I stared at the still closed box. We'd never gone on those runs together. Each time Alex had suggested we try to break in my new shoes, I'd come up with an excuse why it wasn't the right time. I was too tired. My feet already hurt from being in heels all day. I was on my period. I was hungover.

The latter excuse had been my mumbled response on the morning after my birthday party. Somehow alcohol never seemed to affect Alex. I'd feel nauseous the morning after while she seemed to only get brighter and more energetic.

I shut my eyes and exhaled. I should have made her stay in bed that morning. I never should have let her leave the condo.

My eyes re-opened once I'd swallowed back the twin sensations of guilt and remorse. I flipped open the shoebox and pulled out the never-been-worn running shoes from inside. They still smelled new. Alex had taken the time to lace the new shoes for me. I ran my fingertips along the cotton and nylon cords as if I might sense her within their raw materials.

I grabbed some clothes from another moving box that I hadn't yet put away. Alex used to hate when I did the laundry, but I didn't bother with the final step. I exchanged the clothes I'd slept in for a sports bra, t-shirt, socks, and yoga pants. I stepped outside, my new running shoes in one hand, and pulled them on.

I re-adjusted my ponytail as I stood in the unpaved driveway. I'd never participated in an official race, but I knew how to run—one foot in front of the other. Like walking, only faster.

My slow gait was loud and pronounced as the bottom of my shoes struck the packed earth again and again. If I had gone running with her that morning, would it have made a difference? Would the vehicle have struck us both or would the driver have noticed two runners when he or she hadn't seen Alex on her own?

It was a familiar series of questions to which I had no answers. I would never know for sure, but that didn't stop my brain from tormenting me with hypotheticals.

I spotted someone sitting on the swing on the front porch of the farmhouse. As I jogged closer, Lucia's features came into view. I hadn't intended on being away for so long, otherwise I would have left a note.

She stood from the wooden swing as I approached. She hadn't changed back into the clothes she'd been wearing the night before. Instead, she'd taken it upon herself to rummage through my wardrobe for a button-up flannel shirt and a pair of boxers I sometimes slept in. The buttons on her shirt looked to be misaligned—one of the shirttails hung lower than the other—as though she hadn't taken the time to make sure that the correct button had gone into the correct button hole. She'd released her hair from its usual braid, revealing voluminous but chaotic hair. She was rumbled, disheveled, and devastatingly beautiful.

Her dark eyes appraised me and my outfit, much like what I'd done to her. The morning temperature was cool, and I hadn't run hard enough to really work up a sweat, but my cheeks felt flushed and I was sure a slight blush probably crept along my collarbone.

"I thought maybe you were having some kind of gay panic until I remembered you'd been married to a woman before," she observed, "so I chalked it up to plain old panic instead."

"There's no panic," I denied.

She cocked her head to the side as if considering the truthfulness of my words. "Are you sure?"

"Positive."

"I, uh, I feel like I owe you an apology for what happened last night—or maybe, more appropriately, for what *didn't* happen last night."

"It's totally fine." I took her hand in mind. The warmth and strength in her fingers was undeniable.

Lucia looked down at our joined hands. I worried that maybe the gesture was too intimate, but she'd just spent the night in my bed.

"Can I make you breakfast?" she asked.

"I would love that, but I basically used all of my food on vineyard *amuse-bouches* and our dinner last night."

Her eyes narrowed slightly. "I thought you said you had a surplus that you didn't want to go bad?"

"I lied."

"How about breakfast at my place?" she posed. "It's not far."

I quirked an amused eyebrow. "You mean at your dad's house? And with your Aunt Clara hovering around us?"

Lucia grimaced. She shut her eyes and sighed. "You're not making this easy, June."

I wanted to point out that I wasn't the one who lived with her family or that I wasn't the one who'd fallen asleep the previous night, but I bit my tongue instead.

CHAPTER FIFTEEN

"Lucia?" I felt the need to whisper even though I'd been in the wine cellar many times before.

"I'm here."

The voice close to my ear caused me to jump in place. I held my hand to my chest. My heart raced beneath my palm. "Jesus," I wheezed. "You did that on purpose."

A rare smile formed on her lips. Her dark eyes seemed to dance, even under the dim lighting of the wine cellar. "Maybe."

"You run off to top the barrels a lot," I noticed. "Sure that isn't a euphemism for something else?"

Lucia didn't blink. "The barrels need to be topped off regularly. I'm not masturbating down here."

"Will you show me how?"

"How to masturbate?" she deflected.

I didn't take the bait. "Show me how to top off the barrels. I want to help."

I saw the silent struggle in her eyes. "Oh. Um."

She had been reluctant to let me in on any part of the wine-making process. The closest she'd let me to the final product was when I'd dumped wine residue on myself. We'd been busy above ground with new growth, but she hadn't shown me any of the wine-making process ever since.

We'd nearly had sex—or at least that what I assumed the previous night might have led to. We'd slept in the same bed. Could she separate her disgruntled feelings about me as the vineyard owner from whatever attraction was growing between us?

"It's not rocket science," she shrugged. "You're literally just topping off the French oak with reserve wine so the wine in the barrel doesn't oxidize too quickly."

"Can I try?"

Lucia shut her eyes. Her head tilted back and I heard her loud sigh. I would have laughed if not for my determination to learn everything about the vineyard. Lucia's chest filled with another breath that she similarly—loudly—exhaled.

"Okay."

I felt like doing some kind of victory dance, but I didn't want my antics to make her change her mind. So instead of clapping or squealing or something equally tiresome, I schooled my features to look as grim and serious as hers.

"We keep the barrels eighty percent full because fermentation creates a lot of foam," Lucia explained. "It's kind of a delicate balance. The barrels can't be too full or too empty."

"Too full and it won't make alcohol and too empty it will oxidize too quickly?" I guessed.

A ghost of a smile appeared on her features. "You've been paying attention."

I ducked my head, simultaneously proud and embarrassed by the understated compliment. "Just trying to earn my keep," I shrugged off.

"Grab yourself a wine thief," she instructed. "We keep extra wine of the same vintage in steel tanks for the purpose of topping off the barrels."

"What happens if you top off with the wrong wine?" Lucia's story about putting the wrong kind of gasoline mix into her father's tractor came to mind.

"Then you've created a blend," Lucia chuckled. "But let's try not to do that."

I retrieved a wife thief from a shelving unit nearby. The apparatus better resembled a turkey baster, but I was certain Lucia had probably heard that joke every time she gave a tour to our visitors. When I rejoined her at the sixty-gallon casks, she'd already removed the top bung from one of the oak barrels.

"Every winery loses about five to ten percent of their wine to evaporation," she told me. "The dryer the cellar, the more water and alcohol that evaporates in the barrels. That's why we try to keep the humidity at about seventy-five percent," she noted. "Have you ever noticed how moist it gets down here?"

I wrinkled my nose. "Please don't ever say that word again."

Lucia smirked. "What? You don't like it when things get *moist,* June?"

I slapped her forearm, intending to be playful. I must have struck her with a little more force than was necessary; the wine thief she'd been holding was knocked out of her hand and fell to the floor. The glass, and all of the purple liquid inside, shattered on the cellar floor.

I didn't even have time to apologize.

"It was an accident," she immediately declared. She waved her arms and hands as if guiding an airplane's landing. "Not your fault. Not anybody's fault."

I dropped to my knees to pick up the larger shards of glass. I couldn't look at her, afraid that I might start to cry. "I'm such a menace."

June bent down to help clean up my latest mess. "Hurricane June," she murmured.

"I-I'm sorry," I choked out. Emotions of embarrassment and inadequacy struggled for dominance.

"It's really okay, June," she said gently. "That's why it's called an accident." She reached her fingers out and tucked a loose lock of hair behind my ear. Her hand lingered there.

Loud, thumping bass that nearly rattled the structure broke the momentary spell. If not for the distinct low rumble, I might have thought we were experiencing a small earthquake.

"Shit." Lucia cursed beneath her breath. "I forgot she was coming today."

She hopped to her feet and wiped her hands on the front of her jeans. I expected her to offer a hand to help me up, but she turned on her heel and made a hasty exit.

I took a little longer to collect myself. I was being tugged in multiple directions. One moment Lucia was cool and detached towards me; the next, the heat in her gaze and the low burn of her voice might melt the ice caps.

Lucia had already left, so I followed the sound of the bone-rattling bass. The music became louder, but more defined when I stepped outside. I spotted Lucia's quick gait as she stormed across the property in the direction of an SUV I didn't recognize. The pace at which Lucia approached the mystery car suggested that I should do the same.

The black SUV gleamed beneath the high afternoon sun. Chrome accents lined each window, door handle, and the double exhaust spoilers. The windows were heavily tinted, hiding the driver and whomever or whatever else might have been inside of the car. The tires looked almost too large for the luxury vehicle with equally impressive rims. The SUV looked like it could have easily crush my more modest electric car.

I remained close to the barn's entrance. As I stood and stared, Natalie appeared at my side.

"Who is that?" I asked.

"Marisol. She helps with the birds."

"Birds?" I echoed.

Natalie nodded in the direction of the SUV, which no longer played its loud music. "Go see for yourself."

With only slight trepidation, I left the security of the barn's familiar shadow. I crossed the vacant parking lot and joined Lucia by the SUV. A woman whom I didn't recognize began pulling gear out of the back of the crossover vehicle. She didn't address either Lucia or myself. She seemed to be familiar with the property or like she belonged there.

She was a tall woman, slender, and long limbed. Her hair was dark with auburn-colored lowlights. Her skin was tan. She wore dark skinny jeans, ankle boots, and a long jacket that looked far too heavy for the afternoon heat. When she shut the back hatch of her vehicle, she turned on her heel and flashed a brilliant smile in our direction. Dark eyes flashed behind thick eyelashes.

"Miss me?"

Lucia folded her arms across her chest, and I felt compelled to do the same. Her body language indicated this woman wasn't a friend, so I remained suspicious as well.

"You're a little late this year," Lucia coolly remarked.

"I'm not in charge of *veraison*," the woman shrugged. "You know I only go where the berries are sweet."

The woman's gaze traveled from Lucia's sour exterior to my confused visage. "Who's the *gringo*?" she asked.

"I'm June," I introduced. I raised my hand awkwardly. "June St. Clare."

The woman—Marisol—seemed to smirk. "Nice to meet you, June St. Clare. Are you a new farmhand? Maybe the new accountant?"

I looked down at my outfit—work boots, jeans, and a denim shirt. *Did I look like an accountant?*

"June's the new owner," Lucia supplied.

The teasing, amused look on the other woman's features seemed to brighten with new interest. "Owner?" she echoed. "I thought maybe you were a college intern."

My mouth twitched. People were often surprised when I told them my age, but I hadn't been mistaken for a college student in over a decade.

The woman dismissed us and left the back of the SUV for the rear passenger-side door. An involuntary noise of surprise bubbled up my throat when she opened the back door.

"Is that an eagle?" I gaped. A massive bird that looked like it was wearing a hood over its head was perched on a horizontal bar in the back of her car.

"Falcon," Marisol corrected.

She reached inside the SUV and gingerly transferred the giant bird from its perch to her outstretched forearm. When I saw the bird's seriously thick talons, her heavy jacket suddenly made sense. She gently removed the little leather hood that had obscured the bird's vision.

Marisol took a few steps closer to the rows of vines with their heavy bunches of purple-red grapes. She bent at the knee and seemed to fling the bird into the air. The falcon spread its massive wings and launched high into the cloudless, blue sky.

"Woah," I admired.

"I'm going back inside," Lucia announced. She looked to me. "Are you coming? We still have casks to top off."

I watched the large black and white bird slice through the sky. "I-I kind of want to see this," I spoke aloud. I looked next to Marisol. "Is that okay?"

Marisol grinned her careful Cheshire smile. "I don't mind an audience."

I heard Lucia's disgruntled noise. "Suit yourself."

A guilty, conflicted feeling twisted in my stomach as I watched Lucia stomp away.

"Don't worry about her," Marisol spoke. She seemed to read my mind. "I'm sure she can manage on her own."

I returned my attention to the large bird, swooping and gliding just above the vineyard. "So what exactly is happening?" I finally had the opportunity to ask. "This is all new to me," I explained.

"Malachi is scaring away your pests," she told me. "After *veraison*, when the berries mature and sweeten, the birds want to feast. Some vineyards set out poison traps, but Malachi is a natural deterrent that protects everyone involved."

I suppressed a shudder. "He eats the smaller birds?"

"No," Marisol chuckled fondly. "I keep him well fed. He's too full to bother with one of your larks. Think of it like a shark at the aquarium not being interested in any of the other fish in its tank."

"The other birds are really scared of him?"

"Uh huh," she confirmed. "In a few weeks, I won't even need to bring Malachi along. The birds will get used to the sound of my truck. I'll only need to drive by and the birds will rise up and fly away."

Malachi continued to circle overhead. "How do you get him back?"

Another megawatt smile appeared on Marisol's pretty face. "Want to help me?"

I had no idea what that might involve, but I still nodded.

Marisol returned to the back of her SUV. She bent over and reached far inside, offering me an unobstructed view of her own rear. I quickly looked away when she stood and straightened.

Marisol stepped closer and handed me a thick leather glove. "Put this on, cutie."

I stuck my right hand and arm into the heavy glove. The material was stiff and immovable and reached past my elbow.

"Stick out your arm, palm turned to the sky."

I realized what she wanted me to do. "Oh, I-I don't think I can," I stumbled.

Marisol stood behind me and set her hands on my shoulders. Her proximity was nearly as startling as the expectation that I was supposed to let Malachi land on my arm. "If you're scared," she said, her voice smoky and dangerously close, "close your eyes. I'll take care of the rest."

I shut my eyes, but the rest of my body remained rigid. I felt her tug on the arm with the leather glove until it was positioned where she wanted me.

I flinched when the air moved around me. Wisps of my hair lifted and brushed against my cheeks. I experienced a slight pinch and a heavy weight on my raised arm as Malachi landed.

I breathed through my open mouth. "Wow."

"Nice job, June." I opened my eyes at the sound of Marisol's praise. Malachi fluffed the feathers on his wings from his new perch on my arm. I kept my arm stiff and raised.

Across the parking lot, Lucia had reappeared. I wondered if she'd finished topping off the barrels without me. I was too far away to really see the details of her facial features, but her body language remained angry and closed off.

Marisol's voice broke through my mental musings. "How about a drink?" She flashed me a brilliant smile. "Your treat."

"Making friends with the Bird Lady, I see," Natalie remarked when I walked inside the barn.

"Yeah," I said, not really listening. "Have you seen Lucia?" My eyes swept around the barn's empty interior.

"She's sulking in the cellar," came Natalie's reply.

"Sulking? About what?" The word wasn't necessarily unexpected, but I was surprised Natalie had used it to describe Lucia.

"You'll have to ask her that yourself."

I returned outside with two glasses of cabernet, one in either hand, to where Marisol had set up camp at one of the patio tables. Malachi's hood had been returned to his head. He silently perched on the back of one of the patio chairs.

Marisol had removed her long heavy jacket to reveal a low-cut tank top underneath. Her jacket was draped over the back of a chair. She sat with her back leaning against the patio table and with her long legs stretched out in front of her. Her head was tilted up and she squinted into the sun. Unlike Lucia who religiously shielded her skin from direct sunlight with extra layers of clothes, Marisol seemed to revel in the heat against her exposed flesh.

I set the wine glasses on the patio table. "What does that little hat do?" I asked, gesturing to the hooded bird.

"Falcons have exceptional eyesight," she said. "His hood keeps him focused and calm when he's not working."

I eyeballed the bird, uneasy by its relative proximity. My brain reminded me it was a serious predator, but for now it appeared sedate beside its handler.

I sat down in an empty chair, careful to position Marisol between myself and Malachi. "How does a person get into falconry?" I wondered.

Marisol claimed one of the two wine glasses for herself. "I'm from a long family of falconers," she described. "Even Malachi's blood line has been with my family for generations."

She took her first sip of wine and smacked her lips in appreciation. "It's amazing that such a miserable person can make such exciting wines."

Her word choice had me recoiling. "Lucia isn't miserable."

"No?" she considered. "I suppose I don't know her like you do, but she's always in a bad mood when I'm around."

I twisted my wine stem and kept my private thoughts to myself. Marisol could probably tell that Lucia wasn't her number one fan; I didn't need to vocalize that obvious fact.

CHAPTER SIXTEEN

It was a warm July night when Lucia followed up on her promise to set up a vertical tasting for me. The windows and doors to the tasting barn had been left open, allowing a light breeze to ruffle at anything that wasn't tied down. A checkered tablecloth had been draped over the table where Rolando and the others drank their morning coffee. Eight wine glasses—two rows of four—were lined up on the staff picnic table. Each was filled with a few ounces of red wine. Two glasses of water and a small silver bucket joined the wine glasses on the table.

The rest of the open space was remarkably clean. The table that typically hosted the modest coffee bar had been stashed out of sight, and any tools that typically cluttered the production section of the barn had similarly been put away. It wasn't an over-the-top transformation, but it was obvious that Lucia had put in some effort to get ready for the night. It made me feel better about my decision to clean up after work and trade my t-shirt and jeans for a sundress and light denim jacket.

I hovered by the picnic table and touched my fingers to the table cloth. "This looks nice," I observed.

I wanted to tell her that she looked nice, too, but the compliment got stuck in my throat. Her dark, glossy hair was pulled back in its usual braid, but her skinny jeans, ankle boots, and slim-fit flannel shirt were about as feminine of an outfit as I'd seen her in.

She shrugged off my approval. "I wanted to be sure we did your first vertical tasting the right way."

"How does a vertical tasting differ from a typical tasting?" I asked.

"You're technically trying the same kind of wine over and over again in a vertical tasting," she described, "but they're from different vintages."

"Different harvest years," I recalled.

"Uh huh," she confirmed. She gestured to the glassware on the table. "These are all cabernets grown right on the property. The goal is to get a sense of how one vintage differs from another."

"Is there going to be a test at the end?" I asked, only partially joking.

"No written exam, but there may be some oral."

It was a good thing we hadn't started drinking yet, or I would have spit out my wine.

"I can't believe you just said that," I choked out.

Lucia looked pleased with herself and my flabbergasted reaction. "It was too good to pass up."

"After you give the vertical tasting," I posed, "do you offer a *horizontal* tasting?"

"Wow." Lucia blinked and looked a little impressed. "Did you just think of that?"

I shrugged. "I'm kind of mad at myself for not coming up with it earlier, but *anyway*," I deflected, raising my voice, "where do we start?"

All of this talk about 'tasting' and 'oral exams' threatened to bring a blush to my cheeks, but Lucia looked perfectly comfortable throwing the words around.

"We'll go youngest to oldest."

"Are the oldest the best?" I asked.

Lucia shook her head. "Not necessarily. It really all comes down to vintage. Some years are just better than others."

"Why?"

"Different growing seasons," she answered. "Sometimes the weather is too rainy and the grapes don't get the opportunity to let their sugars develop in the sun. Sometimes bud break is delayed by a few weeks or a summer is too hot and the growing season isn't long enough for a high grape yield. It's really just like growing any other crop."

"Except this crop can make you drunk," I quipped.

Lucia offered me a half smile. "But not tonight. We're tasting, not doing keg stands."

I stuck out my lower lip in a slight pout. "Okay, *profesora*." I settled down at the picnic table in front of the two neat rows of wine glasses. "Teach me about wine."

"Okay," she began, touching the base of the glass closest to her, "this first cab isn't ready to be bottled yet. The grapes are from last year's harvest, so it's still figuring out who it wants to be."

"But we can drink it?" I asked.

Lucia nodded. "It's drinkable, but it's very dry and bitter."

I gave the first glass a quick sniff and then took a small sip. "Oh wow," I said, smacking my lips. Even just a small amount of the liquid had produced a dry, almost gritty sensation in my mouth. "I thought it would be more like grape juice, but that's almost like cranberry?"

"It's from the tannins," Lucia noted. "It's naturally occurring in the seeds and skins and wooden barrels. They stabilize the wine and buffer it against oxidation, but it makes your lips stick to your teeth. Wines have highest tannin when they're young."

She picked up the second wine glass from the line. "Young cabs are good—more fruit forward with herbaceous flavors." She took a quick sniff inside her glass. "But most cabs should be left to age at least three years."

"That's a big time commitment," I observed. "Harvesting all of those grapes, but not being able to share the resulting product until much later? It's almost the antithesis of modern life."

Lucia swirled around the liquid in her glass and looked thoughtfully at the centrifugal motion. "The average person doesn't appreciate the labor and love that goes into a bottle of wine. But once you taste a well-aged cab, you'll never be the same. The flavors soften; they become more silky, more elegant." Her eyes swept from the wine glass to me. "Just like a woman."

With anyone else, I would have rolled my eyes at the obvious line. But Lucia wasn't usually a tease or a flirt, especially when it came to the business of wine. If anything, it was her intensity and passion for the industry that made my knees buckle.

"You don't need a big nose or a special number of tastebuds to appreciate good wine," Lucia continued before I could really linger on her words. "All you need is a four-step tasting method. Look. Smell. Taste. Think," she recited.

She held the glass up to the overhead lights. "You're looking for three things here: hue, intensity of color, and viscosity."

"Those are three different things?" I posed, only half kidding.

"Hold your glass by the stem," she instructed. "You don't want fingerprints on the bowl of glassware. Plus, the heat from your hands can warm up the wine."

I followed her lead and picked up the next glass in my row. I was careful to only hold the glass by its skinny stem to avoid clouding up the rest of the glassware with my fingerprints.

She tipped the wine glass to one side, but not enough to spill any liquid. "Look towards the edge of the wine to see the hue. Look towards to center to see how opaque the color is. A red-colored tint indicates higher acidity; more purple or blue means lower acidity. A deeply colored, opaque red wine is typically youthful with higher tannin. Red wines tend to become more pale and tawny as they age."

"Just like a woman," I couldn't help joking.

Lucia shared a quick smile with me, but returned to the task at hand. "Viscosity is related to a wine's sugar and alcohol content. The higher the viscosity, the higher the sugar and alcohol."

"And you can tell that just by looking at the wine?" I wondered.

Lucia nodded. "This is why you see people swirling their wine—well, the ones who actually know what they're doing," she qualified. She swirled the wine, almost violently, while holding onto the base of the glass. "These streaks," she said, pointing to the lines of wine that clung to the inside of the glass, "are called legs or tears. It's caused by fluid surface tension created by evaporating alcohol. Typically, the longer the legs, the higher the alcohol content."

"I'm fresh out of jokes about leggy women," I quipped, "but give me enough time, and I'm sure I'll come up with something."

Lucia smiled mildly. It was clear it was going to take more than a weak comedic routine to distract her from this tasting.

"You're going to smell the wine next," she told me. "The goal here is to create a profile of aromas before tasting it—maybe two or three fruit or herbal flavors, plus any oak or earth flavors."

I picked up the second glass of wine in my row. "So I just smell it and tell you what it reminds me of?"

"Hold the glass under your nose and take a small sniff to prime your senses," she instructed. "Then, swirl your wine and take slow, delicate whiffs. The top rim of the glass will be floral; the lower rim has richer aromas."

I dipped my nose in the bell of the glass and took an experimental sniff. "I'm not sure," I admitted. I worried that the right answer was obvious and I would get it wrong.

"Pick a fruit aroma, and then pick an adjective," she suggested. "Like, strawberry," she offered as an example. "Fresh, ripe, stewed, or dried."

I returned my nose to the glass, acutely aware of Lucia's eyes on me. I wanted to do a good job. I wanted to impress her—to prove I wasn't a lost cause. I closed my eyes and focused. The aroma of the wine was sweet, almost like ice cream.

I opened my eyes. "Black cherry?" I guessed. "Is that a thing?"

Lucia's smile was small, but obviously pleased. "Maybe."

I stuck my nose a little deeper into the glass. "Black cherry," I said again, this time with more conviction. "Ripe. But there's also something earthy." I searched for the right description. "Like rocks. Minerals."

Her silent smile broadened, and I felt encouraged. "You can drink now," she allowed.

I felt some of the tension leave my body as if I'd earned a passing grade on an important exam. "You and Natalie sure make me work for my wine," I wryly observed.

"Anything worth having should take effort," Lucia countered. "You wouldn't enjoy it as much otherwise."

I chewed on my lip as I considered the truth to her words. Over the past few months, she had certainly made me work for every smile, every word of praise.

Lucia held her second glass by its stem. "Okay, I want you to take a sizeable sip and pass the wine all over your palate. But don't swallow until I tell you to."

I took a medium-sized sip. I swirled the wine around in my mouth, not quite like mouthwash, but definitely different than how I typically drank any other liquid.

My eyes followed Lucia's form as she came to sit beside me on the picnic bench.

"Chew it," she directed. She leaned a little closer. "Allow it to touch every nook and cranny inside of your mouth."

I did as she told me. My eyes didn't leave her face. She inspected my reaction to the wine with a barely contained intensity that normally would have made me self-conscious. I watched her lick her lips.

"Now swallow."

I obediently gulped down the liquid.

Lucia shifted on the bench and seemed to sit even closer with the movement. Her voice took on a lower, almost melodic, tone. "Take a slow breath through your mouth and exhale through your nose."

I would have cracked a joke about her being a good yoga instructor, but I was afraid to interrupt the moment with a comedic defense mechanism. Instead, I asked the question nibbling at my brain.

"How many women have you given a private tasting to?"

Lucia pulled back and sat a little straighter. "That's-that's ... what do you mean?" she dodged.

I stared pointedly at her, waiting for an answer.

She turned her face away and sighed. Even her breath sounded annoyed. "Just you."

I arched an eyebrow, not really believing her words.

"This might surprise you, but I don't like many people."

"Really? You?" I said in mock surprise.

"I'm not—I don't know," she huffed. "... friendly? I get impatient and irritated too easily." She fiddled with the stem of one of the wine glasses. "No one has stuck around long enough for me to teach them about wine."

Her vulnerability was unexpected. A flood of complicated emotions washed over me. I tucked my lower lip into my mouth to steady myself. "Thank you."

Lucia looked up at my words. "For what?"

"For putting up with me long enough that we could do this."

My gratitude made her look awkward and nearly embarrassed. She rubbed at the back of her neck. "Sure thing. No problem."

"This wine is good," I observed. "The tannins aren't as intense as the first one." I could have lingered in her discomfort, but I returned our conversation to the wine tasting.

Lucia continued to look grim despite the topical reprieve. "Napa's volcanic soils give the wine a distinctly dusty and mineral character. Wines from the valley floor, like ours, tend to offer more black cherry and lush tannins. Hillside wines produce more acidity, blackberry notes, and rustic tannins."

She recited the details as if giving me a vineyard tour.

The mood in the barn had shifted. The tasting seemed secondary to whatever was currently transgressing.

I fiddled with the stem of my wine glass. I focused on my fidgety fingers. "You must have been really mad about the Mitchells selling this place to have come back early."

"I was pissed," she admitted. She stared straight ahead instead of in my direction. "I thought they'd at least offer my dad the opportunity to make an offer. He deserves it after all the blood, sweat, and tears he's put into this property."

"And instead they sold to two women who couldn't tell a pinot noir from a pinot grigio," I solemnly observed. The corner of my mouth twitched. "Are you still mad?"

"Not at you, no."

"No?" My voice lilted on the question.

Lucia pressed her lips together. "It's getting late. I should probably clean this up."

I blinked, feeling a little blindsided by the abrupt dismissal. "Oh, okay. Do you need any help?"

Lucia stood from the table. "No, I've got it."

I slowly came to my feet and lingered in the space. Lucia was busy clearing glassware from the table. She didn't look in my direction.

I wrung my hands in front of me and twisted my fingers. "Thank you for tonight."

Lucia still refused to look at me. "Sure thing, *Jefa*."

I took my time walking back to the farmhouse. The night sky was clear and dotted with thousands of twinkling stars. I shoved my hands into the pockets of my denim jacket and slowly strolled away from the barn, one foot in front of the other. The evening had left me more puzzled than before. Even though Lucia had shown flashes of flirtatiousness, she'd been mostly serious during the tasting, as if I was an employee that needed training. I *did* need more wine education, but when Lucia had suggested the vertical tasting, I hadn't expected it to better resemble a work seminar.

After the evening-that-almost-was, my anxiety around Lucia had only elevated. If she hadn't passed out in my bed, we would have had sex. But instead of that information putting me more at ease or making me feel comfortable around her, I felt more awkward than ever. There was something between us—unfinished business—but I didn't know how, or even if, I should bring it up. Could I ask for a do-over? A second dinner and sleepover? Or had the moment passed and I would be forced to endure this uncomfortable tension between us for the rest of my life?

She'd been vulnerable, however, about her limited dating experiences and even how her attitude toward me as the vineyard owner was starting to change. But that alone didn't reveal much about how she felt about me in general. Every time I tried to approach the topic, she seemed to shut down and shut me out.

I worried my lower lip as I considered our situation. With the exception of an isolated evening when we'd kissed and had slept in the same bed, nothing similarly intimate had occurred. In fact, the more time that passed, we seemed to be returning to a relationship of employer and employee. I wanted access to her thoughts and emotions, but despite my best efforts, Lucia Santiago remained an enigma.

CHAPTER SEVENTEEN

I heard a quiet knock on the open office door. I didn't spend too much time in the connected office during the workday, but since it was still the only place on the property connected to the internet, sometimes I had no choice. Updates to our social media accounts, updating our website, and responding to requests for private tours and tastings kept me busy when I wasn't needed out in the grapevines.

"Give me a second," I said, not looking away from the computer monitor, "I just have to finish this email."

Between concentrating on spelling and grammar and the sound of my fingertips striking against the old keyboard, I barely registered the sound of the office door closing.

"Did I blow it?"

I looked away from the computer screen and my unsent email. I looked up at Lucia over my blue light glasses. I had perfect 20/20 vision, but Alex had insisted I get a pair since I spent so much time on a computer for work.

"Huh?"

She hollowed out her cheeks. The action made her look more grim than usual. "I didn't mean to pass out the other night."

I pulled off my glasses and set them on the desk. "Oh! I-I know that. It's okay. I know you work hard and have long days."

My ego had been bruised after the Night that Almost Happened, but when Lucia had resumed being all business around me, any flirtations gone, I'd decide it was probably for the best. Office romances were never a good idea, and I probably needed more time to grieve the loss of Alex despite Lily's insistence otherwise.

"But did I blow it?" she asked again.

I dug my teeth into my lower lip and leaned forward in the office chair. "I'm not sure what you mean."

Lucia dropped her eyes to the floor. Her hands—dusty with gold ridge sandy loam—worked against the fabric of her wide-brimmed hat. She looked like she'd come straight from the fields. Sweat had darkened the denim of her button-up shirt beneath the armpits.

"Can I take you out for dinner tonight?"

I sat back in the chair like her question had knocked me back. This was it. This was a decision that was all mine. Did I want this? Did I want to see if this relationship had potential?

"Will you wear your hair down?" I asked. With the exception of the Morning that was Almost After, I'd only ever seen her hair back in her ritual braid.

Her nose crinkled adorably. "It gets in the way," she protested.

"For me?"

Lucia sighed, but eventually relented. "Okay. For you."

+ + +

My palms had grown clammy by the time I heard the knock on the farmhouse front door. I hopped up from the couch and practically yanked the door from its hinges in my excitement to greet the woman on the other side. Dueling emotions of anxiety and eagerness had shared time ever since Lucia had asked me out. I'd rushed home at the end of the workday in preparation for the date.

Date. The word itself made my stomach flip over. God—I hadn't been on an actual date in close to twenty years. I suspected Lucia was no lothario herself, so I didn't really worry that she had much more experience at these kinds of things, but I suspected she had at least been on a few more first dates than me.

Lucia's mouth took the shape of a crooked smile when I opened the front door. She stood a few steps back on the porch, clutching a fistful of trimmed sunflowers. She took another step back so I could open the screen door.

Gone was the chambray or flannel button-up shirts I'd become so accustomed to seeing her in. Her shirt still buttoned up the front, but it was a more professional style than what she typically wore on the farm. The evening was too warm for a jacket, but she wore a navy blue tailored vest over the crisp, Oxford-style shirt. A thick leather belt held colored jeans aloft her hips and tan leather shoes had been polished until they gleamed. Her hair was still damp from a post-work shower, but as promised, she'd forgone her usual braid. Her hair fell in dark, straight layers, cascading past her shoulders to the middle of her back.

"Hi," I greeted. My voice was like a squeak.

"Hi," she returned. Her own voice sounded higher and tighter than usual. Her palpable nervousness put me more at ease.

I pointed to the rustic bouquet. "Are those for me?"

She nodded and thrust her outstretched arm in my direction.

I accepted the flowers and reflexively pressed their petals to my nose. "They're so fresh," I admired.

"I just cut them from my dad's garden," she admitted.

I lowered the flowers a few inches from my nose. "You *stole* them from Rolando?"

"I *borrowed* them," she corrected me. "We can plant the seeds later to give them back."

I quirked an eyebrow, but said no more on it. "Let me put these in water and then we can go."

Lucia bobbed her head and took another step backwards on the porch. Any additional steps would have her falling off the edge.

My eyebrow remained elevated. "Don't run off, okay?"

Lucia's shoulders seemed to swallow up her neck like a turtle retreating into its shell. "Okay."

I let the screen door shut behind me, but I kept the main door open. I didn't know if I expected to hear Lucia's quick footsteps or the sound of rubber tires kicking up graveling, but I felt better about keeping the door open while I fetched a suitable vase and filled it with water.

I set the vase of sunflowers on the coffee table in the living room. I would have to trim the stems down so the long green stalks didn't dominate the vase, but that was a task for later. If I took too much time inside, I worried that Lucia might lose her nerve and run off.

I grabbed my purse and checked my reflection a final time in the oval mirror hanging by the front door. I tucked a particularly stubborn curl behind my ear, and with a satisfied nod at my reflection, I hustled out the front door.

I locked the farmhouse's front door and slung the strap of my purse over my shoulder. "Do you want me to drive?"

Lucia had retreated even farther back from where I'd left her. "No offense, but hell no," came her reply.

My voice lifted. "Don't you trust my driving?"

Lucia's features remained serious. "I trust you, sure, but not that toy car of yours."

"It's not—." I let my protest die on my lips. There was no reason to let lithium batteries or fossil fuels rule the night.

"Not worried about your truck getting dirty?" I teased instead.

Lucia didn't take the bait. "I'll wash it here afterwards and jack up your water bill."

Her dress shoes kicked up dust as she jogged to the passenger side of her green truck, which she'd parked not far from my own car. She opened the passenger side door and gestured with her free hand for me to climb in.

I wasn't into cars, but even I could admit that Lucia's truck was remarkable. The interior of the vehicle was just as meticulously cared for by its owner as its exterior. Reflecting its antique age, a single leather bench served as seating instead of the two captain's chairs and middle console like modern trucks. The dashboard was the same off-white leather as the bench seating, which matched the leather that wrapped around the steering wheel as well. The radio was old—no auxiliary ports, CD players, or even a tape deck—just two knobs, one for volume and the other for scanning the local FM channels.

Lucia shut the door behind me and jogged around the front of the vehicle. She opened the driver's side door and quietly grunted as she climbed behind the steering wheel. With a turn of her keys in the ignition, the engine rumbled to life. The radio's volume rivaled that of the loud engine. Lucia winced and quickly turned the volume down low.

"Sorry," she mumbled the apology.

She drove the truck slowly, barely giving it any gas as the wheels began to roll over loose gravel. She only picked up speed when we reached the paved portion of the vineyard's long driveway. It was obvious that this was her baby; she was particular about its care. I probably should have felt honored she'd let me sit in the passenger seat without taking off my shoes first.

"So what's the story with the truck?" I wanted to know.

"There's no story." Her hands ran along the leather steering wheel as she turned the truck onto the county highway that ran adjacent to the vineyard.

"I don't believe you," I rejected. "No one drives a truck like this by accident."

"It was my dad's originally. He took really good care of it, and now I take really good care of it."

Her answer was simple, but sufficient. I ran my hand across the soft leather of the bench seating. "It's beautiful," I admired.

"I know. It's a real chick magnet," she returned.

I regarded Lucia in profile to determine her level of seriousness. Sometimes she was so abrupt and awkward that I doubted she'd ever made a move on a girl before. I could see her trying to be funny or ironic with the flippant statement and failing at both. But other times the things she did and said made my heart race.

We didn't speak much on the drive into Calistoga, but I was content to listen to the quiet murmur of the radio and the steady purr of the antique truck's engine. Downtown traffic was light and Lucia easily found a diagonal parking spot on the main street.

"Just a second," she told me as she turned off the truck and unbuckled her seatbelt.

I unfastened my seatbelt, but waited patiently while Lucia once again hustled around the front of her truck. She opened the passenger side door and held out a hand to help me get out of the truck. I allowed her to assist me, even though the truck didn't sit very high.

I held her fingers lightly as I stepped down to the pavement. "Is this so I don't scuff up your running boards or smudge the door handle?" I teased.

Her fingers tightened around my own. My breath caught in my throat when she tugged me a little closer. I could smell the clean scent of her soap and the earthy fragrance of her shampoo and conditioner. "No. It's so you know this is a date."

Lucia had been in charge of picking out the restaurant for our first date. It was a small Italian place, off the beaten path, that I probably would have repeatedly overlooked due to there being few internet reviews. It was obvious the location was more popular with locals instead of being a tourist destination. As the hostess led us to our small table in the dimly-lit restaurant, a number of the other seated patrons exchanged greetings with Lucia. It was like she was a local celebrity, and I found myself endeared by the interruptions rather than be annoyed. I also couldn't ignore how good her hand felt in the small of my back as she guided me through the intimately organized tables and chairs.

"You've been here before?" I asked the obvious question as we looked over menus at our table for two. I really wanted to ask if she'd brought previous dates to our restaurant, but I checked my curiosity and insecurities for the moment.

She made an affirmative sound as she glanced over the restaurant's offerings. "I love this place," she revealed. "It's almost as good as my Aunt Clara's cooking."

"Do you cook?" I asked.

Lucia shook her head. "When I'm home, Clara won't let me near her kitchen. It's kind of like the laundry thing," she explained with a grin. "When I'm working at a vineyard in another country, it's very communal. People pool their resources and we tend to have big family-style meals every night."

"That sounds really charming," I approved. "Almost idyllic."

She nodded in agreement. "My dad keeps telling me I need to settle down and establish roots, but I don't know …" she trailed off. "I love the travel and the experiences. I learn something new or think about wine in a different way with each new winery."

A waitress in a white dress shirt and black tie stopped at our table. "Something to drink, ladies?"

I plastered a fake smile to my lips as Lucia ordered a bottle of wine for the table. I hated the interruption; I wanted to hear more about what she did during the off-season. I was genuinely interested in the work she did at other vineyards, but I also wondered what her constant traveling might mean for us—not that there was even an *us* to consider yet. I knew I was getting ahead of myself, but I couldn't let myself fall for a woman who was only available part-time.

"I just want to learn more, you know?" Lucia continued after our server's departure. "I think we can always learn more. The moment you think you've got it all figured out is probably the moment you should retire."

"If that's true, I'll be toiling away at Lark Estates until I die," I mused.

"Don't put yourself down. You've come a long way in a very short amount of time."

My eyes fell to the tablecloth, embarrassed by her kind words. "Thank you," I murmured.

Our waitress returned to our table with our bottle of merlot. She uncorked the bottle in front of us and poured a small taste in the wine glass closest to Lucia.

Instead of trying the wine herself, Lucia slid the glass across the table. "Here," she told me.

My features pinched. "You know I'm no expert," I resisted. The responsibility of approving our dinner wine felt too important, too out of my league.

Lucia smiled encouragingly. "You're not tasting to see if you like it," she assured. "You're only checking to make sure the bottle didn't go bad—that it's not corked."

My body somewhat relaxed. "Oh. I can handle that."

I swirled the base of the wine glass to let it breathe before taking a quick sniff inside of the glass's wide bell. "Plum. Vanilla," I said without thinking.

"Fuck, that's hot," I heard Lucia's murmur.

I glanced up quickly at our server, who continued to stare straight ahead like a stiff soldier awaiting her next command. Either she hadn't heard Lucia's words or she had a masterful poker face.

I took a small sip from my glass and let the lush liquid pass over my tastebuds. I offered another smile to the waitress, nearly desperate for her to leave. "It's good, thank you."

The woman bobbed her head and finished filling both of our glasses. "Do you need another minute with the menu?" she asked, straightening her back.

Lucia looked to me. "Are you okay if I order for us both?"

I surprised myself when I deferred to her. I had never liked it when Alex had ordered for me, but between Lucia's familiarity with the restaurant and how chivalrous she'd been the entire evening, I found myself nodding my assent.

"Ahi tuna arrabbiata to start," Lucia requested. "Then we'll do the pappardelle allo zafferano and wild mushroom ravioli to share."

"Sounds good," our waitress approved. She glanced once in my direction as if to confirm I was okay with the order as well. I nodded again, feeling a little like a bobblehead doll with how agreeable I'd been all night.

"Are you sure that was okay?" Lucia asked when the waitress had finally left our table. "I know you're a grown woman who can make decisions for herself."

She bit down on her lower lip and looked uncertain, but hopeful. My eyes trained on her teeth and mouth. Fuck, I wanted to kiss her. I wanted to grab her by the front of her dress shirt and kiss her across the table. I was rapidly unraveling after nearly four months of foreplay.

"It all sounds wonderful," I approved.

I heard Lucia release a shaky breath.

"Are you okay?" I asked.

She raked her fingers through her long, loose hair, free from the confines of its usual braid, by my request. "I'm fucking nervous, June," she admitted.

I reached across the table and set my hand on top of hers. I curled my fingers around her fidgeting hand and stilled its movement. "I'm terrified."

Lucia quietly chuckled. "Always have to one-up me, huh?" she joked. She stroked the pad of her thumb over the top of my hand.

The arrival of a table runner and our appetizer forced our hands apart. I began to loathe the forced distance that even our intimate table required, but I knew the importance of these rituals. First dates. Candlelit dinners. Getting-to-know-you conversations. If Lucia wanted to woo and romance me, I could be patient.

Lucia served up a few thin slices of quick-seared ahi tuna onto my appetizer plate. "You're going to love this," she anticipated. "It might be the best thing on the menu."

"Fish and merlot?" I questioned. "Aren't we breaking a rule?"

Lucia offered me a mischievous smile. "I won't tell if you don't."

I cut delicately into the tender, fall apart fish. "Tell me something true," I implored. "Tell me something no one would guess about you."

"I can burp on command?" she tried.

I frowned. "Something real, Lucia."

She took a breath. "My dad didn't want me to get into wine. He wanted me to study something more practical—like business—but in the end I convinced him that it was my life."

Her disclosure caused me to lean forward in my chair. "Why do you think he wanted you to do something else? You're obviously really good at it. And probably more passionate about your industry than anyone I've met."

The compliments came easily. I wasn't trying to inflate her ego; anyone who spent any time with Lucia would come away with the same observations.

"That's ... thanks." Lucia looked humbled by my words. "Parents always want more for their kids than they had, you know? This isn't an easy business or even one with a high probability of success. What about your parents?" she pressed. "What do they think about you owning a vineyard?"

"They don't know," I said. "We don't talk."

Lucia's mouth parted. "Oh. I'm sorry."

I waved a dismissive hand. She hadn't unearthed a great secret or poked at a particularly sensitive nerve. I wasn't in contact with my parents. It was a fact, like the sky being blue or the grass being green.

"I have people I'm related to, but they all basically disowned me when I started dating Alex," I divulged. "I haven't spoken to my parents in over a decade and a half, and I don't care to reconnect with them ever again."

"They didn't even reach out to you after Alex ..." she trailed off.

"You can say it," I allowed, "after Alex died. No, I didn't hear from them. But they had no way of knowing anything happened," I reasoned.

"I never would have guessed that about you," she remarked.

"No?"

"You seem so wholesome," she shrugged, "like you would have had this perfect childhood. Or, like, you go home to your parents' house for every holiday and they haven't touched your bedroom since you left."

196

"It was really difficult at first," I admitted, "but I'm at peace with it now." My words weren't for her benefit. They were true. "Alex was in the same situation at me, but even earlier in life. I was at least still talking to my parents when I started college. Alex and her family went their separate ways shortly after her high school graduation. They caught her with a girl and kicked her out of the house. She stayed with a friend until her high school graduation and then got the hell out of that town."

"My mom died when I was nine."

My frown was immediate. "I'm sorry." I had been so cavalier about not speaking with my family, I didn't even think about the make up of hers.

"My Aunt Clara moved here from San Diego to help my dad with the funeral arrangements. It was only supposed to be a short visit," she said with a quiet laugh, "but then she never left."

She toyed with the stem of her wine glass.

"My dad was clueless when it came to raising a teenaged daughter," she disclosed, "but my aunt wasn't much better. She's very traditional. Very old school. She didn't know what to do with me when I showed no interest in learning to cook traditional food and wanted to spend all of my free time in the wine cellar."

I heard her take a breath. "We're really nailing this First Date talk, huh?" She laughed uneasily. "Exes and dead moms."

I licked my lips. I wanted more. I wanted all of her secrets and shame and insecurities laid out before me. But even though we had been tiptoeing around more serious topics for the past few weeks, this was only our First Date.

I leaned into the opportunity for a lighter topic change: "If Napa is an indigenous word," I asked, "how did the rest of the valley get its name?"

I could see the relief and the appreciation for the momentary reprieve cross her features. "Well, St. Helena is named after the mountain," she identified. "Yountville was named after George Yount, the first white settler to plant grapes there. And Calistoga," she said with a wry smile, "was a drunken mix up."

I sat up a little straighter in my chair. "This sounds like a good story."

Lucia leaned closer, almost conspiratorially. "So this guy from New York—Sam Brannon—he bought a lot of land out here in the mid-1800s. He knew about the hot springs, and he wanted to turn the place into a resort town for the rich," she recited. "The story goes that the name Calistoga came after Brannon had a few too many drinks. He meant to say he wanted this place to be the 'Saratoga of California,' but he messed up and said 'Calistoga of Sarafornia' instead. And the name stuck."

"Old Sam must have spent too much time in the hot springs," I observed.

Lucia's lips twisted into a knowing smirk. "Something you two have in common."

I passed my hand over my face. "That was so horrifying."

Lucia leaned back in her chair and took another sip of her wine. "It could have happened to anyone."

"Oh, really? Has it ever happened to you?" I challenged.

"Well, no. But that's different," she said with a cheeky smile. "I know better."

"Excuse me," a man approached our table. I noticed his hair first. He looked like he'd just come from his barber who'd taken just a little too much off the top. "I don't mean to interrupt," he said while interrupting, "but aren't you Lucia Santiago?"

Lucia stared up at the man with the bad haircut. "Depends on who's asking."

He fished into a hidden, inner pocket inside of his sports jacket and produced a rectangular business card. He set it on the table, close to Lucia's silverware. "I'm Jack Horrigan. I work with the Vintner's association."

Lucia glanced briefly at the business card and then back up to him. "We're having dinner."

"I can see that," he acknowledged. "I just need a minute of your time."

Lucia gazed across the table as if seeking my approval.

"It's fine," I assured her. I had no idea what this was about, but I was willing to interrupt our date if it was really that important.

"*Lo siento,*" she murmured to me before standing up. She looked at the man. "One minute," she emphasized.

Lucia and the man stepped away from our table to have a more private conversation. My attention was divided between their meeting and my ahi tuna appetizer. The man spoke with his hands, wildly gesturing, while Lucia's body language remained unchanged.

They were taking longer than a minute. I didn't know if I should interrupt, but before I could make a decision, another table runner brought our pasta dishes to the table. The round serving bowls nearly overflowed with homemade pasta and rich-smelling sauces.

I didn't want to be rude and start without her, but I also didn't want our meal to grow cold. I stabbed my fork into a particularly tantalizing pappardelle noodle from one of the shallow bowls and inelegantly slurped it into my mouth.

"Sorry about that." Lucia apologized as she slipped back into her chair. She grabbed the half-finished merlot bottle and topped off both of our glasses.

I carefully inspected her features as if her face might give her away. "Is everything okay?"

"Yeah. Just a guy from one of the local vintner groups," she said. She rearranged her cloth napkin on her lap. "They try to poach me or my dad away from Lark Estates from time to time."

I gestured to the pasta bowls between us. "I'm sorry I started without you. I couldn't resist."

"I can see that," she smiled. "You've got a little something …" She motioned to her chin area.

I hastily wiped at my face. "Did I get it?"

She smiled, warm and apologetic. She leaned across the table, fingers slightly outstretched. "May I?"

Not really waiting for permission, her thumb swiped at the corner of my mouth. I should have been embarrassed by my messiness, but all I could focus on was the gentle, adoring look on her face.

I wrapped my fingers around her wrist, effectively keeping her from pulling away. I turned my face into her hand and pressed my lips against her palm.

Lucia's nostrils flared. I could practically hear her swallow. "Should I get the check?"

"Yes, please."

The sky had taken on a deep purple color by the time we made it back to the vineyard. Lucia's truck quietly rumbled in front of my house. When she turned off the engine and then the headlights, my throat tightened. I unfastened my seatbelt, but waited for her to exit and round the vehicle. The two other times I'd observed her crossing in front of the truck, her steps had been light and quick. This third time, however, she moved with no urgency. Without the headlights, I couldn't read her features or body language, but there was no quickness to her gait. I took deep breaths while I waited, filling my lungs to capacity to keep my heart from racing out of my chest.

The door opened with a little squeak and, almost routinely, I accepted her assistance out of the truck. I felt in a trance as we made the trek from her car to my front door. Luckily my body knew the way because my brain could only focus on the sensation of her guiding hand pressed confidently in the small of my back.

"I never realized how dark it gets out here," I spoke aloud. Clouds covered the moon, and I hadn't thought to leave on any lights inside or even on the front porch. "Maybe I should ask Carlos about installing a solar-powered street lamp."

I talked to fill the unbearable silence. The air felt heavy. Oppressive.

"Maybe," was all she replied.

We reached the front porch of my darkened home. I fumbled blindly for the keys in my small purse. The sound of metal striking metal echoed loudly in my ears.

"Do you—do you want to come in?" I offered. I swallowed hard. My mouth had become dry. "I've got an open bottle of pinot noir that I don't want to go bad."

"Is this another trick like how you didn't want all that imaginary food in your refrigerator to go bad?"

"No," I scoffed with mock annoyance.

I hated how dark it was. I wanted to see her face more clearly. I wanted to notice the subtle nuances that might indicate how she was feeling. It had been a fun night—not perfect, not without some awkwardness—but I thought it had gone well, and I wasn't eager for it to end so early.

"Not tonight," she said after a long moment.

"No?" My voice cracked on the word.

"No," she said again, her rejection firm, but gentle.

I opened my mouth to spew a variety of apologizes or excuses for my boldness, but I snapped my jaw shut when the wooden boards creaked beneath our feet. Lucia leaned forward, and I did the same. She touched a single finger beneath my jaw and tilted my head up a few degrees. Despite the evening's darkness, I still shut my eyes when

I felt the tentative brush of her lips. She grazed her slightly parted mouth the length of my lower lip. She applied no pressure at first, but the simple movement stimulated me in lower, hidden places.

Her fingertips were light on either side of my face. She gently drew me closer. I sighed into her mouth when she pressed her lips more fully against mine. I whimpered and squeezed my eyes tighter still when she delicately traced the tip of her tongue across my lower lip. Tingles. There were tingles *everywhere*.

"Are you sure," I all but panted, "that you don't want to come in?"

My head was now firmly between her two hands while she nibbled on my exposed neck. "Oh, I want to," she admitted into my skin, "but I'm not going to."

My eyes rolled back when she raked the tips of her canines against the side of my neck. I gulped down a mouthful of muggy California night. "Why not?"

Her mouth left my neck and she straightened to her full height. "Because," she smiled evenly, "it's only our first date."

An unattractive whine bubbled up my throat. "We are grown women, Lucia," I openly pouted.

We'd already spent a night in bed together, even if we hadn't actually had sex. We were well beyond those arbitrary First Date rules, or so I'd thought.

She took a small step backwards—for my benefit or hers, I couldn't tell. She shrugged beneath her Oxford shirt. "What can I say? I'm old fashioned."

CHAPTER EIGHTEEN

I jumped at an unexpected voice behind me: "How was that cold shower last night?"

I turned sharply on my heel to see Lucia and her sly, knowing smile. I didn't have a ready quip and she interpreted my silence for something else. "Oh. Maybe it was just my shower then," she shrugged.

"No. Mine was definitely cold, too," I quickly returned.

Lucia propped herself against the makeshift bar in the tasting barn, and I felt myself leaning in her general direction. Over the barn's usual scents of concrete, earth, and alcohol, I could detect the scent that was all Lucia. She smelled good. *Had she always smelled that good?*

She wore her usual work outfit of jeans and a chambray shirt that morning with her hair in its habitual braid. I was embarrassed to admit that I myself had fretted over what to wear to work that day. In the end, I'd decided on jeans and a buttoned-up shirt, but I'd been purposeful to select a more tailored shirt that attractively hugged my upper body and skinny jeans that highlighted the shape of my calves and thighs.

Lucia wet her lips, and my eyes were instantly drawn to the movement. The tip of her tongue poked out from between her parted lips before she drew her lower lip into her mouth. It re-emerged, wet and shiny like a freshly plucked raspberry. I stifled a telling shudder at the memory of her tongue slowly dragging along my bottom lip.

"You girls ran out of hot water?"

Our dangerous game of cat-and-mouse was broken by Natalie's intrusion into our conversation. Her voice burst the private bubble that had enveloped Lucia and myself, and the rest of the outside world rushed back in.

"You should tell Carlos to check the pilot on the hot water tanks," she instructed.

Lucia stifled a laugh while I cleared my throat. "I'll be sure to do that," I mumbled. "Thanks for the suggestion, Nat."

I turned my attention back to Lucia. "Do you think the casks need topping off?"

Her dark eyes perceptively widened and any earlier cockiness was replaced with surprise. "Oh, uh, yeah. Yeah. You might be right."

"Lucia?" I called out. My voice echoed off of the cellar walls. She had only been a few steps ahead of me, and yet I'd successfully lost her in the wine caves.

"Over here!"

I followed the sound of her voice, or at least traveled in the direction from which I thought her voice had come. I moved through the first room which held our oldest vintages to find her leaning against one of the larger barrels in the second room.

"Hey." Her cocky, knowing smile from before had returned.

She'd been respectful and chivalrous the previous night—even gentlewomanly. But she'd also possessed the upper hand when it came to intimacy. It was time I take back some of that control.

I grabbed the front of her shirt and pulled her in for a crushing kiss. She wasn't surprised by my forcefulness. She fisted the front of my shirt as well and kissed me right back. When I pressed my body against hers, effectively pinning her against a wine barrel, I heard a quiet growl originate from deep in her throat. She spun us around so that my back pressed against a sixty-gallon barrel.

Our teenage make-out session had been fun at our date's conclusion, but just when I'd thought we might finally take the next step, Lucia had put on the breaks. Luckily, she was a really talented kisser. But also—unfortunately—*she was a really talented kisser*. If the pressure of her lips and the movements of her tongue weren't so stimulating, I might not have cared that all we'd done so far was kiss. But I needed more. Much more.

I grabbed onto her hands and moved them to the top of my pants. She didn't require additional instructions as she deftly popped the button on my jeans and pulled down the zipper.

"You'll have to be quiet," she told me in a hushed voice. "The acoustics in here are great for leading large tours, but terrible for sneaky sex."

"You sound like you know from experience," I observed.

She pressed her body against mine and nibbled up the side of my neck. "We've both had previous partners, June. There's no sense in denying our personal histories."

Her mouth felt delicious against my skin, but my brain wouldn't let me completely submit. "So you've brought a lot of girls down here?"

Her hands rested on my hips while she continued to suckle at my neck. "I live with my dad and aunt," she reminded me. "It's not like I could bring them back to my bedroom."

She'd successfully dodged another of my questions. Her response suggested this may have been a regular occurrence, but she hadn't quantified her answer.

"Is there any place on the property where you haven't fucked?" I coarsely demanded.

She pulled away from my neck and grinned. "I'm sure there's a few acres I haven't gotten to yet."

I pushed her away and hastily zipped up my pants.

Lucia looked confused by my reaction. "What?"

"I'm not doing this for a convenient lay, you know," I said crossly.

"Then *why* are you doing it?" she asked. Her voice met the heat in my own.

"Well, I *thought* I liked you," I shot back. "But I'm starting to think I don't know you at all."

I didn't have the opportunity for a grand and dramatic exit before Lucia reached for me. Her fingers snagged around my wrist.

"June. Wait. I'm sorry. My mouth runs when I'm nervous." She took a breath. "I haven't done any of those things."

I blinked a few times. "Why would you lie about that?"

Lucia stared at the concrete floor. "I thought you'd want to be with someone experienced. Someone with more confidence."

"I've only ever been with one other woman," I reminded her. "If anyone should be feeling self-conscious about experience, it should be me."

"I've never dated anyone of consequence," she noted. "You were married for how long?"

"This isn't a competition," I dismissed. "We both have our insecurities. You don't have to pretend to be someone you're not to get me to like you. I like this person just fine."

"Oh, yeah?" Lucia rewarded my words with a lopsided grin. "You like me?"

I snorted. "Don't get a big head about it."

Lucia snagged my hand and began playing with my fingers. "Tell me, June. What do you like about me?"

I didn't intend on inflating her ego, but she looked genuinely interested. "You're hard working. Loyal to a fault. Kind even when you don't intend to be," I listed off. "You're compassionate and conscientious about my quirks. Plus, you're gorgeous."

"Gorgeous?" she repeated. She pursed her lips and looked thoughtful. "No one's ever called me gorgeous before."

"Their loss."

I hadn't been exaggerating or trying to make her feel better. Lucia *was* gorgeous. Despite the boxy, almost androgynous clothes she wore on a typical day, I couldn't help but reflect on the slender yet feminine figure beneath the cotton garments. Her long, jet black hair was so soft and silky I didn't know how she ever managed to keep it in a braid. Her eyelashes and eyebrows were similarly full without needing artificial enhancements. Her nose was long and elegant, proportioned perfectly for the shape of her oval face. Her mouth. I wanted to experience firsthand everything that wide, pouty, generous mouth could do.

She leaned forward as if she expected us to continue where we'd left off.

I turned my head to the side, denying her pursed lips their original target. "No offense, but you kind of ruined the mood."

Lucia pulled back and her mouth twitched. "Yeah. I tend to do that."

"Come over for dinner tonight," I found myself proposing. "You bring the wine. I'll make dinner."

She arched an eyebrow. "Like a second date?"

"Do we have to keep count?" I countered.

"I don't have sex until the third date."

The ridiculous statement nearly caused my voice to raise a full octave. "We were just going to fuck in the wine cellar!"

"I was going to *eat you out* in the wine cellar," she corrected me. "We weren't going to fuck."

I didn't resist the urge to roll my eyes. "That seems like semantics to me."

"Oh believe me, June," she practically purred. "When I'm ready to fuck, you'll know the difference."

I released a shuddering breath. Okay. Maybe I was back in the mood. *Christ.* But I'd never give her the satisfaction.

And it seemed until that moment came, I wouldn't either.

+ + +

"You wore your hair down."

Lucia touched a hand to the side of her head as if she'd forgotten it was no longer in a braid. Her natural, voluminous waves were enviable, like she'd spent the day at the beach, letting the ocean breeze be her stylist. "You said you liked it this way."

"I do! I do!" I confirmed. "Come in!"

I moved out of the way as Lucia stepped inside.

"Something smells good," she remarked.

I looked back in the direction of the kitchen. I'd thrown together a meal of stuffed bell peppers the last time Lucia had come over for dinner. I hadn't been expecting a dinner guest, so I'd had to get creative with whatever I had on hand. This second time around, I'd actually been able to shop and plan the meal.

"It's the lobster risotto," I said. "I hope you're not allergic to shellfish."

"I was actually talking about you," she said with a sly smile, "but the food smells good, too."

I smirked at the compliment. It was a marvel that after months of first resenting each other, that our relationship had grown and matured in such dramatic fashion.

Lucia went out of her way to touch the fabric of my dress. "This is nice."

The dress had capped sleeves with a flowing skirt that stopped just above my knees. I would have preferred something sleeveless, but my suntan was uneven from working in the fields. Lucia was more casually dressed in black skinny jeans and a striped short-sleeved button-up shirt. The sleeves were cuffed and cut high on her thinly muscled biceps. She was better about sunscreen than I was, with no visible tan lines on her arms.

"The last time I wore a dress was probably at my *quinceañera*," she reflected. "I didn't want to, but my Aunt Clara insisted."

"Are there pictures of this miracle?" I teased.

She smiled back serenely. "None that you're ever going to see."

We walked back to the kitchen where my risotto sat unattended. I gave the pot a quick stir and added another ladle of broth to keep the arborio grains creamy.

Lucia leaned against one of the kitchen counters. "Can I help with anything?"

"Want to kill the lobster for me?"

I flicked my eyes in her direction to gauge her reaction. Her normally olive complexion seemed to blanch. "Oh, I, uh …"

"I'm totally kidding," I told her. "I had the lady at the grocery store do the dirty work for me. You should have seen your face though," I teased. "I thought you might pass out."

Lucia crossed her arms across her chest and looked particularly grumpy to have shown any weakness. While I practically lived in that space, it must have been new territory for her.

"I see you're still feeding Gato," she observed. She nodded her head towards the twin ceramic bowls on the kitchen floor, next to the refrigerator. "You're going to spoil him."

"I am not," I rejected. "It's just dry food."

"He's going to get fat and lazy and forget how to survive on his own."

I paused stirring the risotto long enough to shake my wooden spoon at her. "First, I doubt he'd forget how to hunt, and second, even if he did, why would he have to manage on his own?"

Lucia's eyes never left the floor. "I don't know. What if you left?"

I put one hand on my hip and regarded her. "Where exactly am I going?"

Lucia shrugged. "Maybe one day you wake up and realize this isn't where you want to be. Maybe you go back to the city."

I didn't think we were talking about Gato's food schedule any more. I wet my lips. "Why would I do that?"

"I'm just talking. I don't know."

"So I should stop feeding Gato on the off-chance that one day I might not want to live here anymore?"

Lucia grunted.

I touched my fingers to her forearm. "What are you really worried about?"

She finally lifted her eyes to meet mine. "Don't get mad, okay? But this isn't your world. Not like it's mine, at least. And what if one day you realize this was a giant mistake?"

I released a shallow breath. Lucia's words were a lot to process and unpack.

"I don't have a crystal ball," I began. "If anything, Alex's death is a perfect example of how unpredictable the future can be. But it's also taught me that life is precious." I paused to shake my head. "That's such a cliché, but it's true. And I don't want to waste any more time not living my life to its full potential."

I took a steadying breath before continuing. "So I'm going to keep feeding Gato. And I'm going to keep working and learning at the vineyard. And I'm going to keep seeing you, if that's what you want, too."

I watched her exhale. "Oh, okay. Yeah, uh. That ... that's cool."

The smile returned to my lips. "Cool."

We ate dinner at the kitchen table, alternatively flirting and teasing each other or talking shop in between bites. I was pleased with how the lobster risotto had turned out. The arborio grains were fork tender, the sauce was smooth and creamy, and the fresh lobster meat was sweet and buttery. I'd gone the extra step of making dessert— key lime cheesecake—which we ate after dinner paired with cups of strong coffee.

When the food had been eaten and the dishes had been cleared, we moved our date to the living room. Lucia looked over my limited wine selection while I watched her from the couch.

"When you have your own vineyard," I quizzed, "what do you want to do?"

"*When?*" Her eyebrows rose at my choice of words.

"I've seen you. You're one of the most hard-working people I've ever met. You'll make it happen."

The corner of her mouth lifted. "Thanks for the vote of confidence." She pulled a bottle from my wine rack and inspected its label more closely. "For starters, I would make it a collective."

"What does that mean?" I asked.

"Everyone shares the profits. Everyone has a say."

"Are collectives very common?"

"Hardly." She flashed me a brief smile. "Didn't you know that vineyard owners like to keep all of the money for themselves?"

"I guess I missed that memo," I chuckled.

Lucia brought the selected wine bottle and a corkscrew with her to the couch. She sat on the cushion beside me and dug the coiled worm through the wine foil and into the cork below. I watched her strong fingers make short work of the process as if she'd been opening wine bottles all of her life. Actually, she probably had.

She poured several ounces of the cabernet into two waiting wine glasses. When I instinctively reached for the glass closest to me, she stopped me with a light touch to my hand.

"You should never drink a good bottle of wine immediately after uncorking it." Lucia licked her lips. I felt her heated gaze sweep over me. "I want to decant *you*, June."

From anyone else, I might have rolled my eyes. But Lucia had such a passion, close to obsession, about everything wine, that her words made me flush.

"You're okay with us taking our time?" she posed.

I slowly nodded. I felt trapped beneath her intense gaze. "I-I like this. Us taking things slow."

"Is it too slow?" she wondered.

"Maybe? I'm horny as hell," I unabashedly admitted.

"I really want to kiss you," Lucia revealed in a rush. "But I'm afraid I won't be able to stop if I do."

I swallowed thickly. "Would *not* stopping be so bad?"

"It's not our third date yet," she observed.

"You were ready to have sex with me before we even had our first date," I couldn't help pointing out.

"I got wrapped up in the moment," she explained. "We were finally connecting, and then you had that loose eyelash."

I leaned a little closer to her on the couch. "How are my eyelashes now?"

Lucia reached for me. Her fingertips brushed along my cheekbone as if searching for errant eyelashes. "They're perfect," she breathed. She continued to stroke my face. "I don't want to stop this time, June," she said. "I don't want to fall asleep or say the wrong thing to ruin the mood."

"Then don't."

She pressed forward and eliminated the space between us. Her mouth connected solidly with mine, and she groaned at the initial contact. Her feather-light touch remained on either side of my face. Her long fingers drew me in for more.

"Do you want me to stop?" she breathed into my open mouth.

I moved my hands to her hair and lost myself in her lush waves. "No."

"Bedroom?" she spoke against my moving lips.

My fingers dropped to the buttons on her shirt. I unfastened the top button and moved lower for the rest. "Can't risk it."

Lucia shrugged out of her shirt and yanked off her shoes without bothering to untie them first. She started to shimmy out of her tight jeans, but she paused her frenetic disrobing to watch me remove my dress. I didn't have the same buttons and zipper barriers that she did. The dress slipped off as easily as it had gone on.

Lucia stared at me with wide eyes. I stood before her in only my bra and underwear. I hadn't counted on us being intimate that night, but I hadn't wanted to be caught unprepared either. I'd taken the time to shave, lotion, and perfume all over. I normally didn't bother myself with matching undergarments, but I was thankful I'd had the foresight to wear a light blue bra and matching underwear.

Lucia stood from the couch, still halfway undressed herself. Her dark gaze swept over every inch of exposed skin before she set tentative hands on my hips. I nearly shuddered from the simple touch.

"I didn't want to look at you that night at the hot springs," she confessed. "I didn't want to take advantage of the situation. But I'm going to look now, if that's alright."

I bit down on my lower lip. I didn't trust my voice not to wobble. "Okay."

Lucia held me lightly by the hips. Her eyes started on my face before traveling lower. She took in my shoulders and my long limbs. Her eyes followed the curve of my collarbone and lingered in the valley of my breasts. Like a phantom touch, I felt her attention drag down my abdomen and pause again at my underwear. My instinct was to cover up or hide my figure, but her hungry stare kept me in place.

She took one of my hands in hers and she brought my palm up to her mouth. She kissed the back of my hand before turning it over and pressing her lips to the meat of my palm. Her touch, her kisses, were warm and welcomed. I wanted to feel her everywhere.

She slid her fingers beneath my bra straps and slipped them down my shoulders. More kisses followed wherever a new part of my body became exposed. She met my lust-drunk gaze and raised an eyebrow as if seeking approval to continue. I knew it was only a matter of time before I came undone, too. I reached behind me and found the bra clasp in the center of my back. I blindly unfastened the straining hooks and released my breasts in the process.

I heard Lucia's sharp exhale as my bra tumbled to the floor.

"Your pants," I said thickly.

Distracted by my lack of dress, Lucia had forgotten about her own clothes. She eagerly resumed pulling off her pants, but her eyes remained fixated on my naked breasts.

Stripped down to her bra and underwear, Lucia once again latched onto my waist. It seemed like she couldn't get enough of my full hips and thighs. She stroked her hands up my sides, nearly tickling me. Her hands stopped on my breasts, which she cupped and squeezed and massaged. My nipples responded to her more aggressive touch. She trapped a thick nipple between her fingers and pinched until I had no choice but to whimper in need.

She raked her short fingernails across my breasts and down the center of my stomach. When her fingers reached the waistband of my underwear I realized I hadn't really touched her yet. I'd been so focused on her touch, I hadn't done any exploring of my own.

I reached for her bra clasp, but she smoothly evaded my attempt. "I've got it, *Jefa*."

I watched with growing anticipation as Lucia removed her own bra and then wiggled her underwear past her hips and down to the floor. She stepped out of the discarded undergarment, and my attention dropped to the closely trimmed triangle at the apex of her sex.

Lucia sat down on the edge of the couch. I would have dropped to my knees to feast between her thighs, but she beckoned for me to join her on the couch. We could have relocated to my bedroom down the hallway at any point, but I was still feeling superstitious about a change in venue.

She positioned me so my body reclined across the length of the couch. My underwear was the only shred of clothing that remained. It took little coaxing for me to lift my hips off the couch so she could remove them entirely. She rested her weight on top of me, her smaller breasts pressed against mine.

I reached between our bodies and ran my fingers through the short, curly hair above her pussy lips. I loved the way the coarse but soft hair felt against my fingers. Her hips jerked into mine when I stroked my middle finger along her hooded clit.

"J-j-Jesus," she sputtered.

She grabbed my hands in hers and drew my arms above my head. She pressed my wrists into the slightly scratchy material of the upholstered couch. I wasn't exactly pinned in place, but I also had no desire to move.

The window-unit air conditioner that Carlos had installed earlier in the week was no match for the heat being thrown off of Lucia's naked form. She slid against me; she rotated her narrow hips and moved her lower body in small, concentric circles. A slick layer of moisture developed between our bodies that allowed her to rub more easily against me, but with just enough friction where it mattered.

"Lucia," I gasped. My teeth dug into my lower lip. "I'm going to—uhn, I'm not—I can't—I'm … I'm…"

She stopped her lower body movements. "So soon?" She sounded a little breathless herself.

"I w-w-warned you." I struggled to form the words.

"Maybe you're not a red wine to be decanted," she reconsidered. "Maybe you're champagne." She nuzzled her nose against the side of my throat. I felt the tip of her tongue explore the column of my neck. "All of that pressure building up until you have no choice but to explode."

She ground against me again and a fresh wave of arousal washed over me.

"Oh fuck. Lucia—I'm gonna pop," I groaned.

Her words were hot in my ear. "I'll drink your champagne," she vowed. "I'll drink every drop of it."

CHAPTER NINETEEN

I'd always been a light sleeper. As far back as I could remember, the slightest sounds could pull me from even the most tantalizing dreams. So it came as no surprise that even though my brain and body were exhausted from the emotional—and now physical—gymnastics Lucia had put me through, I still woke up to the sound of someone knocking on my front door.

When I initially woke up, my brain struggled to identify the origin of the noise. I carefully sat up, mindful not to wake up the woman soundly sleeping beside me. I couldn't tell the exact time; I'd left my cellphone in the living room and I had no other clock in the room, but the sun still had hours to go before it would be awake. I listened, eyes scanning the darkened bedroom, before I heard the knocking noise again, followed by a muffled voice.

I assumed whoever was at my front door had no intention of leaving without seeing me first, so I grabbed my robe to cover my naked body and quietly headed down the hallway. On my way to the front door, I glanced at the clock in the living room; it was just after 3:00 a.m. The knocking—pounding, really—continued. I was more curious than alarmed by the noise. Who would be at my front door at this hour?

The knocking resumed, and I heard my name being called by a man on the other side of the door. It took me only a moment to recognize Rolando's voice. I tightened the sash around my waist and unlocked the deadbolt.

Rolando looked panicked and sweaty as he stood on my front porch. "The storm," he started. "Lightning." He panted, unable to get the words out.

"Rolando—stop. Breathe," I urged the man.

Rolando filled his lungs with air before trying again. "The Jeffersons' vineyard is on fire."

If I had been groggy or overly tired before, Rolando's words had me launching into action. "How can I help? What do you need me to do?"

"I've collected all of the rakes and shovels from the barn, but we need all hands on deck to keep it from spreading."

I nodded my understanding. "Let me change and I'll drive right over."

I turned to go back inside, but Rolando wasn't finished: "I can't find Lucia. I tried her phone, but ... she's not answering."

I froze at his words. His tone was matter-of-fact and not insinuating, but he had to have known what was going on; Lucia's unmistakable truck was parked directly in front of the farmhouse.

I mustered a response as smoothly as my awkwardness would allow. "Oh, I-I'll get her."

"Just bring her with," he told me in a rush. "I need to get these supplies to the Jeffersons' place right away."

Rolando left me, shell-shocked, in the doorway. I watched him hurry to his own truck which idled in the driveway. He didn't look back in my direction as he got behind the steering wheel and drove away.

I let the screen door swing silently shut. "Shit," I cursed beneath my breath.

I'd never been caught in the act before. No one had ever walked in on me having sex with someone. But Rolando's knowledge that his daughter had spent the night felt a little like that. I didn't really have time for embarrassment though. Regardless of my mixed feelings about my neighbors, if the Jeffersons' fire wasn't contained, our property could be in jeopardy as well.

If I'd had any illusions of a late morning of cuddling in bed, Rolando's visit had shattered those dreams. There would be no surprising Lucia with breakfast in bed or even lazy, languid, morning kisses.

Lucia was still sleeping when I burst into the room.

"Lucia," I hissed.

She groaned, but her eyes remained closed.

I went to her side of the bed and shook her solid form. "Lucia, you have to get up."

She blindly swatted at me, still refusing to open her eyes. "No," she whined. She drew out the monosyllabic denial.

"The Jeffersons' vineyard is on fire," I announced.

At my words, her dark eyes flipped open. And like me, she immediately launched into action.

"Shit. Damn. Fuck." She tossed back the covers, leapt out of bed, and began pulling on the clothes she'd worn the previous night.

I needed to change out of my robe into more suitable clothes as well, but I stood, swaying awkwardly in place. She hadn't thought to ask how I knew about the fire.

"Your, uh, your dad," I said. "He came here to tell me."

The implication of that information didn't immediately hit her. She struggled to get her feet through the appropriate holes of her jeans. She hopped from one leg to another, practically shaking the aged house down to its unstable foundation.

"I can worry about that later," she announced. "Right now we've got a vineyard to save."

The valley tended to be covered in a dense fog most mornings. I feared, however, that what we drove through was thick smoke instead of trapped condensation. Lucia drove through the gates of Silver Stag winery, her features serious and her body visibly tense.

"If the vines are destroyed," she said, "the Jeffersons will be ruined. It's not like a regular crop where if you have a bad harvest you just start over the following season; that's years of grape production lost," she emphasized. "And even if the vines aren't ruined, this year's grapes probably are. Too much smoke will taint the berry. A smoky Syrah can be nice," she observed, "but you don't want your chardonnay to taste like an ashtray."

She pulled past the gray lannon stone visitor center and down a narrow, paved lane. The sun would be starting to rise soon, but the sky was like night, choked thick from the vineyard fire.

The Calistoga fire department was already on the scene. Their giant red trucks served as the lone source of water. They alternated their hoses between the active fire and the vegetation that wasn't already on fire. Without another convenient water outlet to tap into, I worried what might happen when the tanks in their trucks ran dry.

I didn't immediately see Bruce or Darcy Jefferson when I left Lucia's truck. Several dozen figures not in firefighter gear stood as close to the fire as they dared, raking away ground vegetation that might serve as fuel for the fire. I spotted Rolando, Oscar, and Carlos among the men raking and shoveling. A shock of messy silver hair stood out amongst the workers' darker hair; Bruce Jefferson stood shoulder-to-shoulder with my, and presumably his, vineyard workers to salvage what they could.

We each grabbed a rake and joined the long line of workers. It didn't take long, however, for Lucia to become frustrated. "This is useless," she lamented. "We might as well be spitting into the wind."

Her gaze left the uncontrolled fire and passed beyond me. As I watched her features twist in thought, I could practically see the metaphorical lightbulb turn on over her head. "Bruce!" she called out. "Where are the keys to your tractor?"

Bruce looked too distraught to really register Lucia's question. "They're in the dashboard."

Lucia dropped her rake where she stood and jogged in the direction of a giant green tractor whose rear wheels might have been taller than me. I watched her climb up an attached ladder to the tractor's enclosed cab. She settled onto the single seat and the giant diesel engine growled awake.

Oscar stopped his raking and came to stand behind me. "What is Lucia doing?" he asked.

I shook my head. "I have no idea."

The tractor lurched forward and Lucia grabbed the oversized steering wheel. She shifted gears and the tractor picked up speed.

My mouth dropped in horror when the tractor changed directions and Lucia drove directly for the most aggressive portion of the fire—the acreage the firefighters hadn't been able to contain yet. My body sprung forward, and a single, strangled word tumbled from my open mouth: "No."

I didn't get too far before Oscar's tight grip held me back. "Just wait," he instructed me. He only released his hold when my rigid body went limp. I could do nothing but stare, a helpless bystander, as the woman with whom I'd shared my bed seemed to be playing a dangerous game of chicken with the fire.

A new plume of smoke billowed out of the tractor's top exhaust pipe. The engine seemed to snarl; the massive tractor made a hard right turn until it was no longer barreling directly toward the fire and instead was driving parallel with the massive inferno. I still didn't understand Lucia's purpose until I saw something that resembled grey smoke behind the tractor's rear rotary tiller. Only it wasn't smoke. It was moon dust. Gold ridge sandy loam.

I finally understood what she was doing. "She's making a fire line," I breathed.

I heard Oscar's admiration. "Genius."

Once the other farmhands realized Lucia's plan, every serviceable tractor on the property was immediately employed. Not long after, a solid band of bare earth, several yards wide, separated the fire's most hostile flames from its potential fuel.

Lucia and the oversized green tractor bounced back towards its original parking space near the Jeffersons' barn. The engine cut off and Lucia emerged from the enclosed cab. With Oscar no longer holding me back, I was free to jog in her direction. A kaleidoscope of mixed emotions rushed over me. I wanted to throw myself at her. I want to kiss her mouth hard and scold her and be in awe of her. But Bruce Jefferson reached her before I could.

He held out a hand to help Lucia down from the tractor despite her being more than capable of handling the descent on her own.

"That was quick thinking," he openly admired. "I didn't think we'd ever get this fire contained. Not before we lost everything, at least."

Lucia allowed Bruce to help her down to the packed earth. She looked sweaty and her cheeks burned bright. I wondered how hot it had been inside the tractor's enclosed cab, being so close to the hottest burning parts of the fire.

"You're welcome," she returned. "I'm just happy it worked."

"I owe you big time, Lucia." Bruce looked around at the assembled helpers. "I owe you all." His attention returned to Lucia. "I have to assess the damage, but if I'm still in business by the end of the day, count me in."

"Count you in?" Lucia repeated.

"Your union," Bruce clarified. "You have my support."

Lucia's dark eyes widened. "Oh! We didn't help because of that."

"I know," came Bruce's serious and booming voice. "You did it because you're good people. I was being selfish before, only thinking about myself and my bottom line. But that's no way to be."

He held out a dirty, smoke-smudged hand.

Lucia looked down at the gesture with some skepticism. "Is this an offer to not get in the way? Or at you actively going to help?"

"I'm no expert at any of this organizing stuff," he admitted, "but if you tell me which boutique owners you want a meeting with, I'll make it happen."

It wasn't the world. I knew Lucia's goals were so much bigger than having a seat at the table, but it was a start.

Lucia grasped Bruce's hand and gave it a firm shake. "I'm going to hold you to that," she warned.

Bruce flashed his toothy grin. "I wouldn't expect anything less."

The fire still smoldered and burned in some places, but thanks to Lucia's fire line, the blaze had been contained enough that the Calistoga fire department would be able to handle the rest. We packed up rakes and shovels into the vehicles that had brought us to the Jeffersons' property.

I was tired and dirty, but satisfied. After the morning's events, I was hoping for a shower and to go back to bed. I snuck a glance in Lucia's direction. I wondered how she would react to an invitation to join me.

I followed Lucia back to her truck. She walked silently with her hands shoved into the front pockets of her jeans. She walked first to the passenger side and opened the door for me just as she had on our first official date. She held out her hand to help me into the slightly elevated truck. Her fingers closed around mine.

I didn't immediately take my seat. "You scared me," I murmured.

Lucia lifted her eyes to meet mine. She licked the pad of her thumb and swiped it across my cheekbone. "You've got a little dirt."

My face could have been covered in mud for all I cared. "Did you know that would work?" I asked.

"No. It's not like I've had to stop a fire before."

"Then why did you risk it?" I demanded. "You could had been hurt—really badly. Or worse."

"But I wasn't," she replied.

I wanted to say more, but I sensed this wasn't the place or the time for a longer conversation. I finished climbing into the truck and buckled myself in.

Lucia drove us back to the vineyard. She neither spoke nor played with the radio while I tried not to be bothered by the extended silence. When we pulled up to the tasting barn, I noticed Natalie's vehicle parked in the main lot.

"God, we don't have tours scheduled for today, do we?" I lamented.

Lucia shifted her truck into park and turned off the engine. "I don't think so?"

We entered the tasting barn and were greeted by the enticing scents of cooked breakfast meats, hash browns, eggs, and pancakes. An impressive buffet of breakfast foods sat in serving dishes on a card table from storage.

"What's all of this?" Lucia asked.

Natalie set a lid on top of the tray of scrambled eggs so they would retain their heat. "Rolando called to tell me about the fire," she said. "I ordered up some grub from downtown. Figured ya'll would be hungry."

"You're a saint," I breathed.

Carlos, Oscar, and Rolando returned to the barn not long after Lucia and myself. They didn't seem to require the same explanation as we had. With little prompting, they each grabbed a plate and plastic utensils and began to help themselves to the heaping piles of breakfast food.

I lingered back and waited for everyone else to serve themselves before dishing out food onto my plate. By the time I'd finished, everyone sat in their usual spots at the wooden picnic table, leaving me with no real place to sit. I hovered awkwardly a few feet away from the employee picnic table and contemplated my options: should I eat standing up? Retreat to my office where I'd actually have a seat? Or should I dump the food and runaway altogether? Flashbacks of a middle school cafeteria and not knowing where to park my plastic tray filled me with anxiety.

"June. Come sit down," Oscar called to me.

I wanted to point out that there really wasn't room for me at their table, but my grateful feet started to walk toward them, if only excited to have gotten the invite. No one looked up from their respective plates as I tread closer.

I heard Carlos' grunt. "Make room for *Jefa*."

The bodies at the table shifted and squeezed, leaving barely enough space for me at the center of the table. I set my plate down and wiggled in. It was an impossibly tight fit—I couldn't really raise my arms or even bring my fork to my mouth—but I was content to be sandwiched between Carlos and Oscar.

Talking was at a minimum, but everyone—except me—ate with enthusiasm. The morning's events had left me starving, but this sense of belonging had been what I'd craved the most. I sat back and enjoyed the chatter around me; the boys made jokes, Rolando smiled his easy smile, and Natalie's giant laugh filled up the barn. Only Lucia remained quiet, although her silence wasn't unusual. She ate with her head tilted close to her plate and her shoulders slumped forward as if worried someone might try to steal her bacon.

When she finished, she wordlessly rose from the table. I watched her retreating form with curiosity. Her departure had created more space at the table and I might have actually have been able to enjoy my own breakfast, but I found myself abandoning my plate and following after her.

She hadn't gone too far. I caught up with her near the outdoor patio area. She'd removed her socks and soot-stained boots and paced back and forth in the grass.

"That was quite the morning," I observed.

She made a noncommittal noise and continued her manic back and forth. Her silence wasn't uncharacteristic, but it annoyed me. I'd thought we'd been getting somewhere. I'd thought all, or at least most, of the walls had come down. So why was she behaving this way?

She came to a sudden stop. "Do you think we're cursed?"

"Cursed?" I echoed.

"We finally have sex and then the Jeffersons' property caught on fire."

"The *Jeffersons'* property caught on fire. Not ours," I pointed out.

She raised her eyes and scanned the now-clear blue sky. "I don't know. Seems like we made someone unhappy."

"Are you religious?" I asked. "Do you really believe in things like that?"

"No, not really. My Aunt Clara is always trying to get me to go to church with her, but luckily there's always work to be done on the farm so I have a built-in excuse."

"I hadn't been to church since Alex's funeral," I thought aloud. "Although that was her parents' doing. Alex never would have wanted a church service. She thought organized religions were opium for the masses."

"Why did you let her family bully you into have the funeral?"

I shrugged helplessly. "Funerals are for the living, not the dead. I guess I wanted them to have closure even though they'd never really been a part of our lives."

"I couldn't have done it," Lucia decided. She shook her head. "I'm not that nice."

"You were … you were *nice* last night," I observed. The words brought an immediate blush to my face.

This was new territory for me. When we'd first started dating, Alex had been the one to pursue me. She'd been flirty and suggestive, and I the lucky recipient of her attentions. Lucia, however, was obtuse. She seemed to move at a snail's pace. If I was interested in seeing where this relationship might go, I would have to take more initiative.

"I was hoping to be nice again in the morning," she admitted. She licked her lips. "Too bad the earth made other plans for us."

"Maybe we'll have to try again," I proposed. "For scientific purposes," I was quick to add.

"For science. Right."

"What are you doing right now?" I asked.

Lucia raised an amused eyebrow and her mouth curved up at the edges. "Are you suggesting we play hooky from work and test God's Wrath?"

"N-no. I was just asking."

Lucia wrinkled her nose. "I could really use a shower. I feel pretty gross, like I've got soot clogging up my pores."

"Do you want to shower at the farmhouse?" I offered. I hoped I wasn't blushing too much from the offer. It was an innocent question, but one that might result in less-than-innocent activities.

She cocked her head to the side and gave me a shrewd look. "Why do you do that?"

Her response made me self-conscious. "Do what?"

"You call it the farmhouse instead of *your* house?"

"Oh." I blinked. "I didn't realize I did that."

"You do," she confirmed. "I noticed it right away."

I chewed on my lower lip. "I suppose a lot of this still doesn't feel real—still doesn't feel like it's my life."

"What do you think it's going to take to change that?" she wondered.

I shrugged. "Time?"

Lucia took a step closer, invading my personal bubble. "Ask me your question again."

"O-okay." There was a sharpness to her words, demanding and almost aggressive. "Do you want to take a shower at *my* house?"

She grabbed my hand. "Let's go."

CHAPTER TWENTY

There was a beautiful, naked woman in my shower. But I was in my bedroom and not in the bathroom with her. I stared at the clothing Lucia had left on my bedroom floor. She'd worn the patterned short-sleeved shirt from the previous night. When Rolando had shown up at my front door with news of a fire on the Jeffersons' property, she'd had no other clothes to change into.

I retrieved the shirt from the floor with the intention of hanging it on the back of a chair. I brought the shirt to my nose and breathed in deeply. I had expected the shirt to smell and to be in need of laundering. But the fabric was only slightly smoky. Beneath the scent of wild fire, I could detect Lucia's unique scent. The fabric softener she used. The scent of freshly tilled soil. The warmth of a sunny day.

"What are you doing?"

Lucia stepped into the bedroom wearing a bath towel wrapped around her waist and another towel draped over her shoulders like an unwrapped scarf. But besides the towel hanging from her neck, she wore no top. Her smallish breasts moved with each step.

I didn't respond to her question because there was no point. She'd clearly discovered me inhaling her shirt like it was a bouquet of fresh flowers.

She didn't bother teasing me for being caught in the act. She stood in the middle of the room and used the towel around her neck to continue drying off her hair. She rubbed her head roughly with the terrycloth material. The vigorous rubbing caused her naked breasts to move back and forth.

I swallowed hard. *Was she doing this on purpose?*

I crossed the room as if in a trance, hypnotized by the erotic sway of her breasts. She watched my approach with a small, cocky smile.

With no pretense, I pressed her breasts together and licked away the sweet-tasting water droplets that still dotted her flesh. I licked up her collarbone and then down between the valley of her bare chest.

Lucia widened her stance as if to steady herself. "If you keep that up," she said, unable to bite back a groan, "I'm going to have to shower again."

I ignored her lackluster warning. I licked at her nipples, alternating back and forth. I swirled my tongue around each swollen bud before sucking the hardened flesh into my mouth.

"There's a drought, you know." She pulled my hair back so it wouldn't get in my way. I bit down lightly on one of her nipples and heard her sharp intake of air. "I thought you cared about the planet."

I sucked hard on the delicate skin surrounding her nipples until I was confident I'd left a mark.

Lucia breathed loudly through her nose. "June." I heard her resistance crumbling in the single word.

I held her hips and kissed down the center of her torso. My fingers played with the towel wrapped around her waist before I tugged it off completely. The damp towel struck the hardwood floors with a satisfying slap.

I fully expected to have my way with her. I intended on dropping to my knees and feasting between her parted thighs until her knees buckled. I wanted to hear my reserved, and often sullen, assistant winemaker moan. I wanted to bring her to the edge and have her demand more. What I didn't anticipate was her hands pushing me back and onto the bed. I tried to resist, tried to get up, but I only got as far as sitting upright before she was sitting on my lap and straddling my hips.

I drank in her naked form, now lightly resting on my upper thighs. With her legs straddling me, her own thighs were parted wide, offering me an unobstructed view of her sex. I instinctively reached between our bodies, wanting to touch her, but she swatted my hands away.

"Not yet," she told me.

"Are you waiting for another date?" I joked, partly annoyed that she'd rejected my advances.

Her right hand fell between my legs and she cupped me over my jeans. She pressed her palm into me, putting delicious pressure on my clit. I squirmed in an attempt to gain more friction, but I was wearing too many damn clothes.

She continued to rub me over my clothes. "Lucia," I couldn't help my whine. "This isn't going to work."

"Trust me, *Jefa*." She turned my head to the side, exposing my neck. She flattened her tongue and ran it along my throat. "I'm just getting started."

She slid down to the floor—where I had intended to be. She lifted up on her knees as if in prayer. "Take off your pants."

My reflex was to rebuff her demand—to tease her for being bossy—but instead of resisting, my hands went to the top button of my jeans. I popped it loose. Lucia remained at my feet, on her knees. She didn't participate in my disrobing, but she watched my movements with great intensity.

I pulled down my zipper. Lifting my backside from the mattress, I pulled off my pants. They proceeded to turn themselves inside out as I tugged them down my legs. I struggled when the material got caught around my ankles.

"Leave it," she told me. "Now your underwear."

I hooked my fingers beneath the elastic waistband and slowly dragged them off. Since I hadn't been able to remove my jeans entirely, my underwear had to remain around my ankles as well. Lucia watched each step with growing concentration. I still wore my shirt from earlier, but apparently I was undressed just enough for her plan.

She ran her palms up the inside of my thighs and spread me open. Her fingers flexed and she squeezed the tender flesh of my inner thighs. She leaned forward and licked the length of my slit, stopping just before my clit. Her tongue painted circles around the aching nub.

I dropped my hand to her bare shoulder and then to the back of her head. She'd undone her braid for her shower and now her loose, wet tendrils cascaded down her back. I stroked my fingers through her damp hair while she left wet kisses on my inner thighs.

She traced the contours of my sex with the tip of her tongue using a feather-light touch that almost tickled. The light pressure was just enough to keep my interest, but not enough to get me off. I rolled my hips, hoping she would take the nonverbal cue.

She stopped entirely and looked up. "Yes?"

"Lucia," I sighed. "Please."

She maintained eye contact while she kissed a wet trail across my inner thigh. Her dark, wide eyes regarded me, gauging my reaction as her mouth inched closer and closer to where I needed her the most. I tightened my grip in her hair, pulling a quiet growl from her lips.

"Please," I pled again, my voice urgent and rough. I wasn't above begging at this point. After so many months of celibacy, I couldn't handle being teased.

She flattened her tongue and licked to the right of my clit as if eating an ice cream cone. She licked another wide stroke to the left. My body tensed in anticipation of the middle road. She dragged her tongue up my center before plunging her tongue inside my dripping hole.

Her grip tightened on my thighs as she worked her tongue in and out. Her nose inelegantly mashed against my clit with every thrust inside. I didn't guide her head, but I kept one hand firmly clasped against the back of her neck.

My breathing became more labored the longer she drank deeply from my core. My thighs twitched and my stomach tightened.

"Lucia," I gasped. "Oh God. So good. Don't stop. Please don't stop."

My words drove her to increase her pace. She replaced her tongue with her fingers. I flailed and reached for her, desperate to kiss her mouth. I could taste myself on her tongue, lips, and cheeks. Our tongues dueled, and I moaned into her mouth. Still on her knees, she pierced me with two solid, unrelenting fingers. I cried out when she swiped her thumb across my clit.

My body jerked as if being struck with an electric current. "Oh fuck," I cursed.

I rolled my hips in time with her penetrating fingers. I met each thrust with one of my own.

"Yes," she seemed to growl. "Cum for me, June."

"I'm close, I'm close, I'm close," came my chanted promise.

"Cum on my fingers," she pled. "I want to feel you cum."

She rose to her feet for better leverage. She pushed me onto my back, her fingers never losing contact.

I screwed my eyes shut as my head hit the pillow. "It's so fucking good, baby," I cried. I didn't have the bandwidth to dwell on the unintentional endearment. A fire was building in my belly, ready to ignite the rest of my form.

She bent over my body and sucked my clit into her mouth. She gently tongued the hypersensitive bundle while she continued to fuck me with solid, steady strokes.

"Oh God," I choked out. "I'm going to … I'm-I'm … fuck, I'm cumming."

I was still recovering from one orgasm when Lucia straddled my lap for a second time. She pressed her palm into the center of my chest and coaxed me to remain on my back on top of the comforter. I watched her with half-lidded eyes as she positioned her index and middle finger on either side of her swollen clit. She spread her fingers, and with the movement, she separated her pussy lips as well.

She dropped her hips and rubbed her clit against mine. A quiet whimper vibrated in my throat. Her features pinched in concentration as she maintained a slow and steady rhythm. The feeling wasn't as intense as when she'd been tonguing my slit or fucking me with her fingers, but the view was terribly erotic. As she continued to roll her hips and grind against me, I imagined Lucia with a nylon harness fastened snug around her lean thighs and a rigid silicone appendage jutting out from her pubic bone. I'd never used a strap-on before. But on Lucia's toned form, I could already anticipate just how good it might look and feel.

I grabbed onto her narrow hips and took control of the pace. I bucked up into her, pulling a throaty groan from her lips. I held onto her hip with my left hand while my right hand traveled between her thighs. My fingers slipped through her wetness.

"I don't … I don't usually let people do that," she told me between ragged breaths.

"I'm not people. I'm June."

There was only a moment of hesitation before she ground into my stationary hand. "Don't stop," I heard her rough whisper.

Encouraged by her words, I slid one finger and then two into her clenching sex. A strangled noise bubbled up her throat. She held on tightly to my upper arms as I penetrated her. Her grip restricted my movements somewhat, but I still managed to flex my wrist to thrust solidly into her.

I curled my fingers and felt her sex clench around me.

"June," she gasped. "Right there." She closed her eyes and her head fell forward.

I wasn't so much fucking her as she was riding my fingers, but I really didn't care. I only wanted to make her feel as good as she'd made me feel. She wasn't as vocal as me, but quiet sighs had escalated to louder grunts and groans.

Her body went still and then rigid. Her thighs tensed and her features pinched. The fingers around my forearms squeezed me even tighter and her mouth fell open in a silent cry.

I slowed the movements of my hand until the warm, wet pulsing around my fingers stopped.

When she'd better caught her breath, Lucia rolled off of me and onto her back. She rested her hands on her chest as her heartbeat slowed, but she wasn't still for long. She pressed a quick kiss to my forehead before climbing out of bed.

"Where are you going?" I murmured. We'd both been pulled from sleep at a too-early hour and, combined with orgasms, I was beginning to feel the aftereffects of both.

She retrieved her bra and underwear from the floor. "Back to work."

"What?" I sat up, more alert. "No. You've put in enough work for the day."

She deviated from getting dressing to sit on the edge of the bed. She grabbed my hand and kissed my knuckles. "I don't think that making you cum is work, *cariña*," she said with a cheeky grin. "You should stay in bed though. You've earned yourself a break."

My eyelashes fluttered. "Do you really have to go?"

"I do," she confirmed. "Marisol is supposed to be coming by this afternoon. I don't really trust her or that damn bird to be unsupervised."

I propped myself up on my elbow as I watched her put on the same clothes she'd worn the previous night. I would have offered to let her borrow some clean clothes from me, but a nagging question tickled at my thoughts.

"Did you ask me out because of Marisol? I saw you watching us that day."

"What? No," she huffed in denial. "You can hang out with whomever you want."

"So you didn't get jealous?" I prodded.

"I-I … oh, fuck it," she sighed. Her body seemed to droop with defeat. "I didn't like the way she was looking at you; like she had dollar signs in her eyeballs. I didn't want her to take advantage of you." Her nonchalance returned. "But I don't have any claim over you, so do whatever you want."

I swallowed when the words got caught in my throat. "Do you *want* to claim me?"

I watched her slowly wet her lips. The tip of her tongue poked out first before her plump, lower lip disappeared into her mouth. When it reappeared, it was shiny and wet and definitely kissable.

"How about dinner tomorrow?" she proposed. "I'll take care of the food," she told me. "And then I'll take care of you."

"O-okay." My voice shook a little on the word. "No dinner tonight?"

I hoped I didn't sound clingy. We'd spent the last few evenings together, plus we saw each other at work.

"I've got a meeting in the morning."

"What about?"

"It's premature. Kind of a meeting of the minds," she said vaguely. "I'll tell you all about it at dinner tomorrow. Maybe we'll have something to celebrate."

I flopped down more solidly on my pillows, petulant like a child. "I can't believe you're going back to work," I huffed.

"It's not really work if you love what you do," she noted. "Besides," she said, sitting down on the edge of the mattress, "I wouldn't want people to think I'm getting lazy, now that I'm sleeping with the boss."

"You can…" I swallowed hard. "You can be the boss tomorrow night."

I couldn't believe I didn't stumble more on the words.

Lucia regarded me. For the briefest of moments, I thought I'd said too much or had gone too far. She wet her lips before responding: "How about that horizontal tasting?"

It might have been my imagination, but her tone sounded lower and more ragged than its usual timbre.

I sucked in a sharp breath. I had no idea what that might entail, but it sounded very appealing. I couldn't find my words, so I nodded instead.

I hesitated before speaking again. "Will it freak you out if I say I'll miss you when you're gone?"

Lucia rewarded my honesty with a grin. "I'd be hurt if you didn't."

CHAPTER TWENTY-ONE

"Good afternoon, ladies." Rolando entered the tasting barn, the sun at his back. Inside the barn, Natalie and I were going over the upcoming schedule of tastings and special events. Out in the fields, the grapes were deepening in color and building up their sugars. Harvest was still a few months away, but anticipation was building on the farm. "I wanted to go over some plans with Lucia for the younger fruit," he said. "Do you know where she is?"

I hadn't seen Rolando since the morning of the Jeffersons' vineyard fire. It was also the moment he'd discovered his daughter had spent the night with me. I didn't know what he thought or even assumed about the situation. He knew Lucia dated women, and he knew about Alex and my previous relationship. But did he automatically assume Lucia and I were sleeping together? Or did he believe my assistant winemaker and I were just becoming good friends?

"Lucia's at a meeting," I supplied. "I'll let her know you're looking for her if I see her when she comes back."

Rolando bobbed his head, but he didn't directly look at me. It pained me that I'd made him feel awkward when he had only ever supported me.

Natalie regarded me after Rolando returned outside. Her eyes narrowed shrewdly. "Lucia told you about that?"

"Uh huh."

I didn't elaborate the context for how or why I knew that information. I wasn't ready to announce to the rest of the staff that

Lucia and I had been spending a lot of time together after work hours. We'd had sex—really good, really intimate, really intense sex—but until I spoke with Lucia about things like relationship labels and expectations, I didn't want to unnecessarily complicate things by bringing in other people and their unsolicited opinions.

"You're awfully calm for someone who might lose their assistant winemaker to a larger competitor."

I blinked at Natalie's words. "Wait. What?"

"Lucia's meeting. She's down the street meeting with Chateau Barrique. They practically run the zinfandel scene in Calistoga. They've been trying to poach her forever."

I tried to reign in my emotions, but my face must have given me away.

"She didn't tell you what the meeting was about," Natalie correctly guessed.

"No." I shook my head. "She said she had a meeting today. I just assumed it was about the union."

Natalie made a face like a grimace. "My bad. I'm sorry, June."

"No, no. It's not your fault," I appeased.

Lucia could have—should have—given me more details about her morning meeting. About the reason she hadn't been able to spend the night. But instead she'd chosen to keep me in the dark.

Before feelings of self-doubt and betrayal could build much momentum, the barn door slid open and Lucia appeared.

"Honey, I'm home!" she announced. There was a noticeable bounce to her step.

Her clothing was unremarkable that day—she didn't look like she'd just come from a big interview—but I imagined Lucia Santiago wasn't the type to dress up to impress a potential employer. She'd let her wine do the talking for her.

I cleared my throat. "Lucia, can I see you in the office for a minute?"

Her dad was also looking for her, but I had a pressing need to speak with her first.

We left the public side of the barn for the private office. I shut the door behind me.

Lucia sat on the corner of my desk. "What's up, *Jefa?*" She swung her legs back and forth, looking happy and carefree. "Ready for our big dinner tonight?"

I folded my arms across my chest. "Zinfandel?"

I didn't need to elaborate. The eager, playful smile disappeared from her lips. "It's not a big deal—it was only lunch. I was never really serious about the offer anyway," she dismissed. "They've been hounding me for ages to come work for them."

"If they've been asking you forever, why did you finally say yes to a meeting?"

She shrugged with maddening nonchalance. "I was hungry."

The statement was so simple. So innocent. And yet, I couldn't help myself from considering the multiple layers of meaning in those words. It was a literal lunch meeting and she'd gotten a free meal out of the arrangement. But I knew being the assistant winemaker at a boutique winery wasn't enough for Lucia. She wanted more.

"I thought it would be a good opportunity to kickstart the union," she finally admitted. "Maybe I could change the industry from the inside if I worked for one of the major wineries."

"What happened to your dream of owning your own vineyard?" I posed.

I held back my other complaint: *What about me?* It hurt that she hadn't been more transparent.

A dark look crossed her features. "Dreams are for people who are sleeping."

"You can't just give up," I argued.

"I'm not giving up. But not everyone can just swoop in and buy a vineyard because they feel like it." She didn't bother to veil the obvious reference. "Sometimes dreams are just a pie-in-the-sky idea. You might work really hard to make it happen, but the game is already rigged against you. You might wish upon a star, or blow out birthday candles," she continued. "Maybe make a wish on an eyelash or toss a coin in the fountain. But I've got to be realistic," she said with a bitter shake of her head, "I live in the real world."

"Hey, folks. We're not open to the general public." I heard Natalie's voice filter through the closed office door from where she'd remained in the main section of the barn. "You can visit our website though and make an appointment for a private tour later in the week."

The visitor's response was apologetic. "Sorry. We're just looking for June. June Marchand?"

I didn't immediately recognize the second voice, but I knew the last name. I didn't consider my conversation with Lucia to be over, but curiosity won out. I held up a finger, indicating I wanted to hit the pause button, before I exited the office. Although I hadn't intended for Lucia to follow me, she trailed closely behind.

The barn was empty with the exception of Natalie. I figured whomever had showed up couldn't have gone far. I walked to the open barn door to investigate.

I stood just beyond the barn. The afternoon sun was high in the sky and newly hired hands were busy in the fields tending to the vineyard canopy. In about two months, it would be time to harvest the literal fruits of their labor.

A few yards away, a man and a woman held hands, apparently on their way back to their car in the parking lot. I hadn't seen the couple since January. And before that, hardly at all.

"Henry?" I called out.

The man's head jerked up and he turned at the sound of his name. He beamed when he spotted me. "June!"

Lucia turned to me. "Friends of yours?" I could hear the curiosity in her tone.

I shook my head, but I didn't offer more. I was too shellshocked by the unsolicited visit.

Henry and the woman with him walked briskly in our direction.

I blinked a few times. "Henry. And ... and ...."

I couldn't remember the woman's name. I'd only met her once, and it had been at Alex's funeral. I didn't have too many vivid memories of that day. I'd been too overwhelmed, too numb to recall much of anything.

"Shannon," the woman supplied.

"Right. Shannon," I echoed. "Sorry."

"We've been trying to connect with you since the funeral," Henry explained. "We didn't have your phone number and the only email we had was your old work address."

I could tell Lucia was waiting for an introduction. Henry also seemed to be interested in the woman standing beside me.

"Henry, Shannon, this is Lucia," I introduced. "She-she's the assistant winemaker here at Lark Estates. Lucia, this is Alex's brother, Henry, and his wife, Shannon."

Alex's brother and sister-in-law both cordially shook hands with Lucia while I continued to spiral. A tight, foreboding feeling had taken up residency in my stomach.

What were they doing here?

Henry passed his hand over his forehead. It was warm that day, but no warmer than I imagined Iowa was in late summer. "I don't want to bother you at work," he stated, "but do you think we could meet up later? There's some things we need to discuss."

Despite my misgivings, I didn't feel like I had much of a choice. I finally forced a smile to my lips. "Sounds great. Can't wait."

A few hours later, I sat at a small table at a coffee and pastry shop in downtown Calistoga. The air smelled inviting with the strong scents of coffee, chocolate, and other sweet things, but my stomach only felt sour due to the couple seated across from me.

Henry Marchand was nearly the male doppelganger of his younger sister. They had the same serious mouth, wide jaw, and bright blue eyes. Alex's hair had always been long enough to pull back in a ponytail while Henry's hair was shorter on the sides and brushed across his forehead. With the exception of their different length and style of hair, the resemblance was uncanny.

Henry drank deeply from a cup of black coffee before addressing me. "I'm sorry we haven't been able to connect since the funeral," he apologized. "Life got busy."

"How did you find me?"

The framing of my question made it sound like I was a fugitive on the run. I hadn't actively been hiding from Alex's family, but none of them had cared enough to follow up with me in the days after the funeral. No one had my phone number. I'd deleted all of my social media accounts after Alex died, not wanting the pictorial reminder of all that I'd lost. If they'd searched for me on the internet, they might have found my former employer, but my work email had been long deactivated.

"You weren't easy to find," Henry confirmed. "I wanted to check in on you. See how you were doing after Alex died." He cleared his throat. "Imagine my surprise to discover you'd moved on so quickly."

He slid several glossy black and white photographs across the table.

"What is this?" I questioned.

I picked up one of the photographs. It had been taken inside of the tasting barn, during one of our tours, perhaps. Natalie and I stood before a modest-sized group. I picked up a second photograph to find more of the same—me serving wine inside of the barn.

"Did you ... did you have someone follow me?"

"You disappeared," he offered up as his excuse. "We didn't have any other choice."

I looked back and forth between Henry and his wife. Who were these people? They'd never wanted anything to do with Alex in life. Why were they suddenly so involved in her after death?

"I didn't disappear," I countered. "You never wanted anything to do with me—or Alex for that matter."

"Alex was my only sister," Henry said evenly. "She's my family."

I nearly exploded. "Alex was the love of my life!"

Henry produced another image for my inspection. I was no longer in the tasting barn or on the vineyard at all. Lucia and I sat across from each other at the little Italian restaurant. We weren't doing anything incriminating in the photo, but the image itself seemed like a kind of indictment.

"Funny how you found a replacement so quickly," Henry stated quietly.

I felt the air leave my lungs. "That's not ... that's not fair."

"We're willing to compromise with you on this, June. You were obviously a large part of Alex's life. I don't want you to end up with nothing."

"Are you—are you threatening me?" I managed to choke out.

Henry sat back in his chair. "The vineyard. We're going to sell it. We'll return your down payment. There's really no way to know how much of that was yours or Alex's."

"You ... you ..." I couldn't find my words. What Henry was suggesting had blindsided me. I'd expected a tense but civil cup of coffee with the pair. I never imagined this.

Henry took advantage of my continued stunned silence. "It would be a mistake to try to fight this," he said quietly, but calmly. He folded his hands on the table. "You could hire a lawyer, of course, but then our offer goes away. Think on it, June. I know you'll make the right decision."

I couldn't remember how I made it back to the vineyard. My body was numb and my brain was enveloped in a dense fog. I bypassed the tasting barn, not really wanting to see anyone, and drove directly for the farmhouse. Despite my desire to hide from the world, Lucia had other designs. I found her sitting on the front steps of the farmhouse—the steps she'd repaired for me. I felt like she'd fixed a lot more than that.

She stood when I exited my parked my car. I watched her stretch out her legs as I approached. It made me wonder how long she'd been waiting and sitting on my front stoop. "Hey," she greeted.

"Hey." My feet dragged on loose gravel.

She chewed on her lower lip. "How are you?"

My own bottom lip began to tremble. "Not okay."

The tears shouldn't have been a surprise. I'd been blindsided by Alex's family. The rug had been pulled out from beneath me. The wool had been pulled over my eyes. I felt the unbearable weight of every idiom and metaphor.

Instead of running in the opposite direction, Lucia reached for me. A surprised hiccup caught in my throat when she pulled me in for a crushing hug. My breath nearly left my lungs with the force of it.

"Hey, it's okay," she soothed. "Whatever it is, we'll figure it out."

I let her hold me. I didn't think everything was going to be alright. I didn't think we'd figure it out. But I let her try to placate me with encouraging words and her strong arms around me.

I pressed my nose to her shoulder and inhaled. I could smell the earth and her sunscreen and the faint tang of sweat. "Alex's family is going to take the vineyard," I sighed.

Lucia pulled back and held me at arm's length. "What? They can't do that!"

"They can," I said thickly. "And they are. Alex didn't have a will. They get everything."

Lucia's features pinched in confusion. "But you were her wife."

"We weren't …" I sucked in a sharp breath, "technically married."

Lucia dropped her arms and me. "What?"

Without her solid tether, I felt myself floating away. "We'd been together for such a long time that when same-sex marriage finally became legal, Alex thought it was silly to run out and get married."

We'd fought bitterly for several months about if we should get legally married. I didn't want a massive ceremony; I would have been happy with a courthouse wedding. But Alex was stubborn and unconventional. She didn't want the government to legitimize our relationship when we'd long recognized ourselves as life partners. She'd shut me down every time I'd tried to bring it up. Eventually, I stopped trying to convince her it was something we should do.

"But isn't there some kind of common law marriage rule?" Lucia questioned. "You've got to fight this, June. Don't let them bully you."

My shoulders slumped forward. "I don't think I have it in me."

My response brought a deep frown to her beautiful features. "I thought you wanted this."

I shook my head. "I never wanted this. Alex made that decision for me."

"Aren't you letting Alex's family make another decision for you?" Lucia's voice had become agitated.

"This isn't my world, Lucia. You said it yourself."

"Yeah, but that was ..." She swallowed and wet her lips. "That was before."

"You should take that job at the other vineyard," I decided. "You're destined for bigger and better things, Lucia. You shouldn't let this place hold you back. You can reform the system from the inside."

I watched the rapid flutter of her long eyelashes. She looked to be on the verge of crying. "What about ... what about us?"

Her question tore me apart, but I steadied myself and my heart. "I had my chance at love. I can't expect the universe to give me a second one."

+ + +

I left Calistoga nearly as abruptly as I'd arrived. After packing a few essential belongings into the back of my car, my friend Lily's San Francisco condo had been my next stop. I didn't want to linger on the property. I didn't want my forced eviction to be harder than it had to be. I was a coward who didn't want to say goodbye, and one who didn't fight hard enough to stay.

Lily sat on the couch beside me. She set a cup of tea in front of me on her coffee table. "So what happened?"

I exhaled noisily. "You know I'd rather not talk about it."

"And *you* know that I'm not going to take it easy on you."

I picked up the ceramic mug and held its warmth between my two hands. I had no intention of drinking the scalding liquid just yet, but it was an excuse to delay my confession if only for a few more moments.

"I went to Calistoga to honor Alex's memory," I said. "And in the process, I forgot about her." I shook myself to avoid falling apart in front of my friend. "Maybe I can beg my old boss to give me my job back—if he hasn't already replaced me with someone half my age who'll work for half the pay."

Lily set an encouraging hand on top of my knee. "You'll figure it out, June. Time for a reset."

"A reset," I echoed with a wistful sigh. "Again."

élevage

CHAPTER TWENTY-TWO

It was cold in San Francisco, or at least it was unseasonably cold for early November. Lily and I sat at a table for two high above the busy streetscape where other city dwellers were just getting off of work from their desk jobs and were gearing up for the weekend. I wasn't looking forward to anything these days, unless you counted the clawfoot tub in Lily's condo. I'd licked my wounds from her guest room for the better part of the fall season until she'd dragged me out of my cave of misery to have dinner at a restaurant whose owner, Isaiah, was a good friend of hers.

I was still in between places. It hadn't made sense to lease an apartment when I still had my old condo. The current tenants were only subletting, but it didn't feel right making them find a new place on short notice, especially when San Francisco's housing market was so competitive and expensive. Lily had graciously offered to let me stay as long as I wanted in her extra room, so I'd given the couple in my condo until the end of the year to find new accommodations. I didn't want to take advantage of my best friend's hospitality, but the open-ended invitation was a great comfort.

I wasn't back at my old place of work either. I worked from Lily's dining room table as a freelancer and contributed to whatever design projects they kicked my way. It kept me busy, although not really satisfied. But it would suffice while I kept an eye on the classified ads for something more challenging or rewarding.

It struck me that I really had no reason to stay in San Francisco, or even California. After relinquishing Lark Estates to Alex's family, I'd gotten my nest egg back. As part of the deal, they hadn't gone after other assets like the San Francisco condo or my car. And yet, I was living out of suitcases and boxes and working from a makeshift office space. But short of buying a van and living a solitary life on the road, I didn't know what to do or where to go. I was grieving again—not the loss of Alex this time, but rather the loss of me. I'd thought Lark Estates was going to be my new beginning. After an awkward start, I'd started to finally find my place.

But who was I now? What was going to become of me?

"You've got that look again." Lily's voice censured me.

"Sorry." I blinked and shook my head as if to reorient myself to our surroundings. Quiet jazz played in the background. The hushed conversations from neighboring tables created white noise. Utensils lightly clinked against serving plates.

"Where did your brain wander to this time?" she asked.

I smiled, but it didn't reach my eyes. "The usual existential crisis. What am I doing with my life?"

"You know you can take your time," she encouraged me. "There's no rush to figure that out. You jumped immediately from Alex's funeral to a totally new life. Maybe this time you can take a breath before deciding your next move."

I nodded while I fiddled with my water glass. I'd heard her words of wisdom so often that I could recite them by heart. I knew she was right though. There was no sense in throwing my energies into a new project or a new career path if I didn't really want it for myself. The desire for change wasn't enough. I needed to figure out what I wanted.

I couldn't allow myself to dwell too much on Lark Estates and all that it represented. It was supposed to be a new start—a clean slate where I could step beyond my comfort zone and re-imagine my life. I'd definitely achieved that and more with the property, but especially its people. Maybe I should have fought Henry and the rest of Alex's estranged family. Maybe I'd given up too easily. I chewed on the inside of my cheek to stem the unstable emotions that were always simmering just below the surface whenever I let my thoughts linger on the events from the previous few months.

"Lily!" A new voice—this one male—interrupted my most recent emotional spiral. "I'm so glad you could make it out!"

Lily stood and greeted the man—whom I assumed was her friend, Isaiah—with a quick kiss to either cheek. Isaiah was a handsome Black man with a generous and inviting smile. He also happened to be the executive chef and owner of San Francisco's most recent hot and trendy eatery. His white chef's coat fit over a trim yet muscular build. His dark braids were tied back with a thick black band. Because he was a close friend of Lily's, I assumed he was queer. I didn't notice a wedding ring, but he may have taken off any jewelry to avoid injuries while he worked—although I doubted anyone in his kitchen would have to resort to a needle and thread if a finger went missing.

When Lily introduced me, I forced a smile to my lips instead of allowing my thoughts to travel back to a corrugated metal barn in Calistoga.

"I'm going to send over some off-the-menu bites," Isaiah told us. "I got some Dungeness crab this morning; it's so fresh it practically walks itself to your table."

Isaiah's smile and upbeat attitude were infectious. I could feel my previous fog start to burn away.

"I also got in a new red this week," he said with the same enthusiasm. "June, Lily tells me you have quite the palate. I'd love to have your opinion on it."

His suggestion had me rattled. "Oh, I really don't drink wine anymore."

"You *owned a winery*, June," Lily unnecessarily reminded me. "You have more expertise than the two of us combined."

"Fine," I relented with a tired sigh. "Bring it over."

Isaiah left our table, in search of wine and table bites. I could tell Lily was staring at me without even glancing in her direction.

"What?" I bristled.

"You don't drink wine anymore?" she questioned. "Are you really that traumatized?"

"You weren't there, Lily. You don't know."

I had told Lily that my assistant winemaker and I had had sex. But I'd downplayed the nature of my relationship with Lucia, probably out of self-preservation. I hadn't shared with her our all-night conversations. I hadn't revealed how sensitive Lucia had been to my anxiety or how she'd comforted me when I made mistake after mistake on the vineyard. I hadn't told her how protected and special Lucia had made me feel.

Isaiah returned to our table before I could disassemble. He brought two red wine glasses along with the previously referenced bottle of red wine. I didn't recognize the label, but that didn't mean much; it's not like I'd become a sommelier over the past few months.

Isaiah presented us with the unopened bottle. "It's from a new label. The grapes are old," he qualified, "but the label is new. The distributor was really adamant that I give this place a try because they're one of the only cooperatives in Napa Valley."

"Cooperative?" Lily echoed.

"The workers all own a share of the profits," I said, almost automatically, "from the cellar rat who cleans the fermentation tanks, to the arthritic field hand, all the way up to the head winemaker."

Lily looked mildly impressed. "I guess you did learn something up there."

Isaiah uncorked the bottle and poured a few ounces in each of our glasses. "It's a three-year-old cabernet franc," he announced.

"I don't think I've ever heard of a cabernet franc," Lily noted as she stared at the purple liquid in her glass. "Is it related to cabernet sauvignon?"

"It's thinner and less tannic than a cabernet sauvignon," I recited. "It's relatively rare, so it's typically used in blends. There's only about 3,000 acres planted in the whole world, and most of them are in Italy."

"This should be a treat then," Isaiah noted. "Let me know what you think."

I grabbed the wine stem of my glass and took an experimental sniff. Lily noticed my actions and didn't immediately dive into her own wine.

"Teach me how to drink wine, June," my friend implored.

"It's not that hard," I said. "Just follow four steps: look, smell, taste, think."

Lily held her glass up to the overhead light. "I'm looking." She stuck her nose into the bell of the glass and audibly inhaled as she breathed in the wine's aromas. "Smelling," she said, almost like checking off a To Do list. "And now for the taste." I half expected her to down all of the liquid in her glass like it was a shot of alcohol, but to her credit, she only took a small sip.

I took a measured sip myself, enough that I could pass the liquid across my tongue and tastebuds. I was going to tell Lily about Lucia's fun fact that women were genetically better tasters than men—I thought she'd get a kick out of that nugget—but a familiar flavor had me pausing.

I smacked my lips, more in thought than from the wine itself. "It almost tastes like …" I brought the glass to my nose again and inhaled. "It almost reminds me of …"

Lily was the one to vocalize my thoughts: "Bell pepper?"

My mouth suddenly felt dry, and it wasn't from the tannins. "Can I see the bottle?"

Isaiah readily forfeited the bottle to me. I held it so I could better inspect the label. Natalie had once told me you could learn everything you needed to know about a wine just from its label. 2019 cabernet franc. It was advertised as an estate wine from Napa Valley, which meant that all of the grapes had been grown on their property and hadn't been purchased from someone or someplace else.

The vineyard was named *Huelga*, which struck me as unusual or at least unique. Typically Napa wineries had a more romantic-sounding name that evoked a high class or luxurious experience. All of my thoughts collided, however, when I finally read the wine's actual name.

"Does that bottle say '*Alex*?'" Lily had also taken note of the distinct name scrawled across the label. "Wow," my friend marveled. "What are the odds?"

I continued to stare at the bottle. "I don't think it's a coincidence."

CHAPTER TWENTY-THREE

The old signage along the side of the county highway had been replaced and updated. A wistful smile crept onto my lips. I hadn't been particularly attached to the vineyard's previous name, but the new name and new sign were a visual reminder of how much had changed in a short amount of time. The vineyard looked much the same as when I'd first stepped onto the property as its newly appointed owner earlier in the year. Only a few dead leaves and shriveled up berries remained on the vines. It hurt that I hadn't been able to participate in the harvest, but that had been my own fault.

It was a Tuesday, so I was surprised to see so many strange vehicles parked in the normally vacant lot adjacent to the tasting barn. Some larger spots were occupied by conversion vans and extended SUVs with the name of a wine tour company screen printed on the side. Another electric vehicle was plugged into the charger I'd argued with Lucia about installing, so I was forced to park in a regular spot.

I could have called ahead, but I wasn't confident that she would agree to meet with me. I could have been blindsiding her, just showing up unannounced, but then again she might not even be there. She'd told me many times about her lack of roots. Once the grapes had been harvested and their juices set to fermentation, she would be off to another part of the world where it was still growing season.

I slid open the wide barn door and stepped inside. The air was warm on my face and the low din of an assembled crowd filled the enclosed space. I would have guessed I'd interrupted some kind of party, but there'd been no signage to indicate the barn was closed for a private event. I scanned the tasting room for any familiar faces. Groups of female friends and mixed couples gathered around old French oak casks that had been repurposed into high-top tables. I smiled at the thought that maybe Carlos and Oscar had made the new furniture.

Staff whom I didn't recognize rang up wine bottle purchases on one side of the tasting room. Shelving had been constructed to convert the far corner of the barn into a small retail store where guests could purchase full bottles of the wines they had tasted along with various wine-related items like corkscrews and coasters.

Amongst the sea of strangers, I finally spotted a familiar face. Natalie's warm smile welcomed patrons at a separate station that resembled a small wine bar. A few empty stools were positioned in front of the short bar along with what appeared to be beer taps. As I moved closer to the bar I realized that the bar tappers weren't connected to beer kegs, but rather to wine kegs. The few varieties on tap were written on a small chalkboard that hung over the bar.

I stepped toward the bar and waited for my turn. Natalie, unsurprisingly, was affable and gracious to each new patron. She greeted each guest like a life-long friend. When I reached the front of the line, she was busy closing out the previous sale.

"Hey there, what can I get you?"

I waited for her head to raise and for our eyes to meet. "Hey, Nat."

"June! Oh my word! I didn't expect to see you back here!"

Her words had me hanging my head. "I was in the neighborhood…" I trailed off.

Natalie immediately rounded the small bar and left her station. She pulled me into a tight hug and her familiar perfume invaded my senses.

"You're so busy!" I remarked.

"I know! Lucia's been working nonstop to get more foot traffic to the winery ever since she took over."

"Lucia?" I echoed.

"Oh, right. You wouldn't have known," she seemed to scold herself. "After you left, the new owners sold the property to Lucia. She wrote up a business plan and everything to get a loan from the bank. She changed the winery's name, transformed the tasting room, and has been promoting the hell out of this place ever since."

I blinked as I took in the new information.

"Legally it's her name on the mortgage," Natalie continued, "but we're a cooperative now. All of the profits are divided amongst the employees. Once we got our story out there, things kind of exploded. It turns out people want to support businesses who treat their employees well."

I shook my head. "Imagine that."

"She's in the wine cellar if you want to see her."

"Oh, I-I couldn't," I stammered.

"Yes you *could*, and yes you *should*," Natalie all but chastised me. "I've got a bunch of thirsty customers to tend to, so you go on. You know the way."

I wanted to resist more, but there was no point. I didn't need to deny it. I wanted to see Lucia.

I gave Natalie another quick hug before I left her to return to work. I slipped past the crowds and unobtrusively maneuvered around the flimsy barriers that read *Employees Only*. I walked past the giant steel fermentation tanks and the other winemaking machines. Everything smelled clean and disinfected. I silently lamented that I hadn't had the opportunity to see the winemaking apparatus at work. I'd missed out on the vast buckets of grapes being sent through the crusher destemmer. I hadn't gotten to witness the giant juicer pressing the tonnage of berries. I hadn't been able to help break up the pomace cap when the juice was first fermenting. The machines were silent now, but as I walked through the industrial space, I imaged the movement and orchestrated chaos necessary to transform the early fall harvest into its final product.

The temperature dropped a few degrees as I descended the brick steps to the wine caves below the barn. The underground hallways could be a complicated labyrinth; there was a very real possibility that I wouldn't find Lucia. She might finish whatever tasks she had in the cellar and return above ground before I could discover her. That thought put me somewhat at ease. I wanted to see her again, but I had no idea what I'd say to her. I wished she had been in the tasting room so I could have observed her from afar before deciding my next move.

I'd always had a hard time finding Lucia in the wine cellar, so it was only appropriate that I found her right away on the one instance I wanted to avoid her. She stood amongst a mountain of French oak casks. My steps had been light and imperceptible, but I doubted she would have registered my presence if I'd tap danced down the stone corridor. She held onto a clear graduated cylinder in one hand and a wine thief in the other. Her features were pinched with her forehead furrowed in deep thought.

Her hair was pulled back in its usual braid which fell down the center of her back. She wore her typical uniform of blue denim button-up shirt with dark green pants and sturdy-looking leather boots. She'd rolled the sleeves up to her elbows. Her short nails were perceptively stained red around the cuticles. I wondered if I would be able to taste the wine on her fingers if I sucked them into my mouth.

I unintentionally cleared my throat, not to bring attention to myself, but rather to clear the explicit images from my thoughts.

My body jerked when she spoke: "Carlos, this cask is going to need more *Oenococcus Oeni* for the MLF."

I wet my lips. "I'll let him know if I see him."

Lucia looked up sharply at my words. The concentration on her features softened. "June." She offered up my name as if reciting a prayer.

I took a silent, tentative step forward. "Hi."

"Hi. Wow." She shut her eyes momentarily and shook her head. "This … is unexpected."

I chewed on my lower lip. "I know."

Lucia set down the glass cylinder on a nearby barrel. She scratched at the back of her neck. "How have you been?"

I didn't want small-talk. I had questions that needed answers.

"You named your wine Alex."

Lucia's dark eyes widened beneath the dim cellar lighting. "How did you …"

"It was at a restaurant in San Francisco. My friend Lily knows the owner, and he wanted us to try a new wine he was considering."

Lucia's full mouth parted. Her tongue appeared and she slowly wet her lips. "That's quite the coincidence."

It had felt like much more than a coincidence, but I knew there was no way Lucia could have known I'd ever be at that specific restaurant, and Lily swore up and down that she'd had nothing to do with it.

"Why did you name it after Alex?" I asked again.

"Her family sold me the vineyard. They could have sold to a corporation or a hedge fund who would have turned us into grape producers for Two Buck Chuck," she explained. "I thought it was a fitting memorial," she said with an easy shrug. "We're going to name all of our future wines after the important people in our lives. Aunt Clara's demanded that she be next year's blend."

"I have a hard time picturing your aunt demanding anything."

"It wasn't so much a demand, but rather a passive aggressive suggestion."

I found myself chuckling at the description. "Okay. That sounds more accurate."

"I told her the next blend has already been spoken for though. Do you want to try it so far?"

"Oh. I really can't stay," I stumbled. "I-I don't even know why I came all the way out here."

"Hold on. Let me finish with this cask."

"Is that from this year's harvest?" I couldn't help asking.

Lucia nodded. "Do you want to try? It's only a few weeks old, but you can still get an idea of what it might mature into."

I stepped a little closer—as close as I dared with this woman. I didn't want to feel how her body radiated heat. I didn't want to smell the scent that was entirely her. I'd suffered enough for one lifetime without voluntarily putting myself through more.

The open barrel perceptively sizzled as if someone had dropped Pop Rocks into the barrel.

"It's making alcohol," Lucia said in explanation. "It smells a little like warm bread, which surprises people. You normally associate yeast with beer making, not wine."

I took the briefest sniff, only for the purpose of confirming her observation—definitely not so I could smell *her*. I hummed in agreement when the distinct scent of proofing bread wafted to my nostrils.

Lucia dipped the wine thief into the open bunghole and retrieved a few ounces of the liquid. It was a bright, reddish pink, almost like cranberry juice. She retrieved a smaller tasting glass and carefully transferred some of the liquid into the glass like a chemist performing a complicated experiment. The comparison was appropriate; she was a little like a scientist in her laboratory. At this point in the winemaking process, the farming had concluded and the science had begun.

She handed me the glass a little like we were playing Hot Potato. I frowned at the realization that maybe she was just as uncomfortable being around me as I her. The jerky motion with which she passed off the small glass suggested she didn't want to inadvertently touch me.

I took an experimental sniff of the liquid in my glass, but I couldn't smell much over the yeast.

"It's really more about taste at this point," she told me. "The other characteristics—scent, viscosity, acidity, alcohol," she listed off, "will develop over the next three years."

I brought the small glass to my lips and drank the majority of its contents. I swirled the young liquid around on my tongue before swallowing. "It tastes like grape juice. With maybe a little blackberry?"

"Good girl," Lucia approved. I could hear the enthusiasm and pride in her tone. But once the statement had been made, she dropped her eyes in embarrassment. "We, uh, we missed you at harvest time."

"One less pair of hands to put to work, huh?" I weakly joked.

Lucia lifted her eyes to meet mine. "It didn't feel right. You worked so hard all spring and summer, and then you never got to see the payoff."

I was sorry I had missed harvest, too. But I was more sorry to have missed her. "I—."

"What do you think of it?" she interrupted. "It's still a little young, but once it's fully matured, I think it has potential to be something great. I'm calling it June."

I swallowed hard at the admission. "*Lucia.*"

"I had no idea you would ever see Alex's wine," she quickly insisted. "I sent out a few bottles to local restauranteurs. You were right about vineyards needing to make money, not just wine."

The laugh got caught in my throat. "Funny how that works."

"Yeah."

"I-I should go," I said. "You have work to do."

She nodded slowly, but resignedly. "I'll walk you up."

I followed Lucia back above ground. We didn't speak. I started to regret my decision to drive all the way from San Francisco just to ask her about the wine she'd named after Alex. I had her number—I could have called. Plus, she could call her wine whatever the hell she wanted. It wasn't like I owned the name Alex. I began to feel embarrassed by the unannounced visit. Why hadn't I called ahead? Why hadn't I called, period?

We reached the ground level and the barn, which was noticeably more quiet and more empty than when I'd first gone into the cellar. Lucia noticed the change as well.

"Natalie," she called to the tasting room manager, "where did everyone go?"

"I sent them home before the roads got bad." Natalie nodded towards one of the larger windows in the tasting barn.

My eyes followed the trajectory of Natalie's gesture. They widened at the sight of white, fluffy powder steadily falling from the sky.

"Is that ... snow?" I stepped outside through the barn's main door. The air temperature had perceptively plummeted since my arrival. The sky had darkened and a steady snow rained down on the Calistoga day. I held my hands out to capture a few flakes on my outstretched palms.

"I didn't think it snowed in the valley," I thought aloud.

Lucia stepped beside me with her head tilted to the sky. "It doesn't. I can't remember it ever snowing here."

"Huh. Climate change."

We stood beneath the silent snowfall. There was no wind, so the heavy flakes dropped directly to the earth. Even in the short amount of time we had been outside, the snow had already started to accumulate.

"You should stay the night," Lucia announced to the sky.

I turned to appraise her. She continued to stand with her head tilted back as if she stood beneath a showerhead. The imagery made me realize we hadn't been dating long enough to share a shower. We hadn't been together long enough to do a lot of things.

"I'm sure you're a capable driver," she continued when I didn't immediately respond, "but I doubt your toy car is equipped for this weather."

"I'll manage."

"Your car is destined for a ditch," she decided.

As if on cue, my normally capable feet slipped out from beneath me. My ankle boots were functional on the sidewalks of San Francisco, but not on freezing Calistoga volcanic soils. My arms flailed at my sides. Capable hands captured me by the elbows just before my feet completely gave away. Lucia tugged me back up until the soles of my shoes returned to solid ground.

Lucia's strong fingers remained wrapped around my biceps even though I was no longer in danger of falling. The intensity radiated from her serious, concerned features. "Stay," she commanded. "Just for the night."

"I don't want to put you out," I insisted.

"It's no hardship; there's two bedrooms. Besides," she said, "you owe me a dinner."

I'd run out of excuses.

Lucia didn't trust my shoes to traverse the short distance from the tasting barn to the farmhouse, so she drove us in one of the vineyard's covered ATVs. She apologized all the way back to the farmhouse. She'd been so busy with the winery that she hadn't had much opportunity to grocery shop in recent weeks.

I experienced a pang of nostalgia and regret as we drove up to the farmhouse. Only a few months had passed, but based on the changes she'd made elsewhere on the property, I had expected the farmhouse to also look different. Based on the exterior, however, it appeared to be untouched.

Lucia took my jacket as we walked inside. "I don't really cook," she remarked, "but I've got some of my aunt's tortilla soup in the refrigerator I could heat up."

If her aunt's soup was anywhere as good as the tamales she'd made for the bud break party, my stomach was in for a treat. "That sounds great, thank you."

I left my ankle boots in the foyer and followed Lucia to the kitchen. The farmhouse had come fully furnished when I'd first taken up residency. All of the same furniture and throw pillows, area rugs and light fixtures remained the same, almost as if I'd never left. Only a few details like Alex's missing photograph from the mantle reminded me that I had, in fact, left.

When we entered the kitchen, I smiled fondly at the twin ceramic bowls beside the refrigerator. "Has Gato moved in fulltime yet?"

"Practically," she snorted. She opened the refrigerator and pulled out a few plastic containers. "But I don't mind. He's a better roommate than my dad or Aunt Clara."

I sat quietly at the kitchen table while Lucia reheated the soup in the microwave and cut up a few toppings like cabbage, cotija cheese, and slices of ripe avocado.

"The barn looks great," I remarked when the silence became too much. "I love what you've done with the bar area."

"Thanks," she said, accepting the praise. "I had a little extra seed money for some basic renovations. We'll never be as fancy as some of the other properties, but I wouldn't want that for us anyway."

She finished heating up two bowls of her aunt's soup. She sprinkled the toppings into the steaming bowls and set one in front of me.

"You're going to love this," she anticipated. "My aunt's tortilla soup is life changing."

I dipped my spoon into the steaming bowl and scooped up the perfect mouthful. I hummed around my first bite when the rich, spicy broth hit my tongue. "Wow. This is delicious," I complimented.

"The old lady sure knows how to cook," Lucia spoke around her own mouthful. "She, uh, she was disappointed she never got to teach you how to make tamales."

I frowned deeply. "Lucia—."

She held up her hands in retreat. "I'm not going to give you a hard time. I promise. I know you've probably mentally beaten yourself up about it every day without me piling on, too."

"Thank you," I said quietly. That she knew me and my tendencies after only a short time of really being together was striking. It made me regret my decision even more. "So tell me how the collective is going," I directed, eager for a subject change. "And the union?"

"The collective is going great," she nodded before taking another mouthful of soup. "Sales are up from where we were last year at this time. You do-gooders eat up that kind of stuff."

I nudged her under the table with my foot. "Do-gooders?"

"You know the type. All of those white, suburban moms who want to do their part to make a more just society, one glass of wine at a time."

I snorted into my own wine glass. "Professional tip: don't use that in your marketing plan."

"Thanks. How much do I owe you for the consultation?" she teased.

"Don't worry. That one's on the house."

"Good. I don't think I could afford you."

"I don't know. I'm sure we could work out some kind of deal." I stopped myself when I realized I'd gone a little too far. We hadn't spoken since that day I'd left Calistoga, but it felt like no time had passed. I marveled at how easy it was to talk with her, and how quickly I'd unintentionally steered our conversation to suggestion and innuendo. I dropped my eyes to my soup bowl. "How, uh, how is the unionization going?"

"That's been a little slower to catch on," she admitted. "First I was busy with writing my business proposal for the bank, and then it was harvest, and then barn renovations. I'll have more time this winter to refocus on the union though," she said hopefully.

I played with my spoon, dragging it around the bottom of my bowl. "So that means you're staying? You're not rushing off to Chile or Brazil or Australia in the off-season?"

"No. My jet-setting days are over, at least for the moment. There's really too much work right here to be done."

"It's all so great, Lucia," I praised in earnest. "You've done so much in such a short amount of time. You're really making an impact on the industry."

I could tell my words made her uncomfortable. She squirmed in her chair and refused to meet my eyes. "So? Is your life changed?" She waited for my answer.

I knew she was only talking about the soup, but I still hesitated before answering.

"It is."

The snow had stopped by the time we were finished with dinner. I could have made another attempt at leaving, but the evening was inky black and moonless, and San Francisco was over an hour and a half drive away. But even without the less than favorable driving conditions, I didn't want to go.

"Do you want to borrow something to sleep in?" Lucia offered.

It wasn't exactly bedtime, but staying up would mean opening another bottle of wine and more small-talk. I wanted to go back to the way things had been between us. We hadn't gotten to the cuddle on the couch and watch mindless TV stage, but I'd believed we'd been moving steadily in that direction.

I wanted to put on some music and be still with her. I wanted to recline on the couch together and touch her hair and the sides of her face. I wanted to light candles and map her body with my fingertips and bury my face in her collarbone and inhale her scent. I wanted. I wanted. I wanted.

"Oh, uh, that would be great," I fumbled. "Thank you."

"I turned your old bedroom into the home office," she said, almost apologetically. "But I've got the two bedrooms upstairs all set up. You can sleep in your old bed if you want. I've been using it, but you can have it tonight."

"No, that's okay," I insisted. "I can sleep in the other room."

"It's my childhood bed," she revealed, "but it still works."

We walked upstairs together like a silent death march. I waited awkwardly in the hallway while Lucia retrieved an extra set of pajamas for me. I could have slept in my underwear, but the evening would be cold and the farmhouse tended to be drafty.

I exhaled after I shut the bedroom door behind me. The extra upstairs bedroom was spartan but functional. The twin bed that had served as Lucia's childhood bed was smaller than any mattress I'd slept on since college, but I would survive the night.

I stripped out of the clothes I'd worn that day with an eye focused on the closed bedroom door. I wasn't worried about privacy. I wasn't worried that Lucia might bust through the bedroom door and see my naked form. I was worried that she *wouldn't*.

I knew I only had myself to blame though. I was the one who'd run away. I was the one who'd left without a proper goodbye. I was the one who hadn't fought to stay.

I slipped beneath the flannel sheets of the small guestroom bed. I'd never slept upstairs before. I'd hardly spent any time, period, on the second floor. The farmhouse had felt so large and empty that it hadn't made sense at the time to spread myself out throughout each floor plan. It made me wonder how Lucia liked living alone. She'd made the transition from her father's house to living independently. How long had she waited before moving in? Why had she made the change in the first place?

I tossed and turned in bed, knowing that sleep would be hard to find that night. The mattress was comfortable enough, but my brain refused to shut off with the knowledge that Lucia slept just across the hallway.

My body tensed every time the house made a noise. Was she having similar problems falling asleep? Or had she passed out right away?

With a frustrated sigh, I sat up and threw off the covers. I got out of bed before I could let myself overthink my decision. I left the extra bedroom and tiptoed across the hallway. I knocked quietly on the closed door. The latch hadn't fully caught when Lucia had shut the door earlier, and my minimum force caused the door to creak open.

"Lucia?" I quietly called her name with no real intention of actually her waking up.

Her eyes fluttered open and her dark irises slowly trained on me. "June? What's wrong?"

"Can I—can I stay in here?"

Lucia struggled to understand my request. I heard her sharp breath as if trying to rouse herself from sleep. "You want to switch rooms?"

"No." I worried my lower lip. "Can I stay in here with you?"

I heard her quiet cough. "Oh. Okay."

She pulled back the duvet and moved to one side of the mattress to make room for me. I slid into the empty space beside her and lay still while she tucked me in. She pulled the sheets tight under my chin. I hadn't offered up an explanation for wanting to share her bed and she hadn't asked.

"Is that good?" she asked.

"Mmhm," I confirmed.

The mattress was large enough that we had our own space. We could both fit comfortably, side-by-side, without touching. Despite the distance between us, I could still feel her body heat.

"Lucia?"

"Mmhm?"

"Will you hold me?"

Our time together had been cut short by Alex's family's greed and my inability to have a backbone. We'd spent nights together in my bed, but far less than I felt we deserved. Lucia seemed destined to be the big spoon.

"Come here," she said gruffly, but not unkindly. She possessed a particular talent for being rough, but not unkind.

I wiggled closer and she threw her arm over me. I rolled onto my side and pressed my backside into her front. I wasn't sure if snow still covered the ground outside, but there was no danger of being cold inside of Lucia's bed.

"Lucia?" I called her name again.

"Yes?"

"Will you touch me?"

I didn't elaborate, but she didn't seem to need additional instructions. The arm that had been curled around my waist began to move. She stroked her fingertips up and down my arm. Her touch was light, almost tickling me.

"Lucia?"

"Yes?" Her voice noticeably deepened.

I rolled over, turning in her arms. Our noses were so close, they almost touched. I looked down at her mouth and then back up to her dark, shimmering eyes.

"Will you kiss me?"

I heard her quiet intake of air.

I knew my question was unfair. Selfish, even. Just being in her bed was probably inappropriate. I'd left. I'd given up without a fight. I'd run away without standing up to Alex's family. I hadn't fought for the vineyard; I hadn't fought for our budding relationship.

I didn't deserve any of this. I didn't deserve *her*.

"It doesn't have to mean anything," I told her.

Her arms perceptively tightened around me. "But what if I want it to mean everything?"

CHAPTER TWENTY-FOUR

I woke up alone the next morning. I stared at the empty space beside me. I reached across the narrow expanse of the mattress and ran my hand across the cool sheets. I didn't know the hour, but the sun was bright enough outside to tell me that Lucia had probably gone to work. An empty feeling in my gut matched the vacancy beside me. After a few moments longer, I resigned myself to the idea that she'd left without saying goodbye. Now all I had to do was decide if I should do the same.

I retrieved the clothes I'd worn the day before from the bedroom across the hall. I took the time to remake the bed that I hadn't actually slept in and carefully folded my borrowed pajamas and set them at the end of the bed. The steps to the first floor creaked beneath my feet as I descended the staircase. I was feeling morose, sorry for myself, until my nostrils were struck with the distinct scent of bacon. I paused on the bottom step.

"Lucia?"

"Kitchen!" I heard her call back.

My throat constricted at the one word response and my earlier disappointment abated. I descended the remaining step and walked toward the kitchen.

Lucia stood in front of the stovetop, tending to a pan of frying bacon and a second pan of scrambled eggs. Her hair was in its typical glossy braid and she was dressed for work.

"You're just in time," she approved, her eyes never leaving the electric burners. "There's orange juice in the refrigerator if you want."

I remained in the archway. "I thought you'd panicked."

Lucia glanced over her shoulder at me. "No panic. I was planning on bringing you breakfast in bed."

I blinked a few times, taken aback by the sweet gesture. "Oh! Do you want me to go back upstairs?"

Lucia spun away from the stove and pulled out one of the kitchen table chairs. "Take a load off, *Jefa*."

I arched an eyebrow, but I sat down at the table. "*Jefa*?"

Her lopsided grin—that grin that never failed to make my stomach do flip-flops—made an appearance. "Sorry. Old habit."

I settled down at the kitchen table and folded my hands on my lap. "I thought you didn't cook?"

She pulled out a single plate from an upper kitchen cabinet and set it before me. "I don't. But I can heat up things."

She'd certainly heated *me* up the previous night.

I watched Lucia dance around the room as she finished making breakfast, always in motion, never stopping. I hadn't noticed before, but she moved a lot like Rolando. Her steps were light, like a dancer or a boxer. She spooned a heaping pile of hot, fluffy scrambled eggs onto the plate in front of me. Twin crispy pieces of bacon came next.

"There's more if you're still hungry," she told me.

I noticed she hadn't made a plate for herself. Only one place setting had been arranged on the kitchen table. "You're not eating?"

She paused her almost manic dance long enough to address me. "No. I have to get to work."

There was always work to do.

"You should stay though," she told me. "Take your time. Stay as long as you'd like."

She started to fill the kitchen sink with hot, soapy water.

"I can clean up all of this," I offered. "I know you're probably anxious to get to the barn."

She looked conflicted by my offer, but then bobbed her head. "Okay."

She took one last scan around the kitchen as if to make sure she wasn't forgetting anything. I thought she might bolt through the front door without a proper goodbye, but she grabbed the kitchen chair adjacent to me and pulled it away from the table. Its wooden legs scraped against the linoleum floor.

She sat down in a hurry and grabbed my right hand in both of hers. "Stay," she told me. "For as long as you want."

I looked down to where our hands met and then back up to her face. It wasn't exactly a declaration of love and longing, but the force behind her statement had my heartbeat quickening inside my chest.

I didn't know how to respond. And I was too afraid to ask her if she really meant it.

With no place to be, I took my time with breakfast. I drank my orange juice slowly, savoring it like one of our wines. I packed up leftovers into plastic containers. I washed my dishes and the pots and pans in the sink. The kitchen was already clean, but with Lucia's truck in mind, I ran a sponge over the countertops, stovetop, and kitchen table.

Lucia had left the ATV from the previous day in front of the farmhouse. The snow had already melted, leaving no lingering signs that it had ever snowed in the first place. The road was solid and I could have walked back to my car in the parking lot, but I drove the ATV back to the barn and returned it to its usual place.

I pulled my car keys out of my purse. The parking lot was empty except for my vehicle. It was too early to drink wine. Not even Natalie would be on the property yet.

I had a condo, a job, and good friends in San Francisco. I had all of the entertainment and excitement in the city that a person might want. It was practically the queer capital of the world. And yet, I couldn't get into my car. Not yet.

I returned my key ring to my purse and walked instead in the direction of the barn. The overhead lights were turned on, but the barn itself was silent. The employee picnic table—still present despite the other updates that had been made in the building—was empty. I imagined everyone was probably out in the fields. The upcoming winter months meant pruning back the canes and setting out ground cover so they would survive the mild, but still cooler temperatures until April's bud break.

I sat down at the picnic table and sighed. Movement against my right shin had me momentarily forgetting my melancholy. I scrambled to my feet again, panicked that a giant rat had scampered across my foot.

A bright chirping noise corrected my animal misidentification. It wasn't a rat. It was Gato.

The barn cat with the notched ear and white beard rubbed his body against my leg.

"Good morning, Gato. Where's Lucia?" I asked.

Gato gave me no new information, but he arched his back as he leaned into my lower leg and rubbed his body against my calf. I bent over to pet him. His face scrunched up in approval as he let me scratch between his ears.

"What do you think?" I scratched beneath his chin and miraculously kept all of my fingers. "Should I keep looking for her or should I go?"

"I was hoping you'd at least say goodbye this time."

I looked up sharply at the sound of Lucia's voice. She seemed to have appeared out of thin air, but she'd probably only been in the cellar topping off the barrels or working on her blends.

My throat tightened. "Hey."

She nodded at the cat doing figure eights around my ankles. "Looks like he warmed up to you after all."

She held an old rag in her hands. She wiped away the dirt and dust and wine from her hands and flung the piece of cloth over her right shoulder. It made her look like a bartender instead of the owner of a vineyard. The realization that Lucia finally owned her own winery made me a little lightheaded. I was so fucking proud of her, but the praise got caught in my throat.

"Are you taking off now?" she asked.

"I don't know." I wrung my hands in front of my body. I'd been naked with her before, but this moment made me feel even more vulnerable. "Did you mean what you said before? That I could ... stay?"

"Yes."

The word hung in the air. I waited, hoping she might say more.

"Come back to us." Lucia's voice creaked. "Choose us this time. Choose me."

"What would I even do?" I resisted. "You've seen me. I'm hopeless as a farmer and a winemaker."

"Food," she said without hesitation. "You could make food for our scheduled tastings. I've already applied for the permits, but I haven't gotten around to hiring a chef."

"You're just trying to keep me away from the vines," I half-heartedly teased.

Despite my attempt to lighten the conversation, Lucia's features remained solemn and unchanged. "I'm serious, June. You're a fantastic cook. You could make small bites or entire catered meals to go along with our tastings. We could host community dinners and holiday parties in the tasting barn." Her body language became more animated the longer she spoke. "Customers can charge up their electric cars in the parking lot while you cook for them and Natalie leads the tastings."

Lucia took a few tentative steps in my direction. Her ankles wobbled, looking as unstable as I felt.

"Listen, I want you. I want to be with you," she declared. "And I want you to come back to the farm. But I know you won't be satisfied unless you know you're contributing."

I hollowed out my cheeks to keep liquid emotions from escaping my tear ducts. "I wanted to do this for Alex. But a part of me probably wanted to do this for myself, too. I wanted to prove to myself that I could be spontaneous or do something brave and bold. To prove I could live without her."

Lucia grabbed both of my hands in hers. "I'm not trying to ... I don't want to replace her."

"You couldn't."

The wounded look on her face was immediate.

"I don't say that to hurt you," I was quick to insist. "Alex and I were together for nearly twenty years; that's not something you can replace." I took a short breath. "But I'm starting to realize that it's okay to add to my life. I'm not swapping out or diminishing what Alex and I had," I qualified. "It's perfectly acceptable to add something new."

Lucia's features brightened. "Like a blend. You're not diluting or perverting the original wine. You're enhancing the experience. You're making it more complex."

I rolled my eyes at the analogy. "Leave it to you to find a way to relate this to wine."

She shrugged, unbothered by my words. "What can I say? I'm obsessed."

I bit my lower lip. "Do you think you have room in your life for one more obsession?"

Lucia squinted her eyes in a contemplative look. The longer she took with her response, the more my stomach twisted into uncomfortable knots. "That depends," she finally said.

"On?"

She gave me a small, almost embarrassed smile. "Can I still call you *Jefa*?"

I set my hands on top of her shoulders and interlaced my fingers behind her neck. I leaned in closer, fully prepared to kiss her breathless. "How about we take turns?"

ABOUT THE AUTHOR

Eliza Lentzski is the author of lesbian fiction, romance, and erotica including the best-selling *Winter Jacket* and *Don't Call Me Hero* series. She publishes urban fantasy and paranormal romance under the penname E.L. Blaisdell. Although a historian by day, Eliza is passionate about fiction. She was born and raised in the upper Midwest, which is often the setting for her novels. She lives in Boston with her wife and their cat, Charley.

Follow her on Twitter and Instagram, @ElizaLentzski, and Like her on Facebook (http://www.facebook.com/elizalentzski) for updates and exclusive previews of future original releases.

http://www.elizalentzski.com

Printed in Great Britain
by Amazon

82656954R10159